I0822524

KINDRED NØRTH

RUKIS

Kindred — North

Production copyright FurPlanet Productions © 2021

Copyright © Rukis 2021

Cover Artwork and illustrations © Rukis 2021

Published by FurPlanet Productions
Dallas, Texas
www.FurPlanet.com

eBook ISBN 978-1-61450-549-5
Hardcover ISBN 978-1-61450-550-1
Paperback ISBN 978-1-61450-543-3

First Edition Trade Paperback 2021

All rights reserved. No portion of this work may be reproduced in any form, in any medium, without the expressed permission of the author.

Table of Contents

Chapter I

The Wayward Inn

Aging oak floorboards creaked beneath my heavy paws as I stepped inside the threshold of the Inn. They felt good beneath my frozen pads, the well-worn, charming scars of so many other claws embedded deep in the memory of this place. Much like the rings of scarred tattoos along my forearms, they marked the time and experiences this structure had seen.

A sign I'd glimpsed between puffs of cold air and the ongoing flurries outside proudly declared "The Wayward Inn" in four different languages. One was Amurescan, the others were three local tribal dialects. It had immediately put me at ease, because one of them was close to my own. I could read Amurescan too by now, but it was a comfort to know I was welcome. I'd been recommended this trade post, and indeed this particular Inn, but one never knows. We Northerners are not always greeted with open arms, not even in border towns like this. Not since the Otherwolves' settlements had become more numerous than our own.

But from the moment I stepped inside, I knew that would be no issue here. I'd caught the cacophony of voices, sounds and scents from outside; the windows were at least an inch thick of glass (necessary with the cold in these regions, if you were going to risk glass at all) but even that hadn't dampened the noise. And of course, the chimneys had been venting various enticing odors, grilled meat and bread, probably some kind of stew... my mouth was watering already. Hardly odd for me, but still. I thought to wipe my jowls before I stepped in. Big slavering bears made people nervous, even in a place like this.

Much to my delight, I drew nary a glance. A few wolves and foxes were engaged in a rowdy game of cards at the table immediately to the right of the door, but only the foxes spared me the briefest of nervous looks before flicking their tails and getting right back into the argument they had previously been engaged in. It looked like a traveling party of some sort, no real animosity there, just a lot of beer and friendly competition.

My gaze swept the crowded, cluttered dining area, taking in another two dozen or so patrons and at least half a dozen servers, as well as two dogs tending a busy bar. Proudly displayed along the walls were moose, caribou and great stag antlers, butting up against shelves of glittering canned food and a menagerie of wines and liquor, as varied as the guests staying here. The proprietors clearly liked to have a broad variety of food and drink for what was certain to be a broad variety of guests, in a trade hub like this. Anukeetsik, or as it had been recently renamed, "Kingsdale," (don't ask me to explain Otherwolf names, they're all strange to me) was just down river from the Long God Lake, one of the greatest bodies of water in the North Country. It connected via another great river to the ocean, eventually. Or so I'd heard. I'd never been that far east.

On the way here I'd seen some of the Otherwolves' mighty canoes. They called them "barges," and it was no wonder with such a mastery of the rivers they had come so far inland and settled so much land as fast as they had. My tribe hailed from farther north, so we had yet to suffer the ill effects of their incursion, only benefited from trade. And for a fisherman in particular, especially in the winter when I could move frozen fish from far north to the traders here, there was no better time or place to do said trade. I'd offloaded my entire month's catch of salmon in a night; the Otherwolves were hungry for any fish that could be salted for their seafarers. And everyone else in this region had cod. My catch was exotic here.

It had been a gamble, to be certain. I'd come down the river many times before to fish, but never towing such a haul on my raft, and never so far as this. I'd been lucky and only gotten locked in the ice a few days' time further up north, for the most part the river spirits had led me on safely. But if worst had come to worst, I could have hunkered down and lived off my catch through the winter and tried again next season. That's what I'd told my family, anyway.

Of course, I was a bear. I could well understand why my father and siblings, and anyone from my village, would find the journey I'd taken too dangerous. They were otters. Not to say I'd be in any doubt of their skills at negotiating the river, or bringing in a good haul during the spawning run. But as to whether they'd have been able to transport their haul safely… that's less certain.

I'd definitely drawn a lot of attention, traveling for weeks down-river, alone as I was on my raft. But although there had been a few times I'd felt less than comfortable with the sorts of people I'd passed, or the attention I'd gotten at the various stops and camps I'd made, no one had apparently felt up to the task of making trouble for me. And the reason for that was simple. I'd met very few other men, even in my travels, who could rival me in size. Even other bears.

That was thanks primarily to my mixed lineage, split between two of the largest bear tribes from our country. A turn of fate that had nearly doomed a young cub was now my saving grace. And a boon for my otter family, if this run continued successfully. The weight of the coins in my satchel were a comforting reminder of my earlier successful sales, and what it would mean for my family. I'd spend a few days here, rest and eat well, and then I'd re-supply and head back upriver as far as I could before the ice really set. I already had a halfway point picked out, a town called Broen I'd stopped in on the way down where I knew I could hire a guide and a few good mules, and I'd make the rest of my way back home on foot. My tribe was waiting for me. The season had been good to us and we were self-sufficient if pressed, but the coin would be a welcome relief.

The influx of the Otherwolves' goods into our lands had made life easier in many ways. The little ones in particular certainly enjoyed some of the foodstuffs we were able to buy from their traders. And I'll confess, I did too. But it also meant that, in a way, you had to keep up. I couldn't help thinking on that as I walked through this obviously Otherwolf-owned establishment. The foreign canines from across the sea, not quite like the wolves from our lands, had brought many things that had changed the landscape of our world. The first of our hunters had bought a rifle last year, primarily for hunting game. Otters mostly fished, but a little variation in our winter meat was welcome. Usually we had to barter with wolves for it and those trades were never in our favor. Fish weren't much in demand in a land so rich with them.

With the trappings these foreigners had brought, my father thought our best chance was to adapt to the new changes in our world. To ride the current forward, he had said. Not fight it, not paddle hopelessly backwards, like some of the other tribes were doing. He wanted us to adopt as many of the new things coming into our lands as we could. Some of the other otter tribes disagreed with his decisions, and I couldn't say I personally knew what was best. But I trusted my father. These new people had troubled some of the other tribes further east, I'd heard, but it didn't seem like they had designs on our land. Even the ones near our tribe kept their distance. The land we lived on did not give away much, easily. It was probably too remote for them to settle as thoroughly as they had in other places.

That's what my otterfa said, anyway.

We weren't the only tribe adopting some of their ways, either. It was inevitable, of course. I had never fired one of their weapons, traveled on one of their barges or used any of their complicated tools, but I'd eaten some of their food and helped build a small root cellar on our tribe's land using their "bricks," and there was no denying that their strange ways were seductive. I'd never forget the "apple pie" they'd brought us. Oh...maybe they had that here?

One thing was for certain. Before the travelers from across the sea had come, the people crowding this trade post would have looked very different. One glance around this Inn verified what I'd until now only heard the elders speaking of in hushed tones. This was becoming a country of canines.

On the surface, the two different groups of canines looked to be the same people, although I'd heard you weren't supposed to say that to the wolf tribes. Amongst themselves they drew a very serious distinction. But there was no denying that the wolves from our lands, and the "Otherwolves," or "dogs," who'd come in recent generations to colonize and settle in our territory...they were made from similar stock. They could even intermarry and have pups, I'd heard.

My father was intent to get ahead while we still could. And bringing home a good share of their coin was key, if we wanted to do that. The

Otherwolves who lived on our river were willing to trade in goods, but our fish sold for far more here than it ever would up north. And it was high time I began repaying my father's, and my tribe's kindness in taking me in as a cub. So if this is how I could serve my tribe, I was happy to do it.

It also meant I got to travel, which I was finding I greatly enjoyed. In the last month, I'd seen more people than I'd ever seen in my life. And that was just between home and a few towns along the way. This place was the biggest town yet, and I'd only been here a day so far! I couldn't wait to see how lively it would be tomorrow.

The Wayward Inn was lively enough on its own. I had to push aside a few chairs as I made my way towards the bar; as in many dwellings I'd been in before, there just wasn't always enough room for me to walk about without pushing things over. A serving girl—a pretty weasel, I couldn't help but note how she somewhat reminded me of some of the women in my tribe—moved past me with a tray of bread held high, the aroma wafting right past my nostrils and setting me to licking my lips again. She glanced briefly in my direction and I blanched, caught in the act. I lowered my muzzle and nearly stumbled past her, and I swear I heard her giggling.

There were both Tribal wolves and Otherwolves, the latter mostly recognizable by what they were wearing, their odd fur coloration, and in some cases, their bizarre features. The more of them I'd seen, the more confusing the variety. Their pelts were spotted, brindled and even short-furred sometimes, and their muzzles were often pushed in or drooping. As were their ears. I tried very hard not to stare, but you get used to seeing wolves looking *one* way your whole life and it's hard not to be shocked when your whole perception of them changes.

I was hardly one to speak on looking odd, of course. My own pelt was strange, even amongst the Great Northern bear tribe I had likely come from. My father—my adoptive father—had always told me they'd lived in the peaks near our tribe's land for generations, before the Ice Bears had driven them out. They'd gone too, in time. The Bear tribes did not get on well with the Otherwolves. Even the Ice Bears, despite their size, had fared poorly in their skirmishes with the armed Otherwolf communities. Again, rifles made all the difference.

My adoptive mother believed I was the child of a union between the two tribes of bears, before they'd been driven out. But if that was the case, something terrible must have befallen my parents, because my father's tribe had found me clinging to a fallen tree in the river when I was a cub.

My family had never made me feel as though my appearance was something to be ashamed of. But since I'd reached adulthood and begun traveling to fish, and now to trade, I'd learned that to many others, I was... not normal.

It seemed strange to me that in a world so full of such a variety of people, something as small as a brown stripe down my back, or a muzzle that wasn't quite like other bears', would be something of ridicule. But I'd gotten a taste of what it was that unnerved them all when I'd seen my first Otherwolf with a pushed-in muzzle. Just like how I was used to seeing wolves looking one way, the world was used to bears looking a certain way. And I didn't fit that.

It made me mindful even now not to stare. And not to think ill. I wouldn't want them to feel as I had on many occasions when I knew someone was staring at me and thinking how strange I appeared to them.

So when I at last made it to the bar and the woman who greeted me was a stocky Otherwolf with spots over her eyes and muzzle, a short, wrinkly face and small flopped-over ears, I smiled at her and pushed aside my thoughts on what wolves "should" look like. It wasn't even that hard.

"Ain't you a big fella!" she exclaimed with a broad, jowly grin. She finished wiping a tankard in her paws with her apron and put it on the counter for me, gesturing behind her to the various barrels and bottles. "What'll be your pleasure, love?"

I gave an easy smile, instantly won over by her pleasant tone and round, kind features. "Mead, if you've any," I asked. "Please?"

"'Ow'd I know!" she barked out a laugh, turning and gripping the tankard to empty the sweet-smelling drink from one of her smaller barrels. She filled it to the brim and then some, pouring with care to avoid any spill. "You're new in town," she noted as I gripped my drink and brought it to my muzzle, greedy for the brew after so long on the river with nothing but water to drink.

"Just came in off the river," I said after I drained the cup down by half. "Got in a bit later than I was expecting, I was surprised how busy the market was despite that."

"Oh tha'place never shuts down," she chuckled, wiping her hands on her damp apron. "But most'a the rush should be comin' in from there shortly."

I glanced around. "It gets busier than this?"

She just gave me that broad grin again. "Oh, sweetha't. You ain't seen nothin' yet."

She wasn't jesting. An hour later I'd received my dinner, a welcome break from fish. A whole round loaf of bread, a thick slab of butter and roasted venison. By then the place was *alive*. I don't think I'd ever been anywhere so crowded or so loud. Many of the folks I'd seen earlier in the waning hours must have ended their day at the market and come here for spirits, dinner and company. Most were drinking, many were enjoying bread, butter and cheese, but far fewer could afford meat, I noticed. This was a buying season down here, I had to remind myself, not a selling one. Many of these men would be taking to the river or the roads moving their merchandise tomorrow. Winter was sweeping down in from the mountains and it was likely that very few people here would be heading *further* north, like I was planning.

It just meant I should enjoy my time here while I could. My Amurescan was decent. I wasn't usually one for talking to strangers, but I could watch, take in the sights and have many stories to tell when I got home.

More card games had erupted throughout the bustling tables and I'd briefly entertained the idea of entering one, but my father wouldn't have approved of gambling, especially not with the coin I intended to bring home to my tribe. I mean, I *was* my own man now, nearing twenty years in fact, so it wasn't just that I was afraid what he'd think of me if he knew I'd partaken in the Otherwolves' vices. I just wasn't that bold. Maybe later, I thought, I'd work up the courage to meander over to where a few of the bigger lads were arm wrestling. That, at least, was a far surer bet.

A lanky coyote had sat himself down near the fire awhile back and begun playing some kind of string instrument I'd seen once or twice now in the Otherwolf communities. It was sharp and plucky, with a hint of melancholy now and again depending on which songs he played. I liked it after a while, although it took some getting used to.

The nice woman at the bar had gotten far too busy to continue any kind of conversation with, although she did periodically check on me to ensure I got as much mead as I needed. I'd drained my fourth cup and was feeling pleasantly full and fuzzy when a sudden hoot caught my attention.

I turned in time to see a coyote woman taking to the floor with some kind of rough-furred big cat, a stocky man in well-worn clothing and thinning suspenders stretched over his broad chest. He took her by the arm and spun her once, and another few of those hoots went up throughout the crowd, as the coyote playing the instrument cackled and stomped his foot. With that, the music suddenly picked up to a more excited pace.

They were dancing, I realized. Before long a few of the other men joined in on the stomping and one of the women I'd seen earlier serving bread unstrapped her smock and stepped out with a lean young wolf, who began to move with her like the other couple were. It was a lot of quick turns and intermittently holding hands before clapping along to the furiously sawing string instrument. I wished I knew what to call…well, all of it. But regardless, it was engaging. I couldn't look away.

So it happened that, when *he* entered the room, taking his time down a staircase I'd seen earlier but not taken much note of until now, I was looking in his direction. Otherwise I might have lost him amongst the crowd.

On the surface he wasn't much different than many of the Otherwolves here. A bit shorter, slighter of frame, with primarily dark fur except a bit of white around the bottom of his muzzle, a flash of white down his throat, and I think I saw a white tail-tip. But it was more the clothing he wore that caught my eye. Nearly every man here, Otherwolf or tribal man, had come into this place wearing layers. Many of them were heaped in furs, or old leather coats or cloaks. Since it was practically blazing inside with so many furred bodies, the ovens going and a roaring fire in the center of the room, most were stripped down to threadbare, worn cotton shirts, or just the fur on their chests. This wolf had a long, dark coat and a forest green vest, the white cuffs of a long shirt, and breeches beneath it, and he hadn't come from outside.

But it wasn't just the fact that he wore dyed, well-fitted clothing that caught my eye. Clutched in one hand was a head covering…a hat…of a type I'd never seen before. I had to assume it was a hat anyway, based on the ear holes. It was almost like a small bucket, black and with a rim, which is where he was gripping it by.

He seemed as intrigued by the dancing as I was, looking towards it while slowly picking his way through the crowd. Well, intrigued might not be the right word. Maybe more "baffled." Still, I think I saw him smile a bit.

By the time it became clear that he was heading for the bar, I had to remember myself and look away. I was doing the staring thing again and if I didn't stop now I wouldn't. His eyes in particular were striking, I felt them etched in my eyelids even after I averted my gaze. I dropped my field of vision back to my food and brought the haunch of venison back to my muzzle, trying to look more interested in my food than him. It mostly worked.

But then, suddenly, he was beside me. Not in my personal space, mind you, he'd just found a place to squeeze himself up against the bar that happened to be at my side, and it became even harder than before to ignore him. Especially when he deposited that hat on the bar right beside me.

I figured at that point I was permitted to look sideways, at least at the hat. It was fascinating up-close, although much like its owner, more ragged than I'd thought from far away. The man's clothing altogether both looked and smelled of the road, his fine garments fraying at the edges and stained in places. And the musk about him was not much different than most of the other canines here. Just from a cursory sniff, he smelled tired and a little damp. For some reason, that set me more at ease. He was just another traveler.

The bartender noticed him and padded on over towards us, greeting him with a familiar "Finn! 'Aven't seen you since breakfast. You been up there all day?"

"My business can be a cruel mistress, I'm afraid," he said in a surprisingly deep voice, with an accent I couldn't quite place. He was speaking Amurescan, but not like any man I'd heard before. One of his hand paws was resting on the bar very close to mine, and I chanced a glance at it, something out of the corner of my eye making me take note. His fingers were stained. With what I couldn't say, but it seemed dark. Like soot.

"Thas'unfortunate," the bartender tutted at him. "Y'ought to get yourself a proper mistress who'll treat you right. Keep you up all night'n'day for the proper kinda reasons."

He laughed at that. "Perhaps. Once my work is done, anyway. I think a proper mistress would prefer a man dedicated to his work above a lazy one, wouldn't you say?"

"Aye but you need t'make some time for livin', love," she said as she pulled a glass from behind the counter and filled it with something from a pale brown bottle.

He took the glass in one paw and downed whatever the spirits had been in a gulp, before setting it back down and giving a sigh. "Soon," he promised. "Soon, I'll...be done..."

Something about his tone caught my attention and I finally dared to look at him completely. He'd turned away from me, from the bartender as well at that, and his eyes had gone as distant as his tone. He was staring off into the crowd near the door, it seemed like. I would have had to crane my head entirely around, which would've necessitated moving my whole body to the side, so I couldn't see what he was seeing. But I knew the scent I caught from him just then.

Fear.

"D'you need me to get you more ink from town?" The bartender asked him, clearly oblivious to his sudden change of mood while she poured me more mead.

"Yes, please," the man said quietly, "I'm nearly...out..."

Just like that, he'd risen from his seat and folded himself into the crowd, surprising both me and the bartender. All I caught was the white tail-tip as he shimmied between a raucous gaggle of badgers and was gone.

"And he's off again," the bartender sighed, leaning down to scritch at something she had beneath the counter. "Put that'un on his tab too, I guess."

My eyes were drawn to my left, specifically down by where his hand had been resting on the counter. "Do you know where he's going?" I asked.

"What, Finn?" She snorted out a breath, shaking her head. "He comes'n goes since he got here. Spends most o'his time in his room. Some kind of writer, ah think. Or he fancies himself one, anyway." She glanced back up at me. "Why?"

"He forgot his hat," I said, lifting it in one hand.

Chapter 2

A Tussle

Sometimes I do things I can't well explain after the fact. Foolish things. I dare say, even stupid things. Most of the time I'm a fairly deliberate person; my whole family says so. "Tulimak is a good boy," they'd say. "Always my most obedient son," my father often compliments me while deliberately glaring at my otter brothers. The twins are good boys too, of course, just not always as willing to listen to our father as I am.

I wouldn't say I'm a complicated person, either. I try to do right by my family and most other living souls in the world because...well, because I don't see a reason not to. I hate fighting, I don't like arguing and even being the cause of frustration can make me nervous. And when I get nervous, my stomach hurts. Sometimes if it lasts too long, I can even get so nervous, I grow sick. So why would I ever make trouble? It just doesn't seem worth it. I don't honestly understand why so many other people in the world are so angry all the time. Even if they're one of those people who don't care about others, don't they realize how bad it is for *them*?

The point is, I'm not a troublemaker. But sometimes, for reasons I can't explain, I do things that *get* me in trouble. This night was to be one of those times.

If I had to trace my impulse back to one thing, it would probably have been his eyes. It isn't just that they were pretty, although I do like pretty things more than a big bear should. It was more that they seemed so... tired. Drawn. Aching.

I fell down a cliffside once when I was a toddling cub; it's one of my first memories in fact. My otterfa—my father—couldn't help me get back up. Even then, I was too heavy for him to carry, at least while climbing. I had to claw my way back up that steep, rocky hillside, out of the gorge and back up to where my family was calling to me and encouraging me. My father helped me as much as he could and in the end I obviously made it, but I remember being *so tired*. The exhaustion, the way my little limbs burned and hurt for days afterwards, that's what stuck with me the most.

That man—"Finn," the woman behind the bar had called him—had that same sort of exhaustion about him. I can't say exactly that it had been something I'd felt through one sense in particular, it was more an overall feeling. And for some reason it had brought back that memory. That particular one.

Maybe I wanted to reach out. Help him up whatever cliff he was struggling to climb. I know that sounds overly poetic, but I guess that's just how my mind is sometimes. Even in this crowded, busy place, he seemed alone, apart from the rest of the people here. His dress was different, his affect unlike the people here, even his accent noticeably foreign. He looked and felt like someone who was out of place and needed help. I'd always had my family, my adoptive family that is, to help give me that extra leg up the hill when I needed it. Even just knowing they were at the summit, cheering you on, could be enough. Relying on yourself entirely was hard, sometimes impossible.

Or maybe it was that whiff of fear I'd caught on him. It was distinctly that, not apprehension or something else more subtle. Fear had a very sharp prickle to it that made you scrunch your nose back. I had no idea what it was he'd been looking at when he'd quietly slipped back into the crowd. But whatever it was had aroused his fear so quickly, I'd caught scent of it without even trying. Even after he'd left, I felt some of my fur standing on end. This was mortal fear, the same as you'd pick up on the wind of prey you're hunting.

I turned the rim of his hat over in my big paw-pads, looking over the smooth, velvet-clad curves of the odd object. A long line of the fabric was torn and blistering near the edges, and there were a few pockmarked stains. The underside of the rim felt worn and tacky. It was well-used now to be certain, but it had definitely been expensive once. By my best guess, anyway. That only furthered my worries. He'd left it behind. He'd been in such a hurry, he'd left this costly, obviously well-loved possession behind.

Maybe it was for my own sake; the hat after all provided my best excuse to get to know someone in this strange and interesting place. Or maybe it really was just as shallow as finding his eyes pretty, and wanted to see *him* again. But regardless of the reason, I gripped that hat in my paws, stepped down from my stool back onto the creaking floor and began looking for him.

Honestly, I thought it would be harder than it ended up being. Given the crowded nature of this place, coupled with its age and all the various food and drink I was contending with, he would have been impossible to track by scent. But I got lucky. I'd made my way towards the staircase area, thinking perhaps he might have headed back to where I'd seen him descend from, (a silly thought really, if he'd gone back up the stairs I'd have seen him go). But the staircase happened to be near the main doorway into the place, the threshold I'd crossed an hour earlier.

His scent had been no more particular than most others here and the profuse amount of canines didn't help that any. But his voice had been. It was quieter near the door, the din of the establishment and clatter of tin cups and plates fading somewhat as I was drawn towards an unusual sight. There was a crack of bluish-white, a sliver of cold slipping inside, and if I really cupped my ears forward, the hint of voices muffled by snow and wind. The door had been left open. The hostess must not have noticed yet.

One of the people talking outside was unmistakably him. I couldn't make out words, but he had a certain cadence to his voice. And there again was that prickling hint of fear. This time I could *hear* it.

I paused at the door, paw on the cold handle. That familiar feeling welled up inside me, that anxiety of being a nuisance. Of intruding, causing drama or conflict where there might well be none. Whatever was happening outside, whatever had caught this stranger's attention and brought about his sudden flight from the bar—I couldn't know what it was, but it most certainly was *not* my business. And I couldn't even make sense of my rationale for following him to begin with.

I felt this way often, usually in less suspect situations, but it was generally why I didn't speak much in public places, or introduce myself to new people. When you're the biggest, most cumbersome thing in your family, in your whole world, you learn to tread lightly. I hated how much...*space* I took up, everywhere I went. I didn't need to be nosy or loud on top of that.

But something about this night, this situation, just wouldn't let go. It's like that feeling you get sometimes before the weather's about to shift for the worst, or you feel an illness coming on. Something wasn't right.

Pushing open the door, I stepped out into the night air. The street was lit by flickering torchlight, covered in a downy coat of soft snow that furrowed up around my paws as I stepped off the stoop. There were fresh tracks here, more than just one set. I hadn't noticed in my moments of indecision at the bar, but a few of the patrons had clearly stepped outside, not just him. They looked smaller than most canine pawprints, but not by much.

I breathed deeply, immediately catching the unmistakable scent of foxes. I wasn't much for tracking, but I hardly bothered taking heed of their numbers, I could hear their voices tucked between the inn and the building wedged up alongside it, a general store long closed for the evening. There were at least three men speaking, maybe more. That probably should have worried me more than it did.

The worn hat clutched in one paw, I strode a bit more purposefully towards the edge of the building. It was becoming more and more clear the closer I got that there was trouble afoot. I'm not sure what my plan was when I rounded that corner, but at that point I was committed.

A sudden shout and a clamor of activity greeted me almost immediately. I barely had time to open my mouth before a complete stranger—one of the foxes I vaguely remembered seeing inside earlier—stumbled backwards into my chest. I barely felt the impact, but was stunned nonetheless and had begun to ask if he was all right, before I noticed the glint of something in his right hand.

My fur stood on end. He was holding a knife, and not one used for skinning or de-scaling fish like I had. It was long and curved, with a barb that could only serve to do unnecessary damage. I'd only ever seen its like before on warriors or marauders.

Another two sets of eyes stared out at me from the darkness of the alley, catching the torchlight behind me. My own eyes were still adjusting, but I could make out silhouettes. One was canine, one another fox. The fox stabbed a hand out in my direction, shouting, "Wot're you now?!"

I wasn't sure how to answer that question, but in the time it took me to stammer out nothing, the fox who'd presumably been thrown into me got his footing and swung his blade out in an arc in my direction. It didn't even come close to connecting, but I suspect the point was to frighten me back. Which it did.

"He's boltin'!" the one ahead of me shouted. I lifted my muzzle to see the canine, whom I now could see for certain was the man I'd come out here to find, springing low beneath the clawing hands of the man who was yelling. He managed to his credit to duck away from him, but the second man with the knife was still in his way. I was, too. It wasn't exactly a wide alley.

With a start, I realized the fox with the knife wasn't just trying to block him, he had the weapon out with every intent to use it on him. He swung it again, this time at the near-panicked canine, catching the edge of his coat and tearing off a button with an audible pop. His hooked knife served its purpose, snagging in the fabric. He twisted his arm and half his lean body, managing to bring the canine lurching backwards, splayed out on the lightly snow-dusted ground. He hit the dirt hard enough that I felt it in *my* tail bone.

I hadn't been in any real fights in my life, so I can't say I acted fast. The reality was, I had no idea what was going on here, but I knew an unfair fight when I saw one. And this wasn't just some scuffle, the fox with the knife hadn't just been aiming for his coat, someone could get seriously hurt or killed here. Whatever this was over, it needed to stop.

Taking a deep breath and summoning forth a roar I barely ever had cause to use, I bellowed, "*All right, enough!*"

The two foxes, one of whom at this point had the canine pinned down with one foot on his chest, the other of which was still brandishing the knife, froze in place. I was glad at least that I still could have that effect on people. I didn't use my "bear voice" often.

"I asked who you were, stranger," the darker-furred one who'd spoken earlier snarled out. He pulled a knife as well in that moment, smaller and less intimidating than his friend's, but no less lethal if he was any good with it.

The other leaned over and yanked his knife out of the canine's coat, ripping the jacket as he did so. He stepped as far back from me as he could get in the cramped alley, licking a dripping nose and glancing worriedly past me. "He was s'posed t'be alone..." he muttered, his voice thick with an obvious cold.

"Look, whatever your disagreement," I put my broad paws out, "it shouldn't have to end in blood."

"That ain't your place to determine, now is it?" The dark-furred fox replied through his teeth. "Now who'r—"

"He was s'posed to be *alone*, Clay!" the other fox interrupted manically, his back near against the wall now as he clearly made to move past me. I was fine with that, so I gave him a little breathing room. I was twice their size, but unarmed, and I didn't want to fight them if I didn't have to.

The other fox cast him an irritated look and visibly pushed down with his foot, stamping the canine more firmly into the ground. I heard him whimper, and the sound made me wince in sympathetic pain. He must have hurt himself when he fell.

"Let's just talk this out, a'ight? Don't nothin' unfortunate gotta happen," the dark-furred fox said to me in a far calmer tone than his friend was managing. He spread a paw out, the one not holding the knife. "You on the hunt too, friend? We can split the take. I don't like trouble with the Jackwalds."

I arched an eyebrow. "The Jackwalds?"

His eyes widened at that in surprise, then just as quickly a look of resolve crossed his features and he began reaching down for the canine. "Free agent, then? Should've *lied* to me. Now I know you're alone."

I felt rather than heard his friend behind me as he sprung at my back, and I swung my arm out blindly in what was more a fearful retaliation than anything planned. Thankfully in such close quarters I couldn't help but hit, my big paw clapping into his shoulder and spinning him until he struck the opposite wall with a dull thud.

My breath left my lungs in a smoky puff of air, the scent of blood hitting my nostrils. The fox slumped down against the wall, his knife dropping out of his paw, a spatter of dark ichor on the bricks. I barely had time to register what had happened before I heard an unmistakable metallic click ring out in the dead night air. I turned back towards the other two men to find...

The canine had a pistol. He'd had a pistol this entire time?

Now the dark-furred fox finally looked scared. He was lifting his foot slowly from the canine's chest, stepping back away from him gingerly. The man had the weapon pointed at him and he was panting visibly into the cold, his body shivering and his voice wavering when he finally managed to say, "Whatever…they're paying…now…it can't be worth your life."

The fox glanced briefly between the man on the ground and past me, to his friend. And he seemed indecisive for longer than I would've been.

"Is it?!" the canine demanded.

Without any further last words, save a hateful look directed at the both of us, the fox darted towards me and wove to my left and beyond to the street. He paused only briefly to take stock of his friend before abandoning him and making off into the night.

The canine slumped back, the hand he had holding the pistol falling to his side where he let it rest unceremoniously in the snow. He sucked in greedy breaths of air, closing his eyes and leaning against the very same brick wall I'd knocked the other assailant into. A quick glance assured me the fox probably only had a broken nose, he still seemed conscious, just stunned. I was glad for that, at least. I still didn't know what was going on here. Who were "the Jackwalds"? And why had that man thought I was one?

"Thank God for you, friend," the canine huffed out, looking back up at me with those same eyes I'd found striking earlier. Right now, caught in this strange, dangerous situation I had no grasp of, they scared me. He held up the pistol and I briefly bristled, before realizing he was holding it up limply like a dead fish.

"I haven't had powder for this thing in weeks," he chuckled wryly. "Good thing these country lads are pinheads, eh?"

"Finnegan Ambrose, of Ambrose Park," the canine told me over his shoulder as he limped up to the doorway of his room. I followed, mostly out of concern at this point that he'd fall. He was favoring his right leg and his tail was limp, I think he'd mostly fallen on his hip, but I was no healer, so I couldn't guess at what sort of injury he'd sustained. I'd followed him upstairs to ensure he'd make it, after he'd insisted up and down he didn't need a healer and didn't even want to go to the friendly bartender for some alcohol.

But I was giving him a wide berth, because I was spooked. No, that's really not a strong enough word. I was afraid. I hadn't a clue what had just gone down in the alley outside, or who those men were, or who they'd assumed *I* was. This strange man was armed with a pistol he insisted wasn't loaded, but I had no reason to believe him. By all rights, I should have left him in the alley. Gotten my things. Left town. I didn't know much of the world outside my tribe and my river, but I knew enough to realize this man "Finnegan" was in mortal danger, and every moment longer I spent with him, I likely was as well. I'd gone outside because I'd sensed something was troubling him, but I hadn't expected…this.

I'm not sure what I'd expected, or what I'd been hoping for. Less knives, though. Less knives would have been good.

The lock in his door clicked loudly as he leaned into it with his key, stopping briefly to rest against the wood on his elbow and forearm. His head tipped forward. Without thinking, I found myself crossing the distance between the two of us, putting a paw on his shoulder to steady him. He swayed for a moment, then turned to look up at me.

I snuffed back a breath. His eyes were the color of spring shoots, green and clear like lily pads in a pond. I knew I was fixating, but it wasn't just his eyes. He had very striking features overall, and being nearly nose to nose with him now made me appreciate them all the more. But he looked even more tired now that I was so close to him. He wasn't weak because of the injury…he was falling asleep.

"You're a good man, aren't you?" he asked me, exhaustion tugging at a threadbare smile.

I thought he intended to say more, but he didn't, so after an awkward silence, I stammered, "I—I…guess. I try."

He gave something like a laugh, before pushing the door in and moving from my steadying paw, limping inside. His voice continued into the room, but I dared not follow.

"Does the good man have a name?" he asked, maneuvering his way through the small, cramped space. The little room looked and smelled stifling, with no window, only an iron pipe through the center of it that must have come from one of the ovens downstairs to heat it, and his possessions

scattered about in a manner that suggested he'd been here for some time. An overturned barrel with a few planks laid across it seemed to be serving as a makeshift table, pulled up alongside a bowed wooden bed frame with an obviously straw mattress. A travel bag and several worn blankets were bunched in one spot near the barrel, providing a raised area where he obviously sat to work at the table. His laundry, which he was drying, was strung up by twine across two corners of the room, the rest stacked as neatly as one could manage in a place like this on the bedside table. And then there were the papers. Papers…everywhere. I don't think I'd ever seen so much paper in my life. Some of it was even tacked up on the walls, for some reason. My grasp of written Amurescan was poor, I could only read it slowly, so I wasn't sure what they all were at a glance.

The bed creaked suddenly as he sat down on it, and I realized with a start that he was looking at me. "Well?" he asked, tipping his head.

"O-oh!" I glanced briefly aside, having trouble keeping his gaze. "Tulimak."

"Just…Tulimak?" He pronounced it fairly well, given that he'd only heard it once. For an Otherwolf, anyway. They often had trouble with our names.

"Yes," I responded simply.

"You tribal peoples aren't big on surnames, I'd forgotten," he murmured as he leaned back against the wall the bed was pushed up alongside. He twisted his body for a moment, clearly testing his hip. The wince told me all I needed to know.

"You're hurt," I reminded him quietly. "You should see someo—"

"Are you coming in?" He interrupted me, gesturing to where I was still standing in the doorway. "I'd rather you not leave the door open, all things considered."

"Oh," I paused, at this point realizing I had to commit to some kind of decision. And that was difficult. I'd followed him this far because I'd been worried he'd hurt himself on the stairs. And then he'd had that near-faint at the door. But at this point I could walk away and comfort myself in knowing I'd gone above and beyond, done all I could to help the man. Whatever trouble he was in, my conscience was clear. I didn't need to—

He unshouldered his coat, whining softly as he twisted to do so. Beneath the bulkier coat, he wore a tailored vest over a thin cotton shirt, britches and spats. The fact that his outfit was tailored to his figure, and still obviously baggy in places only made it more obvious how lean he was. The scene tugged at a place in me that physically hurt, and I found myself stepping inside and closing the door, if only so I could approach him from behind and help him pull the coat down over his arms.

He glanced back at me as I did, huffing again, like a laugh that didn't quite emerge. "Where do they make big, helpful bears like you? I could have used one throughout..." he paused, "...most of my life."

"Well, you have one now," I said as I gingerly removed his frayed coat and hung it over the bedpost. He gave it a brief, dismayed glance, doubtless seeing what I'd already seen. It was badly torn. Perhaps not worth salvaging. "For the moment, anyway," I said, forcing a smile and doing my best not to make it a scary one. I'd accidentally terrified many young otters with my smiles over the years.

"Yes," he said, suddenly sounding wary. His gaze flicked briefly between me and the door. "Thank you for that. For everything in the alley. Who—" he paused, visibly checking himself. "I'm sorry. I don't mean to sound ungrateful. Tulimak," he again pronounced it correctly. "But who are you, exactly? Why did you come to my aid?"

"I didn't mean to," I blurted out before I realized how bad that sounded. "I mean," I said quickly, as his brow raised, "I mean it wasn't my intention in coming out there. To get in a fight. I-I didn't even realize..." I gestured aimlessly, before sighing. "What *did* happen out there? I really don't mean to pry, it's just—"

"Oh god," he said suddenly, his eyes widening. "You really aren't a hunter."

"Fisherman, actually," I cleared my throat. "It's a certain kind of 'hunt,' really. It has its own challenges, people don't realize—"

"No, I mean," he smoothed a hand over his roughed-up head fur, "a *bounty* hunter. You aren't hunting me. Are you?"

"Why would I be hunting you?" I asked, aghast. "Why would anyone?"

"Aha," he chuckled. "Long story."

"Is that what those men in the alley—the foxes, is that what they were trying to do?" I asked uncertainly. "They were hunting you?"

"Are," he replied tiredly, stretching his leg out on the bed, clearly still stretching his hip. "*Are* hunting me. And they'll be back, I'm certain.

Probably not so long as you're here, but once you leave...You didn't kill that one who hit the wall, did you?"

"No!" I said emphatically. "I mean I don't think...he just had a broken nose. Spirits, do you think it was worse than that?" My mind reeled at the possibility. I'd heard him breathing, he'd seemed conscious. What if I'd really hurt him? I'd abandoned him to follow Finnegan; was that really any better? They'd been the aggressors, sure. But still.

What would my father think of all of this? What would my tribe think? My stomach clenched as my thoughts spun in on themselves.

"Calm down," Finnegan urged quietly, his calm voice bringing me back to the present. I looked down at him and some of my nervousness must have still shone through, because his gaze turned sympathetic. "Look, for what it's worth, you're not in any danger. Those two aren't the first I've shaken, and they didn't seem well-outfitted. I don't think they'll like their luck with you any better the second time around, and it isn't you they're after, at any rate. Honestly men like that, they might give up the chase after a foul-up like that, take their chances elsewhere. Plenty of other work around here."

"You said they'd still be after you," I countered.

He let out a breath, closing his eyes and nodding. "They might wait me out, yes. If the bounty's anywhere near as high as it was last I heard, they might even go in with another outfit. Now that they know where I am."

"Then you need to leave," I insisted, reaching down and grabbing for his coat. "You need to get out of here."

"Not that you're wrong," he said wryly, his gaze sliding back towards me again. "But it would take half a day at least to gather my papers and somehow re-supply for travel, and I'm in no state. Nor do I have the resources any longer. I lost my pony two towns back, my coin's near run out..." He blinked tiredly, his eyes threatening to stay closed this time before he wearily opened them once more. "Is there a reliable post in this area, do you know?" he asked, not bothering to complete his previous statement.

"I don't, no," I said, my claws itching at the hem of my travel cloak. "This is my first time here in this settlement. And I don't really know what 'post' you mean."

"Does it not concern you *why* there might be a bounty out on me?" he asked, tipping his ears briefly towards the door, while still looking at me. I'd been doing the same since I'd come inside, albeit by turning my head.

"I-I don't know what that means," I admitted.

He blinked at that, then simply nodded. "All right," he said, adopting a more informative tone. It wasn't patronizing exactly, but it was close. "Those men outside were hunting me for money. For coin. A bounty is like a reward. Like any other hunter being paid for their catch. Those men were paid to kill me. Or take me somewhere. I'm not sure which."

"I understand war," I said flatly. "Tribal peoples still kill one another."

He held his hands up. "I'm sorry, no offense meant. Language barrier and all."

"You're the only one here with a language barrier," I pointed out. "I'm speaking your tongue. I learned it from a young age and I'm told I'm very fluent. My father said it would be all but essential, considering how many Otherwolves have moved into our lands. He was right."

"'Otherwolves,'" he repeated, something like a smile toying at the edge of his muzzle. "That's right. That's what you all call us. How self-explanatory. I think I like it, honestly."

"Get back to the part where your people want you dead," I pushed. "I've never heard of a 'bounty', but I know what reasons men usually have for wanting other men dead. Grudges. Land. Food." I arched an eyebrow, remembering something I'd heard about some of the Otherwolves in the west. "Gold?"

"You left out 'information,'" he said, gesturing loosely to the room around him. "I'm not *completely* certain who placed the bounty on my head, although I have some ideas…but all I have of value in the world is what you see before you."

I stared blankly at the many papers scattered across his "desk" and around the room. He must have seen the confusion in my features, because he clucked his tongue and said, "I see. You speak it, but you can't read it."

"I—"

"For the best, honestly," he muttered. "This blasted box of papers sealed my death warrant. First the poisoning on the Aranthine, then the hunters…*God*, what a miserable end," he slowly ran a palm down over his muzzle, dryly chuckling. At what, I couldn't understand.

"Wait, hold up now," I stammered. "You aren't—this isn't an 'end'. No need to be so melodramatic."

"If I can at least find a reliable post, I've gathered the most critical manifests, made the most important connections," he continued, speaking primarily to himself.

"You aren't going to die!" I raised my voice. Just a little, but even a little is usually enough, for me.

He turned towards me slowly, looking at me like I'd said something outlandish, rather than what I considered to be quite sensible. "Well, not tonight, no," he replied at length.

"Not…at all," I insisted quietly. "Please. Please just explain to me what's happening to you. I—" I stomped back on my fears for the moment. Letting someone be hunted down like an animal and stabbed in an alley could *not* be the right thing to do, no matter what was happening here. It just couldn't. "I want to help," I finally said.

The canine was silent for a long time. For the first time since we'd met, he seemed uncertain. I could see it in his posture, the stiffness with which he regarded me. I'd been frozen like that more times than I could remember, always thinking and re-thinking over the paths that lay before me. It looked strange on him, though. I'm not sure why.

"Do you know," he finally began speaking again, and as he did so he turned his entire body towards me, wincing, "of the land across the sea?"

"The land the Otherwolves come from," I nodded. "The land you come from."

"Very good," he nodded with a smile. "Not all tribesmen can tell Amurescans and Carvecians apart."

"Those are your tribes, right?" I said, trying to follow along.

"Well, there are a lot of…I guess you'd call them tribes within tribes," he gestured with a hand, waving the explanation aside. "A lot of divisions within my people. And not just the big one between those of us who settled here and those of us who remain living in Amuresca, our motherland. Since the war for independence though, we're certainly two very different peoples. I suppose none of that really matters out here on the frontier, but what's important is, yes, I am from across the pond. The ocean. Sorry, turn of phrase."

I just nodded. "I noticed you speak differently than the rest of the Otherwolves here."

"Good ear," he seemed to approve. "Same language, but yes, Carvecians have their own…flavor of dialect. Hard for even me to make out sometimes."

"You came from across the world," I said softly, the realization hitting me like a solid blow to the chest. This man wasn't just an outsider like the traders that came down the river. He was as foreign a person as I had ever met.

"I suppose I did," he said, not seeming to realize the significance of that. "Unpleasant journey, but luckily or unluckily for my sake, I had the benefit of spending much of it in such poor health, I hardly remember the months at sea, except that they were miserable."

"I'm sorry," I say, resisting the urge to pat his head like he was a child. It was an urge I often had for some reason around folks who were smaller than me, which was of course, most people. "That sounds awful," I knitted my paws in front of me instead. My impulse to touch others was very normal back home with my otterfa and my tribe, but they'd told me to resist doing so out here in the world.

"Yes well, poison will do that," he muttered bitterly.

"You're certain you were poisoned?" I asked, dubiously. If there's one thing I knew about poison from speaking to our village healer about it, it's that it was the first thing many people tended to assume, when the usual culprit was generally spoiled food.

"I'm certain," he said in a tone so dark, I dared not question it further. "And in any case, the two gentlemen we just encountered in the alleyway should be all the proof I need that someone is out to kill me, yes?"

"I guess so," I conceded. "But why? You said you had some idea, but not entirely?" The man's statement was among many he'd made tonight that had confused me.

"I dug into a very important man's affairs, back in Amuresca," he said, all mirth gone from his voice now. He was staring at nothing, irises blown wide in the dim candlelight. "The trail brought me this far."

"Trail?" I echoed.

"I'm hunting something too," he snarled.

"Information?" I guessed.

He looked back at me, and all I saw was a wolf. The softness was gone.

"The truth," he growled out.

Chapter 3

Off We Go

I blinked blearily against the cruel white light of morning, so much infinitely brighter thanks to the fresh coat of snow. My bed groaned beneath me as I shifted, rolling to my side to face the window.

Around me were the sounds of others sleeping, five other single men and a family of weasels, the last being the ones who'd ultimately woken me up. They were trying to be considerate while getting dressed and gathering their things, but the children were chattering amongst themselves as children do, in conspiratorial not-quite-whispers.

My head was pounding, but that also wasn't their fault. I'd stayed up far too late last night in Finn's company, discussing what our plans for today would be. I was usually an early riser, but I also usually went to sleep early and I was not one of those kinds who did well on little sleep.

The weasels were packing up from the rooming house before sunrise, likely to avoid having to do so while all of the other larger, single men were changing and relieving themselves and…all the other necessary and unnecessary things men did in the morning. I couldn't really blame them, the mother and at least two of the children were clearly women. My father had prepared me for finding accommodations in Otherwolf towns, so I didn't make any blunders. Usually rooming houses like this one had separate areas for families, but most of the town's lodging was full up and this family must have just taken what was available.

I'd chosen the accommodations here for the same reason they had – everything else was occupied. But I actually had a lot of coin on me, even if I didn't look it, and it was probably best to pack up and move out before the loose assortment of strangers here started rousing. I preferred to trust people, but after last night, I'd take no chances.

I'd slept in my clothing, so after washing my paws and face, giving my fur a quick brush with my claws and tucking my few possessions away into my travel bag, I made my way out into the commons area. It smelled of oatmeal and eggs, and most mornings I would have relished the simple fare, but there was a knot in my stomach that had yet to uncurl from the goings-on of the night before. My life had changed overnight.

Now when I stepped out into the bustling, bright town and took in all the various sights, sounds and smells of the community waking up, it was less giddy excitement I was feeling and more apprehension. I found myself checking every alley, glancing at every fox I passed to make sure it wasn't one of the two that had attacked the night before. And worse yet, it had been dark, so it was hard to remember their faces.

Finnegan had said he was being hunted. Which means it might not just be the two foxes. He'd also mentioned poisoning, he'd said those two men weren't the first…and then there were these "Jackwalds" the fox hunters had thought I was a part of. I still wasn't sure what or who they'd been referring to.

By the time I made it back to the Wayward Inn, I was a balled-up knot of worries and fears. And while that wasn't entirely a new feeling for me, that didn't make it any easier to handle in the moment. Why had I agreed to help this man again? I could leave. I could go back home right now—

"Tulimak!" His voice carried somehow across the noisy din of the morning crowd emerging from their rooms and gathering for breakfast. I lifted my muzzle abruptly from where I'd been sullenly tucking it against my own neck fur, shocked to hear him down here. I saw a distant black paw waving at me from the bar and quickly hustled my way across the room, being less careful than I normally would have. At some point along the way I bumped a chair with a small cat of some sort in it and got an irritated "hey!" for my trouble. I apologized profusely, then continued on my way.

And there he was, sitting at the bar, one lean leg draped over the other, his threadbare tapered vest and well-fitted britches still somehow managing to make him look far more elegant than anyone in this place should. He wasn't wearing his coat or his hat, but had a gold chain hanging out of one pocket I hadn't seen there the night before, and he looked…better. The way he was leaning his thin frame against the bar suggested he was still favoring his hip, but he looked much more rested, his fur was groomed, and he smelled of someone who'd bathed recently. The soap was clearly inexpensive, but pleasant, likely whatever they provided here. It reminded me I could use a bath, myself.

He greeted me with a long canine smile as I approached, and I couldn't help but gawk at him for a moment before gathering my senses. The sheer nerve of him to look so composed when I was so…not.

"We agreed you wouldn't leave your room until I came to get you this morning," I blurted out, trying to cover the quiet panic in my voice as I glanced around the room.

"I had to pay my tab," he explained in an easygoing tone, looking sidelong at the bartender, the same woman from last night. She wasn't paying much attention to us, focusing on getting a tray of drinks and steaming bowls ready for one of the servers.

"Besides," he waved a paw, "this place is safe enough. I highly doubt those two would start trouble in a crowded establishment. The owner here's a mastiff…something something…mongrel mix. He's big, got a bunch of big boys, too. They keep the place pretty peaceful."

"Those two," I paused when one of the servers passed nearby us, and dropped my voice to a whisper as I moved to stand beside him, "those two men from last night found you here. And they got you outside somehow." I paused. "Why *did* you go outside? You saw something and then wandered off. If you'd stayed by the bar, by your own logic—"

"I was heading for my room," he explained, leaning his cheek ruff against a palm. "The staircase happens to be by the door. They cornered me and forced me out. My fault for panicking and trying to head upstairs. You're right, I should have stayed right here," he tapped the bar at that with his knuckles. "But I was more worried about my, ah…"

Realization dawned. "Your papers," I supplied.

He shrugged haplessly. "The truth dies with those documents up there, not with me. I mean ideally, it would be best if we both survived, but I had to prioritize."

"What could be so important that you'd risk your life over it?" I asked, settling my weight on the stool beside him. This was a point we'd discussed last night, but all he'd given me were roundabout answers that really answered nothing.

He looked up at me, giving me an even stare. "Aren't there things you'd be willing to die for?"

"People, maybe," I countered. "I don't know about 'things.'"

"I have my reasons," he assured me. "And in any case, I wasn't counting on dying. I only had a suspicion those two were hunters, because I thought I'd seen them tailing me while I was out in town a few days prior. I didn't know it was going to go south that fast."

"'South'?" I quoted back uncertainly.

"Uh…it's like saying 'poorly,'" he explained. "Or 'going wrong'. I don't entirely know the expression's provenance. Maybe referring to Hell? Because it's so far down. Ha…" He cleared his throat, seeming to realize I wasn't following. "Never mind. In any case, this whole trip *has* been a road to Hell for me with all the trouble I've had, but as I was saying, I have my reasons to be taking such risks. They're rather personal, is the thing."

"I," I paused, "I want to honor that. I do. But I also want to help you."

"A fact which I greatly appreciate," he said, putting a paw over mine while still maintaining eye contact with me. The combination was almost overwhelming and set my mouth immediately dry. How did a starving little wolf manage something so easily with a stranger I couldn't even do with my family most days? I had to admire his boldness.

"R-right," I stammered out, embarrassed at myself and finding I immediately had to avert my gaze. I allowed my paw to remain beneath his. The heat was comforting. "But," I pressed on, "it's going to be hard to help you if I don't…understand things."

I heard rather than saw him consider that and after a quiet "hmmm" of a hum, he patted my paw and replied, "Fair point. And I'd hate to leave you in the lurch. I assure you, it's primarily for your own protection. I don't intend to ask for your help for long and I'd rather not get you involved any more than necessary in this whole sordid affair. But you did say you'd help me make my way to the village of Broen…"

"It's not so far out of my way," I nodded. "Broen is up-river twenty miles or so to the northwest, then another ten on foot. I was always planning to discard my raft up there once the ice set. Also it's exhausting and not really worth it to row up-river for long periods of time. The waters near here are mild, but they can get tumultuous the further up north you go."

"I have to admit, I don't much like the idea of my documents traveling via river," the wolf said with a slight grimace. "But they made it across the ocean and I've got a beaver skin bag that I was assured was water-tight."

"If we get dumped for whatever reason, you won't care about the documents," I promised him. "You'll be too busy re-learning how to breathe in ice-cold water."

"Spoken like a man who's experienced it," he said, arching an eyebrow. "You any good with that raft?"

"I've only used it for a season," I admitted. "But I've never lost control of it. I was very careful on the way down here and the current moved me along much faster then. It's just that ice can get tricky. Hopefully we won't encounter any."

Finnegan looked towards the stark white windows and presumably the fresh snowfall outside.

"It's not cold enough yet," I assured him. "The water, when it moves like it does in a river? It doesn't freeze as easily. It has to get very, *very* cold before it will begin to ice over. Right now that should only be happening up-river."

"Well, you can pray to your spirits that that doesn't happen," he muttered.

"I will," I nodded. "But the spirits of the river will not protect us from what is inevitable. If we are not clever enough to know when it is wise to take to the water, and when it isn't, that's our own failing."

"Harsh," he chuckled. "Your spirits don't sound much different than our 'God', honestly. What with the cruel ambivalence."

I knitted my brow. "It's not cruel. It's just that some things must be our own responsibility."

"All right, I don't want to get pulled into a discussion on theology," he sighed, rubbing his brow and smoothing back his ears. "Got enough of that back home. And I've never been much of a Godly man to begin with. He and I disagree on a few sticking points."

He hopped off the stool at that and immediately went weak in one knee and buckled, catching himself on the bar. His jaunty mood suddenly gone, I put a paw on his shoulder to steady him while he winced through the obvious pain he was in.

"You *really* need to see a healer," I reiterated my words from the night before, concerned.

"I've had worse, I assure you," he shook his head, hissing through his teeth for a few moments as he steadied himself. "Just a bit of a fall."

"Onto a cobbled street," I pointed out. "Hardly soft earth. And you don't strike me as much of a warrior."

"Hnh, duly noted," he grinned, winking one eye open at me. "Although I fail to see how that would have helped me."

"That's because you're not a warrior," I repeated. "Most tribal warriors learn how to fall without hurting themselves. As much."

"Not a skill I ever thought I'd need," he said defensively. Then with a slump, "You're right, though. I'm in over my head on this particular caper and the sooner I can admit that, the better."

"'Caper'?" I repeated, as I helped him slowly back to his feet.

"Uhh…quest? Job? Mission? I don't know, it's really none of those. I'm not sure what," he stretched out his lower back with a grunt, his tail bristling as he did so, "to call this. 'Disaster' is probably the best word that comes to mind. I've had a few scrapes in my unfortunate life, but this one certainly takes the crown."

"So, the papers…" I said again, pointedly.

"Right," he started towards the stairs. "Follow me."

We made our way back up to his room. When he unlocked the door, I was taken aback by the state of things inside.

"When did you pack everything away?" I asked as I stepped inside, noting the bare walls and stripped bed. Somehow the mess from the evening prior had all but disappeared, save a few ink stains on the makeshift table, some mangled quill pens and a few crumpled and torn sheets of discarded paper left crammed in an empty chamber pot. At least I hope it was empty under all that paper.

"One thing I've gotten rather good at over the last few months is leaving no traces," he said as he approached the bed, where one large, worn beaver skin bag was stuffed to bursting. "I suppose for you tribesmen it would be like—" he began to struggle to close the bag, "covering your-nngh…tracks."

I approached him from behind, unable to watch him fight with the bag any longer. I leaned down over him and with one paw, pulled the straps closed.

"Seriously," he sighed, grabbing for the handle while looking back over his shoulder at me. "Big, handy bear. Where have you been all my life?"

I flushed in my ears, which I was thankful he wouldn't see from where he was standing. "Here," I murmured, reaching down and grabbing the bag before he could. "You shouldn't carry that."

"Careful, it's heav—" he turned and cut himself off as I lifted it over my shoulder with ease. "Oh." He blinked. "Right."

"My size is more a hindrance than anything, most of the time," I said. "But it's helpful at least for tasks like this. And pulling up nets for fishing. And rowing." I looked around the room. "Is this it?"

"As it turns out, documents are rather easy to pack down," he said as he donned his torn coat. No other choice, really. "And I haven't much clothing left that's serviceable. I had more when I left Amuresca, but that was months ago and the journey's taken its toll." He glanced down at his state of affairs, blowing out a breath through his nose. "I look a fright. Most highwaymen could muster more class."

"Your clothing is still finer than most anyone else in this town," I insisted. "You look fine. Honestly, it might do you well to stand out less, given the state of things."

"'Fine' is not 'refined,'" he moaned. "But I suppose you're right about that last part."

"Finnegan," I caught his attention by using his name. He stared up at me, ears perked. "Before we leave this room, I want to know what I'm carrying in this bag." I watched as his gaze fell, then sighed. "Please."

"If you wish," he shuffled a bit on his feet, then slowly sat on the edge of the bed. After a moment I did the same, setting our bags down.

"Not all of this will make sense to you, since it concerns foreign affairs," he began, looking up at me.

There was that eye contact again. How was that so easy for him?

I nodded. "I will try my best to follow along."

"There's a man in Amuresca – a loathsome man," he said, with bile on his tongue. "A Pedigree Lord. That's a man of great importance in my country, a man with a title and land, a lot of resources." He looked to me to make sure I wasn't confused, then continued. "This man..." he went silent for a few moments, gathering his thoughts. "This man betrayed someone very important to me." Silence again, then, "My mother."

I watched as his frame went tense, his ears tucked back against the scruff of his neck. His eyes in contrast were sharp, like they were last night when he was talking about finding "the truth." I believed him.

"Do you understand the importance of marriage?" he asked.

"I've never been married," I said. "But yes, I understand why it's important to pledge yourself to someone, to forge bonds between tribes. There are many reasons it's important."

"I'd wager to guess they're different here than they are in Amuresca," he said dryly. "But suffice to say, bloodlines and bonds are *very* important where I come from. Especially the Church-sanctioned kind. And if you break them or—worse yet—never have them, the consequences can be dire." He began to count off on his fingers. "Opportunities, money, how you're treated by the law, and *shame*." He really emphasized the last word through his teeth. "Shame over there is like an art form. Everyone delights in wielding it, on every rung of society. Even the Priests."

"That's awful," I stated simply, because I didn't know what else to say.

"It's also not the point," he shook his head. "The point is, this man, this Pedigree lord, made promises to my mother. He used her. And then he refused to marry her. He left her saddled with a pup and a sullied reputation, which for some reason she had to bear alone, even though he's the one who lied to and deceived her. That sound right to you?"

"No," I said softly. I hesitated for a few moments, before murmuring, "So he's your fath—"

"*Please*," he said emphatically, turning his sharp gaze on me. "Don't use that title. He doesn't deserve it."

"I'm sorry," I said quietly. I brought a paw up to my forearm, suddenly uncomfortable I'd literally forced this all out of him. It's no wonder he hadn't wanted to talk about it.

"My mother died some years ago," he said, his tone cold. He fished the gold chain out of his pocket, tugging free an expensive-looking pocket watch. I only even knew what it was because I'd seen one at a trade post, once. "This was all he gave her when they parted ways. She passed it on to me and after she died, I decided I'd throw it back in his face in Highvolle. That's when I found out how the old man makes his gold. He owns a Mercantile Fleet that's registered with the Crown itself, and runs goods between my country and yours."

He paused, "But here's the thing." He looked down to his bag, then back up to me. "I have connections in Highvolle and while I was digging into the man to find out how I could confront him somewhere that'd be the most public, the most humiliating place I could find...I stumbled on some pretty damning information about what his ships really move."

"What do you mean?" I asked, my stomach knotting. The intensity of his gaze was beginning to unnerve me. His eyes were beautiful in the right light, but not when he was angry.

"People," he said, licking his teeth. "He's a slaver. And I can think of no greater punishment for that demon than airing his true colors for all the world to see."

Finnegan's words hung over my head like a storm cloud for the remainder of the day, their implications beyond what I could imagine. My knowledge of slavery was limited to a tribal custom known as "Fanruk Wela," which was fundamentally different in many ways than what he'd had to explain to me. I hadn't even known the Amurescan word at first, let alone its equivalent.

Fanruk Wela was a practice whereby one tribe took female prisoners, usually from war or other skirmishes, and forcibly married them to their men. It was often used as a means to make alliances, ironically, and to spread blood between tribes. Especially rival tribes who might have little other reason to meet peaceably. Once their women were married into the opposing tribe, it was generally agreed-upon that there was little choice but to begin negotiations for a peace, or to forge bonds for future communication and trade.

While I understood the reason for the practice, at least in theory, I felt fortunate that my own tribal leader, my otterfa, found the idea outdated and abhorrent. Even among some of the most old-world tribes, traditions like Fanruk Wela were beginning to fade away.

And these days in the few places in the North Country where it still took place, it was usually more done out of adherence to tradition and had often been negotiated in advance. Some couples used it as an excuse to find romance across tribal boundaries. Sometimes species boundaries.

Even in the worst cases though, in whatever far corners of the North where the practice was still in full swing, still completely non-consensual, once the woman was taken and forced to marry, she became a part of the tribe. I couldn't speak to the conditions those women lived under, but they were *supposed* to be treated as family. The whole idea still made my skin crawl, though. To think of it happening to one of my sisters…it was no wonder our tribe had outlawed it.

What Finnegan had described was something else entirely. People treated like beasts of burden, like work animals. Not for the purpose of expanding your family or your tribe, but to be bred and bartered for, worked until their bodies broke down, until they were no longer of "value." No rights to any kind of life outside of the purpose they'd been bought and sold for. If there was a similar tradition amongst the tribal peoples of the North Country, I had never heard its' like.

I suppose that didn't mean it didn't exist, though. People could be terrible the world over, as much as I hated reflecting on the fact. I'd been fortunate enough not to glimpse the darker side of life, growing up in my little tribe. But this trip was proving a fast lesson, and one that was perhaps overdue.

This "slavery" sounded hideous. Unthinkable. And apparently, according to Finn…very commonplace, in the world beyond our lands.

"Our people fought a war to end the practice, generations ago," he said as we moved through the bustling open-air market that Main Street had become. He paused near a vendor with a cart full of late season root vegetables, mainly carrots, and began looking over some of the thickest ones, turning them over in his paws and presumably looking for blemishes.

"A war?" I asked, peering over his shoulder. He'd donned his hat again, which made it hard to see his face from above. "With another tribe?"

"Another country," he corrected me. "Mataa. Enormous Nation to the south of Amuresca, and our biggest economic rivals. Wasn't the first war, either. Our countries have been nipping at each others' heels throughout most of known history. Usually over religion, land, resources…same things your people fight over, I'd imagine."

I nodded at that, picking up one of the carrots and giving it a sniff. They smelled fresh and they looked good to me, but I'd thought wolves primarily ate meat.

"But the last big one was specifically over slavery," he continued. "Two centuries ago? I think? Something like that. Two centuries ago, the Church passed an edict banning the sale or ownership of 'high-minded creatures'. Which basically covers any person who can make their own decisions and speak. You know, discounting the mentally infirm and whatnot."

"What happens to them?" I asked, not liking the sound of that.

"Wards of the Church, or their families," he said, shrugging. "Whoever will take care of them. But if you're wondering if they get taken advantage of, the short answer is 'yes'. The Church has work-camps and workhouses *everywhere*, where they warehouse the 'infirm' and 'heretics', and they have some broad interpretations of those words, let me tell you. I've known a few blokes unlucky enough to do time in one of those places, it's as good as slavery."

"So what is the point?" I asked, uncertainly. "Of outlawing it if it happens anyway?"

"Moral superiority?" He chuckled, for some reason. "No, no…I mean, that's the reason given. The Faith is built on this ladder structure of death and rebirth. The thought is, if you're a good lad and you follow the doctrines, tithe generously and pray to the big dog in the sky, you get to slooooowly but surely clamber your way up the ladders in each successive life. Until eventually you're born as one of the Chosen People, the Pedigrees. And they can 'ascend' when they die. To be with God."

I blinked, trying to follow all of that. "Didn't you say your father…"

"Yeah, he's one of the ruling elite," he said bitterly, looking up at me. "Which is just proof it's all bullshit, as far as I'm concerned. These are supposed to be the least sinful, the most perfect people. One step on the great celestial ladder away from true salvation. All they've got to do is live pious, make pups with the right people so other Chosen People's souls can have vessels to be born into, and then die a righteous death. You screw anything up along the way and you get kicked back down the ladder. But my father's still right up on top. What does that tell you?"

I tried to process that. I wanted to be respectful of someone else's beliefs, but it *was* confusing.

"By the logic of The Faith, my father did the right thing by turning his back on my mother and marrying some Pedigree woman instead. The 'righteous' and 'holy' thing," he said distastefully. "Pedigrees breed for purity, of body *and* soul. You don't want a tainted pup, or you're delivering a soul to an unworthy vessel."

His tail, which was usually rather lively, had gone uncharacteristically still while he spoke of his faith. I took that to be a bad sign. I wanted to say something comforting, but found my tongue stuck in my throat. I still didn't want to offend.

"Anyway," he said, shaking his head and moving on just like that. "Moral superiority might be the excuse, but it's not really why they banned the sale of people. The real reason was rats."

"I-okay," I said uncertainly.

"Rats are the most prolific peoples in most countries. Maybe not here, but give it time. Trust me, they're survivors," he said with a chuckle. "They tend to be numerous wherever they are, but they're also some of the smallest, and the most overlooked people. They also tend to get blamed for a lot of diseases, fairly or unfairly. I'm no Physician, so I can't attest to the truth of that either way. Seems to me like it's more that it's easier to get sick, what with the...poverty, and all. But for all the aforementioned reasons, they're at the bottom of the damnable ladder. And not just in Amuresca. In Mataa they call them 'untouchables'. In our country they're the farthest away from God, if you believe the Priests. They don't get a fair shake. Anywhere. So they're poor, not well-regarded, have trouble finding good employment or good relations with other species. They mostly stick to family groups, caravans and slum cities, they aren't even allowed to own land in most places. And they get enslaved a lot. Or at least, they used to."

"'Owning' land is a very Otherwolf idea," I said.

"Hey, don't look at me," he shrugged. "I haven't owned much of anything throughout my life I couldn't carry on my person. Land ownership's pretty rare unless you're wealthy even amongst canines in my country."

"I'm sorry, you were telling a story," I said, hoping he'd still continue. I'd never gotten to listen to stories from an Otherwolf before. This was so new and exciting.

"There was a Revolution," he said. "Again, this was centuries ago, and my history's better than most, but I only know it in vague terms. There was a rat who rose to prominence in the Kadrush, our 'North Country' basically, and returned to Amuresca with a taste for rebellion. She inspired rats across Amuresca to take on the Pedigrees. Can you imagine? And they were really making a dent apparently, because that's when the Church passed the edict. They claimed it was about giving all peoples a fair chance to better themselves in freedom than they'd have in shackles, and climb that celestial ladder. But really, it was because of the rats. At the time *most* of their population were slaves and abolition was their chief demand."

"And then your country," I paused for a moment, "fought another country?"

"It was a case of 'if we have to play by these rules, so do you,'" he explained. "Once Amuresca abolished slavery, we started falling behind Mataa economically. Things balanced out eventually; they tend to when suddenly a huge portion of your population is generating industry and spending money they didn't have before. But there were growing pains in the beginning, since so much of our economy depended on slave labor before that. Mataa's industries still do. They still haven't *really* abolished slavery. We fought this whole holy war with them over it, which was really over *money*, mind you," he added that last part around a hand like it was some great conspiracy, "and we made them sign this worthless treaty to bring the fighting to an end, but it basically only abolished slavery there in *name*. Slavery is very much still alive in Mataa, they just call it something else now, and use legal loopholes to insist it's something other than what it is."

"It still sounds like a good thing," I stated, thinking carefully about all this new history I'd been given. I believed him, he really had no reason to be inventing all of this, and what chances would I ever get again to learn about the world so far from my home? "This war," I clarified. "Even if it was done for the wrong reasons."

"War's never a good thing," he said solemnly. "But I see what you mean. It probably would have been, if it'd stuck in any meaningful way. But the

Huudari Tribes—that's what the people in power in Mataa call themselves—figured out that if they just called slavery 'indentured labor' and attached contracts to the work, they could essentially keep the practice going. And they have. And Eamon is taking advantage of that."

"Your fath—" I stopped myself. "The man who sired you?"

"Yes." He placed two carrots he'd at this point meticulously picked out back in the wooden box he'd found them in, fixing the frayed edges of his coat sleeves. I watched him, perplexed.

"Just a nervous habit?" I guessed. I had a few of my own.

"Huh?" He looked up at me, seeming surprised. "Wh-no. I just, ah, can't afford produce."

I looked at the scrawled prices on the cart, arching an eyebrow. Sure, they were a *little* expensive, but that was hardly surprising considering they were some of the last fresh vegetables pulled from the ground, probably stored in a root cellar somewhere.

"I haven't been able to afford anything fresh in a while," he sighed. "I've sold just about everything I can. I had no idea what a trip across the New World was going to cost me when I set out, but I've gone through almost all of my savings at this point."

"Well once we're on the river I have fish," I offered, which immediately set his ears shooting up. I had to laugh when his head whipped around to stare at me, his eyes gone wide. "You," I chuckled, "looked like a young otter there for a moment. I've never seen a wolf so excited for fish."

"Oh, we Amurescans love our fish," he assured me. "And it's 'dog,' by the way. We prefer there be a distinction."

"Oh," I cleared my throat, my eyes roving his very…very wolfish face. And ears. And fur. Although I suppose he *was* small for a wolf. "I'm sorry, I-it can be hard to tell sometimes."

"You're forgiven for being confused," he replied. "My mother was a wolf. And I do carry her features more strongly than I'd like—what has gotten into you?" He balked as he took in my sudden smile, which I can only imagine from his expression, was showing off more teeth than I intended.

"I'm sorry," I put up my paws. No, no good either. Huge claws. I put them down, hiding them behind my back. But then there was the rest of me, which was no less intimidating. "I'm sorry," I repeated. "I've just never met someone else with, with mixed lineage. I'm also, well, my parents were two different kinds of bears."

He looked me over, seeming perplexed for only a moment before just snuffing. "Huh. Didn't know that could happen."

I nodded, pointing to the darker fur around my eyes. "You can mostly see it where my fur turns darker." I'd seen Great Northern bears and even one Ice Bear, and it was clear I carried the bloodline of both. My fur was not pure and white like the Ice Bears; my undercoat was brown and cream-colored in places, especially along my spine and flanks, as well as my muzzle and eyes. And my muzzle was shorter, like the Great Northern bears.

He tilted his head. "Seems pretty minor. But I suppose to an outsider, the differences between some dogs and wolves would be minor, too. In any case, it's pretty common amongst dogs. So you absolutely have met mixed blood canines, you just don't realize it. A lot of dogs have wolf blood, and vice versa."

"I've heard you were the same people, once." As good a time as any to get the truth of that straightened out.

"A *long* time ago," he said. "It's a pretty important distinction now." He stressed that part in a very no-nonsense way that I took to meant I might have offended him and he was getting frustrated having to repeat himself. So I just nodded. Whatever the difference was, other than strictly appearance, between the wolves and these "dogs," I would try to respect it.

But he'd said his mother was the wolf, so…that was confusing. He preferred to identify with his father's lineage? Why? He certainly didn't seem fond of the man. He didn't even seem fond of the society he came from.

I reached down and started grabbing up an armful of carrots. It wasn't my place to wonder such things about something so personal to another. As it was, I'd pushed him to talk to me about the matter of why he was being hunted, which had proven to be very personal. He'd even warned me it was personal, and I'd overstepped and insisted anyway.

I mean, I suppose I *was* putting my life on the line for him. So had it really been overstepping?

Oh…I hated thinking this way. I kept gathering carrots, while my mind spun with self-doubt. Had I made the right choice? Had I made *any* right choices since I'd met Finnegan? How many more choices would I make wrong in the future?

"Tulimak," his voice snapped me out of my reverie, and I paused and looked down at him. He was looking at my arms, which were now laden with carrots. "Are you, ah," he looked between the vegetables and me, "getting all of those?"

I looked down at the armful, then to the vendor, an older boar woman who was hustling over to us with a broad grin on her snout. "You like them, right?" I asked Finnegan. "We can make stews while we travel, to keep our fare varied. I hadn't known wolv—dogs liked vegetables like this, but you seemed to want some."

"I love carrots," he admitted, his ears splaying for some reason, like he was ashamed to admit it. "But I haven't the coin."

There was something about his demeanor that seemed false. His stance was more subdued, tail almost between his legs, ears splayed as they were...it was cute, I couldn't deny that. But he didn't *smell* subdued, if that makes sense. He felt as sharp and acute as he had been a few moments earlier, but he was adopting a more submissive posture. The two didn't fit together. It almost reminded me of my otter siblings when they were begging me for a fish. Except this was a full-grown man.

I couldn't deny it was effective, though. And for now, I didn't see a reason not to let him win me over. I would have bought the carrots anyway.

I patted him on the head between his ears, and to his credit he only looked moderately irritated. I smiled down at him, "I'll get us the rations we'll need for the trip. Feeding you won't cost me much more than feeding myself. I probably eat four servings to your one."

"I wouldn't doubt that," he muttered as I moved past him and deposited the stack of carrots down on one of the boar's empty carts and began asking her about her potatoes. Another import the Otherwolves had brought here, and one that I very much enjoyed.

As the sun rose further in the sky, we gathered what I imagined we'd need for the trip. I'd always been planning to use today to re-supply anyway, I was just purchasing a little more food now than I'd originally intended to. And really, in the end it wouldn't have much effect on the coin I would bring home to my tribe. I'd done well on my fish, better than my father and I had expected when I'd set out. And with Finnegan along, I might even make better time going upriver, if he was at all able to help with rowing.

I tried to focus on those thoughts and not lingering fears about hunters around every corner, while we perused the market. We—or well, I—purchased fresh, fluffy griddle cakes drizzled with butter, and if you'll pardon the expression, Finnegan wolfed his down with a relish that made me smile. There weren't many better feelings in the world, I'd wager, than feeding someone and watching them enjoy it, especially if they'd been long denied. I found myself looking forward to cooking for him, wondering what I could make with our limited ingredients and one small iron pot. I wasn't really much of a cook, just knew how to keep myself fed on long trips. I hadn't thought I was going to have any kind of company on the trip home and while solitude suited me fine, I discovered I was looking forward to it.

After a few hours of gathering supplies, sharing a meal in the town square and watching the oblivious hustle and bustle of the frontier town, and not a single man attacking us, I was finding my calm again. Finn seemed to be right. If anyone else in this town was hunting him the way those two men had been, they weren't showing themselves with me around.

I'd long known, of course, that being so big had its advantages. It was no mystery to me that bears were often feared and almost always given a wide berth, wherever they went. And that wasn't *just* because of our size. The bear tribes had fearsome reputations as unflinching, stalwart bastions of the tribal alliance, wherever they lived. It's part of why we were becoming so rare. My father said they'd resisted the incursion of the Otherwolves more than any others. It's likely why I'd been found abandoned and what had ultimately become of my parents.

Of course, I'd never know for sure.

But living a relatively peaceful life as I had up until this point, I hadn't ever really had a use for a fearsome reputation or even for my size and strength. It had come up occasionally doing physical labor back home with my tribe, but more often than not, it was a hindrance. Now for the first time, I was able to put my lineage to use for something. Even if it was just to scare people off. The fact is, I'd gotten lucky with the fox the night before. I wasn't trained to be a warrior. I barely had the stomach for dressing a hare, let alone hurting and potentially killing *people*.

Hopefully, the intimidation factor alone would be enough. That was probably what Finnegan was counting on and it was comforting to think we'd gotten through the worst of it.

I found myself looking at him again while we walked down towards River Street, my satchel resting heavily over my shoulder. I tried to obscure my glances and make them look natural, but I must not have been as subtle as I thought I was being, because he caught my eye on one particularly long look and crooked an eyebrow.

"Crumbs?" he guessed, pawing at his muzzle a bit and shivering his whiskers.

"Oh, no," I assured him quickly. He brushed his hands up over his fine-featured snout and removed his hat to sweep back his ears and the ruff of fur between them.

How to put this?

"I was just thinking, ahh," the words embarrassingly came out in a sort of croak, and I was left wondering why. "You said you favor your mother's looks more strongly than you'd like. I…take it you mean you look more like a wolf than you'd like?"

He sighed through his nose, with the air of someone who didn't like being reminded of something. "Yes. That is what I meant."

"I know, somewhat at least, how it feels to look different than everyone else around you," I explained softly. That got his attention. He turned his green gaze on mine. "I just wanted to say, regardless how the wolves, or the Otherwolves see you…I think your features are very striking. I-in a good way," I added quickly.

He gave me a long, searching look, tilting his head just slightly. I felt like something had shifted in his gaze, like he was seeing something differently than before. Whatever it was, he said nothing for a long moment, then simply gave a "hmm" of consideration.

My stomach did that thing it does sometimes where it felt like it had lifted inside me, but it wasn't quite discomfort. I'm not sure what it was. Apprehension, certainly. Why? It had just been a simple compliment.

Maybe because he was a stranger. A man outside my tribe. A foreigner? But that didn't mean I shouldn't show kindness towards him. Or indeed, in this case, honesty.

Had I *needed* to say that to show kindness, though?

Probably not, I decided. But I'd wanted to, and for some reason I hadn't hesitated like I normally would have. I'd really wanted to compliment him. So I had. It was done, and it had felt right. Maybe I just wanted to comfort someone else with mixed blood who knew the sting of looking different. Nothing could be wrong there.

What I didn't expect was for him to answer me the way he did.

"You're a rather striking fellow yourself, Tulimak," he said after a considerable silence had passed between the two of us. There was a quiet, careful hesitance to his voice, which he kept rather low. But when I turned to look down at him, he was staring back at me, smiling coolly.

I didn't know what to say to that, so I just muttered a quiet "thank you," and we made our way to the river.

Chapter 4

Unfamiliar Waters

For the rest of the afternoon, I could feel the canine's eyes on my back, whenever I wasn't looking at him. You get a sensation for that sort of thing even as a predatory species, an awareness that you're being sized up. Any time I turned to regard Finnegan, he'd just smile wanly at me, apparently neither ashamed of being caught, nor too awkward to lock eyes with me. The man was *never* awkward, which for someone like me, would have been miraculous growth. For him, it seemed effortless. Even while we took the mile-long hike down the riverbed towards where I'd stowed my raft, with nothing but precarious deer trails and ice-slicked stone and mud, he moved with a confidence that belied his size, (and if I'm being honest, his physical abilities). That's not to say his footing was always stable, he just never seemed deterred.

But then, I was fast learning that Finnegan was the sort of man whose every step had purpose, or at least, that was certainly the impression he wanted to make. I wasn't well versed with the world, but I'd always thought myself to be a good judge of character. Since I'd met him, he'd wasted no time in deducing who I was, how I might be able to help him, and he'd told me just enough about himself and his task to ensnare me, but little more. I didn't begrudge him any of that, nor did I doubt his sincerity. The men hunting him had been proof enough that he truly needed help, and he spoke so passionately about his cause, I had to believe it was genuine. But I'd be a fool to be led around by a man I'd met a day ago without at least taking stock of what he'd permitted me to know and what else might remain unsaid.

One thing was very clear. This was a wolf...dog? Wolfdog? With a clear direction in life. My otterfa would have called him "driven." That intense gaze of his was a permanent fixture and it suited his equally intense personality. Even while injured and so clearly far from the society he called home across the sea, he managed to keep that confident air about him. And no matter how hard I squinted, I honestly couldn't tell if it was an act, or if he was truly possessing of the certainty he put off.

Despite this, he wasn't lacking for charm, either. Helping my otterfa at the trade posts over the years, I'd met plenty of independent, confident lone men. And while I respected the sort of assuredness it took to venture off into the wilds and trap for months at a time alone, they didn't tend to be much for conversation, and their demeanor was usually what I'd call "gruff" at best. Finnegan was generally pretty merry and pleasant to talk to, when you weren't discussing his much-loathed kindred across the seas. As we walked, he talked to me about a great many things, none of any real importance, just light conversation. Fish, for one. Because I'm boring and we were near the water, so of course I talked about fish...but it didn't matter that I was boring, or that I earnestly took a delight in explaining the spawning habits of salmon, because he listened to me enrapt all the same. I suppose to him, my very mundane life here might have been exotic.

I wasn't usually much of a talker. Even with my family, I'd always favored listening. But in the short afternoon we spent together readying for our trip, I found I couldn't bear the silence that would occasionally pass between us. I'm not sure if it was an anxious need to fill the space with words because I was traveling with a stranger, or if it had more to do with the fact that he seemed to want to listen to me as much as I usually gave way to listen to others. Finn was not lacking in questions for me to field, or anecdotes of his own, (yes, even about fish) but when I'd say something, whether it was about food, the trip or whatever else came to mind, his big black ears would snap up and he'd look at me and listen. It was oddly thrilling to have the foreigner's attention. I'd barely ever spoken this much to anyone outside my tribe, let alone someone from another land. And if he was merely feigning interest, he was doing a convincing job.

The mile hike up the river took a few hours, primarily due to the fresh snow and ice and the occasional breaks we had to take for Finnegan to rest. I was carrying all of our possessions by then. He obviously didn't have the endurance for travel that I had, but it was more than that. His injury was bothering him. He clearly didn't want me to notice, but I could tell.

We came to a stop near the upturned, gnarled roots of a fallen spruce that had grown too close to the banks of the widening river. Nearby was a clutch of birch, a trio of the young, peeling white trees. My marker. I began sniffing about.

Finnegan gave a heavy sigh as he lowered himself to sit on a curled root that absolutely would not have supported my weight. He brushed off the fresh snow first, apparently not so exhausted that he was willing to have a cold, wet rear. I heard him wince even though I wasn't looking his way at that moment, a low, almost imperceptible whine through his teeth.

I turned to regard him sympathetically. "I hope it's not a broken tail-bone," I murmured.

"Not hardly," he assured me. "I didn't fall *that* hard. It's more in my hip, in any case. Sort of twinges down my leg, and I can feel it in my back whenever I have to stretch or bend," he sighed, looking frustrated. His green gaze flicked up to mine. "You must think me quite the fragile lad. Can't even take a slight spill in an alley."

"You fell on *cobblestones*," I felt my brow crease, and immediately tried to unfurrow it. It always made me self-conscious for some reason when I could feel the folds of fur on my face. So unlike my sleek-furred family members. I plodded over towards him and sunk down to one knee, putting a hand on his shoulder gingerly as I took stock of the way he was sitting. As if I'd glean some way to help. I was hardly a healer.

He glanced at my paw on him, and I realized how big my hand looked against his lean, small shoulder. I withdrew it, immediately.

"Why do you do that?" he asked suddenly.

To say I was caught off-guard was an understatement. I hadn't expected him to...to call me out for the transgression. I'd removed my hand-

"I-I'm sorry," I said, humiliated, looking anywhere but him. "I shouldn't have touched you without your permiss—"

He snorted. Actually snorted. It was a laugh, I realized after a moment. And a pretty undignified one. When I looked up at him, he wasn't bothering to cover it, either.

"Not that," he guffawed. "I'd say we're pretty well past impropriety at this point. You scraped me off the ground while I was getting the shite kicked out of me by two blokes in a back alley. You've been helping me carry my overstuffed satchel all day, and soon we'll be sharing what I suspect will be tight confines on a...is it like a canoe?" he guessed.

"It's a timber raft," I said, my long claws itching at my palms where they were curled.

"Lovely," he said, unconvincingly. "Well look, regardless of my accommodations while traveling with you, they're a fine sight better than dead. Which is what I'd be without your intervention. So you have absolutely earned the right for an occasional companionable pat on the shoulder." He chuckled. "Really, more, if you want."

I arched an eyebrow at him. Sometimes his comments didn't make a whole lot of sense to me. Cultural differences, I suppose. "So...I haven't offended you..." I ventured.

He rolled his eyes, and stiffly got to his feet. "No, Tulimak, you haven't offended me." He sighed after a brief pause following that statement, like something I'd said, or not said, was exhausting him. "Damned if you're not a hard bloke to read." He muttered the last part as he headed towards the bank of the river, flexing his unclad toes in the rocky, wet soil near the edge of the water. I couldn't help but notice the way the shallow tendrils of water trapped in crevices along the banks were beginning to freeze.

"We should try to make some progress with what's left of the day," I said, abruptly fixing my mind on the task ahead. Travel, I could do. I knew how to travel. I knew this river. Navigating this new friendship would have to wait.

I heard his footsteps crunching through loose stone and ice as I moved off towards the clutch of birch trees. "How much more of a walk, then?" he asked, his voice fading a bit into the wind as I put some distance between us. It was going to snow again tonight. I could smell it.

I felt around in the fresh snow with my foot, until I found what I was looking for. A forked stick, half-buried in the frozen soil. I reached down and wrapped both paws around it, and began to pull upwards.

"What in God's name are you—" he began, then gasped audibly as the snow spread before me in a wide patch began to shiver and lift upwards, sliding down off the buried, half-frozen expanse of stretched hide I'd laid out days ago over my possessions. It was actually the watertight, cured skin of two bull moose, sewn together with beaver skin cording. It was a simple tent really, or at least it made up the roof of the lean-to I used when I slept. It would come in handy tonight, if my guess on the weather panned out. It wasn't nearly as comfortable as a tipi, but it served to keep the elements out and went up quickly. It also made for a good cover to hide my things under.

I shook the cumbersome hide out as well as I could, unknotting it from where I'd tied it to the unique stick. Good thing I'd anticipated the snow, without the marker it might have been hard to find. I heard Finn approaching from behind me, padding carefully through the snow-covered underbrush. "Is that—" he began.

"My cache," I said with a grin, looking down proudly on my hidden treasure. My raft had weathered the cold well, it didn't look like any of the lashings had snapped, and nothing had gotten at the frozen canvas sacks I'd buried in the snow alongside it, which I happened to know were full of salmon I'd saved for my own enjoyment on the trip home.

Finnegan seemed less impressed, his ears drooping a fraction.

"What's wrong?" I asked, looking down at him.

"I-I just, I don't mean to offend," he gestured helplessly at the lashed timbers. "But it's…it's just timbers tied together. There are holes, even. Spaces."

"Here and there," I shrugged. "I'm sorry it's not a canoe, but my father can't spare those. And anyway, they're too small for me."

"Will it even float?" he asked dejectedly.

I chuckled. "How do you think I got here? I'll show you, but it'd be easier if I had your help launching it, and we need to be ready to get onboard once we've got it to the bank, all right? Help me find the oars, they're buried around here somewhere…"

I began digging about, as he asked almost disbelievingly, "'Oars'?"

"Well, yes," I said. "We're traveling up-river. It's not a fast-moving river, but we'll still need to row."

"And you were going to do this alone?!"

"To be honest, this is my first time making this trip alone," I admitted. His expression following that was so aghast as to be almost comical. I tried not to laugh and only half succeeded. "Don't worry," I tried to assure him, patting his slumped shoulder again, this time with more confidence. "I promise you it won't be as hard as it sounds."

It was just so great to get out on the water again. There was such familiarity in it, such comfort. The river wasn't exactly "home," but it had been a constant companion throughout my life. Indeed, it had brought me to my eventual adoptive family. In a way, it had delivered me to my parents, like a healer bringing forth life into the world.

Finnegan seemed less enamored.

From the moment he'd set foot on my raft, unstable and panic-stricken by the time I settled my bulk aboard, he'd found more and more reasons to be dissatisfied. His clothing wasn't suited for long periods of sitting and crouching, and looked to be made of cotton and wool, so it would soak up the cold water. And there was simply no way to avoid getting a little wet now and then on the raft. I wore a breech cloth and a cloak I could tie back when I was on the river, both made from water-resistant pelts. Just like my otter family. To be fair though, our fur was made for the water and the cold, too. Mine somewhat less-so than my otter brethren, but still far better suited than Finn's seemed to be. Even now, as I glanced back briefly at him, he looked miserable and shrunken in on himself. Coupled with the fact that he was underweight for any man, woman or child living in the north in the winter, he'd suffer from the cold on this trip. We'd have to make frequent stops so he could warm himself by a fire. And once the snow started falling, we'd have a whole new problem.

As unfortunate as it had seemed at the time, our meeting in the alley might have been fate. I don't think he would have made this trip on his own. A lot of foreigners tended to underestimate the winters in this part of the country.

Well, that confident air about him had lasted all of the walk here, at least. The realities of traveling by river looked to be dampening his spirits.

"So if I-nnhh...said...at any point...that this is harder than you made it sound," the wolfdog grunted again as he sunk his oar into the cold, churning river, "would that be trite?"

"Sorry, I never learned that word," I called back over my shoulder at him. "Is it another way to say 'whining'?"

There was a marked pause from my companion, followed by a quieter, "Touché."

"That one I definitely don't know," I informed him chipperly.

"That wasn't even Amurescan," he assured me with a sigh. "I don't know why I expected you'd know it."

"What language is it?" I asked, hoping that perhaps conversation might cheer him up some. Luckily or unluckily for us, some of the fastest-flowing waters were actually here, closer to this part of the river. We had a few hours navigating through the worst of it, (which wasn't even that bad this time of year, really, not like in the spring during the melt). It was unfortunate that it would be over the first leg of the trip, but at least we wouldn't have to be rowing so hard through a winter storm.

"A dead one," he said, and I heard him dipping his oar back in. I had to slow to match his pace, which was fine. The water was choppy, but we weren't moving against a particularly fast current and I was enjoying watching the scenery go by. This close to Otherwolf land, we were passing a lot of game trails, homesteaders and even a few other canoes and rafts. None of the famed Otherwolf barges yet, though. I'd been hoping to see more of those.

I nodded. "There are a lot of words, phrases and paoken—that's hand-signs—we use in our tribe that are from tribes that no longer exist. Lost to time, to disease or famine, or..."

"...to us?" he guessed accurately.

"Well not you, specifically," I reasoned.

"Look, I know this isn't worth much," he raised his voice to speak up just enough that I could hear him clearly over the sound of the oars and the water, "but you don't need to do that, all right? Excuse it all. Just let me apologize, whether it changes anything or not. We both know what's been happening to your people at the hands of mine," he said it matter-of-factly, his voice dipping to a regretful tone. "I'd rather not pretend otherwise. Even if I haven't personally had a hand in it, it seems...I don't know... disingenuous to tiptoe around it like *you're* worried about offending *me*."

I was silent for a while, uncertain what to say. My impulse was to again assure him he bore no guilt, but the truth was, that wasn't entirely what I felt in my heart. The Otherwolves were all benefiting from their incursions into our land, whether they intended to or not. And just because I liked some of the things they'd introduced us to, and my father had decided to adopt many of their ways, that didn't mean my otter tribe wouldn't still be better off if they didn't have to worry constantly about losing their land.

"Well then," I cleared my throat. "For whatever it's worth coming from a tribal orphan, because I can't speak for my adopted family...I'd rather none of that get in the way of our friendship."

"Fair enough," he replied. I felt him shifting his weight around, likely to avoid the water splashing up between two particularly gnarled and ill-fitted logs that ran the length of the raft. The water always found its way up between those two...I'd have to seal them better when I got home.

"You know," Finn said, breaking me out of my thoughts, "you said your lineage was mixed, but you never mentioned being adopted. Makes me feel a bit foolish for complaining about my family." He paused. "I mean, not really. I meant everything I said about the man who sired me. But still. I was at least raised by my mother."

"As was I," I said with the briefest of smiles. Thoughts of her always brought with them a certain warmth, like sunlight in the morning. "I never knew my blood mother. My adoptive mother was all I ever could have asked for, though. I don't feel I've been denied anything."

"How old were you when you lost her, if you don't mind me asking?" he asked gingerly.

"She returned to the earth two springs ago," I replied.

He didn't ask me how she died. I was glad for that.

"...it was more like three years, for me," he said after a time. "Feels so much more recent."

I had no reply for that. I felt exactly the same, some days more acutely than others.

"But, so," he paused, "that must have been your adopted mother, then. If it was only a few years ago."

He seemed confused, so I clarified, "She's the only mother I've ever known. She'll always be my mother. Just as the man who took me in will always be my father."

"Oh," he was silent a beat. "Do you ever think about them? Your real parents?"

"My real parents were—"

"All right, I get it," he sighed. "Your blood parents, then."

"Of course I do," I said softly. "What they might have looked like, how they might have raised me, what it would have been like to grow up in their tribe…but…it just wasn't to be. Whatever befell them, the river spirits saw to it that I was guided safely into another life. I try to be grateful for that, and not think about what might have been."

He didn't reply for a time. Then he coughed, a smile in his voice. "You'll forgive me for not entirely buying that. You seem like an overthinker. I've known you half a *day* and I've yet to watch you make a single decision without some degree of agony."

I rolled my eyes. "All right, yes, fine. I think about it all the time. I don't know that I'll ever…*not* wonder at what might have been."

"Understandable," he said knowingly. "A life denied is a hard thing to come to terms with."

"I was being earnest about being grateful, though," I insisted. "It's not that I feel I should have had *more*, I just…it's more wondering about what could have been *different*."

"Nothing wrong with wanting more," he said, shaking his oar out as it caught in something below the water's surface. I turned when I heard him grunt and watched him struggle with it for a few moments. "Snagged," he got out between grit teeth as he struggled with it.

"Could be a sunken tree, or fishing nets," I said, turning my bulk carefully so I could lean closer to him without tipping the raft too badly. I put my oar down, then reached over him and moved my arms alongside his, taking hold near his hands so I could test how thoroughly it was stuck.

"Definitely a fallen tree or something of the like," I confirmed as I shifted my grip to knock the oar beneath the water's surface against whatever it was snagged on. I looked down at the canine's black muzzle from above and saw his green-eyed gaze drift upwards towards me for a moment. I moved in closer against his back and gripped one of his hands with my own, guiding it so he could move the oar as I had. "See?" I directed. "See how it moves cleanly to the side then stops abruptly? If it were snagged on a net, it wouldn't 'knock' like that. It's caught against something. Probably roots or interlocked branches. Snags feel more like you're pulling something. See?"

"Hmm," he hummed, testing the oar again. His back pressed against my cloaked chest. I thought he meant to lean into me as leverage to pull the oar out, so I braced my arms against his to help.

"Turn the oar," I suggested. "Whatever you've gotten it lodged in, it must have found a way in to begin with. You just need to find the angle it'll come loose at."

He didn't bother with the oar, though. If anything, his grip on it relaxed.

"You're warm," he murmured.

I sucked in a breath. "Wh—"

The churning water a foot from our raft exploded, a sound cracking out across the river and the surrounding countryside. At first, my instincts screamed that it must be cracking ice. But it was louder, more like thunder. And of course, the river wasn't frozen over. It took me longer than it should have to register what it was I'd heard. By then, Finn was at rapt attention and was grabbing me by the cloak, pulling me.

"Get down!" he snapped. I struggled to comply, flattening myself as much to the surface of the raft as he was. Which wasn't accomplishing much. I was too big to take cover behind our lashed-down bags like he was.

"Finn, I can't—" I felt panic freezing up my body. "Who's shooting at us?!"

"Someone must have followed us from town," he deduced rather obviously, his eyes scanning the nearby riverbanks. Of course, he was right. I just wasn't thinking rationally. "Make your silhouette smaller," he commanded me fiercely. "As flat as you bloody well can!"

"I'm trying," I whispered, not sure why I couldn't get my voice out full-throated. It's not like keeping my voice low would help us. The reality of our situation was settling in fast, and fear was seizing my body. We were almost in the very center of the river, the only object in what was essentially a clear line of sight from every shore. And the shores here were thick with pine and spruce, debris from the river and brush, all with a fresh coat of snow. Finn at least must have thought the shot came from the right bank, but that still left a lot of ground our attacker could be firing from. And if they were camouflaged well enough, we'd never see them.

What's worse, even if we did, we'd have to slowly make our way to shore while getting shot at before we could do anything to defend ourselves. And our oar was stuck!

"They probably followed us from town and waited until the right moment to jump us," he spat. "We gave them a perfect chance, going out on the water…damn. Tulimak, grab my—"

Another shot crackled across the cold landscape, this one gone far wider than the first, puncturing the water ahead of us. Finnegan and I both flattened ourselves to the raft regardless.

I glanced past his prone form to where I was still gripping the oar in one hand, and considered releasing it. I'd lose an oar, but…

"I'm going to let go," I told him. "At least if we let the current take us, we'll be a moving target."

"No, keep us steady," he said between grit teeth. He turned to his stomach, crawling a foot or so past me and reaching out for where his satchel was leaning against our supply bags.

"Why?" I asked, uncertainly. The bulk of our bags, mostly full of carrots, potatoes and frozen fish, were all the cover we had out here. He couldn't reach past them for his satchel, so I inched my arm out to do so for him, pulling the strap to his hand

"Hang on, I'm counting," he said distractedly, pulling his satchel clumsily towards himself, the strap snagging a few times on the uneven surface of the raft.

Ten seconds later, something struck one of our bags and blew off chunks of canvas, potato and I swear, some of the fur along my back. Through the shock of it, I barely felt the pain.

"A little under thirty seconds," he gave a "tch" noise between his teeth, as he dug into his deep beaver skin bag. "Fucking cocker…got to be a percussion musket. That or he's a better loader than he is a shot."

"What?!" was all I could say.

He finally yanked something out of his bag…the pistol I'd seen him with that night, I realized. It was housed in what looked to be a hip holster that he hadn't been wearing, likely for my benefit. To be fair, traveling with an armed man might have made me too nervous to consider it. He was either masterfully falsifying confidence again, or he knew what he was doing with it too, because not a moment after he'd gotten it free, he began frantically tinkering with it. It looked like he was opening it up? For all the little I knew about fighting, I knew even less about guns.

"It means it's a nice weapon," he clarified. "An expensive one. Someone other than the foxes is hunting me. If they'd had a gun like that, they'd have used it."

"I thought you said you had no powder!" I exclaimed. "Why bother with yours?"

He took a moment to inspect the weapon once more before closing it up, seeming content. "Good, still dry. What do you think I spent the last of my coin on?"

He risked lifting his head after that, peering over one of the sacks of frozen fish. I began to beg him to get down, when another shot skipped across the water, this one coming close like the first, but not managing to peg our raft as the last had. My back felt wet.

"Got him," he growled out, and *stood,* stepping out from behind cover to the edge of the raft.

Before I could do anything—as if there was anything I *could* do in this situation, a thunderously loud noise broke from his outstretched hand, far louder than I'd ever imagined up close. He held the weapon out still and straight in front of him, like he was a stone statue pointing towards some distant horizon. I had never actually seen a gun fired so close to me before. It looked and felt like a pronouncement. That's the best way I can honestly think to describe it.

There was a very distant noise I could only barely hear over the sound of the river and the pounding of blood in my ears. It might have been a voice. If it was, they were none too happy by the sound of it.

"Nicked him at best," he snarled, letting his pistol fall at his side. "Tulimak, can you get us moving? I don't know if that's put him off entirely."

I nodded numbly and re-focused my attention on the oar, turning it in my palm like a key, until I found the right angle to free it. As it came away, I pushed myself to my knees and grabbed the other oar, spinning them both up into the air then digging back into the water for the most powerful stroke I could manage.

We were getting out of here as fast as my arms would take us.

The hunter took no further shots at us as we began moving upriver again, this time at a much less leisurely pace. We traveled in silence for a time, Finnegan facing down-river all the while, his ears pivoting from place to place, gaze firmly fixed on the banks we'd left behind.

"He shot at us four or five times," I said at length. "You got him in *one*."

I'd meant it as a compliment, but he only shook his head. "No, I didn't," he said regretfully. "I took too long to aim. He was taking cover when I got my shot off. I might have grazed his shoulder, but that's all. I'll take it, though. Looks like he's thought the better of it. You can probably slow down."

"This is the least I can do," I shook my head. "I was no help, and I was supposed to be the one protecting *you*."

"Yes, well I'm sure the only reason they waited to take me out was because I had a big bear with me on land," he tried to assure me. "Besides, I essentially used you as a blind. Oh, hell...Tulimak," he kneeled down suddenly, and I felt his paw on my back. I winced when it found its way to where that burning wet feeling was. His paw came away bloody.

"My winter coat and skin are thick there," I insisted at his look of worry. "I hardly feel it."

"You're bleeding everywhere," he said, looking down at his bloody palm, ears tipped back. "Please don't lie to me. I-I don't have any medical... shite, are you going to make it?"

I actually laughed, only wincing a little. "I know this is hard for you to imagine," I insisted, "but I really am fine. It's going to bleed, but I can feel it didn't penetrate deep. My body is different than yours. I have more I can afford to lose."

"I'd heard bear and some big predators were a bit more durable," he said uncertainly, his paw gingerly stroking my shoulder near, but not over, where I'd been grazed. "Are you sure?"

"I wouldn't play hero," I said soothingly. "Look, if you want to help, tear off some clean cloth from my bag, I have a spare breech cloth there. Press it to the wound for a while and it ought to help stop the bleeding."

He started looking through my bag diligently, murmuring as he did. "Hurt yourself often? You sound experienced."

"Like I said, my skin is thicker than yours," I said, pausing and stabilizing the oars long enough to unclasp and remove my cloak. "I scratch and tear it up sometimes without realizing it. Especially in the winter, when I've fattened up some and my winter coat comes in."

"We truly live in different worlds," he chuckled nervously, the conversation lightening the moment for both of us despite the fear we both clearly still felt. "In Amuresca no one would *intentionally* fatten themselves up for a season. It's the land of…corsets and girdles…" I heard him tearing cloth, and soon he was pressing a small bundle to my back.

Silence passed between us for a time. "This is a first, though," I said. "I've hurt myself plenty over the years, being as big and cumbersome as I am, it happens, you know? But I've never been shot."

"The lead shot itself didn't do this," he said. "You're lucky. It probably grazed our bags and caught you with debris of some kind. Trust me, if you'd actually been shot, a little fat and thick skin wouldn't have made much of a difference. We'd be dealing with a whole different problem, now."

"I've seen a bad gunshot injury before," I said quietly. "The Otherwolves near my tribe hunt in our forests, sometimes. Accidents happen."

He was still pressing the cloth to my wound, but his free hand was gingerly stroking my opposite shoulder. It was unnecessary, but I found I quite liked it, so I didn't ask him to stop.

"I'm sorry this is happening," he said at length, voice laced with honest regret. "I-I didn't mean to get anyone else involved."

"I'm glad I did," I replied emphatically. "I'm no warrior…obviously… but whatever good I might be to you on this leg of your trip, I'm glad to give."

"How can you say that?" he asked incredulously.

"If what you said was true, I know I'll have done something important," I explained. "You're trying to help people, with your papers. I don't understand it well, but if I can do a good thing just by helping you get to Broen, it's where I was headed anyway. I'm so used to receiving good will, it's high time I paid some of it back."

"It's all true," he said solidly, squeezing my good shoulder. "You can be assured of that."

"I believe you," I nodded. I glanced back at him, managing to smile a bit through the discomfort. "You talk about your…quest…like a hero of song. No one could doubt your passion."

"Ha," he huffed, his ears tipping back, muzzle lowering somewhat. "I don't know about all that. I'm...this whole thing was borne from self-interest."

"It clearly isn't in your self-interest to keep pursuing it now," I pointed out.

"I don't know," he said vaguely. "Sometimes I just don't know my own mind well. Maybe it's...spite...that's kept me going? Lord, that sounds awful. I know I'm not nearly as charitable as your sweet words make it sound, though."

I leaned back to look at him over my now bare shoulder. His hand was still resting on it. "I think," I said carefully, "that it's probably natural to have doubts, given what's happened? I have doubts all the time, over everything, really. But what you're doing sounds right to me."

"What we're doing," he corrected me.

"I'm a glorified ferryman," I reasoned.

"You got hurt helping me," he said, again with that woeful tone. He looked up at me, eyes wide. "It's a small list, the people who've bothered that much on my account."

It seemed a dramatic statement, but much like his many other dramatic statements, it sounded sincere. And that thought made my chest twinge, not unlike it did when I saw one of my younger siblings get hurt. I wanted to make it not so.

This was why I wanted to help him, I realized. Why I'd continued to help him since we met, despite my better judgment.

Why I was well and truly in trouble.

I forced myself to look away, down the expanse of river ahead of us. "Did you see who he was?" I asked, partially filling silence, partially because I was honestly curious.

"The hunter who shot at us?" he asked. "Not well. He wasn't a fox, the tail was wrong. He was wearing a pale cloak, or a jacket of some sort, which doesn't bode well."

"Why?" I asked, confused.

"Means he was prepared enough to camouflage himself against the snow," he said. "Means he's a professional. At least, more so than the lads in town. He looked tan, what little of his face and tail I caught. Other than that, it was hard to tell."

"How did you know he'd be on the right bank?" I asked, remembering.

"I guessed," he shrugged. "Accurately, as it turns out. Town was on the right side, and we hadn't passed any bridges."

His answer was simple, but impressed me all the same. I wasn't always capable of such insight. Not without more time to think it over.

"How was his tail shaped?" I asked suddenly, something occurring to me.

"Long," he paused. "Longer than a canine's, anyway."

"And tan?" I snuffed out a puff of warm air into the chill.

"...you have a thought," he surmised.

"It sounds like a lion hunter," I said, not able to hide the edge in my voice.

"There are lions here?" He honestly sounded as though he hadn't known.

I nodded. "There haven't been any tribes for years now. Tend to be solitary, stick to family hunting parties, or take up residence with a different species' tribe. There aren't many of them left in these parts, but I know a few who come to trade with us from time to time."

"...and?" he pressed after a few moments.

"You should hope it's the young lion who traps game in the mountains," I told him. "And not a *lioness*."

"I certainly couldn't distinguish their gender," he sighed. "I just... assumed it was a man. Why?"

"If it's a well-armed mountain lioness in these parts, it's probably Odina," I said solemnly. "She is not a woman you want hunting you. I don't know her well, but my father does and he's told me enough about her to be wary."

"Ideally I don't want anyone hunting me," he chuckled, then cleared his throat, his tone sobering. "But you look worried. I'm guessing I should be worried."

I nodded sagely, still not turning to face him. I could feel him grow tense though, through his hand.

We passed the longest time in silence following that since we'd met. Despite the palpable air of fear we were sharing, which had been bound to catch up with us eventually after our brief bravado following the near-death incident, Finn stayed close at my side. Eventually he was shoulder-to-shoulder with me, close enough that I could feel him shivering. I couldn't reach out to him as he had to me though. Not if I wanted to keep rowing.

My shoulder was beginning to ache and the first drifts of snow were touching down and disappearing on the water's surface, when he finally spoke up again. I'm not sure how long it had been. Hours.

"If I am to die in the coming days," he said softly, "at least it will be in good company."

"I'm not as prepared for death as you seem to be," I admitted, letting the vulnerability I felt slip into my tone. "So let's try to avoid it, if we can. Maybe you injured her. Maybe she's given up. Maybe it's not even her."

"Maybe," he conceded. But I could tell he was only saying it for my sake.

That prompted me to look down at him where he was hunkered against my side. He'd drawn most of his body into his coat, feet pressed together, ears limp. The shivering when it came was sporadic, but pronounced.

Taking only a moment longer to decide, I pulled one of the oars up and began to twist the other. "We're going to make camp," I declared.

"Have we put enough distance between us and her?" he asked, glancing behind us.

"I honestly don't know," I confessed. "But I need to rest my shoulder."

It was true, but it wasn't why I wanted to make camp and I think he knew that. Still, he didn't question me. He just moved closer against me, took up the other oar, and nodded.

Chapter 5

He Awakened Something

It took twice as long as it should have for us to drag the raft through the icy mud of the river bank in the waning twilight. Our bodies were in misery by then, the hours of fear and tense alertness taking its toll, as our vigor had long since abandoned us. I'd chosen the reed bank precisely because it was marshy and the overgrowth would cover most signs that this was where we'd pulled ashore, but it was a long, shallow shelf, which meant we were dragging the timber raft through half a foot of water and two feet of mud and weeds. The oars were no use to us, and we ended up having to sink ourselves into the half-frozen slurry and struggle against the sucking sludge and numbness in our lower legs as the water soaked into our clothing and fur.

For all that I tripled him in strength, Finnegan was giving it all he had, gritting his teeth as he dug his heels into the icy slime and the sharp, frozen grasses bit at our flesh. I couldn't even say he was the one holding us back; we were both injured at this point, and the effort required we use our shoulders and hips, so neither of us were at our best. I could feel blood soaking through my fur again, and several times the wolfdog had to stop and squeeze his eyes shut, gritting through the pain.

My heart stung watching him. I could tell he was worried about me too, but neither of us dare spoke. Dragging the raft was causing enough noise in the otherwise unnaturally still, quiet air. The world was subdued and soft as it only was while a heavy snow fell. Hopefully it would muffle our sound from the woods.

The knowledge that the hunter might be not far behind us was ever-present. I'd never known this kind of anxiety, and I'd known most kinds. But I'd primarily lived my life in fear of social recriminations and embarrassment, humiliation...that sort of thing.

This was a fear so new, it was hard for my mind to make sense of it. This was primal. Our tribe had never been at war, and we'd never faced a serious plague, or a famine. There were the dangers of everyday life, but they were rarely so acute. The few times someone had died unnaturally in my life, it had come on suddenly. It had never been so looming as this.

I had never been hunted before. The knowledge that someone out there now wanted me dead, wanted us dead, and had the means to do it... had *tried* to do it...was surreal. It was beyond anxiety. I almost didn't know how to feel.

As we trudged up onshore and I began to un-lash our belongings, I reached down to my stomach and pressed a hand against the spot beneath my ribs that always hurt when I was most anxious. Oddly, I found my stomach was calm. Hungry, but not twisted in knots, as I'd expected. For whatever reason, the fear of death was not giving me the stomach pain I was so accustomed to.

I didn't know what to make of that.

"Hey," Finnegan's whisper came from behind me. Something cold pressed to my wound, and I realized he was holding a handful of snow against where I was bleeding again. My back shuddered a bit at the contact. "Sorry," he said softly. "Can't have you bleeding a trail up to wherever we're going to camp, though. We have got to get that bound up somehow."

I hefted one of our supply bags and his satchel up over my good shoulder. "We have to get the lean-to set up first," I told him. "Shouldn't be hard, there are a lot of big spruce here. We just need some fresh boughs and a fallen sapling or two."

"I trust that you know what you're doing," he nodded. "Lead the way."

I looked up the nearby embankment. "We need to find somewhere hidden from sight from the top of that ridge there. If she moves at night at all, I don't think she'll come down through the wetlands here; she'd get bogged down like we did. She'll probably stick to that rise there and scan the shoreline. That's what I'd do if I were hunting game. Help me hide the raft. The snow will probably do most of that for us, but we need to make sure it doesn't leave a silhouette."

We brought our supplies to shore and then went about the process of covering the raft with whatever detritus we could find. Thankfully the reeds caught a lot of washed-up logs, branches and dead, tangled, unidentifiable river plants. All of it was half-frozen and brittle, but that really didn't matter for purposes of camouflage. It did however make the process of pulling it up and dragging it over the raft harder and saw that our hands were numb and caked in mud by the time we were done.

"I'd thought my jacket was bad before," Finnegan spoke lowly with a dry chuckle. "Little did I know." He straightened up after dumping a tangle of roots over the raft, wiping his muddy paws on his equally mud-caked britches. Then he reached for where he'd deposited his hat—which he somehow had managed to hold on to throughout all of this—dangling from where it was perched on a tall cattail. He'd hung it there while we worked like it was a hat rack.

He plopped it onto his head with purpose, straightening his ears through the two well-fitted holes for them and tipping it into a roguishly askew position, before flashing an equally roguish smirk.

It was frayed, dirty and ridiculous-looking. But he somehow managed to pull it off.

I smiled despite the aches and pains. I don't know how I could have ever been put in this situation without his arrival into my life, but if for some reason I'd had to endure this trial alone, all of this would have been so much less bearable.

A sudden, new worry gripped me. We were taking pains to not be found tonight. If we managed that, the rest of the trip might be uneventful. What if we were fine and nothing more happened until we reached our destination together? After I got him as far as the next town, we were supposed to part ways. But that had been before all of this. I couldn't possibly let him make his way alone, now.

But then, what had really changed? I knew he was hunted before. The very night I'd met him, he'd gotten hurt by men who likely meant to kill him. How had I ever accepted the idea of leaving him behind in Broen?

There it was, reliably. That knot in my stomach, slowly tightening. But why now? Did the concept of doing what we'd both already agreed was my part in this somehow scare me more than death? What more was I hoping for? It was abundantly clear I wasn't even much good to him. *He'd* been the one to defend us on the river today. Just because I was big and stronger than him didn't necessarily mean I'd be able to protect him.

I didn't even really understand where he was going, or his reasons for why. I knew what he'd told me, but the specifics were still confusing. He'd come halfway across the world pursuing these "truths" of his, and I really had no place in his story. I'd played a small role in this foreign, strange tale and that would have to suffice. I was ferrying him on one leg of his journey. I'd always have that.

What more did I want?

I wanted to know what was going to happen to him. Obviously.

I watched him massaging his freezing hands together, impossibly green eyes staring down into his palms as he blew into them. Despite the pistol I knew was both on his hip and re-loaded, he looked so fragile. But there was a ferocity there, too. It's what kept his eyes sharp, even in the waning light. His fate was as precarious as a man standing on a cliff's edge. If I turned and left him now, I'd never know if he fell. I couldn't stand the thought.

I was letting my mind weave every dramatic fear it could conjure. This is just what it did when left to its own devices. But one thing was certain—when I got this worked up over someone, it was usually a family member, a loved on. Not a stranger I'd only met a day ago. What *was* this?

He was staring at me. Smiling uncertainly. "Are you alright?" He asked, a slight huff of a laugh in his tone. "You look *intense*, suddenly."

I averted my gaze. "Fine," I said, shortly.

"I know you lost a lot of blood, but you can't pass out on me, all right?" He wiped his hands together once more, sucking his feet out of the mud and making for the shore line. "I can't carry you out of here."

I nodded and followed him. Once we made it to the shore, I gathered up our few essential bags and we began to make our way down the thin strip of woodland beneath the rise, looking for a well-hidden spot to make camp. I'd like to say we found something perfect, but luck was not entirely with us. No large upturned trees or dug-out rocky crevasses. Not even particularly dense tree cover, which made sense this close to the water, really.

What we did manage to find was an area thick with young pine trees, still not large enough to have cleared much of the forest floor around them. They made for a darker patch of woodland that was littered in pine needles and fallen boughs, and I was too tired to look any further. My desire for comfort won out over my desire for the best possible hiding place. Here, at least, there were plenty of fresh boughs to construct the lean-to and the ground would be a soft place to lay our aching bodies for a time. It was nestled enough against the rocky rise that it seemed to be mostly out of sight from above, but it was still not too far a sprint from our covered raft.

I set our things down and Finn accepted my choice without a word. He was trusting me, knowing few of my considerations. I could only hope I hadn't failed us both.

I opened my own worn rucksack and pulled out my brush axe. Finnegan took in the sight of it with a soft whistle. "Didn't know you carried a weapon on you," he said, as he began to shrug out of his jacket. We were soaked through, so our clothing was doing little for either of us at that point.

"It's not for people," I insisted. "Or even game." I scanned the grove, selecting two larger pines that were near enough to one another. "See if you can find some dry branches," I called back to him.

"I doubt anything out here in this weather will be dry," he replied as he unbuttoned his vest and left it open, his white undershirt plastered to his lean chest.

"Look for dead branches fallen and caught in the boughs of live ones," I instructed. "The snow above on the live branches can shield them, and the dead wood will burn better. It's the best chance we have."

I hacked away the lower branches on the two trees I'd selected, clearing a few feet on each and collecting the boughs. I'd brought my oars, tucked under my arm, up from the shore, and found two crooks of the remaining branches on which to lodge them at an angle. Then I lay boughs out between them, creating the basic shape of our lean-to.

It was barely big enough to shelter me, and we'd have to share it. But it was the best I could do. If I set the two supports too far apart, no bough would be long enough to stretch between the two. And my tent hide was essential to keep the snow out and the heat in as well in as possible, and it was only so large.

Normally I'd take an hour or two to construct my lean-to each night, taking care to ensure it was as comfortable as possible so I could be certain to get a good rest in. Tonight, the more I swung the brush axe, the more my body screamed at me to lie down. I knew that in time it wouldn't give me a choice in the matter.

As I began scuffing through the dirt under our ramshackle shelter, looking for and tossing any sharp rocks I found aside, I heard Finn returning. He knelt down beside where I was hunkering, depositing an armful of brown, fragile branches and sticks. Some of it looked like it might be dry enough to burn, most of it probably wouldn't. But I had no doubt he'd found what little there *was* to be found. There'd been a snow the night before, as well. Finding anything dry right now would be a struggle.

I hadn't been planning on relying much on fires on the way home. It was nearly impossible to keep dry kindling on the raft, and most of the time I wouldn't have been nearly so wet when I settled in for the night. But given our circumstances tonight, we had to try.

He shook the shed pine needles off his arms, glancing up through the dark canopy of snow-covered branches. "If we can even get a fire going, do you think she'll see the smoke?"

"Not with so much snowfall," I shook my head. "But we can't keep it going all night. Just long enough to dry off and warm ourselves." I struggled back to my feet, trying not to show the shudder in my legs. "Help me spread the hides out over the top of the shelter," I said to him, gesturing to where the large covering was folded with our things.

Together, gripping either end, we sloppily covered the lean-to with the bull moose hides. It was large enough to spread end to end over the whole lean-to, with a long piece in the front that could be tied up or flopped down over the opening to try and keep some of the heat in. It was moderately effective. Nothing like the dug-in clay bank homes of my otter tribe, or the 'brick' and wood structures the Otherwolves built, not even as decent as a good tent or tipi, but it was portable and went up quickly.

While I continued to stamp down and clean up the area inside the lean-to, Finnegan sorted through the kindling he'd found and selected what seemed the driest. I showed him how to dig out a small pit to place it in, using primarily my claws, and talked him through the process of steepling the sticks together, which he did very exactly and carefully. He was probably just trying to make himself useful, but seeing him commit himself to the simple task so diligently was endearing all the same.

I stripped a few of the remaining pine boughs of their needles and made a carpet coating the already rather soft forest floor that would be our sleeping area, then unpacked my old furs to lay over it. My rucksack was also watertight, like Finnegan's, and had my most essential gear in it. The furs, old sheep hides, were hardly plush, but they bundled into the rucksack well enough and that was more important.

When it came time to see if I could get a fire going in the little pit we'd dug right alongside the opening of our lean-to, I'm fairly certain both Finn and I held our breath. I struck the flint and fire steel for a good few minutes, repeatedly, without anything taking.

Eventually, Finn sighed and reached deeper into the lean-to where he'd stowed his bag. He disappeared for a few moments while I continued in vain, trying to get the fire started. When he returned, he was crinkling something in his hands.

"Try this," he held it out to me. It looked like a crumpled ball of—

My eyes widened. "Isn't that…?"

"It's not an essential document," he insisted softly. "It's just some of my notes. And anyway, it's no good to anyone if we die of exposure. Right?"

I took that chance to observe his physical state. It was worse than it had been at dusk. Decidedly worse. He was shaking violently now, body stiffly convulsing now and again as a full shudder racked his figure. He was bearing it with as much dignity as was possible and I doubted the cold would actually kill him, but there was a chance he'd suffer some kind of frostbite to his ears, or worse.

I wasn't much better off, I realized. My body maintained heat better, but not when I'd been wet this long. Not while I'd been panting and exerting myself.

I took the crumpled paper from him. With the aid of it, all it took was one strike to get a flame going. It was like a miracle.

A miracle we had to keep feeding to ensure it paid off. The fire was hesitant to take a hold of even the driest kindling we'd found, the cold and the wind beating it back whenever it seemed to be growing. We fed it four more of Finn's papers before we'd really gotten it to a survivable size.

Once we had a fire though, everything just seemed to feel...better. Less terrifying and oppressive. It chased away the dark and the cold, and slowly returned the feeling to my paws.

"God," the wolfdog crooned, flexing his toes and fingers in front of the flickering warmth. "My kingdom for a cup of tea right now." Before I could ask, he flicked an ear at me, smiling. "It's just an expression."

"I may not have tea," I said, leaning over him for a moment to grab at one of the frozen sacks I'd had on the raft that I'd dragged to camp with us. "But I do have fish."

"That's right," he brightened considerably at that, only growing more so when I untied the bag and reached in to snap loose a few of the frozen salmon. I broke one clear in half, leaving the tail bit in the bag, but I hardly cared. "You mentioned that," he said, eyes gone wide as I slowly settled the two...or well, one and a half...frozen fish on a flat rock I'd set near the fire when I'd first dug the pit. I had a skillet somewhere in my bag, but I didn't care enough to go digging for it now. I'd removed the rock from the lean-to area earlier, it would do in a pinch.

"I packed them with ice as soon as I caught them," I assured him, "and it hasn't gotten warm enough to thaw them since, so they're still very fresh. You could honestly eat them as they are if you wanted."

He leaned his arms over his knees and watched the ice begin to slide off the scales as they started to cook, shaking his head. "I've always preferred my fish cooked."

We sat there in companionable silence for a time, his eyelids settling heavily at half-mast as we watched the popping fire begin to sear the salmon skin. "Back home," he cleared his throat quietly. "Back home you *have* to cook the fish, if you've caught it in most any port, or any major trade river. The waters in our rivers have gone strange. Sickly. Too many people, too much drainage, all...trickling down. It's no surprise, when you see how the streets get in the slums. Hell, even in the better parts, sometimes."

He stared into the fire for a while, passing the silence peaceably. The salmon skin began to crisp, and he inhaled the scent, closing his eyes. I felt the pull of my own eyelids, my head drooping briefly.

"It's not like that here," he said suddenly, pulling me back to wakefulness. "I mean, it's wild. Uncivilized. Brutal, even. But it's unspoiled. Clean."

"I'm curious how you can say that when we're covered in mud," I pointed out, combing out some of the dried dirt on my fur with my claws. At least it was drying.

"There's a difference," he insisted. "Only someone who's never walked the shite-caked, moldering streets of the Risers in Highvolle could say that."

"What's the difference?" I asked uncertainly.

"The difference," he sighed, "is between mud and filth. You put enough people—especially poor people who've got no choice except to rag pick, burn refuse and eat vermin—cram them into tent cities and windowless, ancient ruins of buildings, and that's what you get. Filth. You know why they call it 'The Risers'?"

"I'll be honest, all of this is completely unknown to me," I admitted, leaning an arm against one of my knees and shaking my fur out a bit so it would dry faster. "Like hearing stories of the realm of spirits."

He laughed at that, coming out a bit hoarse, but earnestly amused-sounding. "Oi, you really *don't* know my world, then." He tugged himself with some difficulty out of his vest, then even more slowly, the fabric catching on each still-wet clump of fur, began working his shirt off. His voice relaxed, somehow more at ease, like he wasn't watching his words as carefully. I swear, even his accent changed, becoming less annunciated. "The Risers are like...hm...like the ditch the gutter empties out into. D'you know what a rain gutter is?"

"I...think so," I said, thinking back on some of the Otherwolf buildings I'd seen, both in the towns I'd visited and the small settlement they were building on my otterfa's land near the river. "It's like a sluice."

"Sort of," He waved his hand. "It controls the flow of water anyway, so you're half-right. I won't even begin to explain cesspools or nightmen to you. Suffice it to say, cities like Highvolle are choking in their own shite, filth water and viscera from butchers, fishmongers, even our own dead citizens, from time to time."

I couldn't hide the horror on my face. He just nodded at me. "I know," he sighed. "It's just what happens when so many people live so close together, I suppose. Anyway, it all has to go somewhere. And water doing what water does, it all flows down. Eventually to the rivers, but along the way… the Risers. It's what they call the lowest ring of the city, where most of the runoff pools. The houses have to be lifted, or the lowest floors shelled out, because it's just permanently full of that mire and muck, nowadays." He shut his mouth for a few moments, staring into the fire. Finally, hesitantly, he spoke again. "That's where I hail from. Home. Or at least, it used to be."

Remembering his flippancy earlier in the muck of the reed bank suddenly made a lot more sense. It twisted up my fond memory of watching him plop his hat on his head, like he hadn't a care in the world. I'd thought he was just trying to find cheer in a dismal situation…not that he was honestly accustomed to this.

"There's a grim comfort in mud and death, for me," he said with a false smile. "It's all I've ever been told I'm entitled to. By everyone except my mother, anyway." He finally freed himself of his soaked shirt, standing and spreading it out on the ground in front of the fire. I wish we had somewhere to hang our clothing, but it would freeze regardless where he put it. I didn't have the heart to tell him yet.

"But," I looked down at what had clearly once been a fine garment, "your clothing. Your hat…"

"Second hand," he chuckled, "all of it. And if I'm being honest, probably stolen or pawned. I learned how to put together a good outfit from my mother, though. And my uncle Mikhail. Well, more like…family friend. I always called him 'uncle', though. Like family. And the man knows how to look posh on a budget." He leaned back to sit again, wincing as he stretched out a leg. He seemed to think nothing of leaning against me, his heat bleeding into mine where our fur touched. "How you present yourself to the world is more important than substance, sometimes. It's better for someone to *assume* you're of means than to be of means and not look it, in most interactions. Gets you started off in all intercourse with a marked advantage. You clearly took note of my appearance when we first met. Kindly disposed you towards me, didn't it?" he asked knowingly.

I blanched, looking away. "It did," I confessed.

"I've always tried to make the most of whatever I've got," he said, smoothing down the fur on his fine-featured face and running his palms down his neck ruff, straightening it out. "For those of us born to poverty, sometimes our bodies are *literally* all we have." I felt his eyes on me. I hesitantly looked back at him. His muzzle was shockingly close to mine, his eyes alight with the reflection of the fire.

"You, Tulimak," he said, reaching across the short space between us, and laying a hand on my bicep. "You use your big body as a tool, right? You understand."

My mouth felt dry, and I wanted very badly to…I don't know. I thought perhaps to move back from him, because that was my default when I felt I was too close to someone else's space. A lifetime of bumping into people, nearly stepping on people, shoving people, just generally being *too big* had taught me never to get this close. Finnegan didn't give me a choice though, he existed within my space effortlessly, bending and shaping his interactions with me around my hulking figure. Sometimes using me as a shield, sometimes as a support to lean on or to warm himself near. He always had a convenient reason.

What more did I want?

That thought had been pounding in my head since the realization on the river shore. It felt like a thing misremembered, like something was on the tip of my tongue, unfulfilled, and I just couldn't put the pieces together to know what it was. So much had happened in a few days' time, it was easy enough to pass the feeling off as confusion that would abate once this whole nightmarish endeavor was over and I had time to process everything that had happened—and nearly happened—to me. But for now at least, it was like a muscle cramp, a tensing in my chest that wouldn't ease. I was on the precarious edge of something.

And I couldn't shake the feeling that Finnegan knew exactly what it was.

The way he looked at me even now was expectant. And I didn't know what he was waiting for. I didn't know what to say, what to do. I felt helpless.

He'd asked a question. At least try to answer that.

"I…don't know," I admitted, feeling useless. "I-I guess. I *want* to understand you better, Finnegan," I said earnestly.

He leaned back, perhaps sensing my discomfort. "Hm," he moved his gaze back to the fire. "Let's hope we survive the night, then. I'd like the chance to get to know you better, too."

I looked away again. "I think you've got me pretty well figured out. You seem insightful. And it's not like I'm all that complicated." In truth, I felt completely laid bare around someone as worldly and knowledgeable as him. There was next to nothing about myself I hadn't already told him. And that's because there…honestly wasn't much *to* me.

"I'm not so sure about that," he replied quietly, his voice softer still against the muffling atmosphere of snow falling all around us. I normally liked the world like this, when it got quiet and subdued. But for some reason tonight, it only served to enhance my fear, uncertainty and yearning. I was achingly tired, but couldn't surrender to exhaustion.

I tried to remind myself that this anxiety I was feeling right now was rational…we were being hunted. But some part of me knew that wasn't the only reason for it.

He was looking at me again. I glanced at him out of the corner of my vision. He was leaning back on his palms, his chest and belly fur bare and drying in the warmth of the fire. His fur was sleek in places, layered and heavier in others, specifically over his shoulders and clavicle. Remnants of his wolf heritage. That white patch down his throat went further down still, peppering his upper chest and reappearing lower on his abdomen. Otherwise he was almost entirely black, save the one little bit on his tail-tip. No wolf had that kind of coloration.

His body couldn't decide who or what it was. Like my own, brown fur bleeding into white down my spine, the mask over my eyes. We were straddling two peoples, trapped forever in our patchwork bodies—he'd called mine a "tool." Said he used his to his best advantage, even if it wasn't very much. He'd been intending to say, I suppose, that we were both making the best of our unfortunate circumstances of birth.

But the implication there was that we were, both of us, unfortunate.

And to be honest, though I'd always been self-conscious of my big body, wanting desperately to fit in more with my otter siblings, I'd never thought overly about being mixed. My problem had always been that I was a bear, not an otter. Perhaps being mixed is why I'd not been raised by my bear family, and in that case it *was* unfortunate. Not because there was anything wrong with my otter family, but because there were many things I'd simply never learn or experience without other bears in my life. But I'd never thought about it in that way. I'd always bemoaned other things about who I was.

For Finnegan, it wasn't about his size or how well he fit in physically with his own people. It was all about who his parents had been. Our circumstances were similar in some ways, but wholly different in others. And that's probably why we dealt with them differently. I couldn't hide my lineage under fine clothing, or falsify the kind of confidence he wore like a second skin, so I didn't bother to try. I was always acutely conscious of how different I looked from everyone around me, but I didn't try to fit in as he did. I didn't have that option.

But, I'm not so sure either of us was either right or wrong in our approach to how we felt about ourselves. My otterfa, who was easily the wisest person I had ever known, had told me many times that I would never find a place in the world where there wouldn't be people looking on me with cruel eyes. It seemed a hard lesson when he'd first explained it, but being an adult now, I understood. Cruelty was everywhere, in all peoples, in every land. Even if I'd been born fully white-furred, or even born an otter, there would always be someone who would think white-furred bear, or otters, were ugly. People would think less of me for being big, for being small, for being a tribesman. It was inescapable.

If Finnegan's fine clothes made him feel better about his lineage, about the flaws he clearly saw in himself, that was good. But I wished he could see him the way I did, not because of a fine shirt or vest, but right now. Even muddy in places, stretched out on my tattered sheep furs, tousled fur drying in the crackling firelight, he looked beautiful.

Oh.

Oh, spirits.

"The fish is done," I said suddenly, snapping my eyes away from his. He blinked dazedly at me—how long had we been staring at each other? How long had I been staring at *him*?

"...uh-huh," he said from behind me, his tone oddly wry and amused, again like he knew something I didn't. I fussed with the hot stone, using my claws to move it closer to us. He watched me as I did, the amused look eventually just fading to mild disappointment. I was left once again wondering what I might have done to offend him. But of course, I knew. I'd been staring again.

What was wrong with me?

I had some ideas. But I hadn't any life experience to compare them to. So I wasn't sure.

We ate our fish in silence. Finnegan seemed very pleased with his half a salmon, but I barely tasted mine. I was starving, but my mind just wasn't on food.

I must have been eating slow and was certainly lost in thought, because at some point I lost track of Finn and nearly jumped out of my skin when I felt cold press against the wound on my back again.

"Calm down," he eased, kneeling down behind me. "I'm just cleaning this up a little more. Seems to have stopped bleeding. Good thing too, because I don't know how we would've wrapped it. Your shoulders are… fshhh…" he made a noise through his teeth which I didn't know the meaning of, but I could only infer it meant "too big." I slumped a little, and he slapped my opposite shoulder lightly. "Don't move," he chastised. "Let me work." He reached outside the lean-to and balled up another handful of snow, packing it down in his palm before returning to the wound.

"You know healing?" I asked, curiously.

"Not in the slightest," he chuckled. "But I've gotten in enough scuffles throughout my life to know cold's good for swelling. And that it's bad if you leave little chunks of fish in a wound."

"Is that what did it?" I asked, incredulously.

"Yes, sorry to say," he sighed, "you were injured by exploded, frozen fish chunks. To be fair, it was the shot that really did the damage. But what a story, eh? I would lead with 'there was this one time I got impaled by a salmon….'"

I laughed, my back shaking, and he batted at me again. "What'd I say?" he scolded me.

"I'm sorry," I couldn't stop grinning. "You're ridiculous."

"Don't let that get around," he snorted.

I smiled again, taking note of his knees on either side of one of my haunches. Working up some nerve, I reached down and gingerly touched one. "How is your hip feeling?" I asked.

"Awful," he admitted. "But considering what we put ourselves through today, hardly surprising. And the cold isn't helping."

"You should take your britches off," I said without thinking about it.

There was a pause. Then a *far* too amused, "I should, should I?"

"They're...soaked through," I explained quickly, suddenly immensely glad he was behind me and we weren't face to face. "Our clothing's going to be frozen in the morning regardless, but there's no reason we shouldn't allow our fur to dry."

He hummed in consideration. "You make a fine point, honestly."

I knew vaguely from my travels that the Otherwolves were a bit more hung up on modesty and preferred to cover more of their bodies than most tribesman, and Finnegan certainly fell into that category, since he covered himself ankle to wrist most of the time with multiple layers of clothing. So I tried to give the man his privacy while he stripped out of his soaked trousers. I myself wore little more than my breech cloth over my lower half, but I wanted to honor his cultural traditions.

As it turned out though, it was unnecessary. And counter-productive. He'd been behind me in the cramped lean-to grunting and struggling with the wet garment for over a minute or more before he whined out a call for help.

"Please," he groaned, "I've been bested!"

Turning, I took in a truly pitiable sight. The wolfdog had...*half*-managed the task, but the combination of wet clothing and wet fur, along with the fact that he was clearly having trouble bending without being in pain, meant he was trapped midway through the process, lying on his back. I tried not to snort out a laugh as I gingerly untangled and dragged the remaining length down off his legs. He shook the last of the offending garment off with a growl, kicking it needlessly and presumably accidentally out into the snow. Then he groaned, flopping down onto my sheep furs.

"Just leave them there," he grumbled, stretching out his limbs greedily. "I never want to put them on again."

"You'll change your mind about that in the morning," I assured him, sighing and hunkering down to crawl outside just far enough to grab them and spread them out beside his shirt. They would also be frozen in the morning, but they might at least be a little more dry.

I took a moment to look up through the dark canopy to the flurries silently drifting down between the cracks in the grasping branches. It was impossible to say how long the storm would last, and were I on this journey alone and unhindered, I would probably have hunkered down here for a few days.

That would have been nice, I thought. To be here with Finnegan, passing time in our little snowed-in shelter, cooking fish, talking and being amused by his antics. I think I would have really enjoyed that.

But we'd have to leave in the morning, no matter what. If we weren't found in the night, that is.

When I kneeled back down to make my way into our little sanctum, I had to stop for a moment to catch my breath. Finnegan had rolled over to lie on his other side, the hip that wasn't bothering him presumably, and that meant his back was turned to me and the fire. The firelight threw the contours of his lithe figure into stark relief, the path down his spine marked by layers of slightly thicker fur with hints of silvery-white that caught only in the light.

He shifted, stretching out a long leg and rubbing at the prominence of his hip, down the curve of his thigh.

I was all at once, stunningly, and acutely physically aware of *what I wanted.*

The realization froze me in place and sent my mind reeling. How—why was this happening? Why now? Why *him?* Why here, of all places, when I couldn't escape or ignore what was coming over me?

I stayed there, kneeling in the snow, not knowing what to do. For far too long. Long enough that snow began to gather on my shoulders, and in time, Finnegan called out for me.

"Tulimak?" he murmured, paw still rubbing at his hip. "Please don't worry me. If you're relieving yourself or something, just let me know you're all right out there?"

"I—I'm fine," I said, getting back on all fours and crawling back inside slowly, remembering that yes, we were still being hunted and he had every reason to be concerned.

Bigger picture. All of this...

...whatever this was...

...it would have to wait. We still had to get through the night.

I tried so hard to put whatever space between us I could. But it's as though circumstance and the elements themselves were conspiring to make my life tonight an anxious misery. And Finnegan wasn't helping, whether he realized it or not.

"You can get closer, I don't bloody care," he mumbled, fumbling back with a paw to grab at me blindly. I moved forward an inch or two at best, just enough so that my back wasn't against the flap of our cover. When I didn't entirely close the distance, he did, giving a contented noise. "You're like an oven," he chuckled. "Thanks for blocking the chill from outside."

"I-I…" I don't know what I'd been planning to say.

As it turned out, it didn't matter. For all that I was on edge, Finnegan was apparently not. Because his breathing evened and he very obviously drifted off not long after that.

By all rights, I should have, too. I ached, I was exhausted in every way a person could be. But I lay there awake for some time, trying to make one very important decision.

What to do with my arm.

The last time I'd ever slept beside someone, I'd been a cub. Once I'd started getting really big, I'd gotten my own sleeping area and eventually, my own living space. I literally couldn't remember what the feeling of a warm body next to mine felt like, let alone how I was supposed to position myself to not get in their way. If I lay my arm on my side it would fall in the middle of the night regardless, if I bent it back I'd be sore in the morning, and my shoulder was *already* sore, so…

As so often happens when you're overthinking something and tired, it was in the midst of deliberating whether or not it would be all right to put my paw over his hip that I fell asleep.

The night was long, restless and punctuated by dizzy moments of waking to a sound outside, or a half-remembered dream. There was a warmth in my arms I was unaccustomed to and it both comforted and frightened me, intermittently.

Sometimes that warmth would move closer in against me, or shift away, leaving the spots it had occupied to grow cold. I'd reach for it and sink my paws into soft, pliant fur and more besides. I stretched my fingers out over the expanse of that warmth, feeling the leaves of fur between them. I breathed it in, the scent slowly becoming dreams. But I knew they were dreams. There was a comfort in that. The waking world was so much more complicated.

In my dreams, the discomfort and pain in my body was dissolving. Slipping away, being replaced by far more pleasant sensations. The tenseness in my muscles, the anxiety always tying me up in knots, unraveling almost visually, coming apart. My paws were kneading that soft heat, stress slipping away and falling off me in rivers.

In my dreams, that warm feeling was pushing back. Curling against me like licking flames. It was only a dream, so I was permitted this. I touched and was touched back.

Something far more acute and pressing jarred me through my half-conscious state, pulling me forcibly into the waking world. A noise, and simultaneously a feeling. A sound like a gasp, punched-out beside-against? -me. And an all-consuming *need*.

"Auhhhh, *fuck*," Finnegan's growl of an utterance were the first real words I heard upon fully waking. "So this's happening, after'all..."

It took me a few seconds to come to grips with the reality of what I'd woken to. The lean-to was cast in purplish twilight, so the sun was only barely making itself known somewhere beyond the tree line. I could vaguely feel the chill air threatening outside, but that was because of the intensity of the warmth pooling in my chest, stomach and lower, from every inch of my body in contact with my bedmate's...and right now that was every inch. I had the wolfdog pulled in against me, both of my arms caging him in, my palms spread flat over his hip and stomach respectively, fingers and claws buried in his fur. We were still lying with his back to my chest, there was hardly room to do anything else, but the curve of his body was fit so snugly against mine, he was almost off the ground.

And even through the fog of my waking dream, I could feel how hard I was between my legs. Pressed between *his* legs.

Which meant he sure as hell felt it.

As I tended to, I panicked. In fact, I was about a second away from shoving him away from me and backpedaling out into the snow...when his paw slipped down beneath my loosely-tied breech cloth, and gripped me.

And everything pretty much stopped working at that point. My voice, my body, my mind.

His paw was feverishly warm as it closed around the base of my sheath and slowly stroked upwards, gripping slightly more snugly as it moved towards my tip. When he gave a gentle squeeze there, I whined out a breath, and I swear to you, he chuckled.

He chuckled.

That, at least, alleviated any worries that he was doing this...I don't know...out of fear? I was, after all, holding him in my arms. Despite my inner turmoil, I somehow still hadn't managed to let him go.

"Wasn't sure," he mumbled, his words drawling out lazily. I had no idea what he meant by that, because my mind was too busy screaming that I should do something, anything, soon, because he'd begun to move his paw again and oh-

...oh...

His palm was so much softer than my own and so much smaller, his fingers wrapping around the expanse of me, each running upwards at a slightly different pace, following the motion of his hand.

My jaw was hanging open and I knew some very bear-like noises were escaping me, despite my best efforts to stay silent. I dared not look down, except of course the many times I *did*, and the sight was not helpful in calming my racing heart, or the coiling tension in my lower extremities.

I should be stopping him.

Why wasn't I stopping him?

What I did was...lie there...shivering despite the heat...and let him touch me for what amounted to a very short time, when all was said and done. I know this for a fact not because I was at all keeping track of time, but because when I stiffened my arms around him and came messily with the most bear-like noise yet, he seemed pleasantly surprised.

There was that chuckle again. It sort of sounded *smug*, but I'd be hard-pressed to tell you for sure, because I was lying there weak and shaking in the wake of what had just occurred.

I was still in that state of shock when he slipped his hand free and patted my own where it was still pressed against his belly.

I didn't entirely know what he meant, so I did the only thing I could think to. I let go of him finally, releasing him from my hold. He shifted a bit, arching his back and stretching out a leg, grimacing as he did so. Then he glanced over his shoulder at me, one ear half-tipped, expression bemused.

"You could've just asked last night, y'know," he huffed.

"What just happened?!" I finally managed to exclaim.

Chapter 6

Against the Current

No one came for us in the night. Nor that morning, while we packed and loaded the now muddy and thoroughly frozen raft. Cracking it out of the reeds was no easy task, but I relished the chance to have something difficult and all-consuming to focus on.

My body still ached, but the pain in my shoulder and the stiffness in my joints were welcome. They distracted from the lifting feeling of vertigo I felt every time my thoughts returned to what had happened in the lean-to.

It felt like I was falling into something unknown. That's the best way my mind could interpret the feeling in my chest, the somehow both exhilarating and terrifying panic that gripped me whenever I re-lived it in my mind. Falling.

I couldn't make sense of it, but yet somehow, it all finally made sense? So much about myself that had long been an enigma to me had snapped into place. What it was I'd felt...been feeling...about Finnegan was just one part of it.

Since I'd hit adulthood two years ago, I'd tried not to think about how my future was shaping up to be so much different than my otter brethren. Everything came about naturally and normally for them, within the prescribed lives the otters of my tribe were supposed to live. They'd hit adulthood, the shaman would visit and they'd get their markings, then they'd choose a trade, or marry. Sometimes both in the case of the most industrious young women and *all* the men, save those few that became devoted guardians for the tribes' pups. And even still, that was a trade in and of itself. One of my cousins had even become a shaman. Her path had been a bit different than most, but still accepted, honorable, even. And we'd long known she had a deeper connection with the spirits, so we'd all been prepared for it.

But nothing about becoming an adult had felt natural or normal for me. Everything had been through that barrier of difference, of not being an otter. There were rites of passage like hunting my first deer, or navigating the rivers, that I'd managed just fine. I'd followed in my otterfa's footsteps and become a fisherman, something I certainly had a knack for, and I'd gotten the first of my markings. But building my dwelling had been difficult, since it had needed to be thrice the size. I'd had to learn to work with leathers and hides simply to clothe myself, as nothing the tribe made was sized properly for me. My aunts tried, but...

I was used to not "fitting" into just about everything around me. Even if my family did not begrudge me for it and in fact were quite accommodating and eager to have me stay in the community, (having a bear around has its advantages, they'd say) I knew that try as they might, there were certain things they'd simply never be able to give me, no matter how much they loved me.

Marriage, lifelong companionship of any kind, was not something I'd find as easily as my otter brethren. I'd have my extended family, but starting a family of my own was not as guaranteed as it was for my brothers and sisters.

I'd long assumed, (and my otterfa had assured me) that I was just delayed on my path to such fulfillments because of the obvious barrier of species between me and most tribal women I'd ever met. Part of why my tribe had encouraged me so readily to be the one to take this trip was, I surmised, for the chance that I might meet another of my kind out in the world. And I was only twenty years of age. Many men my age were yet unmarried; it was not as unusual as for a woman, perhaps. But men were expected to take a bit more time to settle in their younger years.

And to be fair, I'd met few other bears in the world, even in my travels. Three so far, to be exact, all male. So, the fact that I'd never felt that yearning that most young men apparently felt was perhaps unfortunate, but not unusual. My circumstances were unusual. I hadn't had the opportunities most might have had.

Was I confused? Was that it? Was my body confused? Because I'd been raised by otters, raised apart from other bears? This wasn't what a bear should have wanted, I knew that much. Certainly not in *this way*.

But I'd never felt this way about an otter, either. To be fair, almost all the ones I'd known were my family. And most of the otters from other tribes I'd met over the years were older traders who were already married.

But Finnegan wasn't an otter. He was smaller than me, certainly. Closer to an otter's...size? Was that why this was happening? No. No, that was silly.

Had I *ever* felt this way about anyone else before?

The answer to that was complicated. About any one person? No. Not that I could remember. But vaguely. At least in the back of my mind, although I had not known or understood what I was feeling at the time, I had felt this...I'm not certain what to call it. Attraction. Before. And I had experienced desires of the flesh in the past, of course. But they'd never been clear. Taken no specific form. Just notions of nameless, faceless people some buried part of my mind wanted to...know...in this way.

I'd even met people throughout my life I'd found beautiful, I could clearly remember thinking so. But it was hard to remember if it had been a more general admiration or something more specific, like, well...

Like how I'd felt last night. How I'd let a dream overtake my reason, had violated any and all physical boundaries between myself and my bed-mate, a-and then...

I glanced back at the wolfdog as he finished lashing down our bags, tugging at the hem of his frozen coat disdainfully. For about the hundredth time today, I wondered if he was angry at me. He certainly hadn't seemed it. But I couldn't make sense of that man. Finnegan had been outright flip-pant. Confused, really, by my state of shock all morning. He was acting like nothing unusual had happened between us.

I couldn't understand it.

I was fortunate at least that he'd not held it against me. I'd *grabbed him* in his sleep. Buried my paws, my claws, in his fur. I'd held him against my body and...and...

Calm, I tried to tell myself. We still had to keep our wits about us. The hunter must have rested to nurse their injury, or otherwise held off on moving due to the weather. Maybe they'd given up. But so far, our luck hadn't been that good.

Either way, we had to get going again.

I saw Finnegan checking his pistol meticulously as he stood there in the frozen reeds, steam puffing out his nostrils. It was easier to take stock of him when I knew he was distracted and not focused on me. He had that look of intensity about him that he got sometimes, but it was more directed at the weapon in his hand. He still didn't seem angry, or in a foul mood. Just focused on the task in front of him.

He looked handsome as ever.

How could he not be angry at me?

A terrible thought occurred to me then. Bits of memory came back to me spanning our acquaintance, the many times he'd seemed expectant of me. Almost…bracing.

Had he determined this was just somehow expected of him?

No. No, that was a ridiculous thought. How would anyone expect *that?*

I couldn't shake the notion, though. Even as we counted off and began shoving the raft back out onto the river, aided in the morning by the sheen of ice over the shallowest edges of the water. I lumbered aboard and held a paw out to him, clapping it around his arm and pulling him up onto the raft with me.

The raft pitched forward as I landed on my rump with the momentum of tugging him aboard. It sent us both sprawling. He might have slipped right off the icy timbers if I hadn't slung an arm around his waist and steadied him against my side.

He blinked rapidly and stared up at me a moment, his eyes blindingly green in the morning sun.

Then he gave a cavalier smile, breath puffing out his mouth, and twittered out a needlessly dramatic, "My hero."

I snuffed, averting my gaze. "You'd hardly have drowned in two feet of water."

"No, but I'd be wet again," he said, shaking out and toying with the still crispy edges of his coat. "And I'd like to avoid that until we have to shore this thing again, if you don't mind." He disentangled himself from me at that and moved towards one of the oars, taking it up and kneeling on one side of the raft, beginning to push us away from the shore.

I stayed on the other side of the raft, although nearer to the center so we'd keep the weight even. We were compensating with some of the bags, too. "Finnegan," I began to say, as I took up the other oar.

"If I had to guess," he cleared his throat noisily. "I would say I must have clipped her more than I realized. Or him. Still not certain on who it was, after all. Something must have occupied them last night. That or we hid effectively."

"Finnegan…" I sighed.

"Let's not get too cocky, though," he pushed back his coat, revealing the holster beneath. "We'll need to be more alert today. Weather seems to be clearing, so if they're still out there hunting, they'll be on the move today. And the path we're taking is unfortunately rather easy to follow."

"*Finnegan*," I said a little more vehemently.

He was silent, finally. But then he had been last time I'd tried. So we were at this stalemate again.

Pleadingly, quietly, I asked again, "Why can't we talk about it?"

He wasn't looking at me, but I could see from his rather expressive and large ears how guarded he must have felt.

More silence. Again, I implored, "…Finn?"

"This just isn't the sort of thing you *talk* about," he snapped, not angrily, but more…worriedly? It was hard to tell when he wasn't looking at me. "All right?"

I dipped my oar into the water slowly, aware that the current would soon take us if I didn't begin to row. Cautiously, I asked, "Why?"

He sighed, taking up his own oar. "You just don't," he said, submerging the oar.

"But," I stammered, "but I have so many questions."

"God help me," he pinched the bridge of his muzzle, then all at once, nailed me with that intense gaze of his. "Look, I thought you were…"

I looked at him imploringly, waiting to hear whatever wisdom he could impart.

His gaze softened and he looked away from me, down at the water. "I thought you were more experienced," he finally said. "I don't know why I thought that, in retrospect. Shit."

"So," I felt my chest clench. "You *are* angry."

That got his attention back on me and he went from frustrated-looking to concerned, all at once. "No," he insisted. "No. I mean...maybe at myself. But not at you."

I stammered, "What does that even mean?"

"It means I might've mis-read things, that's all," he blew a breath out through his nose, rowing slowly on his side. "And reading people is something I usually pride myself in, so I feel foolish."

"'Mis-read'?" I knew the words, but not the context he was using them in.

"Saw something that wasn't there," he clarified. "In you."

I looked down into the calmer waters we'd found ourselves in this morning. This stretch of the river was not nearly as wide, being surrounded on both sides by rocky, more mountainous land. The trails here were tough, especially in the winter. The river was the best way to travel. This was our best chance to make ground and outrun our pursuer. I dug my oar in deep.

"Whatever it was you saw in me," I said quietly, "it was there. And even I didn't know it until last night. But it was *definitely* there."

He made a noise at my statement that sounded like a groan and a sigh mixed together. "Yes, that much was obvious," he muttered, "from the first day I met you."

"What?" I asked.

"That you fancied me," he said around his own hand, like saying it aloud was taboo. To be fair, I suppose it was. I'd never seen or even heard stories of something like this. I wonder then...

"How did you know?" I asked, relieved that we were at least talking about it, now.

"Oh, you get a feeling for it after a while," he rolled his eyes. "Especially when the people ogling you are as *subtle* as you were."

I stopped to consider that. After a few moments had elapsed, I glanced sideways at him, and took note of his expression. "Oh," I said, "that was sarcasm."

"Glad that didn't need a translation," he muttered.

"But then," I said uncertainly. "You didn't 'mis-read' me. If you guessed that, you were right. Clearly."

"That isn't what I meant," he said flatly. He gave me a beat to ask the obvious question, then filled in for me. "I more meant that I thought you also knew what you wanted. I thought we were communicating without words."

"*That* needs a translation," I said, confused.

"It means exactly what it sounds like," he stated matter-of-factly. "I thought we had come to an understanding."

"Without words," I repeated, uncertain I was hearing him correctly.

"That's just how these things are done," he said, again in that snappish tone. I flinched back a bit. He tipped his ears back, looking awkwardly away from me again. "Look, I'm sorry," he said emphatically. "I didn't realize how new this all was to you. I never would've—" He stopped himself suddenly. "Tulimak, how old are you?"

The question was an odd one, but I didn't mind telling him. "I don't know my exact birth time, but nearing twenty," I answered.

He closed his eyes, "Oh thank god. You're so big, I-I just…assumed you were a grown man. I might be a louse, but a cradle robber, I am not."

"How old are you?" I couldn't not ask, after he'd asked me. I'd been assuming this whole time we were around the same age, but I didn't really know how to look for markers of age in canines, save probably gray fur around the muzzle. Probably?

"I have a decade on you," he told me. Then, "Thirty. I'm thirty."

I nodded. Finn did come off a bit more mature than me, to be fair. But a lot of that I'd attributed to his being more worldly, more traveled. Discovering he had ten years on me didn't surprise me as much as I'd thought it would, though.

"You seem to understand…all of this," I said hesitantly. "Much more than I do, anyway. Can you please at least tell me *why* you don't want to talk about it?" I suspected I knew the reason, but I wanted his answer all the same.

His eyes dimmed and he slowly churned his oar through the water. When he spoke, his words came out wary. "Because it's dangerous," he said, stating exactly what I'd been afraid of.

My heart sank, but I'd known. There had to be a reason no one had ever told me this was a path my life might take. There must have been a good reason why I'd never known two men could…

"I don't know your culture well," he admitted, speaking lowly. "But where I come from? Admitting to this sort of thing can get you thrown in a work camp. Jailed. Even hung. And my people brought their Faith here, so presumably the laws aren't much more allowing in the colonies—pardon me," he corrected himself, "'Carvecia.'"

I opened my mouth, but he cut me off. "And before you ask 'why,'" he sighed, "it doesn't matter why. Procreation, religion, some think it's emasculating, I suppose. Ask a Priest, they'll give you a hundred reasons they think are important. But all that matters is—that's the way it is. It's not worth losing your life over."

"But you still..."

"I do whatever I can get away with," he chuckled. "But I'm good at getting away with things. I'm savvy. No offense, but you're not. So, if you've got the predilection, fine. But you do it out in the woods, or with someone you trust in a private room. Treat it like it's a crime, because it *is*. And don't. Fucking. Talk about it."

He turned, gesturing at me. "You're a big, strong lad. Find yourself a wife, and if she isn't scratching the itch, get what you need on the side. If I learned anything from my time spent amongst the Pedigree, it's that a marriage can shield you from the consequences of all manner of immoral behavior. Wives give you credibility." He turned back around, leaning to the side to stretch his hip out. "Throw in some cubs while you're at it. No one'll blink."

"That's," I opened and closed my mouth several times before settling on, "a lot."

"Yes, sorry," he conceded. "Maybe too much information at once there. But now I feel responsible, like I've got to warn you of all of this."

"I appreciate it," I assured him, quietly. My mind was spinning, running through all the new information. One question immediately surfaced, though. "Is...is this what you've done?" I asked him. "All of that?"

"What, married?" He literally snorted. "No, no. My lifestyle doesn't really suit married life and I wouldn't want to subject any woman to it besides. No. Now don't get me wrong, I've known my share of women. Enjoyed their lovely company," he toyed at the hem of his vest at that, likely an old habit when fussing with his garb might have done him *any* good. "I love women. Was raised by them, in fact, so I usually prefer their company to other men, if given a choice."

"You were raised by women? Only women?"

"Ah, my mother's..." he paused, "...coworkers. We lived in a cooperative house, of a sort. Pooling resources, sharing chores and child-rearing, you know. Good for safety too, in the Risers. There were a few other children, and my uncle Mikhail for a while. But yes, I suppose mostly women."

"An Uklashan," I said, prompting a bemused look from him. "A female tribe," I clarified. "Sometimes when the men are hunting or warring, or when a tribe has lost all of their men, an Uklashan will be formed. An elder mother will take the position of Chieftain and all roles in the tribe will be re-assigned, regardless whether they are meant for men or women. The tribe survives that way until the next generation is grown, or until favorable matches for young women can be found. Some of them choose to remain Uklashan for generations though, and take war orphans to grow their numbers."

He was listening to me, enrapt in that way he had been the day before. I was certain now it wasn't false; he was just a curious man and he earnestly seemed to want to file away the things I told him.

"U-klah-shan," he sounded it out, again taking care to pronounce one of our words correctly. "Huh. That's fascinating. I suppose our cooperative was a little bit like that, although planned that way from the start. Men were...discouraged in our neighborhood in general, unless they were there to trade."

"Why?" I asked, intrigued.

"Bad experiences in the past," he waved a hand. "Men tend to take advantage of my mother's trade, and none of them really contribute to the work load, if you know what I mean."

"I don't," I stated plainly.

"Of course you don't," he gave me a wry smile. "You're as pure as fresh snow."

"But you said you had an uncle..."

"You never met my uncle," he chuckled. "He contributed, suffice to say. And he was considerate, kind. Not one to take advantage. We had a whole community there, I guess sort of its own little village. Found family, you could say. We took care of one another, did the best we could in shite circumstances."

"That sounds like a good village," I smiled.

"Den of sin and heretics, as far as the rest of the city's considered," he snuffed. "But yes, they were good people. Are." He looked down, at that. "I haven't been back since my mother died. I'm one of those men that would be taking advantage, these days. I found a different trade."

"You have a trade?" I was aware the subject of our conversation had diverted from the main topic, but I was learning so much about him all of a sudden, I didn't want to staunch the flow. If anything, since last night, I wanted to know even more about him. Everything he would tell me.

"Man my age has to have a trade," he said dismissively. "But it's not an easy one to explain. Especially not to someone who doesn't understand our world."

"Please try," I encouraged.

There must have been something about the plaintive way I asked, because he took one look my way and cracked after a few moments, relenting. "I'm a...mediator. Of a sort. I help settle disputes."

"Like a wise man?" I asked uncertainly. He was still fairly young, though.

"I'm not sure what the equivalent would be in your culture, so that's probably as close as we're going to get," he said. "Amuresca has a lot of old traditions that Pedigree society in particular likes to cling on to. My trade fits into a particular niche, a need that rich men with big mouths like to exercise before they think the better of it. Like I said, it's hard to explain to an outsider. But it hardly matters any more. I gave it up when I began this journey and it's looking as though I won't survive it, so..."

My brows furrowed. "Finnegan, we're making good progress on the river. We're going to make it to Broen. We'll outrun the hunter, and..."

He was shaking his head. "I want to stay optimistic, I really do," he exhaled. "But my final destination is a long way off and my best chance now is to find a reliable Post somewhere and hope. This whole business of trekking halfway around the world as a courier for these documents was... high-minded, but it isn't turning out well."

I took a breath. "Where is your final destination, Finn?"

He gave me a long, steady look before replying, "Arbordale."

"All the way in the south?" I gasped. "I've never even known someone who's been to the southern sea."

"You probably have," he assured me. "A lot of the traders in town have likely done business there; it's the Nation's Capital. But I understand your reaction." He sighed. "I had two choices for this trip. The route by sea around the east side of the world is faster overall, but two months longer on the water. In *good* weather, and the weather in the Somanta is rarely good. I...*hate*...traveling by ship. I can't even explain to you how horrible it is if you've never tried it before."

"I've grown up with the river," I said, "but I've heard the sea is different. Much larger. Much deeper. Storms that lift the water as high as some trees."

"Ugh," he groaned, presumably at the memory. "Please don't remind me, if you want me to keep my breakfast down. Now, granted, I was contending with the effects of poisoning throughout most of the voyage I did take, but even when I recovered, I was never truly well. They say you get your 'sea legs' after a time, but it never quite happened for me."

"You'd mentioned the poisoning earlier..." I said, trailing off intentionally, hoping he would expand on that story.

"If I'd taken the Eastern route, I would have arrived directly in Arbordale," he said. "But, hearing of the land route, I figured the extra few months travel time would be worth it. It also *should* have cost less. But this country is...not like home. There are few roads, it's outright lawless in places and the terrain is—challenging would be putting it mildly. I vastly overestimated my chances of making this trip alone. To be fair," he ascertained, putting a hand up, "I didn't know at the time I'd also be hunted along the way. Or that I'd lose my pony. *Or* that I myself would suffer the climate so poorly and be forced to hunker down in townships so often. It's been a long series of misfortunes."

"You traveled halfway across the world," I said, feeling the urge to reach over and put a paw on his shoulder. I resisted. "It's remarkable you got so far on your own."

"I would have researched the trip more thoroughly if I'd had the time." He dropped his hand against his knee. "But certain events led me to realize I needed to be anywhere but in Highvolle, and fast. Lad like me comes to appreciate when it's time to skip town. All the better that I had a destination in mind."

"You were being hunted in your country too?" I asked.

When he turned to look at me, he seemed tired. "Not quite as literally as the folks here seem to do it. Not like game. But someone clearly wanted me dead."

"The poison," I surmised.

He nodded. "Dangers of a busy pub," he muttered. "I'll never know who slipped it to me. Or even how. I'd have to guess my drink, though. And the more I've thought on it, the more I've been certain it was someone working or serving there. I ordered an Islander Caife, that's…essentially just coffee, whiskey and sugar, and whoever poured it was generous with the whiskey. Too generous. They were trying to cover the taste of whatever they put in it." He set his jaw in a grim line. "It worked."

"You wouldn't even be safe if you went home," I realized aloud, the air leaving my lungs.

Finnegan just shook his head again, slowly. "I dug up something my old man doesn't want known," he said, that hint of anger creeping back into his voice. "He wants me dead, and he's got the resources to see it done. I like to think of myself as a resilient man, but I'm up against a lot of coin, here. And the bastard runs a shipping Cartel. I wouldn't, but even if I wanted to, I couldn't hide from him if I tried. His bloody tentacles are stretched between both these continents. Maybe if I went to Mataa… although apparently he's buying his 'merchandise' from there now."

He continued talking, but my thoughts were preoccupied with the most pertinent of the new knowledge he'd given me. Mainly the most important fact: I couldn't even convince him to give this up. It wasn't just some grim resolve, although it certainly seemed that too. He had no choice but to see this through now. If I was understanding him correctly, the only way he'd live through what he'd learned about his kin back home was if he revealed his illegal trade to—presumably the law in his lands?

If that was even enough to stop this man. What kind of father did all of this to their own son?

I began to understand his hatred more than I had before. I'd never known my parents, but they'd either given me up to the river, or met some untimely end that kept them from being in my life. And I'd no memories of them to resent or regret.

Finnegan knew this man he shared blood with, and importantly, was known *to* him. It wasn't as though his father didn't know it was his own son he was trying to have killed. I knew little of their relationship other than what Finn had told me concerning his mother, but I didn't need to know any more. Anyone who willingly inflicted all of this on their own blood, whether or not they *chose* to acknowledge them as family, lacked something inside that made most people whole.

"I want to help you," I blurted out, my mouth only somewhat ahead of my thoughts. But I'd pretty well decided by that point.

His ears perked and he arched an eyebrow. "You…are," he said uncertainly.

"No, I mean," I sighed, "I can't bear the thought of leaving you in Broen, at the mercy of these people."

"I'm hardly defenseless," he said, patting his hip where his holster rested.

"With all due respect," I looked him in the eyes, "you need to make up your mind on that."

He blinked at me and for once, had nothing to say.

"Are you going to give up and send your papers along with a courier?" I asked pointedly. "Or are you capable of carrying them the whole way yourself? Because in one breath you're speaking of how doomed you are, and now you're trying to assure me that you'll be fine. Which is it?"

He seemed stunned. It took him some time spent visibly gathering his wits to reply. "You're really holding me to task," he chuckled nervously. "Damned, Tulimak. I—I was just trying to make you feel better, is all."

"Don't do that," I said vehemently. I didn't use my "bear voice," but I put some bellow into my words, enough that I saw him lean back a hair. I took heed to lower my tone when I continued, "I'm not a child just because I'm ten years your junior. We live difficult lives here, too. Perhaps I've been more fortunate than you, but that doesn't mean I don't understand and don't…feel…the consequences of action and inaction. If I were to leave you in Broen, I would always think on what became of you. We may be recent acquaintances, but," I looked down at the water sloshing against the creaking timbers of the raft, "I've gotten to know you. I would always remember you. For...many reasons."

I heard, rather than saw him shift, uncomfortably. He didn't reply, but I knew he was listening. He was a good listener.

"I don't want to have this regret," I said quietly. "You've given it to me. Don't try to take it away with paltry words. I want your honesty." I looked back up at him at that. "Can you complete this journey of yours alone?"

He lowered his muzzle slowly, hands knitted at the frayed knees of his trousers. "I don't know," he admitted at length. "But the odds are...not in my favor."

I breathed in slowly, then let the breath out through my nose. I took up my oar once more, pushing back into the current. We'd been listing for a time now. "How can I help?" I asked.

"If we can lose this hunter, that would be a start," he said, taking up the other oar with an obvious twinge of pain. The rowing involved a lot of leaning to the side, which was clearly hard on his hip. "But Broen is more connected to the roads and trade than the last few towns I've been through, and they found me there. Honestly the closer I get to Arbordale, the better the chances I'll be found by another soldier of fortune."

I considered that. "Then you should take the game trails," I reasoned. "Stay off the roads and away from Otherwolf settlements."

"I haven't any maps of alternative routes," he said. "And anyway, I don't trust my ability to find my way on game trails. I'm moderately well-traveled, but in Amuresca everything is mapped and populated, there are road and sign posts, very few uncivilized plots of land left...here, everything is still so wild."

"My father would know what to do," I scratched behind one of my ears, thoughtfully. "Perhaps we should skip Broen. Continue on to my home. It's farther north than you probably want to go, but it would be safer."

He tipped his ears back, "Tulimak," he cautioned, "I shouldn't have to explain to you why that's a bad idea."

"If we can outrun her," I said, jerking a thumb backwards to denote the distant hunter, "no one would know or suspect you'd be going further upriver. Your father knows where you're headed, right?"

"Don't call him that," he said softly, although there was no real anger directed at me there. Then, "Yes. Yes, he'd have to know the reason I've come this far is to report him to the authorities at the Trade Commission in Arbordale. He's too well-seated in Highvolle. I'd stand no chance there. But here, he's a foreigner. I don't know what the Trade Commission will have the power to do. It's doubtful he'd ever be arrested. Even if they *could* take a warrant out on him, he'd have to set foot on Carvecian soil for it to take effect. But they could seize his holdings here, crumble his slave trade and cut him off from all of his markets here. It would still be financially crippling and that would be enough to satisfy me."

He looked to me. "But none of that would be worth bringing his far-flung wrath down on your family, Tulimak. I don't want anyone else caught in this hellfire. This is between me and him, and anyone foolish enough to come after me. It's bad enough that you've gotten involved."

I smiled slowly at him, which seemed to confuse him. "What?" he asked, glancing about like I must have seen something he hadn't.

"I was worried," I admitted. "Especially after...last night. I thought there might be a chance you were..."

Ever canny, he seemed to understand. "Using you?" he filled in.

I nodded. "I'm sorry."

"No, it's," he sighed. "It's understandable. And I'm not going to deny I saw the benefit in our meeting from the start. But I only would have taken that so far. It was rather cute having a big bear bodyguard when I was worried about a few skinny foxes. But then, when we got shot at on the river and you got hurt..."

"I'm fine," I lied unconvincingly. My shoulder was still hot and aching.

"Don't try that on me," he said, snorting. "Look, you were talking about regret. I've been thinking about that a lot too, with the shadow of death hanging over me for the last few months and all. Really gets a man to thinking about his worth. Which in my case, is literally all in my own mind, because I sure as hell haven't gotten much reinforcement from the world at large."

I wanted to reach over and embrace him, hearing those words. It wasn't just that they were profoundly sad, it was how much he clearly meant them.

"If I'm going to die any time soon," he murmured, "I want to do so knowing one thing, above all else. That I'm a better man than my—" he cut himself off. "Than that man. And *he* uses people."

"You're passing up a safe haven because you don't want to endanger my family," I said softly. "And I'm practically a stranger to you. My family even more so. That's not a sacrifice most people would make."

"We'll figure something else out," he promised, giving me a weak smile. "I don't want to leave you with regrets, Tulimak."

I smiled back. For a time, we rowed in silence. It wasn't long though before I had to put words to what had been gnawing at me this whole morning and afternoon, and what had ultimately started this conversation.

"So if you weren't," I gestured with a paw at nothing, "trying to...I—I don't know...win me over? Why...this morning..."

He gave me a long look, and for a few moments I was worried I'd offended him, until he finally guffawed. "Are you honestly asking if I whored myself out to you to keep you around?"

"I-I didn't—" I stammered.

"Relax," he laughed through his nose, showing his fangs through his amused grin. "I'm not upset. Honestly, you don't even understand why that's as funny as it is to me." He straightened up a bit, tucking the oar under one arm so he could use his other hand to smooth his fur back and flare out the ruff around his neck in that way I'd noticed he did whenever he was taking stock of his appearance. "Let me ask you something," he said, giving me the side-eye, "why did *you* wish to engage in such a thing...with me? Because there was no mistaking *your* interest."

I dropped my gaze to the water. "I wish I knew," I admitted.

"Well there you have it," he chirped. When I looked back up, he'd set back to rowing. "Who can say why we enjoy the things we do? Maybe it's how God made us. Maybe it's just as random and ultimately meaningless as eye color."

"Eye color doesn't...seen random," I reasoned. "Most people have similar fur patterns to their parents. Eyes, too."

He shrugged. "So perhaps it's in the blood? Considering how much stock the Amurescan Faith puts in bloodline, you'd think they'd entertain that possibility. But no, it must all be sinful, *unnatural* desires, tantamount to spitting in God's face!" He shook his fist at the sky for dramatic effect, then waved it off. "Look, the point is, it hardly matters *why*. I enjoy the company of women too, as I said earlier. I've never stopped to question why *that* is. I see it as a blessing, an...expansion of my options for earthly pleasures. And there often aren't many of those to be had, so I try to make the most of those that are available."

"I wasn't asking why you'd want to in general," I said uneasily. The truth was, that part still didn't make much sense to me, either. It *did* seem unnatural, at least based on everything I'd seen in my life. I wasn't a child, I understood by now that mating brought pleasure, but I also understood that the reason for that particular gift the spirits had bestowed on us was to encourage procreation. And two men couldn't make young together.

But I didn't want to offend him. So I continued, "I was more curious why you'd want to…with me."

He seemed to hesitate a beat, before saying, "You demanded honesty, so shall it be."

I held my breath.

"I'm not *usually* so quick to jump into bed with people," he said, then amended a moment later, "all right, maybe sometimes. But my point is, I try to be careful about it. Growing up where I did doesn't make for a particularly trusting individual. But," he gave a hapless smile, "when the alternatives are freezing to death, I make exceptions. And I'd already noted that you'd taken a certain bumbling, adorable sort of interest in me—"

I groaned.

He patted my shoulder from across the raft. "Take heart. Social grace is overrated. Transparent emotions won't win you any points in politics, but you'll never be misunderstood. There's something to that."

"I'm more humiliated that you realized something I hadn't even realized myself," I muttered.

"It's easier to see some things from the outside looking in," he reasoned. "Anyway. I noticed, I suspected, went back and forth on whether or not I was correct in my estimation. And then the confirmation woke me up in my sleep."

I couldn't possibly have been more uncomfortable.

"And considering death felt like a real, imminent possibility," he continued, "I saw no reason not to accept the offer and indulge in something amidst this quagmire of cold, pain and fear that might actually feel good. It really is that simple."

"But you didn't," I said haltingly.

He looked at me, surprised. Recognition dawned on his features after a flash. I wanted to bury my muzzle in my hands. A laugh bubbled up from his throat and he physically turned to look up at me. "Ah, I understand now! You're upset because I didn't, what, partake myself? Oh, that's why you thought I was just doing that to keep you around, isn't it?"

At least he hadn't guessed at the other reason it had been eating at me. I could hold on to that.

He smirked at me, leaning over my way enough that I had no chance except to look at him. "Or," he cooed, "are you worried I'm not attracted to you?"

Well, there went that.

"You poor, sweet bear," he said around continued chuckles. "If it weren't for the fact that it would overbalance the raft and dump us in this freezing river, I'd show you how wrong you are."

I swallowed, at that.

"For one, you didn't exactly give me the chance," he said pointedly. "It wasn't but a moment after…everything…that you began to panic. And from there it was hard enough just to calm you down."

"I'm sorry for that," I said, now thoroughly humiliated.

"Again, I shouldn't have assumed your experience," he said, his tone genuinely concerned. "We should have talked more. I'd take it back if I could."

"No," I said quickly. He smiled, presumably at the suddenness of my response. "No, I wouldn't want to take any of this back," I said, meaning it. "Not meeting you, not any of our time together, and not…that. Regardless how briefly we travel together, I've learned a great deal over the last few days. About a great many things."

I finally got up the courage to look at him again. "And I appreciate you talking to me about all of this. Even though you've said several times now how you don't prefer to."

He locked his gaze with mine. "It is literally the least I can do."

When we settled in to sleep that night, not exactly as wet as we'd been the night before, but still not dry, (and the temperature had dropped further despite there not being a storm, so it somehow felt worse) I was almost too tired to feel awkward.

Almost.

We'd rowed through every lit hour of the day, trying to make ground. My shoulder hurt nearly too much to bear and I could tell Finn was in pain, as well. There was no question that all either of us wanted to do was sleep, but still, despite that, I felt a twinge of uncertainty in my stomach when Finnegan began to undress.

We hadn't really resolved anything. I'd enjoyed our conversation and the ones that had followed throughout the day. Truth be told, I just enjoyed talking to Finn. Even if it was on dark subject matter, or things that made me uncomfortable. I would still rather be taking this trek with him, pursued and fearing death, than be peaceful and alone on my way home.

That realization was shocking, to say the least.

I couldn't account for whatever was happening between us. This foreign man was peeling me back, revealing pieces of me I hadn't known were there. That thought alone...I was no poet. No storyteller. I'd hardly spoken so much aloud this *year* as I had in the last few days.

What was happening to me?

It was, like this trip had become, unexpected, frightening, and exciting. I felt as though I'd passed the marker for a new trail, a new stage of my life. And whether or not he knew it or appreciated it, Finnegan was the one who'd ushered me into these new realities.

I'd always be grateful to him for that, regardless what happened.

I couldn't help but notice his body shaking as he got the last of his clothing off. It made that knot in my stomach seem less important. I simply couldn't *afford* to sit here worrying while someone right beside me was suffering. All of this introspection was making me selfish.

I lay down beside him and reached forward, wrapping my paw around his hip and dragging his body back against mine. He began to say something, but ceased when I wrapped my other arm underneath him and pulled him in close. All he did after that was let out a long breath, going lax in my arms.

This? This was easy. This all made sense to me. Caring for another person, sharing the comfort of warmth and touch together. There was nothing complicated about it.

Finnegan made a low noise, a rumbling groan, and I realized that without so much as considering it, my paw-pads had been running circles over his hip bone. I tried applying a little pressure and he groaned more audibly.

I ran my paw further down his thigh, feeling the contour of his body, bone and sinew. His fur felt different from mine in many ways and his figure was so much leaner, so different in build than my own. I found that I quite enjoyed touching him, even simply in this way. And since he seemed to be enjoying it too, I kept it up until his breathing slowed.

By then I was falling asleep, myself. The last thing I remembered doing was draping my cloak over the both of us.

Chapter 7

Broen

The next morning, I woke to pain. Burning, itching, intense pain. I'd actually roused many times throughout the night as it got noticeably worse, but exhaustion had given way to deeper sleep eventually. At least, until daylight broke into the lean-to, and the combination of pain and light overwhelmed all of that. My body could no longer rest.

I knew from the aching weariness in my limbs and the queasy feeling of full-body weakness washing over me as I attempted even the slightest movement, that I was not well. And it was all radiating from the wound on my back.

Finnegan was gone, but I could hear him outside, milling about. With a heavy grunt, I willed myself to my knees and crawled out into the daylight, squinting against the sun. I saw his silhouette and heard him approach before his figure came into focus, carrying something over his shoulder.

"I figured to hell with even trying for a fire this morning," he said as he trod through the snow into camp, clearly coming back from the river. "If these fish are safe to eat frozen, let's do it. I'm tired of just carrots—hey," he paused, putting down the small sack he'd brought with him, presumably with our breakfast in it. "You look like death."

"What?" I asked, hazily.

"Sorry, it's an expression," He shook his head, crossing the distance between us and kneeling in the snow, reaching for me tentatively. "You don't look well. The edges of your eyes are red, your nose seems dry..."

"I don't feel well," I supplied unhelpfully, rolling my shoulder with a wince. "My wound is acting up."

"The wound you weren't particularly worried about?" he chastised, sighing and tapping my arm lightly. "Lean down, let me take a look."

I did as instructed and he scooched around to my side, peering at the injury on the back of my shoulder for a while in silence. After a time, I began to worry. "What does it look like?" I asked, nervously.

"Like an injury," he said, sounding lost. "I don't know, Tulimak. I'm not a Physician. It looks redder than before?" He sniffed. "And it smells different. Worse. Not putrid, but not good."

"I'm not a healer either," I said, wiping my paws over my eyes, trying to get the world to look less muddy. I hardly felt like I was in serious danger, but I certainly did feel a little ill and the spot hurt a lot worse than yesterday. I didn't know what that meant.

"Hell, you're not going septic on me, are you?" he asked, voice laced with concern.

"I don't know what that means."

"It means the wound's not clean," he said, then after a brief pause, "as far as I understand it, anyway. Like I said, I don't really know much about this, but sepsis is something we'd worry about in the Risers a lot, any time we had an open wound for too long."

"Is it dangerous?" I asked.

"You don't come back from it," he said quietly.

Fear lanced through me. Death had been hovering over us for the last few days, but I'd thought—I don't know. I'd thought I'd be shot maybe. Which I suppose I was, but I hadn't thought of this graze as being enough to kill me. I thought if we were going to die, it would be quickly. The idea of disease had never entered my mind, even though it really should have.

It's how my mother had died. My otter mother.

"A few years ago," I said quietly, feeling Finnegan perk up from beside me, his ears going up, "some kind of disease came through our village. A few of our hunters came back with it after a trip and before long a dozen of us were sick. My mother worked with our medicine woman, our healer, sometimes. Mostly delivering pups, but she thought she could help." I looked down, stretching my shoulder and feeling a fresh wave of pain come over me. "She caught it, too. They all died. Everyone who got the disease. I wasn't allowed to see her, even towards the end."

Finnegan was looking at me now, his gaze full of sympathy. I wiped my nose, turning my muzzle towards him. "A man from the nearby settlement came and told us what to do to avoid anyone else getting sick. We had to leave food in a basket outside their door and water in a bucket. My father couldn't even be with her. When it...was over...we had to burn the hut they were in. We couldn't even bury them. Just the ashes." I drew in a shuddering breath. "I hope this isn't like that. I'd hate to put my father through that. Again."

The wolfdog said nothing for a while. When he spoke again, he did so with a far-off look, although he was technically still facing my way. "My mother also died of illness," he said, then snuffed, "although I suppose that's not much of a coincidence. I think Mikhail once told me it's how half of all people who die before their time meet their end. He was very...aware of it, given his profession."

"Was he a healer?" I asked.

"Not exactly," he said with a sigh. "He and my mother, and...well, most everyone in Ambrose Park are Courtesans. I know you don't know the word," he said before I could speak up. "Just think of them as entertainers. Personal entertainers. They travel a lot for their job and spend time with a lot of different men. Including a lot of military men and sailors, so it's a risk. Everyone picks something up eventually. That's why Mikhail got out of the work while he was still healthy enough to do so. Sometimes you get lucky like that and find someone who can take care of you, so you can stop working." He wilted a little. "That never happened for my mother. She caught something that...lingered...a long time. She stopped the work when it got bad, but the disease was untreatable. Better medicine and coin for a real Physician would've made all the difference near the end, but the man who sired me refused to send aid. He'd long since disavowed us by then. I started working, making as much coin as I could, but..."

He curled a lip at that, revealing clenched teeth. "The thing about working to make life better for the people you love," he said with some difficulty, "is that you're not around to enjoy the time they have left. I wasn't home, when..."

I instinctively found myself reaching for him. When had that become so second nature for me? Why was it so easy to touch him, when I'd spent most of my life terrified of moving into most peoples' space with my big body?

I grasped at nothing for a moment and dropped my hand. He noticed and went to reach for me, but I yanked my paw back. "No," I shook my head, suddenly feeling the need to put distance between us. "M-maybe you should go. I don't want to make you sick."

He let out a breath and darted his hand forward, catching mine. It clenched around my paw like iron. I'd never known he possessed such strength in his arm. "Tulimak," he said intently, "I can't catch blood poisoning from you, if that's what this is. I know that much, at least. You need to have a wound."

"But you do," I insisted.

"My humors haven't been exposed," he insisted. "I'll be all right."

He said it with such certainty, I had to believe him. I swallowed, and at length, nodded.

His expression softened and he released his grip on my paw some, turning it in his, then squeezing it again. "And we don't even know that's what this is," he pointed out. "So it's a little early to resign yourself to death. Certainly not on my watch." He released my hand fully at that point and stood, with purpose. "Now get up. Help me pack camp."

I did so, albeit much more slowly than him. He turned and grabbed up the bag he'd brought with him, doing an admirable job of covering the wince as he bent over. "Are you hungry?" he asked. "You should try to eat."

"It's hard to tell," I said honestly.

"You are," he stated, pulling one of the frozen fish out of the bag. "We didn't eat last night, so you must be. You need to eat to keep your strength up. Do you think you can do that for me?"

I nodded, taking the frozen salmon from him. He pulled out the other, a far smaller one, and began to gnaw on the tail as he moved towards where his coat was lain out, the fish dangling from his mouth as he spoke through his teeth. "I can pack us up. Just eat and try to wake up some, all right? We need to get back on the river and I need you at your best there."

I nodded, head still a bit muggy. But something about his sudden determination caught me off-guard. He was acting far more purposeful than we had any right to be, considering we still didn't really have a firm destination in mind.

I must have said that part out loud, because he replied, "Yes we do. We're going to Broen."

"But the hunters looking for you..." I trailed off.

"You need a Physician," he snapped. "To hell with them. I have a pistol and I'm pretty damn good with it. We'll manage."

"And the one following us?" I said pointedly.

He pulled free one of the oars holding up our makeshift lean-to, collapsing the pine boughs, the hide, and the layer of snow atop it all at once. And then he fixed me with his sharp gaze. "Didn't you hear me?" He began to lift a corner of the hide, shaking it out. "Now eat."

I did so, finding the ill feeling in my body was subsiding enough so that I could stomach eating. Maybe it was because I was waking up. Maybe it was Finnegan's sudden command of the situation, making me feel more at ease.

"I don't know how well I'll be able to row today," I admitted. "But I'll try my hardest. I hope I don't slow us down."

"Tulimak, I don't care if you do," he said in a clipped tone. "I don't like living through my mistakes more than once. We go together, at whatever pace we can manage. I am not leaving your side until this passes, or until we've gotten you help."

That was clearly the end of the conversation and I knew by the bark in his tone not to question him further. I'd noticed it in the past, but at times like this it was even more evident. Finnegan had a surprisingly deep voice for such a slender, small man. Or well, smaller than me, which I guess wasn't saying much. I suppose amongst canines he would have been average.

I found I rather liked his answering my uncertainty with certainty. Even if I suspected some of it at least was false, there was a comfort in surrendering to his demands at a time like this. I wanted someone to take charge, because I simply didn't have the energy to. And I wanted very badly for him to be right, as well. It was harder to quiet the doubts that constantly plagued my mind when I was alone, but with someone with such a strong personality reassuring me, I found my anxiety receding. Certainly not entirely, but enough that I felt better.

That feeling improved further after the meal, just as he'd predicted. It had been a safe prediction, to be fair. We got back on the river and that day passed as well as could be expected, given the situation. Rowing was difficult. Painful. But Finnegan was giving all he had and the gap between us was closing. We found a pace eventually that I could slow to match that was easier on my body. The wolfdog clearly struggled through mounting exhaustion to compensate, but he did so with quiet determination. I had to admire his resolve.

There was a lot I was beginning to admire about him.

Spirits, how I wanted more time. I wanted to know more of life, more of this feeling, this yearning growing inside of me.

I wanted to know Finnegan Ambrose better than I did now.

I tried not to think about how the destination we were determinedly racing towards was also the place we were set to part ways. Tried not to think about how or why I could justify knowing this man longer. Survival was the goal right now. Planning past that was pointless, until we knew there *was* a "past that."

I'd originally intended on us giving up on the raft after we passed the Twelve Sisters' Rise, a break in the earth where twelve large rock formations split the land. We passed them on that third day and kept moving up-river. As painful as rowing was, the concept of carrying our possessions with my shoulder the way it was the remaining ten miles it would take by land to reach Broen was simply inconceivable. Broen *was* along the river, it just wasn't as direct a route to get there. It would take another two days as opposed to the one it would have normally taken me in good health on foot, using the game trails.

Thankfully, other than aching from the exertion, I didn't feel any more ill by the close of the day. Just very, very tired, and very sore. I hardly made it to shore before I had to sit and despite my protestations, in the end, Finnegan pitched almost the entirety of our camp. I had to help steady the oars and spread the hides, but he did all the labor aside from that. He'd picked up on it fairly quickly for someone who'd only had a few days' experience making camp. He even managed to start a fire, although he once again used some of his papers to do so.

"How much farther?" he asked, voice thick with fatigue as we watched the salmon laid out on a stone in the fire crackle and sizzle.

"Tomorrow," I said drowsily. "We should...end of day..."

He leaned forward and spitted one of the fish on a sharpened stick, holding it out to me. "Eat," he insisted quietly.

The next morning, I felt much the same. Which was to say awful. But I suppose not *more* ill-feeling than the day before. Just intensely tired. All my body wanted to do was stay lying down in that lean-to, warm and still. Sunlight was filtering in through the hide flap, and not meager morning light like had been many mornings prior. It was stark daylight outside, which meant we'd slept for a long time. And all I wanted to do was sleep *even longer*.

As bad as I felt, the little world inside our lean-to was still so comforting. Unlike the evening before, I'd slept soundly the whole night through. Which might have accounted for why I was, at the very least, not getting any worse.

The reason for our deep and restful sleep was abundantly obvious, at least as far as I was concerned. Every night prior, Finnegan and I had slept with our backs against one another, or back to front, putting as much distance between us as we could in the small space. I'd obviously closed the gap in my sleep the one night...but we'd *tried* to have some kind of propriety in the tight quarters. As meager a bubble between us as we were able to, anyway.

It was pointless, really. We'd crossed every boundary that mattered already. Finnegan had been hesitant since we'd talked to come anywhere near that kind of closeness again, and I suppose a part of me was glad for that. But the nights were getting colder and last night when we'd pulled the worn sheepskin over the two of us, and the cold had persisted, the futility of the distance we were putting between us had been too obvious to ignore.

This wasn't about whatever I felt for Finnegan, it was about common sense and survival. If I'd been well, the cold would have been something I'd have easily endured. But it was one more pain we didn't need right now.

Without so much as a word to one another, we'd drawn in close and folded our bodies around each other. It had so immediately made sense

and felt right, I was tempted to believe a spirit was guiding us. But it was probably something a lot more basic than that. Instinct.

I'd not slept this close with anyone since I was a cub. Even now, in what I'm fairly certain was the early afternoon light, the canine was still pressed against my chest fur, arms tucked up against me, nose puffing warm air along my breast bone. He was wrapped in one of my arms and the solid weight of him was quickly lulling me back to sleep. I forgot about the throbbing pain in my shoulder, the nagging fear we were being followed, and allowed myself to bask in the moment.

This was the kind of comfort, I thought, that married people must feel. Not that I wanted that with Finn (obviously, it would be sheer insanity to think I could marry another man); it was just the only thing I could think of that might compare to this total feeling of peace with someone who wasn't related to you. I was glad I got to know what it felt like this once, even if it wasn't under the most ideal circumstances. There were many comforts you could only have with a wife, and this was one of those things I thought I might never experience. But here it was, unexpectedly.

Of course, I'd experienced another "comfort" reserved for marriage with Finn by now, as well. And I hadn't stopped thinking about it just because I was ill.

In his sleep, alongside me as close as he was, I was able to study him in great detail with the advantage of not feeling awkward for staring. Every moment, I found a new interesting thing about him. Like how his eyelashes were longer than mine, or that some of his whiskers were bent. The various spots he had dashes of white through his fur, his throat, his tail-tip, lower down his stomach there were even a few soft, whisper-fine tufts of lighter fur.

There were areas I was pointedly trying not to look, of course. Which was unnerving to consider, because I *shouldn't* be as awkward as this about seeing another nude man. Looking at a man's sheath should have been normal. It most certainly should *not* be making my throat catch, my body grow restless. Focus on something else. Anything else.

Intriguingly, he had scars. At least a dozen so far that I could see. Three of them were on his face, one on his ear, the rest on various parts of his body I could see. They were hard to spot on the previous occasions I'd seen him with his clothing off, both because it was dark and because of his dark pelt. But on his face, joints and limbs in particular, where his fur was shorter, I was able to make them out. Most of them looked older, pink lacerations or divots in the skin that were shinier and missing some fur. In a way they almost reminded me of my markings, which had been burnt into my hide. But these clearly had not been intentional. They were old injuries.

A few might have made sense, given what he'd told me about his difficult childhood. But so many? It was unexpected. I'd have to ask him about them some time.

Some time. In the next day. Because after that…

I shook my head slowly, trying not to think about it for now. I should get a little more sleep, if I could. Even if it was getting late in the day, I clearly needed it. And Finnegan wasn't even up yet.

He was, actually. At some point I'd gotten lost in my thoughts and failed to realize his eyes had opened. He yawned slowly, his tongue curling, body flexing against mine.

"Mnnhhhh," he groaned. "It's bright out."

I opened my muzzle to say something, but he was already shifting up onto his elbow, fur tousled and flattened against his cheek on one side. He brushed at it sleepily with his claws, making a half-hearted effort to preen down the black tufts.

"Finnegan," I said suddenly, my words coming before my thoughts had caught up. "Are you certain you can't get this illness from me?"

"We don't even know for sure that you have it," he said, voice deep and still thick with sleep. "And you've been able to hold food down, so I'd say that's definitive. We just need to get the wound treated before it gets worse." He reached down and pressed a palm to his back, stretching his hip. "Why?"

I'd asked. I had to answer now, or it would seem strange.

My eyes darted away from his as I spoke. "You…said you felt the same things for me that…I felt for you."

That got his attention. I wasn't looking at them, but I could feel his eyes become more intense, more awake. "That's vague," he said, tone far too comfortable for something that was so hard for *me* to get out. "You mean attraction?"

"Yes," I said simply.

"Then yes. Although we're both in a poor state of affairs currently, physically speaking—"

"Can I kiss you?" I asked, forcing myself to look him in the eyes when I asked.

To say he looked shocked would be an understatement. It took him a full three blinks before he replied to me, and when he did it was with a bemused, "Why-ever are you asking n—I am a *mess*." He gestured down at both of us, really, but he was clearly mostly referring to himself. And presumably the mud and grit in his fur, the scent of exhaustion and river water soaked into our bodies, and the stale odor of woodsmoke permeating the lean-to from last night's fire.

I smiled, though I'm not really sure why. "You always look handsome."

"That's true," he said, without missing a beat. "And I'm not saying no, exactly. But why now?"

"We're going to reach Broen tonight," I said with certainty. "And once we make it to town, I may never have another chance."

My forthright answer had the desired effect. He immediately seemed to realize the truth in the statement and leaned up on his hands, humming thoughtfully. "All right," he said. "You make a fine point. But I've one caveat."

"A what?"

"A demand," he clucked, leaning over me.

"I—uh," I stammered, "all right."

Maybe I shouldn't have agreed to it so quickly, without knowing what it was. But when he smiled at me, that long canine smile that went up into his cheek ruff, and leaned down over me, those forest green eyes boring into mine, I was certain I'd give this man whatever he wanted. Which was probably a bad idea.

Oh, I was done for.

I reached up to cup my paw around his cheek, amazed by how perfect the contrast in our fur color looked against one another. I wanted to see more of him…against me…

He was speaking.

"I don't actually, ah, kiss people often," he said, his voice uncertain. It was rather cute to see him awkward about something. Anything. "It feels like it's something more reserved for people who are important to you, not dalliances. And I've had more of the latter than the former. So..." he cleared his throat, looking at me, his ears tipped back slightly, "you have to swear to me that you're not going to leave me with awful, tragic memories, all right? Because I'll remember this, I'm certain I will, and the bad memories I already have of people who've been important to me haunt me enough as it is."

He said it all so matter-of-factly, like he was making the simplest of requests. He obviously knew the demand was a farce, what guarantees could I possibly give him that I wouldn't let something unfortunate happen that would leave him with depressing memories? But despite how nonsensical it sounded, I understood what he meant completely. And it gave me some insight into him I hadn't had before.

"There's only so much one man can take," he said with a smile that didn't fit how tired his eyes looked. He laughed, dry and weak. "I just... don't prefer to have any more regrets than I already do."

"Finn," I said with a huff, smiling as I realized I'd stumbled on at least one thing I could explain to the more worldly canine. "Memories of people we've lost are like...stories. Some parts make you sad, but it doesn't make the rest of the tale worth any less."

"Sage wisdom," he said in an unconvinced, dry tone. "But I'd like to spend whatever time I have left on earth not being sad, if that's all right. I've had enough sadness in my life."

"I believe you," I said quietly, my thumb brushing over his cheek. "But I think you know I can't promise you that."

He dropped his gaze, and after a time, spoke again. His voice was very small. "Just don't die because of me, then."

"I'll do my very best not to die at all," I promised. "At least not any time soon. I have a lot left I want to do."

He nodded and closed his eyes for a moment, leaning in to my palm. "Then I guess...it's all right."

That was it. He'd given me permission. I'd been the one to ask, so I couldn't back down now. That would somehow be even more awkward than attempting it and failing. Oh spirits, could you fail to kiss someone? If anyone could, it would be me.

He'd said he hadn't done this much before, but then any experience he had was more than mine. How miserably would I compare to his standards? Why had I been certain enough to ask for this in the first place? Where had all my confidence from a few moments ago gone?

His eyes were boring into mine, the color of spruce boughs and mountains in spring flush. I could not possibly invent enough metaphors in my mind to describe his eyes. They were the first thing that had drawn me to him, and now they were inches away, looking into mine expectantly. And for just this moment, I knew I was allowed to want something, to take something, and that he was willing to give it. There was such a...*calm*...in that certainty.

There it was.

Still holding his chin in my palm like a lifeline, I leaned in the few inches remaining to touch my muzzle to his. It didn't matter that I was twice his size, or that we were different species. Or that we were both men. His muzzle was soft and pliant against mine, and it only took a short span of brushing fur and whiskers together before we found an angle at which our barely open mouths met. I felt him on the tip of my tongue, dragged his scent through my nostrils, tasted him. I was overwhelmed by him, over-

come by how his presence was dominating my senses, so much so that I barely noticed when his tongue slid over my own. But I hardly needed a coherent thought to know what to do from there. I wanted more of him, more of that. So I reciprocated, opened my muzzle more for him.

And so it went for…I'm not certain how long. But when we pulled back, it was because we were both panting for air. I felt dizzy, my limbs loose and heavy. Finnegan looked more disheveled than before, and as the haze began to fade from his eyes…surprised.

"Damn," he said at length, words almost slurred. "I was expecting something sweet and simple, from you. Little peck on the muzzle. There *is* a bear in there somewhere, isn't there?"

"I…" I was momentarily considering an apology, but I dismissed it before I got it out, remembering every vivid detail of the kiss and how very *mutual* it had most certainly been. Still, I wasn't going to be held entirely accountable for it. I gripped his paws, speaking to the baffled looking wolf-dog. "Finnegan…" my mouth was dry, but I persisted, "I—I'm really…fond of you. And I'm worried about you. I'm worried about what's going to happen in Broen. I still want to help you somehow, a-and I don't know how, but I do know that I have…I feel…" I knitted my brow, frustrated. "I have all of these *feelings*," I settled on the simplest, bluntest way to impart how confused I really was, because there really was no better way to say it, "that I don't understand," I continued, helplessly. "I know we have to go to Broen. But I'm afraid we'll part ways there, and then I'll *never* understand…"

I let the thought run out intentionally, hoping he might explain in words what I simply didn't have the means to. But he said nothing, only looked down at our hands for a long time.

"We have to get moving," is what he eventually said, instead. "You need treatment. Broen isn't far, right?"

I swallowed back my disappointment. What had I expected him to say, really?

"Less than a day," I said softly.

He nodded, standing and releasing my hands slowly. "We row until we arrive," he announced, quietly but firmly.

What then? I wanted to ask.

But I didn't.

We arrived at Broen when the day was late and the whole world was purplish-blue, the snow catching the final colors of daylight as it faded over the mountains. The lights of the large town were spread over the small valley on which it resided, the docks along the river ringed with lanterns. I didn't bother to hide my raft this time, we simply pulled straight up to the town and tied it off, alongside canoes and the sorts of larger boats the Otherwolves favored. There was even a small barge.

Our raft was, by far, the smallest and most ramshackle craft here, and a few stoats cooking fish and a pot of potatoes over a crackling fire had a good laugh at our expense as we wearily stumbled onto the docks. I made sure to gather up everything we still had of value, because I wasn't certain any of it would still be here if or when we returned. I'd never had intentions of taking the raft all the way up-river to my tribe, anyway. The water had become peppered with ice over the last day or so as the temperatures dropped. It would soon freeze.

Despite it being dark, the dirt road alongside the docks was still bustling with activity, mostly men trying to make the most of the last waning hour to unload supplies, or gather water in bucket lines. A cattle dog with a herd of mules was bringing them in for a drink before he presumably turned them in for the night.

And there were a lot of women about, for some reason. At least half a dozen, moving between firepit camps that had sprung up around the docks, some sitting with the groups of men, talking, laughing, and drinking. We passed a wolverine amongst a group of Otherwolves, wearing a bright, if mud-stained, checkered dress. She was smoking a pipe and gave me a long look when I stared, lifting her muzzle to me as if challenging me to say something. I quickly looked away.

"I've never seen so many women out at night in an Otherwolf town," I said quietly, leaning down to Finn as we walked.

He glanced briefly up at me, arching an eyebrow. Then sighed. "They're working, Tulimak. Don't stare."

I shut my mouth and dropped my gaze to the ground, mortified. He was right. I forgot sometimes how my curiosity about the world beyond our tribe might be inappropriate. These were people going about their lives, not a spectacle for me to behold.

We were passing rows of drying and salting racks for fish and I'd been keeping my gaze firmly on the dirt, so when someone approached us, I didn't notice until she was right up on us. Finn clearly had though, grabbing my arm and pulling me to a halt.

It was a woman. A coyote, by the look of it, lean and just a bit shorter than Finnegan. She was wearing an Otherwolf dress with burgundy checkered patterns on it, over a dingy white petticoat and blouse, and a leather corset. She was the most uncovered female I'd ever seen outside my own tribe, with her sleeves and most of her top pulled down to just below her shoulders, so that you could see the slope of her breasts.

I was briefly worried I'd somehow offended her too, until I noticed she was smiling. Although she was primarily focused on Finnegan.

"Saw you sizin' up Gina o'er there," she remarked, gesturing in the direction of the wolverine. "She's spoken for t'night but I ain't."

"We're not interested in company," Finnegan said politely. "We have business in town."

"Ah've got a place in town if you prefer," she said, tugging at one of her sleeves. I wanted to tell her that doing so was just revealing more of her chest, which must have been accidental. It was so cold out. "Or a'least, I can. For a few pence extra, I know a place I kin get us a room."

There was something in her tone…she was smiling, but also shivering a bit. And her voice had a waver to it, a weakness in her throat. It wasn't desperation, but it was close.

"That's not—" Finn began.

"I kin handle two," she insisted, wiping her nose. "Even the big lad. Ah'll be good t'you both."

Finn had gone silent. I wasn't certain what it was the woman was offering, but I doubted very much that he was planning to take her up on her offer. But that wasn't it. He was staring past her. I followed his gaze and caught sight of two eyes in the dark, peering out from behind one of the drying racks.

The coyote woman saw where we were both looking and snapped her head around, calling out. "Ben, no. I told y'to stay near th'fire…" She frantically looked back at us and did a quick curtsy, hustling back towards what I now realized was a small child. A little coyote boy, clearly only a few years old. She bent down and picked him up, shockingly walking back towards us once she had him on her hip, her tone placating. "Ah'm sorry, lads. He won't get'n the way, ah promise. He's quiet. He won't touch none'o your things. He knows better."

I had hardly known what to say before, I was even more at a loss now. I looked to Finnegan and found him equally silent. Only he looked different, now. Where he'd been polite and calm before, now he seemed…pained. It was impossible to say what was going through his mind or why, but his eyes were unfocused, jaw tense.

"Do you not have a place to stay tonight, otherwise?" he asked of the woman, at length.

"I don't 'ave fleas, if that's your worry," she insisted, far too quickly. "I stay at the Church nights I can't find board. I'm clean. M'boy's clean, too."

Finnegan turned to regard me. "You have coin, right? To pay the Physician? We'll need at least a few silver."

"I have coin, yes," I said, uncertainly.

He turned at that and unbuttoned, then fished in his coat pocket and produced a few pence, the copper flashing in the firelight from the nearby camps. I happened to know it was probably all he had left. He held it out to the woman and after a brief pause, she took it.

"Four's all I can manage," he said quietly. "Not enough for your services, but you said you could find board for a few more, so…get somewhere warm."

"If I wanted charity I'd go to the Church," she said, seeming quietly offended. All the same, she pocketed the coin and readjusted her son on her hip. "I don't s'pose the tribesman there's willin' to part with some of that silver, then?"

"Let's go," Finn said to me, walking around and past the woman. I followed behind him, glancing back behind us as we left her. She stared at us a further moment, then began to move back towards the camps.

I thought about asking Finn what exactly had just transpired, but he seemed in a dark mood, all of a sudden. I walked beside him in silence as we made our way into the lantern-lit town. After some deliberation, I put a paw on his shoulder and squeezed it. I didn't know what to say, but he seemed sad, and it was all I could think to do.

He reached up and gripped my paw back and held it for a brief time, before easing it down off of his shoulder.

We'd entered Broen's main street. It was far more intimidating, far more foreign to me than any place I'd been before. There were people of all stripes (sometimes literally) milling about in the night market area, moving in and out of rooming houses and inns, sitting on the sprawling porches and leaning on paddock posts. Broen wasn't just some frontier town; it was a major trade post. My father came here to trade for goods our tribe needed sometimes, but I'd intentionally avoided it to sell my fish, since my fish would catch a much higher price further to the east, where they were less common.

I felt somewhat more comfortable being here with Finnegan, who seemed not at all flustered by the civilization around us, or the menagerie of different people. And this was at dusk. During the day it must have been...I couldn't even imagine.

I didn't have long to take in the sights. We bypassed most of the main street on our way to the trade district, which was not hard to find. There were signposts up on the few street corners that comprised the square that was the town, (built around animal paddocks abutting most of the inns and rooming houses, as many towns were), and Finnegan seemed completely able to read them. Unlike the sign on the Wayward Inn, these were only in Amurescan. Which I could sound out if I took my time, but I was mostly good at picking out familiar words for inns, food, drink, words I already knew. It would take me a good long while to make sense of all the signs in this place. It was, after all, still a second language for me, even if my father has insisted all of his children become as fluent in it as possible.

I'd never been gladder for that than I had been throughout this last week.

"That has to be it," Finnegan pointed ahead at a shop window with a complex word I couldn't immediately make out, and a weathered, painted sign on a plank that looked like a jar of some sort.

"Ahh...p-p-ah—" I tried my hand at reading the word, squinting.

"Apothecary," he finished for me, looking mildly surprised. "You can read Amurescan?"

"Not quickly," I said bashfully. "My sisters are all better at it than me."

He readjusted the strap of his heavy satchel over his shoulder, glancing down at his bag and holding it closer to his body. "I had no idea. Come on."

The doorway into the small shop, built into the side of a larger building with two other shops in it, was clearly built for a smaller species. We found the door open, thankfully, but the main area was a cluttered, V-shaped counter ringing a ten-foot room, at most. There was barely room for Finn and I to stand in the center with our bags and look around at the shelves of molasses-brown bottles and jars. The counter was equally cluttered with various-sized glass containers of tinctures and spirits, dried herbs and many different sizes of gauze and linen. The air inside smelled like nothing I had ever experienced before, sharp and bitter, stinging to the nostrils. And beneath it all, the unmistakable coppery edge of blood from somewhere nearby.

A bell above the door had rung as we'd come in, and we heard the sound of someone making their way down the stairs from the second story. The man that emerged through the doorway behind the counter was a striped Maine coon cat, with a thick fur beard and sharp, triangular ears.

I recognized him immediately.

"I'm sorry if you were closing down for the night..." Finnegan began.

"We never close here at Carlton's Apothecary and Barber Surgeon," the cat snuffled, pulling down a stained smock from a nearby peg and tying it across his belly. He wiped some crumbs from his thick fur, flicking his whiskers. "Although you did catch me in the midst of supper, so apologies for the wait. Now." He placed his meaty paws on the counter. "What ails you? Here for a night tonic?"

"I'm...not sure what that is," Finn admitted with a slight chuckle. "But no. We had a..." he glanced up at me,"...bit of a hunting accident."

"Couldn't be too bad if you're still upright," the cat guffawed, lifting a section of the counter and shimmying through it, just barely. "But let's have a look."

I put down our bags, looked once to Finn, who nodded at me, then kneeled down to be at the cat's level and slowly pushed back my cloak to reveal the wound on my shoulder. Even moving the cloth aside stung, and I let out an audible hiss.

"Ahhh, I see," the man moved around behind me, his hands prodding at and pulling taut my hide around the injury, which hurt like hell. But I suppose he had to get a better look. He took some time, even leaning in to sniff at the wound, before stepping back and nodding. "Corruption of the humors, yes. Hmmm. We'll need to purge the wound, sear it, and prescribe you a tonic."

I saw Finnegan wince out of the corner of my eye.

"I remember you," I said quietly. "You came to my village once. Told us how to stop the illness our traders brought back from spreading."

The cat's eyes widened marginally. "Ah, yes. That strange disease that afflicted so many tribes along the river. I traveled to many villages…many towns…" He patted my arm, indicating for me to stand. "Never seen its like before. Hope I never do again."

I stood slowly and he continued, "Well, when we don't know the nature of the beast, fire is always the best method. Purges all impurity, all sin. We'll employ something similar for this affliction of your humors. I'll just have to get the brand ready…"

I blinked. "Wh-what?"

"C'mon upstairs, if you can fit," the cat chuckled, leaning down and grabbing up a leather bag from behind the counter.

I watched him head upstairs, my shoulder still pounding with pain from his prodding at it, and fear now setting in fully.

"I've never been treated with Otherwolf medicine before," I said quietly.

"We can't let it get worse," Finn put a paw out, taking mine. "I'll be with you. You can endure this."

Swallowing, I nodded. And we made our way upstairs.

Chapter 8

Standoff

That acrid, astringent smell increased as we climbed the stairs to the second story. And the unmistakable stench of old blood accompanied it, not overwhelming, but lingering, like it had sunken into the wood of this place. The quarters upstairs was as limited in space as the downstairs area, essentially just a hallway with three doors off of it, the first of which we entered.

The treatment room looked as though it doubled as a spare bedroom he let out to patients sometimes, with a worn straw mattress on an old frame in the corner, one small, uneven table, and a chest of drawers. There was also, intimidatingly, a chair in the very center of the room with fraying leather straps built into the arms and a lot of suspicious stains marring the headrest. It had an odd array of metal pieces near the center, a few locking hinges that probably leaned it back, if I had to guess.

"Ughh," Finnegan grumbled beneath his breath. "Reminds me of the time I had a tooth pulled."

"I do that, too, if you've an irksome bugger that needs out," the cat said chipperly. He moved towards the potbelly stove near the far end of the room and opened it, reaching into a cone of what looked like small fire pokers nearby. He extracted one, looked over the end of it, then repeated the process several more times before he apparently found the one he was looking for. Then he inserted it into the stove and hustled back out down the hall, presumably to get something else.

I had a feeling now that I understood what he'd meant by "sear" the wound.

Finn had put his paw on my shoulder again, the uninjured one, and I turned to regard him. He looked worried for me.

"You actually seem fairly calm," he noted, dropping his voice. "You know what this treatment will entail, right? Do you need a translation?"

I shook my head. "No, I understand. He is going to burn the wound closed."

Finnegan gave a soft huff, "So resolute. I won't lie, I'd be pissing myself."

"I'm just glad there's a simple treatment for this," I said. "And anyway, it took weeks of hide-burning to finish my markings. This will probably be much faster."

"Oh, right," he rubbed a hand over his muzzle. "Damn, how didn't I think of that? I've been staring at them for days. Seems obvious now that you mention it—those are burned in?"

I nodded, mostly paying attention to one part of what he'd said. "You've been…staring at them?" I asked, voice as low as his.

He slowly smiled.

We both heard the cat approaching us, and he removed his hand from my shoulder probably faster than he needed to. When the apothecary came back into the room, he was carrying a brown glass bottle and removing the stopper with an audible plunk. He gave it a sniff, then nodded, handing it up towards me.

I looked at it uncertainly, then slowly took it from him.

"Payment first, if'n you don't mind," the cat cleared his throat. "Two silver for the medicine, two for the treatment. You'll want to drink at least a third o'that now. Help keep you calm so I can work, help with the pain."

I reached down into my shoulder bag and dug for my coins, pulling out a handful. The silver were obvious, thankfully. Some of the copper pieces were worth different amounts and I wasn't good at telling them apart yet. I sifted out four coins and handed them to him.

While I did that, Finn leaned in and sniffed the bottle, arching his eyebrows. "What exactly is *in* that?" he asked.

"Carlton's Patented Pain Tonic," the cat announced proudly. "A proprietary tincture to treat the discomfort of all ails, and induce a calm and painless euphoria—"

"It smells mostly like whiskey," Finn muttered, in a dry tone.

"Aye, that's the base," the man affirmed. "Also Laudanum, castor, a bit of hashish—"

"Bloody hell," the wolfdog exclaimed, glancing briefly at me. "Tuli, maybe drink that *slow*, all right? Have you ever even had whiskey before?"

"We don't trade for whiskey. My father doesn't believe in it," I said, warily. "He says it makes men crazy."

"Your father sounds like a wise man," he agreed.

"Do as you please," the cat shrugged, setting down a bucket on top of the stove that I'd just realized he'd also brought in with him. It was half-full of water, and had a rough-looking rag slung over the side. "But you'll be wanting my tonic to endure the treatment. Believe me."

"I've sat through branding before," I said, "I know what to expect."

"It's not the brand you'll be wanting it for," the apothecary promised lowly.

He was right. The worst part of the treatment, by far, was having the wound scrubbed and cleaned. The man used what I'm fairly certain was an intentionally coarse rag, (woven from horse hair or something like it) scathing hot water and lye soap, and scoured the wound raw, washing it in nearly boiling hot water in between each successive round.

I was lying on my side on the chair, the wood creaking beneath my weight, praying to the spirits that it be over. The whole while. I'd had a few sips of his tonic before the cleaning began, but midway through, Finn sympathetically offered me more, and I took it. The tincture was muddying my senses somewhat, but I can't say it was euphoric. It was mostly making me even more tired than I already was, but the pain saw to it that I stayed well and truly conscious.

I'm not sure how long it all took. It was thoroughly dark outside by the time he approached me with the brand. At that point the pain was already blinding, but he gave me something to bite down on and I closed my eyes and pressed my muzzle into the headrest of the chair, thankful at least that this probably meant it would soon be over. I vaguely felt Finn take my paw where it was slung over the edge of the armrest.

And honestly, though it can be hard to compare physical pain sometimes, especially when remembered through the haze of years…the searing brand on my raw wound was in fact far worse than receiving my markings had ever been. Likely because the area was already so exposed. But it was blissfully short. I'm not sure if I cried out…I probably did. I think I should be forgiven if I did.

The apothecary said he'd give us an hour or so following the treatment for me to recover my senses. He offered me the bed to rest in, but I didn't want to move. I just wanted to lean there on my side in that chair and pray to the spirits that the pain fade faster.

Finn talked to me, quietly and calmly. His voice kept me grounded, comforted me with its cadence. It didn't even matter what he was saying.

I could tell by his demeanor that unfortunately, this situation was not new to him. He'd already told me how his mother had been sick, so…I could take a guess why he had experience comforting someone who was ailing. As time passed, the minutes stretching as long as they could, as the burning fire on my shoulder blade oh-so-slowly began to lessen, I started to think about that a lot more. My mother had died six days after catching the affliction she'd been trying to treat in someone else. At the time those days had seemed long, but in retrospect, I'd essentially seen her healthy one day, been uncertain for a week, and then she'd been gone.

Finn said his mother had lingered. For how long? Long enough to request and be denied the coin to comfort her in her illness, apparently… by his own father.

Losing my mother had seemed the most tragic, unfair thing that could happen to someone, from my perspective. I'd been outright angry about it for a long time, and I'd had many talks with my otterfa, trying to make sense of it. What kind of purpose it could possibly have served, why the spirits hadn't seen fit to save her, even though we'd prayed and prayed…It had me questioning so many things, wondering how I'd ever live on without her. And I *had* a father, who still loved me very much and had tried so hard to fill in the gaps my mother had left when we'd lost her.

I turned my head slowly to regard Finn. In the low light of the room, the wolfdog's eyes were intense and dark, lost in a sea of black fur peppered with those small scars I'd seen the other night. His lean, elegant muzzle and strongly-defined, angular features had always been attractive to me, even when I hadn't known that's what I was feeling. But seen in another light, they could be frightening. There was a ferocity there, a fury, which I often interpreted as determination or focus.

But I knew the anger that came from watching someone you loved… die. Helpless to stop it. And whatever it was he had endured with her, it had not only lasted far longer, he'd gone through it being denied the comfort and love of his remaining parent. The man who should have loved her. And him.

What did something like that do to a person?

"I know it must feel enormous," he said, soothingly stroking my good arm, "but the mark's not that big. Size of my palm, at most. And it will probably shrink as it scars."

I shook my head slowly. "It's an honor," I managed, through a dry mouth. "To be wounded…protecting a friend."

Finnegan's brows lifted and he smiled softly. I swear I heard his tail brush the floor.

"I'll get a marking…for this," I said hoarsely. "An honorific I never thought…I'd earn. A warrior's emblem."

"All right," he chuckled, "but give it a little time before you go burning yourself again. We all like to look good, but health comes first."

"I'll have such stories thanks to you," I said. "My family will want to hear everything about this trip."

"Hopefully not *everything*," he said with a knowing smirk.

I went silent at that, realization setting in. "Oh spirits," I groaned, "I hadn't even thought about how I might talk to my family about…"

"And you're not going to start," Finn affirmed. "Remember what I said? You don't talk about it. To anyone."

"But I tell my father everything, we don't have secrets."

"All right, this is probably not a good talk to have when you're out of your mind with pain and…'tonic,'" Finn cleared his throat, stroking back one of my ears. "Are you feeling up to moving yet?"

"…I think so," I said at length. I attempted to sit up slowly and mostly managed, despite the world spinning and my body badly wanting to upend itself. Finnegan stabilized me by the arm, and I took my time getting my bearings.

The apothecary returned some time later with a tankard of fresh water from the well outside. I gulped it down greedily. I hadn't realized how thirsty I'd become. The water, and likely just being vertical, helped immensely with the dizziness.

More than just an hour must have passed, (at that point I was having trouble keeping track) because by the time I was really able to walk well again and was feeling capable of leaving and finding a place for us to actually spend the night, it…wasn't really night any more. At least, it looked as though it was beginning to grow more blue than black outside. Dawn was probably an hour or so away, and we'd certainly taken up enough of the apothecary's time.

The Maine coon seemed pleased with the transaction however, and more importantly, with his work. He reminded me to keep the wound as clean as possible and to drink the tonic to help me sleep and improve my humors, but assured me that it would heal in time. He suggested that I not overly exert myself for the next few days and showed us back down the stairs.

By the time we made it down to the storefront area, I was dead on my feet. Our bags were still there in the locked shop, although I recalled I'd left the oars on the raft. We'd need them to set up our lean-to. Probably down near the docks, alongside the other travelers who'd taken to using the area as a camp site. I'd seen a few good spots near the wood-line where we could pitch. We'd have to sleep through the day, but that hardly mattered. Finn had to be as tired as I was. Or well, maybe not *as* tired. But tired.

Those were the only thoughts going through my addled, exhausted mind as we stepped out into the chill early morning air. Fresh snow had fallen at some point last night, not very much, but enough to coat the town in a shallow dusting. We'd have to stamp down an area for camp, I thought vaguely. I wasn't thinking about the troubles we'd had, or what the next day would bring, or what would become of Finn and I from this point forward.

Everything, absolutely everything, came rushing back into my consciousness with a vengeance when a gunshot split the snow-muffled silence.

The door behind us clapped shut, the apothecary wisely bolting back into his residence. The bleating of a small flock of sheep receded back into their pens in a nearby enclosure, and Finn and I both froze in our tracks.

I nearly stumbled down the two shallow steps to the cobbled road, but his arm shot out to steady me before I fell.

There was an upturned patch of blackened dirt and snow not ten feet in front of us, right in the middle of the road. It was close enough that the intent was clear, but not so close that they might have missed. Not unless, whoever they were, they were a terrible shot.

"Should we run?" I asked in a whispered, frantic tone, my breath puffing out into the air. "Go for cover?"

"No," Finn said softly, holding a palm out. "Stay completely still."

He was staring straight out across the road, very intently at something. I followed his gaze slowly, and caught sight of the man.

There was a lone figure standing on a porch across the street, staring back at us. He was wearing simple mountaineer's clothing, a cotton shirt with leather breeches, suspenders and a brimmed hat drawn down over his features. He was feline at least, that I could make out, and had a rifle held in his hands, but it wasn't pointed at us.

"Why aren't we running now?" I asked Finnegan, again in a whisper. "He already fired."

"No, he hasn't," he said with dead certainty, his eyes scanning the street. "Do you see any smoke? Look for smoke from their powder. He isn't alone. Whoever else is with him, they're re-loading right now. And *he* still has a shot, if he chooses to take it."

Finnegan shifted his paws a bit further apart, turning his body slowly to the side and gingerly brushing back the edge of his coat. But at that point, the man on the porch spoke up, and began descending the short staircase down to the road.

"That's enough, Ambrose," he called out, padding slowly across the street towards us. He lifted his chin, revealing a very young face. A mountain lion. He was barely grown, skinny and fawn-colored. I felt like I'd seen him before, but it was hard to place. Maybe when he'd been even younger.

He stopped a short distance away from us, tail curling and flicking from side to side. He pushed up one edge of his hat, looking Finn over. "You *are* Ambrose. Aren't you?"

"I haven't a clue who you think I am or what you want," Finnegan said, and I noticed with some shock that he'd shifted his voice, or rather his accent. The one that set him apart from the Otherwolves I knew. He was doing an admirable job of it, too. If I hadn't met him before, I'd never have picked his voice out as being foreign. "But my friend and I have done you no ill. Please don't hurt us."

"C'mon now," the young lion spit on the ground, cracking half a smile. "A man as defenseless as you play at would've a'least put his hands up. Show me now. Show me 'ow innocent'n helpless you are."

I saw Finnegan's jaw tighten, but he didn't move. Didn't raise his hands. I looked between him and the lion, wondering what could be going through his mind. Shouldn't we do as the man with the gun said?

"Aye, thought not," the lion snuffed. "Mmhh. You look juuust like yer picture. That artist did you right. N'the bounty papers didn't miss no details. Down to the eyes...and that fancy grip on yer pistol there."

"Did they tell you who you were hunting?" Finnegan asked, voice deadly low. And he'd given up the charade of masking his accent.

"That they did," the young man nodded slowly, before glancing briefly back behind him...somewhere. "That's why m'ma got set up well and proper this time. She's got a clear shot at you, half-blood. No tossin' river to foul things up."

"Your mother is Odina," I said suddenly, before I realized the words had left my mouth. That got the man's attention, although his gaze kept flicking back to Finn.

"How d'you know my mother?" he asked curiously.

"She comes to trade with my father," I said. "Chieftain Takoda."

He seemed to digest that, his hands shifting on his rifle, showing the first sign of nerves any young man his age should rightfully be feeling in a situation like this. "You're Takoda's son?" he asked, nose twitching. "The bearchild?"

I nodded. "My name is Tulimak. What's yours?"

The mountain lion looked again briefly to Finnegan, his gaze darting back and forth, hands gripping his rifle tighter. "Sawyer," he said, distractedly. "We didn't know who you was when we fired on you. Thought you was just some gun for hire."

"I barely know a thing about firearms," I said, trying to sound less tired and drunk than I felt. The pain was still there too, my shoulder throbbing with each pound of my heart.

"Why the hell are you travelin' with this'un?" he asked, denoting Finn with a flick of his rifle.

I opened my mouth before I really knew how to answer the question. What could I say that would help us, here? The reason we were traveling together, after all, was *because* he was being hunted. Apparently by one of the local hunters my father's tribe knew. Which wasn't that strange when you thought about it long enough, but still.

Should I tell him why there was a bounty out on Finn? That would take a long time to explain. Probably more time than we had.

"Look," Sawyer said, addressing me and taking a step in my direction. "Ain't no reason this has to go down bloody. Why don't y'just—"

I heard, and saw, next to nothing. Only felt the barest hint of motion beside me and a flash of movement. And I do mean a flash. In an outright *stunningly* fast gesture, Finnegan had somehow drawn his pistol and pointed it directly at the mountain lion's head.

The boy was as caught off-guard as I was, having been talking to me, he'd looked away from Finn. For a few seconds, at most. That's all it had taken.

I was on Finnegan's side, and it frightened even me.

Sawyer didn't have his own gun raised, only held in his hands, so he was caught dead. He went stock still, flinching back as one might if they expected they'd be shot any second. But thankfully, Finnegan didn't pull the trigger. Not immediately, anyway.

"Finn..." I started to say, my voice probably *far* too loud, but my blood was rushing through my ears.

"Tulimak, stand back," the wolfdog cautioned. "Last thing we need is for you to get fresh viscera in your wound."

"You *wouldn't*," the young mountain lion said, obviously trying to keep his voice calm, but only partially succeeding. Plenty of the fear was coming through. "She's got her sights on you boy, let me tell you, an—"

"Try me," Finnegan rumbled from somewhere deep in his chest. "You think I won't shoot a kid? You think I won't take you out with me? You carry a firearm, you become fair game, as far as I'm concerned. And I haven't got much left to lose, lad...so by all means..." he advanced a step, closing more of the distance between them. "I'll take my chances on a rifle at, what...

ten yards? Twenty? Versus a pistol three paces away? God knows I've had worse odds in the past."

"Finn, no, please," I begged quietly, splaying my palms out, although I did not know what I planned to do with them. I just wanted to stop *this* from happening.

"Tulimak, look away," he commanded quietly.

"She'll kill you!" the boy shouted.

"If she hits, maybe," he replied, voice dead calm. "Did you *really* think a standoff would make me flinch? You said you knew me." He took another step forward, and the mountain lion another step back. I heard someone else move, somewhere down the road. Quiet footsteps in the snow.

"Finn—" I tried to warn.

"I hear her," he murmured, then louder, "Last chance. Leave. *Both* of you." He fully cocked the hammer on the pistol. "Or your son dies."

I could see her now, silhouetted against the pale, muted blue mist of snow lifting in the wind on the empty street. She had a rifle raised, and wasn't far. But she was still much farther from us than Finn was from Sawyer.

My heart was hammering. I wasn't even certain who I was more afraid of any more. I didn't want to be here, watching this. Being a part of this.

I didn't want to watch Finn shoot this young lion. No matter the threat to our lives.

And I believed that he'd do it. I wasn't even sure why. There was just something in his tone that prickled my instincts, made me feel the intent in his words.

Like he'd done this before.

"What if I were to shoot the bear?" a rough female voice called out.

Finnegan had been still as a statue until that point, his gun arm unwavering. But he shuddered at that and one of his feet shifted. Unlike Sawyer, he didn't move his gaze from his target. But he inclined his head ever so-slightly and raised his voice to her.

"Why would I care?" he asked coolly.

The words stung, but I knew he was trying to bluff her. I wondered if I should move…but he'd told me not to. Still, things had changed. There had to be *something* I could do.

"Odina," I called out. "My name is Tulimak. You've traded with my father—"

"I know who you are," she asserted, slowly approaching us, becoming more visible through the morning haze. She was a tall, stocky woman, much as I remembered her. She was dressed similarly to her son, practically, in men's clothing, and had two heavy straps supporting a large pack she carried on her back. She wore a heavy, worn duster that had clearly seen many years of weather. Her tail rigidly twitched from side to side as she walked, keeping her balance as she held her rifle aloft.

I swallowed. "You've always had good relations with our tribe. I know my father likes trading with you—"

"You threw your lot in with that one," she stated matter-of-factly. "I don't know why and I don't care. If you want to rectify that mistake, now's the time."

"Give me a chance and I'll explain why," I said, holding up my paws and trying to put myself between her and Finnegan.

"Tulimak..." Finnegan growled out a warning.

"Weak pretense there, Ambrose," she called past me. "You two use each other's given names, and we've been stakin' out the apothecary since my son saw you go in last night. You bothered seeing to the bear's injuries... and now he's standin' in the line of fire for you. You really want his death on your conscience? Got a lot of others weighin' on you by now, I'm sure. So maybe what's one more?"

"I—what?" I glanced back at Finn. And this time, his eyes had moved. Only momentarily, but not at me. He'd just closed them for a moment. He opened them a few seconds later, and slowly...slowly...waved the pistol at the young mountain lion, in the direction of his mother.

The teenage boy skittered the few feet to his mother's side and moved partially behind her, pulling his own rifle up, finally. Finn had followed his movement with his firearm, and now the two groups were just staring down their barrels at one another.

I looked back to Odina, who had relaxed some now that her son was at her side again. She kept her rifle up, but tipped her chin towards me. "Relax, bearchild," she said in a far less gruff voice than before. It sounded *almost* motherly. "I wouldn't've shot Takoda's boy. I have far too much respect for your father."

I breathed out a sigh, but Finn cursed behind me.

"Fuck you," he hissed out. "You *already* shot him!"

"And whose fault was that?" she retorted, like she'd been ready for it. "How was I to know you'd suckered a local boy in somehow? What manner of spell did you cast on this sweet'un to string him along? Takoda's told me about him, he's a good boy. No reason he should be involved in any of this. I'm sorry I fired on you, child. We didn't know."

"Are *you* all right?" I asked her, prompting an outraged look from Finnegan. "I—it's just that, we were pretty sure Finn hit you."

"I *did*," he said with angry certainty.

"Aye, he did," she agreed. "The wardens warned us you were a crack shot, but I thought for sure, on a river-tossin' raft…well, it was a graze, anyway. Got me on my right." She glanced down at her duster, which I now realized had a stain and a sizable hole in it just along the right side of her ribcage.

"This time I'll be a lot more careful," Finnegan said, his tone icy.

"All right, enough of that," the mountain lioness said dismissively. "Seems t'me at this point we're at an impasse, and I'd rather we settle things one way or the other before the law in these parts starts to take an interest in our activities."

"That won't exactly shake out well for you," Finn said. "The law in Broen is my people. Who do you think they'll side with in a dust-up like this? Some *feline* woman, or the *canine* she's menacing?"

"I'd be happy t'let them take us all in," she replied evenly, apparently not at all flustered by his words. "Then I can show them the bounty papers I've got on you."

Finn went dead silent at that, gritting his teeth.

"Your friend there's the solution we're both seeking," she continued. "A means to work this out without spillin' blood."

It took me a moment to realize she was talking about me. "I—I am?" I said when it was obvious everyone was looking at me.

"You're taking him up-river, aren't you?" she asked knowingly. "To your tribe. Which means he'll be in Chieftain Takoda's care."

I realized where she was going with her questioning before Finn did. He mostly looked confused, and was beginning to say something when I spoke up, "Yes," I said quickly. "Yes. That's where we were headed. How did you know?"

"Ain't much else up-river," Sawyer finally spoke again, sounding a little less scared now. A little.

"Just the settlement they've been building on Takoda's land, and Broen here," Odina added. "If we hadn't found you here we would've gone up that way even not knowin' who you were. Not many other places you could've been headed."

"How did you beat us here?" I asked, realizing they must have been here for quite some time to have been able to follow us, wait outside the shop and lay an ambush for us.

"We took the deer trails," she said, as though the answer were obvious. "The river winds, takes a day longer at least. I didn't know I'd hit you, but figured chances were good you'd stop here regardless."

I'd known that, of course. I felt foolish for even asking. But it had been a long few days.

"I'm guessin' it's not the bounty you're interested in," she said, nodding her rifle at Finn. "But whatever your interest in this half-breed is, we can negotiate it with your father."

My eyes widened. "You'd be willing to do that?"

"I know once I explain things to him, he'll see it my way," she said evenly. "Takoda's a sensible man. We can talk business and mediate how to handle this in your village. In a way that gets no one killed."

"We're not—" Finn began.

"Fine, yes," I raised my voice over his, and the wolfdog blinked at me in shock. "That's good by me. My father will know what to do here."

"Can we talk?" Finn snapped quietly, from behind me.

"Later," I promised him.

"Later might be too late," he insisted.

"I am not going to stand here and watch either of you shoot each other!" I exclaimed, summoning what I could muster of my bear voice. My throat was dry and I was still hoarse with pain and addled by whatever drug I'd been given. But it still worked.

The nice thing about rarely raising your voice is that when you do, people tend to listen.

"Enough people have been hurt by this already," I said, quieter. I looked into Finn's eyes and his expression slowly gave way. "My father will know how to handle this. I know he will. We are *not* just going to hand you over, Finn."

The canine haltingly lowered his pistol, and his gaze from mine. "All right…" he said at length. "Sure."

There was something non-committal in his tone, like he didn't believe me. I wanted to say something to assure him, but it was at that point that Odina spoke up again.

"We'll be keeping an eye on you for the duration of the trip, if'n you don't mind," she hoisted her rifle up over her shoulder. "But you can keep your own camp…and that piece o'yours."

"Just try to take it from me," Finnegan growled softly.

"Oh, I will," she promised. "In time."

We made camp just as we'd planned down by the river, while most of the rest of the town was just starting to wake up. Pitching our lean-to was a blur for me, I was beyond exhausted and had needed to drink more of the tonic just to muscle my way through the agony of lifting some of our things and making it back down to the river.

Finnegan once again did most of the work to set up our campsite, and I leaned against a nearby tree on my good side and drifted in and out. He went about the task in complete silence, the air surrounding him dark and agitated. I couldn't imagine what was on his mind after all that had happened, but considering I was having enough trouble staying conscious and he didn't seem to want to talk, it felt like a good time to give him some space.

At some point he woke me and I crawled into the lean-to and barely made it onto the sheepskins before sleep took me. I vaguely felt him settle down beside me, but not as close as we had been the previous nights. I didn't need the added comfort to sleep, though.

I don't know how long I was out, before an overpowering physical urge woke me. My eyes opened to bright yellow light streaming in through the hides, my eyelids nearly sealed together, mouth dry, nose dry, everything parched. My body ached, but it seemed mostly residual; my shoulder actually *did* feel a little better. Not good, certainly, but not like it had before. When I flexed it, the pain didn't radiate all the way down my back. It felt more contained to the burn now.

What had woken me, though, was the overwhelming need to relieve myself. I realized groggily that I hadn't last night, I'd just gone straight to sleep. And I'd had a lot to drink after the treatment. The tonic seemed to parch me, for some reason. I knew I should probably drink some more water now, while I was up.

That thought just made me need to relieve myself even more, so I stiffly got up and crawled out of the lean-to, making my way for the woods. It wasn't far, we'd camped right on the edge of the tree-line to afford ourselves some privacy from the other campsites. Also because we needed trees to set up the lean-to.

Once I was done, I made my way down to the river, which also wasn't far. I could hear the distant sounds of the other other campsites and beyond that, the bustle of Broen. But here, things were quieter. And we should have been alone.

Except we weren't.

The young mountain lion saw me approaching and didn't bother to hide himself. He was sitting on a boulder near the edge of the river, whittling something with a pocket knife. It was hard to tell if he was making any progress, or what it would be. Currently it just looked round.

I gave him a long look before I leaned down over the edge of another of the boulders along the bank and just stuck my face in the water, letting it wash away some of the stale, dry feeling around my eyes and my nose. It was freezing, of course, so I lifted my head back out immediately and shook, before lowering my muzzle back to the current and drinking for a time.

Sawyer began speaking while I was still drinking.

"I don't know under what falsehoods that'un imposed himself on you, young'n," he sniffed. "But you ought get out from under his sway before this thing's done."

I lifted my head and shook again, before glaring in his direction. "I'm pretty certain I'm older than you."

"Ah'm fourteen, and nearly full grown," he said stubbornly. "Been a man longer'n you have. Ma says you only just left your tribe, that you ain't been out in the world more'n a year."

He had me there. Something was bothering me, though.

"*Why are you still speaking to me in Amurescan?*" I asked in Nontawlik, the northern tribal language that almost every tribesman I knew in the area spoke.

He balked a bit at that and when he answered me back, did so imperfectly and slowly. "*Don't speak tribe speak well. Mother said it's less important now. It's their world.*"

His answer made me sad, but I couldn't argue the logic in it. The mountain lion tribes, much like the bear tribes, were all but dissolved. At least everywhere I knew. They'd been small to begin with and fiercely territorial, so they'd been some of the first to meet with the Otherwolves' aggression.

"Is that also why you have an Otherwolf name?" I asked, switching back to Amurescan since it seemed to make him more comfortable.

He nodded. "Ma says I fit in better like this. Anyway, you're the one travelin' with one of 'em. And a criminal at that."

"Just because there's a price out on his head him doesn't make him a criminal," I said with a sigh, reaching back down into the water to wash my paws.

"No," he said in a clarifying tone, "killin' people is what makes him a criminal."

I lifted my head slowly to stare at him.

"He didn't tell you why there's such an enormous bounty out on 'im?" the young lion asked me point-blank.

"He..." I tried to find the words to explain what I knew. What Finnegan had told me.

What Finnegan had told me.

"He's a murderer," Sawyer said.

My field of vision shrunk. The sound of the river seemed to intensify, or maybe it was the blood in my veins, growing to a roar that filled my skull. But it was still not loud enough to drown out the mountain lion's next words.

"He killed some rich man across the ocean, in their home country. And two more since he made landfall here. Shot 'em all dead in the street." His eyes softened with some sympathy. The pity I saw there made me feel sick. "You didn'know, did you?"

Chapter 9

Trust

My mind was a blur as I stumbled back towards the lean-to. It's hard to describe what I felt. I was physically shaking, my stomach clenching in knots, waves of uncertainty and apprehension washing over me in equal measure.

It couldn't be true.

I'd told Sawyer I didn't believe him. Upon first hearing his claims, it had seemed obvious that he was just trying to sow distrust between Finn and I so that I wouldn't try to convince my father to release him into their custody.

Or, it could have been a lie they'd been told. The bounty put out on Finn could be full of lies, and they'd have no way of knowing any better.

It couldn't be true.

But a frightening number of things were playing through my mind, coming together like some grisly tapestry. And the picture they were creating was dark, but compelling. Especially when I looked at it all as a whole.

It couldn't be true.

But the truth had always been there, if I really thought about it.

From the first day I'd met Finnegan, I'd sensed he was hiding something from me. Many things. And he'd only begun revealing them bit by bit. But there were still so many facets of the man I'd been traveling with, that I'd grown so strangely attached to, that I couldn't make sense of. Until now.

His story was just the sort of righteous, worthy cause for an adventure you'd tell someone if you wanted their help. And that's the part I'd really believed, until now. Because he spoke on it with such *passion*. Maybe that part *was* true. Maybe…it was hard to believe he might have lied about everything concerning his family.

But did I really have any evidence? Of any of it? We'd been carrying a bag he insisted contained documents proving the whole of his tale, but I'd never read any of them, and we'd already lost several to the fire. Granted we hadn't had much time to go over them, but it's not as though he'd ever offered.

If the story about his father and mother was true, why had he come halfway across the world to punish the man?

Finnegan had a pistol. A weapon he rightfully shouldn't have had, upon reflection. It was expensive, not just because it was a firearm…it was a particularly *expensive*-looking firearm. And he'd talked about how he'd been born in poverty, and how desperately he'd needed money for his mother's treatment. What about that weapon? It must have been worth a small fortune.

But moreover, he'd had a pistol, presumably before he came to our country. Which means he'd been armed when he was in the same country, possibly the same city, as his father. If there was one thing about his tale I absolutely did not doubt, it was the hatred he clearly had for that man.

Had he killed his father?

That, at least…I suppose I might have understood. It would have been a terrible thing. An immoral thing, certainly. But putting myself in his position, given what he'd experienced, (if true) I couldn't say what I might have done.

But he could have told me. He could have *told* me the truth, in that case. I would have listened. I'm not sure if I'd known right off about a man killing his own kin if I would have still consented to travel with him, but…

And maybe that had been the point. I wanted to believe he'd deceived me because he was frightened, because he'd needed my help. I wanted to believe it had been for a good reason.

The things we'd been through, the things we'd done together over the last few days…

I deserved to know. If this was true, I had *deserved* to know.

The one real thorn in my paw, the point on which I kept returning that made my gut sink through the earth, was his remarkable skill with the weapon. It was something I'd avoided thinking about throughout our travels, and now it was *so obvious*.

Finnegan had never mentioned being a soldier of any kind and he clearly wasn't a hunter. Why else would he be so steady a hand, so knowledgeable about firearms, unless he had considerable experience with them? I didn't understand pistols or rifles well, but I knew enough to know they were difficult and dangerous to use, even for an experienced bearer. But Finn had always been so focused and calm when he'd had occasion to use his pistol. I vividly recalled watching him stand, steady as a pine, and aim for the shoreline. The memory of his startling speed drawing the weapon, just hours ago. He'd known how to handle Odina and Sawyer on both occasions they'd fired on us, too. Known whether or not they'd fired based on smoke, how long it might take them to re-load. Now that I was thinking back on it, he'd checked and cleaned his pistol meticulously every morning after we'd camped. He'd used up nearly all of his remaining coin to purchase powder, instead of food.

And I'd been *so* worried he was really going to kill Sawyer. He'd hesitated, but… I feel like if it weren't for Odina's intervention, he might have.

I realized, in the mire of my thoughts, that I'd made it to the lean-to. It had really only been a short walk from the river. Close enough that Sawyer could keep an eye and an ear out for us if we were to flee.

I stared at it for a long time, my fingers brushing my palms, my body so on-edge I thought it would simply break. Every fiber of my being wanted to run away from this. From all of this. What had I gotten myself into?

I could run, I realized. Our supplies were outside, save Finn's bag. I could take some of our food, (my food, really) get back on that raft and go as far up-river as I could before the ice set. I could leave Finnegan here, with the mountain lions. I could go home.

I had every reason to.

Except that I'd always regret it. I knew myself and despite all my fear and apprehension, all of my awkwardness and anxiety, I knew I couldn't be the kind of man who ran from something like this. I wouldn't be able to face myself. I'd always wonder if I was wrong.

Whatever the truth was, Finnegan should have told me the full extent of it by now. But if I ran, I'd be running from that truth. And even if it was unpleasant, I had to know. Because I had to make the right decision here, or know at least that I had tried to.

I steeled myself and kneeled, pushing aside the flap and going back inside.

Finnegan was awake. Not just awake, but upright, leaning back against one of the trees the lean-to was pitched on. He looked indescribably tired, slumped and hollow-eyed. Like he hadn't slept at all.

"I heard," he said in a hoarse whisper.

My heart stopped.

"So, it's true?" I asked, in a voice so small it was hard to believe it had come out of me.

He looked towards me, sidelong. "That I've killed people? Yes." He dropped his gaze to where his hands were sitting lifeless and uncurled in his lap. "Although your man has the number wrong. It's actually eight kills now, all in all."

I felt a spike of anger rise inside me. "Are you boasting? Doesn't that *bother* you?"

He closed his eyes slowly. "Of course, Tulimak. It's just..." he seemed to search for the right words, "...hard to...to cope with. If I let myself fully feel it. I try not to think about it. It's the only way."

"If you've killed people, Finn," I said, hardly believing the words were leaving my mouth, "you *should* feel something. Even if it were at war, o-or... like with Odina. If you were defending yourself."

"The last two," he murmured, "the ones in Stuttgar...those were bounty hunters. Like Odina, or the two foxes. I had no choice there, I *was* defending myself. They came after me, they shot my pony, they cornered me on this bridge, and..." he sighed, running his hands over his muzzle. "What does it matter? It feels pointless to even make my case."

"It isn't pointless, Finn," I insisted. "I want to know. I *deserve* to know."

He looked back at me at that and there was a flicker of something across his features. "You do," he agreed quietly.

"So why have you kept all of this from me?" I pleaded, desperately. "I—I...was *really* beginning to feel that I knew you."

"Because I didn't want to lose your respect," he said bluntly, if quietly. "Even if we parted ways here, I didn't want you to know this part of me. I wanted to know you'd be out there somewhere, thinking I was a better man than I am."

"Finn," I put my paws to my knees, digging my claws into my fur. "If there was a good reason..." I clenched my jaw. I couldn't say I'd accept it. I didn't want to make that promise, without knowing the specifics. "Any reason," I said softly. "Any reason that I could...understand. I want to know. Why? Please tell me why."

He was silent for longer than made me comfortable. The air in the lean-to felt hot and constricting, like I couldn't really breathe it. But finally, just when I thought it was more than I could bear, he responded.

"It's hard to explain," he said.

The anger returned. I lifted my head, speaking between my teeth. "*Try*," I growled out.

He opened his muzzle for a moment, then shut it. When he opened it again, this time to speak, his face looked tense and drawn.

"I've never lied to you, Tulimak. I swear on my mother's grave. I have tried to be as honest with you as I could. There are just some things about my life that are hard for me to talk about. Not just because of the language or the cultural barrier. Because...I'm ashamed of them."

I stayed kneeling where I was, giving him time to continue speaking. It was clear he had more to say.

"Remember when I told you I had a trade, back home?" he asked, although it was clear he required no answer. "As a mediator, of a sort? That wasn't...a lie. But it also wasn't the whole of it."

"That sounds like an Otherwolf expression for 'a lie,'" I said, sternly.

He huffed. "You're not wrong. But it wasn't just my shame that kept me from explaining my...profession. It's a hard tradition to explain to an outsider. Because honestly, it's barbaric and stupid. And it's not something I ever saw myself getting involved in. But an opportunity came my way when I was desperate for money, and..."

He held out his hands, helplessly, gesturing at nothing. Then he dropped them back in his lap and let his breath out slowly. "I'm a Professional Second, Tulimak. Or at least, I was. Back in Amuresca." He must have felt my uncertainty, or knew what he'd said would make no sense to me. "A

Duelist," he amended, in a subdued voice. He finally summoned the nerve to look me in the eyes, searching for any signs of comprehension. "You still don't understand, do you?"

It was frustrating to be proving him right. "No," I admitted. "I know some of the words, but not what you mean by them."

"I shoot people, for money," he said. "Or at least, I used to."

"Like a bounty hunter?" I asked uncertainly. If the men he'd killed were criminals, surely he'd have told me that earlier.

"No, not like a bounty hunter," he sighed and slowly turned to face me. "In Amuresca, there is an old tradition whereby men who wish to settle disputes...arguments...over various things, they...fight one another. To determine who is in the right."

"That would only determine who is the better warrior," I pointed out.

"It's even less sensible than you realize," he muttered. "Because men with enough money can, and often do, simply pay someone else to fight for them. They call that man a 'Second.' He fights in their stead, against their opponent. Often another Second. In five of the duels I took part in, I was simply facing off against another man like myself. A stranger. Although to be honest, they were all strangers to me...even the men who fought their own battles. I was just a hired hand. I never really had any stakes in what the duel was over, save the coin I was being paid and my own survival."

"That doesn't make any sense," I said, baffled and disturbed.

"It never made much sense to me, either," he agreed. "It's an ancient, brutal tradition that usually solves very little, except wounding or killing one or both of the participants. There's some thought that Pedigree Lords used to duel to *avoid* larger battles that might cost many more lives, but those times are long past. Nowadays it's primarily engaged over social slights, or a woman. Or 'honor,' which is especially hypocritical when the Lords in question employ men to fight for them. It's more like a cock fight, a spectator sport."

"Then why do it?" I moaned imploringly.

He tipped his ears back. "The money," he replied simply. "It pays like nothing else a man like me can aspire to. The medicine my mother needed near the end of the wasting rot that took her...it's from Mataa. Imported. Illegal, in fact, which just made it more expensive. But it was the only thing that eased her pain."

"You could have sold your weapon," I said, recalling my thoughts from earlier. "Instead of using it to...to kill. For coin." That part still didn't make sense to me, and it was hard to say, in reference to this man I'd grown so fond of.

"Tulimak, I only have this pistol," he explained, "because of the first duel I agreed to be a Second for."

I didn't say anything, but I kept my gaze pinned on him, saying wordlessly what he had to know by now. *Explain.*

"One of the men," he sighed, "that my mother used to work for. They were very close. I guess you could say he was her primary patron. He obviously wasn't the man who'd sired me, but for whatever reason, maybe because he had no sons of his own, he didn't mind my coming to the estate with her. We'd spend weeks there. I loved it," he admitted. "It was in the country. Sprawling grounds, so many places to play. His stable hands and gardeners had children my age. You could really breathe the air..." he looked nostalgic for a short time. "He had no sons, like I said, but he'd been a military man when he was young, and I think he'd always wanted to pass on some of his knowledge. So every now and then, while my mother wasn't occupying him, he'd take me out on the grounds and show me what a fine soldier he'd once been. And he'd let me try things I never would have had occasion to learn, back in the Risers. Like fencing. And shooting."

He leaned forward, knitting his hands over one knee. "I never took to the foil well. But for whatever reason, I was a natural with a pistol. It's the only thing I've ever discovered that I have a real gift for. God, if he exists, gave me nothing else."

He drew a breath in through his nose. "When I was thirteen I started looking for a trade, and there weren't many opportunities available to me. I considered enlisting, I tried my hand at getting a few apprenticeships, none of which I was chosen for. I didn't have any desire to, but I wouldn't have even been able to follow in my mother's footsteps and be a Courtesan. Not as successful as my uncle Mikhail, in any case. Black fur is frightfully commonplace in Amuresca, and I'm too wolfish besides. My mother at least had a beautiful white pelt," he looked bitter. "But I inherited my father's fur, more than anything else."

He looked up at me again, as if to ensure I was following along. I was so far, so he continued. "I thought I had time. Until my mother's condition became apparent and she couldn't work anymore. We got by for a time on the kindness of our neighbors, but that couldn't last. And this disease, Tulimak…God," he narrowed his eyes, expression pained. "It *ate away* at her. Rotted her face out, until you could see *bone*."

I wanted so badly to reach for him. I had to fight everything inside me, remind myself that once again, no matter how hurt, how earnest, how heartfelt he sounded, they were all just words. Still just words.

But spirits, it was hard. The emotion laced through his voice was undeniable. If he was lying to me now, he was summoning forth deception I hadn't known a soul was capable of.

"I was *so* desperate," he continued, solemnly. "I sent letters to all of my mother's prior patrons, to see if any of them were willing to show some compassion for her condition. This Lord, the man who once showed me how to shoot, he was the only one who got back to me," he held up a finger, "and made me an offer. Apparently, sourcing a Second from the lowest rungs of society is fairly common practice. He thought nothing of asking me to shoot his rival for him. I was hesitant at first, sure, but he offered me *so much money*. More than I could earn in years doing any other kind of trade available to refuse like me. I didn't see that I had a choice. I would have done anything for my mother." He stared me straight in the eyes. "Anything."

This was why I'd wanted answers. Because I'd suspected there might be some reasoning that would explain things. I'd worried it might be something muddy like this. Complex. Hard to make any kind of judgment on. So much of this was so difficult, nearly impossible, for me to understand. But I was determined to try.

"You said you killed eight people," I said softly. "Or, well, including the two hunters who came after you here. Which I have no reason to disbelieve, and…I can forgive you for that. Or at least, I *would* have. If you'd *told* me about it, rather than hiding it from me." I let out a shuddering breath. "But you said eight, Finn. Not three. Your story only explains away the first."

"That first duel was so simple," he said in a single breath. "I went to his estate. I hadn't touched a pistol in five years, but it didn't matter. I practiced on his property for a day or so before the duel, picked it right back up. And when the day came, I shot that man dead. He didn't even graze me. I was so resolute, so certain in my conviction. I figured if two men were going to fire on one another that day regardless, it ought to at least be for a good reason. It was so easy to convince myself of that."

"How do two people fight with pistols?" I asked, having trouble picturing this.

"You stand a set distance apart, wait for a count, and then fire on one another," he explained matter-of-factly. "If no one hits, you move closer, and repeat. You do so either until first blood, or death. Although since most duels now are done with pistols instead of blades, death is a lot more common than it used to be. I didn't shoot dead six people right on the spot. I've wounded over a dozen. It's just that some of them died after the fact."

"You just stand there and shoot one another?!" I exclaimed, horrified. I couldn't *think* of anything more insane. This is how Otherwolves won arguments?

"It can be more nuanced than that," he shrugged. "Honestly, a lot of people just don't show up in the morning, or lose their nerve before the count. You can admit defeat before things have begun and avoid the whole mess. Once I started getting a reputation, that happened to me a few times."

"A reputation?"

"Dueling is legal in Amuresca, Tulimak," he explained. "It's legal here, in fact. So yes, if you make it your profession, it's good to build a reputation. It doesn't just get you more work, it can intimidate people. Frightened people have unsteady hands. So even if they elect to go through with the duel..."

"Why not stop after the first?" I pressed. "You said you won. Did he not pay you?"

"Oh, he paid me," he said, glancing down at his holstered pistol. "And he gave me that pistol, besides. Out of gratitude. It's specifically a dueling pistol, that's why the barrel is a little longer than most."

"Then why?"

"The money I made was enough to care for my mother for a while," he said. "But the disease she had was...a lingering one. And she continued to need medicine. For years. More and more, as time went by. It was the *only* thing that kept her calm and stopped the pain. I just wanted her to have peace." His voice sounded strained on the last word. "I thought about selling the pistol, but I realized I could make more over time if I just...kept winning duels. And I did. I've never missed a man at ten paces. I've been hit, but—"

"You've been shot doing this?" I balked.

"No one who's done this for years on end hasn't been shot at least once," he muttered. "A few grazes, two bad ones, but I came out the other side. I still have lead in my hip."

I put a paw up over my eyes for a moment, swiping it slowly down my muzzle. "Of course," I murmured.

"Luckily I've always been kind of scrawny. But I've also intentionally stayed lean to keep a slim profile," he explained. "Helps more than you'd think. Many of the men I've gone up against are Pedigree or well-paid Duelists, both of which live the good life and…eat well, suffice it to say. When you're half their size, you're half as wide a target."

"You were killing complete strangers, Finn," I emphasized, my voice strained.

"Don't you think I know that?" he replied with a bit of a snap in his voice. He immediately tipped his ears back and looked ashamed of his defensiveness, though. "I didn't," he said, visibly trying to calm his tone, "know…what else…to do. It seemed…what I was meant for."

"It can't possibly be," I said softly. "Killing for *no* reason can't be what anyone is meant for."

"I don't know," he said darkly, in a defeated tone. "As far as most of the world is concerned, a person like me is worthless. Low-bred, guttersnipe son of a whore. But as a duelist…" he got a distant look, narrowing his eyes. "I was a force to be reckoned with. Am. A force to be reckoned with," he corrected.

"I thought you were a force to be reckoned with before I knew all of this," I said quietly.

He looked up at me, surprised.

"Finnegan, you're one of the most passionate people I've ever met," I said sincerely. "You made me care about something I knew *nothing* about until just last week. You drew me into your story, into this quest of yours, and made me consider leaving my home, leaving the world I know, *just* to be with you. To help you see this goal of yours through." I hunched down, leaning in closer to him, my voice plaintive. "Was that all a lie?"

"No," he said firmly, and immediately. "I told you, I haven't lied to you. Not *once*. I fucking meant that."

"So this bounty out on you," I said. "It really is because of your father?"

"Of course it is," he said indignantly. "That man knew my profession. He had the gall to mock me for it, the one time we met after I put my mother in the ground. As if any of it, *any of it*, would *ever* have been necessary if he'd just lived up to his responsibilities!"

His voice had risen to a crescendo over the end of his statement, and I let him, without flinching. I could *feel* how much he wanted this out of him. The anger was coming off of him like heat off a stone, his green eyes burning, even in the dim lean-to.

I had so many conflicting feelings. So many. But overwhelmingly, I pitied him. I wasn't entirely certain of my trust for him. He'd kept this facet of who he was a secret from me all this time, and it was no minor thing… but I believed his anger. I believed that he'd been terribly hurt over the course of his life and I had no reason to think he'd invented the reasons why. Everything seemed to fit, now. In a way it hadn't when I'd been missing pieces.

The question was, how did I feel about him now that I knew all of this?

There wasn't an easy answer to that. But one thing I knew for certain was that my perception of him had fundamentally changed. And I needed to think on all of this, come to make sense of it all somehow, and learn how I felt about him all over again.

I'd already been contending with so many new feelings over the last week, things he'd brought out in me that were forcing me to confront who *I* was. It was so much, all at once. I hardly knew where to start.

"I don't know how he used his channels on this continent to get a bounty out on me here," he muttered. "I suspect I know which duel he's citing as a 'murder.' The last man I shot, the duel wasn't officiated properly. There was some question as to the credentials of the man overseeing it, and the young deerhound I killed was from a prominent family who were demanding an investigation. I got the hell out of town before things got bad. Which," he paused, "maybe I shouldn't have done. Upon retrospect. But I've learned to fear what Pedigree families can do with their money and station, whether they're in the right or not. I didn't want to be hung over a job."

"You said you were just the hired gun," I said, still trying to make sense of this ritual of theirs. "Wouldn't they come after the man who…started the…argument? 'Duel'?"

"He was also a Pedigree," he said pointedly. "It's messier when families of means go at it. Simpler to make a point by offing the pawn, someone no one'll miss. Less chance of continued retribution, too."

"No offense, Finnegan," I said, exhaustedly. "But your country sounds awful."

"So yeah, there might be a legitimate warrant out for me," he let out a breath. "That or he *lied*. Not exactly difficult for a man of his means to forge a warrant. But he knew I was digging into his financials. I'd gotten a whiff of how dirty his business dealings were years ago, when I managed to get one of his associates drunk and talking. At the time, I won't lie…I was looking for a way into his Estate. I was angry, Tulimak. So angry. But the bastard never went anywhere in public without an armed escort."

"You *were* planning to kill him," I nodded.

"I didn't, for the record," he growled out. "I got as far as his grounds once, got a look at what my mother and I should have had, and…" he trailed off. "He had other children. Purebloods, of course. But still, just… kids…" He turned his chin aside, posture slumped and small. "I'd only lost my mother a few months earlier. I couldn't do it." He gave a snuff. "I can kill a man I've never met before, who might have a family of his own. But I couldn't put that *bastard* in the ground, because for once, I had to confront what I was really doing. Pretty fucking cowardly, hnh?"

"If anything," I uttered, "I think it's the least cowardly thing you've admitted to so far."

He looked up at me at that. And scowled. "I'm not a good person, Tulimak. Don't try to reason that I am just because you're attracted to me, and you want me to be."

"Is this," I paused, "why you wanted us to part ways?"

"I told you, I didn't want you knowing all of this," he said. "I've enjoyed being with you. Truly. Not just because…well, because you *are* a good person. But…because for a while, I got to pretend I was one, too." He lifted his ears ever-so-slightly. "I'm the only person left alive who will ever ultimately care what I've done with my life. What I've made of myself. I don't want to…be…" he swallowed heavily, his jaw trembling, "…*this*."

"Then," I steeled my nerve, and reached for him. Not his hand, but his shoulder. "Don't," I said simply.

He looked up at me with a fragile tremor, like some part of his expression was about to give way. "I can't undo what's done," he said, quietly. "I lived that life for years. I've taken eight souls. Wounded twice as many."

"I don't understand your people's ways," I said, putting my feelings on the matter as kindly as I could. I'd accepted at this point that I needed to think on this all much more before I really decided how I felt about this 'dueling' practice. And I wanted to know more, too. "And my tribe has not gone to war for many generations. I've never experienced war. So I can't say I even have an understanding of killing, as my people see it. But killing to protect, or even to ease the suffering, of one's family…I can't say I wouldn't be willing to do the same. I'd have to be put in that position. And that's a thing I never hope to face."

My expression softened. "Whether you did the wrong thing by taking on this 'profession' or not," I said, "or by continuing it for so long…the fact that you had to make such an awful choice at all isn't fair. It wouldn't be right for me to judge you the same way I would someone who had more options in life and still took so dark a path."

His shoulders and gaze lifted marginally. I felt bad cutting him down after I'd managed to lift him up some, but I continued.

"That being said," I sighed out. "I don't care how many times you say you didn't lie to me. You hid this from me. Intentionally. You had a lot of chances to explain this to me and you chose not to." I tightened my jaw, knowing the betrayal was showing in my features. "If we'd just travelled together for a few days Finn, I might have understood that. But you…let things…happen…between us…"

The wolfdog curled in on himself, the shame evident in every part of his body. His tail was tucked, ears folded back, knuckles tense where his hands gripped his knees. "I'm sorry," he said quietly. "I didn't…think…"

"I deserved to know who you were. Who you *are*."

He nodded slowly. "You did. You do."

"Is the guilt why you're doing all of this?" I asked, honestly uncertain what he'd say. It was clear what I wanted him to say. If he kept feeding me what I wanted to hear, I wasn't certain I could repair any of the trust I'd had in him.

He seemed to think about that for a long while. "Maybe, on some level," he reasoned, "I'm hoping to be redeemed? But. I think it's more about... not just revenge, but certainly that. I want to ruin what he values most, without having to hurt his family. I want to ruin his reputation, his business, his respect amongst his fellows. I want them to know what a monster he is. I know he'll likely never be brought up on charges for any of this, or lose enough of his fortune to be forced to live the kind of life we did. But I want..."

Again, silence. He tipped his head back, clearly thinking. It was so strange to see the wolfdog uncertain about anything. Lost for words.

"I don't just want him to have less," he stated. "I want him to *be* less. And I want to show him, and maybe myself? That I can be more. I can at least be a better man than *him*, if nothing else. I can put a stop to the worst thing he's ever done and is continuing to do. It's a sort of redemption I guess, but also I'll be kicking him in the teeth. It just feels like it's the only thing left for me to do."

I felt the hint of a smile finally come to me, albeit briefly. Not because he'd professed his noble aspirations, but because he'd admitted to his selfish, angry reasons for them. It was real. It was the truth.

It was a start.

"Finn?"

His ears perked and he looked at me expectantly.

I took in a breath. "I want to know everything," I said.

He blinked. "What? 'Everything'?"

"Everything you haven't already told me," I said. "Anything that might affect me. About this bounty, any part of your past that might end up mattering to us now, here. Anything about your plans to bring these papers in. Everything that might involve me. Or my tribe." I shifted to sit cross-legged, getting comfortable. "I don't expect you to tell me everything there is about yourself. Everyone has things about themselves they'd rather not share. But things like this? Things that might involve armed and dangerous hunters shooting at me? Those things, I need to know."

He let out a long, staggered breath, slowly closing his eyes. "All right," he agreed.

Chapter 10

Proof

"Hey, can you show me how to quick-draw?" Sawyer asked. The young lion had been sitting on the fringes of our camp all morning, replacing his mother, who'd taken a shift last night. Unlike her son, she'd kept her presence quiet and hadn't engaged with us at all. But she also wasn't hiding. I'd heard her, smelled her, knew full well she was there, all night. She wanted us to know.

I was busy packing our remaining supplies for an extended trip on-foot, which was different than just lashing them in place on our raft. They needed to be less cumbersome, more tightly-bundled. I'd be carrying most of them and one of my shoulders was still injured, so I was paring down to essentials.

Finnegan was tending the campfire, stirring the hearty stew of carrots, potatoes and half a chicken we'd purchased in town. After we'd spent an additional night in Broen, (mostly sleeping, after Finn and I had a *long* talk) I'd been feeling a lot better. There was still so, *so* much we weren't- couldn't deal with, right now. My impression of Finnegan was forever changed, I had many questions still to ask, and I wasn't at all certain how I was going to explain *any* of it to my otterfa. But Odina's arrival into our lives meant we didn't have all the time we'd need to parse that all out, and I'd decided we had no choice right now except to focus on the present. A good hearty meal felt like a real necessity before we made the trek to my tribe. When I'd noticed they were slaughtering a bird a few campfires over, I'd offered to purchase half of it off of them for double what it was worth, just so that we didn't have to go to the market. They'd readily agreed.

I was only vaguely listening in on the chattering young Sawyer while he'd been pestering Finnegan all morning, who'd mostly been ignoring him. The teenager must have been profoundly bored to be trying so hard to start up conversation with the man they'd been hunting not days ago. Finnegan was having none of it.

"You're inside the boundaries of our camp again," he muttered. "I'd appreciate some space."

I heard rather than saw the mountain lion take a few steps back, then sit, likely again on the stump he'd been favoring nearby. "What're you cookin' there?"

"You're not getting any of our stew," the wolfdog replied tersely.

"I don't want yer bleedin' stew," Sawyer groused. "I want y'to show me how to pull a pistol that fast. I ain't ever seen anything like that before, but I'd 'eard it could be done."

I turned, taking in the sight of the young lion as he leaned forward, elbows on his knees, rifle unceremoniously tipped against his side. He was looking at Finn, who was cocooned in his dark coat against the cold, stooped over the soup like a miserly, grouchy old man. The illusion was completed by the most ornery expression imaginable, focused squarely on the young, impudent lion like he could burn him with his eyes if he tried hard enough.

"C'mon," the teenager pleaded. "Can I just see it again? Maybe I kin pick up some tricks."

"I don't. Do. Tricks," Finnegan said emphatically. He stood slowly, wincing as he stretched his hip. "You want a lesson?"

The expression on the mountain lion's face said he most certainly did. I began to wonder when I was going to have to get involved in this.

"Never pull a weapon, any weapon," Finnegan said, "unless you intend to use it."

He turned and began to make his way back towards me. I saw Sawyer move a second before he did and began to raise my voice to cut off what would *certainly* be a bad thing.

Sawyer stood quickly and tried to reach for the pistol on Finnegan's hip, but before I could shout at him to stop, Finnegan had clearly felt his presence behind him and whirled around to face the lion. His gun was in his hand in a flash, just like two days ago in the street. It was almost too fast to follow. I was again astounded that anyone could move so quickly.

"Whoa-haha—" Sawyer back-pedaled, chuckling nervously.

"Lesson *two*, you little wanker!" Finnegan snapped, advancing on the boy. "Never *fool around* with a loaded firearm!"

I was on my feet by then, approaching the two of them. "All right, enough—" I growled out.

"That was amazin'!" Sawyer exclaimed, for some reason thrilled by the turn of events. But then, he'd gotten what he wanted.

Finn seemed to realize that suddenly, dropping his pistol with a disgusted noise, stalking back towards our lean-to after holstering his weapon and wrapping his coat back around himself.

"Please show me how t'do that?!" Sawyer called after him.

"No!" came the muffled response from inside the lean-to, where the wolfdog had retreated.

I began to make my way back over there as well, before I noticed Odina standing near the edge of the clearing. She was leaning against one of the few maples in the area, casually. I was worried for a moment that she might take issue with the fact that Finnegan had once again pulled a gun on her son, but she seemed relaxed. She was smoking a pipe, just watching us. And she had that odd pack over her back again. Looking at it now, it actually more resembled a big basket of some kind. My tribe made baskets like it, otters were usually well-known for their reed weaving. But it stood out because it was shoulder-holstered and large. I couldn't imagine what she used it for, where a normal backpack of some sort would have sufficed.

Considering what had just happened and that soon, I'd be bringing her to my tribe, I thought it might be best if I made sure we were still on good terms. So I crossed the small clearing towards her, stopping a few feet away. She levelled a placid look my way, slowly blowing out a smoke ring.

"*I'm sorry about that,*" I said in our language since I knew she spoke it.

"*You've nothing to apologize for, bearchild,*" she said, tapping her pipe against the nearby tree. The pipe weed she was smoking reminded me of the kind my father smoked sometimes and made me nostalgic for home. It's possible she even traded for or bought hers from our tribe.

"Finnegan's not," I paused, "in the best of spirits, right now."

"He is facing the consequences of his actions," she said, shrugging. "I wouldn't expect him to be happy about that."

I decided now wasn't the time to argue the semantics on that. Instead, I said, "Your son's being precocious, but that's no excuse. I'll try to make sure he keeps his temper in better check in the future."

She gave me a searching look. "You think you can change an Otherwolf's behavior? Oh, child," she blew out another puff of smoke. "You really **haven't** been in the world long."

"*I don't know,*" I admitted. Then, something occurred to me. "*You didn't intervene,*" I pointed out.

"My son is growing into a young man," she waved a hand. "I can't pick him up every time he falls, or he'll never learn. I watched. If I thought your 'friend' had any intent to actually shoot, I'd have gotten involved."

"Then you've realized he's not just some heartless murderer," I reasoned. Maybe this was a chance to make some ground. "Were the circumstances of how he came to have a bounty out on him ever explained to you?"

"No, and I don't really care to know them," she said point-blank. "I need that bounty. And it's triple if I bring him all the way to the southern lands alive. Those are the only facts I need to know."

"Why did you shoot at us, then?" I asked, confused.

"Less coin is better than none," she reasoned, then smirked. "And I was aiming for you. We thought you were just some guide he'd taken on, remember?"

"Maybe don't tell my father that part," I muttered.

"I've always been honest with Takoda," she said, shifting the straps over her shoulders to put her basket-pack down. "This time will be no different. He gets the full story."

Something about the basket caught my eye. There was a small opening in the side facing out, only large enough that I'd be able to fit a few fingers through. I was perplexed what it could possibly be used for, until I saw a pair of eyes staring out from inside of it.

Odina noticed my gape-jawed stare and casually reached down to lift the lid off the basket. "*You may come out and meet Tulimak,*" she said, extending an arm down.

The tiny child who clung to her thick arm as she lifted her out was a fawn-colored, tufty-furred little mountain lion, with oversized ears and an even more oversized tail. She had her mother's eyes, deep mahogany brown, and lighter fur along her facial features that reminded me of Sawyer. But her overall hide color was lighter than both of them, suggesting she must have had a very light-furred father.

She was, to put it mildly, one of the cutest little creatures I'd ever seen. And I'd grown up with otter siblings.

She clung to her mother's leg once she set her down, staring up at me with those big brown eyes, clearly intimidated, but also curious. I lowered myself to my knees by habit, something I'd learned to do amongst my otter brethren.

"*This is Nuka,*" Odina said, stroking her daughter's head. "*My young one.*"

I looked up at her. "You gave your son an Otherwolf name, but her a Tribal name?"

"They both have tribal names, Sawyer simply chooses not to use his," the mountain lioness said.

I looked back to the little girl, who had boldly begun to approach me and was reaching up to gingerly pet the fur on my arm, near my markings. I let her do so for a time. I'd gotten quite used to being around small children, given my upbringing, but that didn't mean I was about to scoop a stranger's child up into my arms.

No matter how badly I wanted to.

"She's beautiful," I said earnestly. "But you had that pack with you the other night. Do you bring her with you…everywhere?" The rest was unspoken, but it hung there. Do you bring her with you while you hunt people?

"I have no choice," Odina said plainly. "We have no land any more, no place to lie our heads except the road. For some jobs, I can leave her with Sawyer. But when I need him, she must come with us. She's safer on my back than she would be hiding somewhere, alone."

She was probably right about that, but the explanation still left me feeling concerned. The little girl was wrapping a hand around one of my fingers now, toying with the long claw. When she looked up at me again, she smiled, and it felt like my heart ripped in half.

We could have destroyed this family. And it wouldn't even necessarily have been the wrong thing to do, given that we were fighting for our lives.

It just felt like the world wasn't supposed to work this way. What was right and what was wrong, anymore? A week ago, I thought I'd known.

Now, I wasn't sure.

When I re-joined Finnegan in the lean-to with two steaming bowls of soup, he looked pensive. He took the bowl from me all the same, quietly. But he didn't immediately begin to eat. I did.

Things had just...been like this, since the talk. Whereas before I'd spent nearly every hour awake with him talking, eager to listen to his stories and his wisdom, and he eager to hear my thoughts on whatever it was we found to speak on, now we measured our words more. When we did speak, it felt important. But serious. Always serious. No pleasantries. And it wasn't that the spark between us was gone, exactly. Just tempered. There was an uneasiness between us that I knew hinged mostly on me, and my feelings. I'm not sure exactly how I knew, but I felt that I had the power to lift it, to dissolve the tension between us, if I chose to. It was an odd feeling, knowing you were the one *causing* such a rift. But it also felt warranted.

I wasn't sure how long I could go before I gave in, to be honest. It was hard to intentionally hold yourself at arms' length, to protect yourself like this, from someone you wanted and preferred to be close to.

And I did still want to be close to him.

Despite everything I'd learned, or maybe because of it, my feelings for Finnegan were still deepening. They weren't all positive; the good was so entangled with the bad it had gotten hard to separate the two. It was complicated.

The strangest realization that I'd come to, primarily thanks to some very illuminating introspection, was that some part of me enjoyed how dangerous Finnegan was. It wasn't that I wanted to be hurt by him in any way, but more that my life before meeting him as opposed to now had been so much smaller. Finn had brought a world of experiences with him and as awful as some of them had been, I wouldn't go back.

It was exciting. It felt twisted to admit that, even inwardly. But it was true.

The more he'd told me about his life before this and the task ahead of him, the more I'd wanted to know. And the less I wanted to part ways with him. I was still very confused about my feelings for him, personally. But the thought of going back to my life with my tribe as it had been only a few months ago, even though that would clearly be the safer option, made me feel hollow inside.

"Kid doesn't even use a pistol," Finnegan muttered, randomly. "He barely ever bothers to hold his rifle correctly. Muzzle's covered in dirt."

I glanced at his bowl, then said, "Eat your soup."

He slowly brought the bowl to his muzzle and sipped some of the broth. I watched him for a time, before getting back to my own. "He's impressed by you," I said. "Wants to be as skilled as you."

"He shouldn't be," Finn murmured.

"*I'm* impressed by you," I admitted, at length. "I don't particularly like firearms, but...you are a master of your craft. In a way. How did you get so fast?"

"Becomes second nature after a while," he said, plucking at a piece of carrot with a claw. "But in Amuresca it's more about accuracy. I was already an expert marksman by the time I was twenty. I only started practicing the draw when I knew I'd be coming to Carvecia."

"Why?" I asked.

He sighed. "Dueling is different, here. In Amuresca duels are officiated, for one. Everything is planned out more precisely, time, place. The rules are enforced more. And you draw first, then there's a count." He finally ate a chunk of carrot, which would be the first solid food I'd seen him eat in two days. "Here, there's a count...*then* you draw. Or at least, that's what I've been told. But it sounds like it's looser overall. More chaotic. It's about reflexes, more than accuracy. I thought I should be prepared for that. I practiced a *lot* on the voyage over. Wasn't much else to do, since I could barely leave my bunk. My innards were revolting, but my arms still worked."

Knowing him, I could imagine him practicing the same thing hours on end, for days and days. Finnegan was intense, driven, and probably a perfectionist.

"You were prepared to engage in these duels here?" I asked, before chewing on a piece of chicken.

"Death seems to follow me," he said morosely. "I wasn't planning to make a career out of it here, but I thought it might be a possibility. Anyway, it hasn't really ended up serving me well, save at the bridge in Stuttgar. And even then, I got the ever-living shite beaten out of me taking on the second man. I only have the one pistol. One shot."

"How did you...?" I asked, trailing off.

"I got lucky," he admitted. "Managed to get him against the railing and tip him off-balance. He fell over the side." He said it staring straight at me, like he wanted to gauge my response.

I stared back at him, then continued eating my soup.

"For what it's worth," he said. "They weren't trying to capture me, Tulimak. They were trying to kill me."

"I know," I said softly. "Although Odina says your bounty is worth three times as much if you're delivered alive to the south."

"Thrice as much?" he repeated, disbelievingly. "*Why?*"

I shook my head. "I don't know. But it means she prefers you alive. Which is good."

"Yes," he agreed, staring down at his soup.

"You really need to eat," I urged quietly. When he continued to simply look down at the food, unmoving, I said, "You know, you probably would be dead now, if not for these skills of yours. Which means no one would be looking into these documents. That's something."

"Like I said, my 'skills' haven't availed me much," he said. "They don't equate well to the real world, where people don't stand in a field and wait for you to shoot them. I mean hell, when you first met me, I was about to get my bell rung by two mangy blighters armed with little more than pocket knives. They just stuck one of them in my back and shoved me outside, and I could've drawn on one and hoped he didn't realize I was out of powder, but then the other would have gotten me from behind. Literally all it takes for me to be as helpless as a newborn lamb is *one more man* than I'm accustomed to."

"It was two-on-one, Finn," I said. "Now we're two."

He looked at me, ears lifting slightly, hopefully.

I smiled. "Eat," I reminded him. "Or your fur will get thin."

That seemed to get through to him. Self-consciously, he brushed back some of his cheek ruff, like he was checking it. Then he began to eat the soup in earnest.

The final stretch of the journey to my home village would take five days. The brief rest we'd taken, the extra day we'd encamped in Broen, had done wonders for me. Whatever the affliction that had taken hold in my wound, it was well and truly gone. The apothecary, for all his eccentricities, had done good work.

I'd spaced out drinking the tonic far more than he'd probably intended, but that meant I still had plenty left when we began our trek, which would prove to be a decent remedy for the remaining pain. And honestly, I think it had done more than that. Once I'd begun drinking less of it in the days immediately following the initial treatment, I realized it had surely affected my overall character. It made me think less, or rather overthink less, about saying what was on my mind. In the case of what I'd learned about Finnegan, loudly and angrily.

He'd since assured me I had not been at all "out of line," which apparently meant "in the wrong." But I did reflect on how much more severe the drink had made me. Maybe in this case it had been for the best. It's not as though I'd said anything that wasn't true. But I didn't like the version of me the harsh spirits brought out. My otterfa was right about liquor.

Or maybe I was using it as an excuse and the anger I'd expressed was all me. It was so hard to say. Either way, what was done was done and even now, I had to admit I was still a little angry. The fact that Finnegan was being contrite about it all should have satisfied me some, but it mostly made me frustrated for some reason. I think because the whole situation was so…confusing this way.

If Finnegan had been a lying con artist criminal who'd strung me along as a protector so he could skirt the law, I'd be on my way home now feeling stupid, but resolved.

But what he truly was, I couldn't build a clear picture of. Not yet. Was he lying? I didn't think so, at least I *wanted* to believe him, but I knew enough of the world now to know I was naïve. Was he a criminal? Even he didn't seem to have the answer to that, and even if he was, how much did that matter to me? The Carvecian laws had done nothing to protect my people and he was a foreigner besides. Amurescan law was so far-removed from my world, I hadn't even known about this 'dueling' practice.

Did I believe his story?

Would it even matter soon? I was once again facing the inevitable, that we would be parting ways in a short time. One way or the other, we couldn't be together for long. I was taking a risk by bringing him to my family as it was. My only comfort was that I knew Odina and she knew my father and seemed to want to maintain good relations with my tribe.

Beyond who he was within his own story, I wanted to at least figure out who he was to *me*. Was he a friend? An interesting acquaintance I'd met once, that I could tell my children about some day? The things I'd felt for him, would they be unique to him? Had they somehow tainted or changed how I'd see relations like that in the future?

Would I ever feel the way I'd briefly felt for him, for someone else?

Did I *still* feel that way for him?

That last one was especially hard, because I was of two minds about it. There was no longer any denying the physical attraction. I might have been self-conscious about my big, cumbersome body, but I knew at least in this case what it was telling me. There was no getting around the thoughts, the *dreams* that had been unleashed in my mind. If anything, I was growing more certain by the day about that.

But there was no future with Finnegan. And I might have been inexperienced, but I'd always thought these feelings were meant to go together with other, more lasting ones. My otterfa had explained it very clearly to me, that these yearnings were allowed, were part of being a man. But that they should accompany other feelings, like respect, loyalty, a desire to protect. All things I would someday feel for my wife.

Perhaps even more frighteningly, what if I *did* feel those things for someone like Finn? Even if and when the wolfdog left my tribe, what if this happened again, with another man? What then? I couldn't...marry...a man.

Would I ever feel this way about a woman suitable for me to marry?

I'd asked the canine everything I could think of about himself over that last day we'd spent in the tent, and he'd answered me, even when it had seemed hard. In retrospect, there were a few things I wish I hadn't asked. Things about his mother. And what her profession truly entailed.

But I certainly understood it all much more now than I did before.

I hadn't asked him about these fears of mine, though. These worries about my future beyond him. Because for one, he'd already told me back on the raft how to handle this problem, if it did indeed become a problem. He'd said get a wife, (as if that were so simple) have children, and never talk about what we'd done together.

And for two, what could he possibly tell me that would help? He'd already given me what he deemed to be the best advice and he was probably right. I didn't need to know as much as he did about the world beyond our river to know these feelings I had for another man were unusual. I'd never even known they were possible until I'd met him.

Although thinking back, really digging through my memories, I suppose I might have suspected…

Finnegan had traipsed into my life, whisked me along on a dangerous journey with him, told me stories of a world beyond that was crueler than I could have imagined, and revealed a part of myself that might haunt me for the rest of my life. And yet still, strangely, that wasn't what I was angry at him about.

I was angry he hadn't told me more.

Here we were yet again, moving towards a destination, and that destination could and should separate us. And here I was again, mind spinning, trying to think of ways I could keep him from being taken away, somehow. Not just because I was afraid for him. I just knew there was… more…between us. Even while I was angry and frustrated with him, I had so much empathy for him. And I had so many more questions that he might have the answers for.

I didn't want to lose him. I didn't want to know he was being dragged off towards an uncertain fate…without me by his side, to protect him.

Respect, loyalty, a desire to protect.

Oh no, oh no. No, this was a bad path to go down.

As if I *could* protect him, I chastised myself inwardly. I had to look at this logically. Finnegan didn't even really *need* my protection. For the whole of the trek over land, I don't think Odina or Sawyer considered me a threat even once. But they certainly still kept a wary eye on Finn. All of the other more earth-shaking revelations from this trip aside, one humbling lesson I needed to take away was very clear.

Size wasn't everything. I guess even though I'd long felt awkward and uncomfortable in my body, I'd assumed somewhere in the back of my mind that at the very least, my bulk would be an asset to my smaller loved ones if the time came that we were put in danger. Indeed, it often came in handy with my tribe, performing tasks far more easily than the much smaller otter folk were capable of.

But in a world full of firearms, it meant very little. In that world, Finnegan Ambrose was a terror, and I was just a larger target and potential victim.

But would he be alive right now if not for me?

Would I be alive right now if not for him?

I hardly knew what to do with myself, with these thoughts, these feelings. I spent most of the trek up-river in a haze, wanting more than anything to talk to my otterfa. As childish a notion as that was, I wanted it more than anything. My mind was more tumultuous than it had ever been and the object of that storm was walking beside me every step of the way.

Finnegan was similarly quiet and contemplative, and I believed, troubled. He was having the other half of this maelstrom play out in his mind. I wanted so badly to know what he was thinking.

I could have asked. But seeing as I didn't know how to put my own thoughts into words, it hardly felt right to demand he give me more answers than he already had.

Odina, Sawyer and their little girl kept a decent distance from us throughout most of the trek. I was grateful Odina afforded us that respect and that her son was listening to her. I'd been worried he and Finnegan might fight the whole way, or that Sawyer's immaturity might grate on Finnegan enough that there would be some kind of incident.

It was only on the third day that Finnegan noticed Nuka, and only because she'd bounded on ahead of her family and gotten close enough to us that he'd briefly been spooked by her.

He'd nearly drawn on her, too. Had his coat pushed back right up until he'd seen her peering out from behind a tree.

Honestly, given our situation, I couldn't blame him for that sort of instinct. But it scared me. It would have been so easy to make a mistake.

What shocked me was that it seemed to scare him, too.

"...fuck..." he breathed out, like he'd just come up for air under water. "I could've—"

I put a paw on his shoulder. I could feel him shaking. His muzzle was drawn in a thin line, ears quivering. He let out another breath after a few long moments, thrust his hand down to his holster and deftly pulled out the pistol, lifting it up to his shoulder, held by the grip backwards.

It took me a moment to realize he was offering it to me. Uncertainly, I took hold of it and slipped it away from his hand. "Are you sure?" I asked.

"My nerves are shot to hell," he said, voice wavering. "I don't trust myself. And they're going to take it from me when we make it to your tribe, anyway. You may as well keep it. Sell it, if you don't want it. It's worth a decent amount of coin, even out here."

"Finn," I said, trying to sound more confident than I was, "we haven't spoken to my father yet. He might be able to talk them down."

"Uh-huh," he said, noncommittally.

The crunching of heavier footsteps approached us and soon Sawyer came into view, rifle slung over his shoulder. He called out, "Approachin' from th'east," before he came in closer to us, clearly heading for the little girl. She was still standing partially behind a spruce tree, peering out at us curiously.

Specifically at Finnegan, who was also looking at her. I'd told him about her days ago, but this was the first time they'd met. It was hard to gauge his reaction.

"Sorry about'er," Sawyer said, easing up behind the little girl and loosely curling his tail around her, protectively. "She's practicin' stalkin' up on folk and she's got good enough at it tha'even I lose track o'her sometimes."

He seemed to read the tense silence that followed and just nodded, putting a hand down on her shoulder and trying to turn her back. "Anyway. We'll get outta yer fur."

"Wait," Finnegan said suddenly, surprising the mountain lions. And me, if I'm being honest. He slowly kneeled down, lowering his bag to the ground as well. He looked across the ten feet that separated us towards the little girl and asked, "I'm sorry...Nuka, was it?"

The little lioness nodded.

"Did I scare you?" he asked, quietly.

She shook her head.

"Good," he forced a smile. "I'm sorry, all the same." He reached down towards his bag and opened it, pushing aside a few things and digging about for a moment, before he found what he was looking for. He pulled out a long, green ribbon and looped it around his fingers a few times, bundling it.

"Your mother and brother would probably have given this to you eventually anyway," he reasoned, looking right up at Sawyer, "after they take possession of everything that's on my person." He looked back at her, and held it out. "But I'd like to give it to you myself, if that's all right."

Nuka looked up at her big brother, who simply shrugged. "Jes'a ribbon. You can take it."

She needed no further nudging. She darted up to Finnegan and gingerly took the ribbon, turning it over in her hands with a growing smile.

"When we wear cloth spats," he said, patting his ankle to indicate the leather calf and ankle guards he currently wore, "we use those to tie them. I always fancied green. Enough there to use for a dress or something of the like, though."

She looked up from her new trinket at him and gave the kind of bright smile only a child's capable of. "Thank you," she chirped in somewhat accented Amurescan.

"You're welcome," he smiled back, a little more genuinely this time.

"Actually, while I'm here," Sawyer cleared his throat. "Ma's been sayin' we should hunker down early tonight. Snowstorm comin' in."

"Or we could just move on ahead of you, and lose you," Finnegan said sardonically.

"I'm fine to camp now, actually," I said, setting down my things. "Shoulder's aching. We should arrive late tomorrow, regardless. Another hour won't do us much good."

So, we made camp and Finnegan started a dinner for us. We were down to fish and potatoes, which didn't exactly stew well together, so tonight it looked as though it was just going to be fish. We'd been able to keep them frozen even since we'd left the raft thanks to packing them in snow at night. And the freezing temperatures in general.

We'd run out soon, exactly as I'd planned for. Initially I'd saved enough for myself on the trip back home, but I'd been eating about two thirds as much as I'd planned on, so that Finn could eat. It hadn't been a hardship, really. I'd just lose a little more weight this winter.

Finn hadn't been eating or sleeping well since our talk, so it was a relief to see him finish his meal and almost immediately fall asleep in the lean-to, even before the sun had set. I guess the exhaustion finally caught up with him.

It also meant we had as little awkward silence between us as possible, which admittedly, had been bothering me, too. Before all of this, I'd loved talking to him at night. During the day, while we were traveling, really any time we were together. But all of our talks since Broen had been tense and dire, by necessity.

And that closeness we'd had was marred by discomfort, by mistrust.

I found myself sitting near the campfire, thinking on that. And my eyes drifted to his bag.

He'd left it just outside the lean-to with our other bags, covered by the branches of a thick-needled pine. I could hear his even breathing, just feet away. He was out to the world.

He rarely let that bag leave his side and he'd never offered to show me its contents. Of course, I knew primarily what was in there. Documents. The ones that supposedly proved his story, that he'd brought all the way across the ocean. The ones he intended to use to prove his father's misdeeds.

My grasp of the written Amurescan language was poor, but I *could* read it. How much would I be able to make sense of them, if I took a quick look? Could I at least discern they were what he'd said they were?

Was it right to go through someone's possessions like that?

No, I told myself immediately. Of course it wasn't. But maybe this was a special circumstance. I'd been hurt, physically hurt, at this point. I'd put myself through a lot for him. I was about to bring him home to my *family*.

I needed to have more than just his word to go on.

Making up my mind in that moment, I reached over for the bag and dragged it as quietly towards me as I could, unclasping it carefully. I stamped down any further misgivings I might have had and reached inside for the bound stack of weighty papers, encircled with twine. I made sure to undo the knot, rather than cut it, so I could bind them again when I was done.

Spirits, I was covering my tracks now, was I? This was feeling less and less warranted every second.

Still, at that point they were in my hands. And I began to look over them, slowly turning one to the back of the pile, then the next. The first two were folded three ways and looked to be letters written to someone. I recognized the name "Eamon" immediately, which I vaguely recalled had been the name he'd given me for his father. It was followed by another name, "Lancaster." I was briefly confused, then realized Finn had likely taken his surname from his mother, not his father. So far, so good.

I spent quite some time trying to decipher the letter. The script was flowing and fine, but that only made it harder for me to read. To make matters worse, it had gotten a bit wet in places, so parts of it were blotted out. I picked out a name that was mentioned many times, which was far simpler than Finnegan's father's, "Gezan." As far as I could gather, the man who'd written the letter—presumably this "Eamon Lancaster," since that was the name signed at the bottom, was asking this "Gezan" about a shipment of livestock.

I didn't realize how long it had taken me to make out even that much, before Finnegan's voice pierced the still night air.

"Have you gotten to the ledgers yet?" he asked, nearly right beside me. I almost jumped out of my skin.

I looked over at him guiltily, being caught in the act and all. But he was just sitting on the other side of me near the fire, drawing his knees up to his chest, looking exhausted. He made no move to stop me from reading any further.

"I-I'm sorry—" I stammered.

"Stow it," he muttered. "If you really were, you wouldn't have done it. Here," he reached over, taking the stack away from me and sorting through it. "Look over Eamon's letters to his Fleetmaster in Arbordale all you like, but what you really want to see are the ledgers. I'm sorry I didn't show them to you earlier, but I didn't even know until we made it to Broen that you could read our language." He extracted a few papers from the stack and handed them to me.

I took them slowly, while he kept speaking. "The rest are mostly my memoirs," he sighed. "Of this whole escapade. And Eamon's history with my mother, with me, with Ambrose Park in general. I don't know how much *my* account of any of that will matter to anyone, but I thought I should write it down for posterity all the same."

I looked to him, arching an eyebrow.

"In the very likely case I die," he explained, then stared back into the fire. "I thought, you know...someone should hear my story. I guess that's a little grandiose of me, eh?"

"Not at all," I assured him. "Every person's story is worth telling. There are stories in my tribe for every member, current and many generations past."

"I suppose you'll care, then," he said, leaning back on his hands. Then, quieter, "That's something."

"I'm confused," I stated, my eyes sweeping the dense logs I was trying to read through. "I'm not...saying you're lying, Finn, but...that letter, and these papers here all seem to talk about 'livestock' a lot. Horses, mules, cattle."

"That's what's on the books," he nodded.

"But that's not what you said..." I trailed off.

"The thicker paper, with the seal on the top?" He pointed. "Those are the official Dockmaster's logs, for each vessel. Turn a few pages. Pull out some of the thinner, more yellowed ones. Those are the logs from the Mercantile house itself, private logs. Got into some real dodgy situations getting those, let me tell you."

I did as instructed and got to the pages in question. After a cursory sweep of the page, I said, "still livestock. Again, horses—"

"Ah-ah," he shook his head, "look three columns over. Those are the Captains' notes from each vessel, on the state of the cargo. Usually, they'd use it to indicate when they take cargo on, if it's already been damaged, waterlogged, gone rotten, what have you. Read what's written there."

I did so, slowly. "Male. Tw-enty...years of age. There-a-bouts. S...suitable...for...labor." I paused, then moved down to the next. "Female. Four...teen. Years of age. Suitable for...ho-use...work."

I lifted my head slowly, reality sinking in. I felt Finnegan's gaze on me, his green eyes catching the firelight, flickering like embers.

"You should see how young they think is 'suitable for companionship,'" he said, tone dead and lifeless. "So you tell me, Tulimak. How many fourteen-year-old mules do you think would make good maids?"

Chapter 11

Tawnahowac Village

It seemed impossible after the last month I'd spent in the world, after my life had so fundamentally changed, that home would not be similarly changed. But there it was, almost precisely as I remembered.

Almost.

We made it to the river late the next day and followed it several more hours, already beginning to see all the familiar places I'd known growing up. The water was icing over fast, but I could still see signs of my tribe, markers etched into boulders along the banks, remnants of deer trails we used to forage and even occasionally hunt, and eel weirs cutting the river into sharp V formations in places. We passed spots I remembered where we'd taken down beaver dams, fallen trees I recalled clearing and hauling home and foraging spots where in warmer months, we'd found blueberries.

The waves of nostalgia and warmth washing over me would perhaps not have been so strong if not for the hardship I'd endured on this trip. But as things stood, I was just *so* glad to be home. As the promises of familiar comfort grew nearer, I began to wonder why I'd ever left.

And then I spotted the first of the longhouses in the distance and my heart lifted. I could see trails of smoke rising, I could smell roasting pine nuts and fish, and I could hear voices on the wind. My language.

It's the first time I'd not felt like I was out of place in a month. I can't tell you how comforting that was.

The first of my family members we were greeted by were two young otters, Anoka and Panuk, siblings from one of my uncles' families. In a way, they were my cousins. But I considered most everyone in my tribe to be my cousins, really.

The two were out ice fishing in the waning hours and seemed shocked to see us coming out of the wood line. Panuk rose and stared across the snow-covered reeds towards us for a time, before shouting my name and bounding across the bank towards us.

As he drew near, he began to slow, catching sight of our strange group. Only for a moment, though. "*Tulimak*!" he said again, huffing out breaths of air through his whiskers. "*Your father will be so surprised—you are early! And*," he glanced past me for a moment, "*bring us…guests*." He seemed uncertain about the last bit, perhaps a bit nervous, but Panuk had always been curious about outsiders, so I knew he'd give them the benefit of the doubt. Behind him, still lingering near the shoreline, was Anoka. She looked considerably more worried.

Most of the women in our tribe were more wary of Otherwolves and outsiders in general. I couldn't blame them. We'd had…well suffice it to say, we did not send the women into the nearby Otherwolf town to trade anymore. Not even supervised.

Speaking of the town…

I glanced past him for a moment, unable not to take note of the new structure that had risen up along the banks of the river, nearby. It looked half-constructed and strange, with an enormous water wheel. I'd seen mills before, of course. The Otherwolves had perfected some kind of method to grinding their maize and other grains harnessing water. It was fascinating.

But that structure hadn't stood just a month ago, when I'd left. And it was quite far from the Otherwolf settlement.

On our land.

A lot of trees seem to have been cleared for a field as well, which stretched the distance between the new construction and the distant settlers. Had they laid claim to all of that, already? Why had my otterfa allowed it?

Panuk was still looking up at and past me, expectantly. I realized belatedly I hadn't yet answered him.

"Yes, sorry," I shook my head. I gestured behind me. "Odina and her family, and...ah...Finnegan...must speak with my father."

"Are they here to trade?" he asked uncertainly.

"No," I said, clearing my throat. "It's hard to explain. It concerns Otherwolf matters."

"Ah," Panuk nodded, gathering his cloak around his shoulders. "Well then, if it's all right, Anoka and I will move on ahead and let him know of your arrival. And your guests. We will welcome you near the canoes."

I nodded. "Thank you Panuk."

He headed back towards Anoka, glancing back once before speaking lowly to her. They gathered their things and began moving along the bank, towards our village. When I turned back to the group, Finnegan was looking back at me curiously and Odina was still staring out towards the Otherwolf town, for some reason.

"That was all Huudari to me," Finn cleared his throat.

I blinked at him a moment, then realized what he must have meant. "Oh. Oh, I'm sorry. I didn't mean to hide anything from you, it's just that only a few of us in the tribe speak Amurescan."

"I caught your name," he approached, "that was about it. No need to apologize, by the way. I'm the unilingual prat, here."

"We didn't discuss anything important so far," I assured him. "My cousin was just asking why I brought guests home, whether you're here to trade—"

"Your 'cousin'?" Finn balked, looking back down the river at the two otters as they walked off.

"Well not by blood, obviously," I reasoned.

"Wait a minute," he huffed out a brief, dry laugh. "Are they all...otters?"

"My tribe?" I asked. "Well...yes. Other than me. I told you I was adopted."

"I thought you meant by other *bears*," Finnegan exclaimed.

"We should move on," Odina spoke up, walking past us down towards the river. Sawyer followed, his gaze also on the mill for a while, for some reason.

He looked to me. "I don't remember that bein' here last we was about these parts to trade."

"No, it's new," I said. "Very new. It wasn't even here when I left home. It's going up fast."

"Mmmhhh," the mountain lion gave a strange noise of discomfort.

"What?" I asked warily. "What aren't you saying?"

"I think ya know," he said with a tip of his hat, before hustling off to catch up to his mother.

Finnegan moved beside me, looking up to me uncertainly. He said nothing, but I could sense he had something he just wasn't putting to words.

"Finn—"

"Look, I don't know the laws in this country," he sighed. "But it's odd they'd be building in the winter, is all."

"What do you think it means?" I asked, suspecting I already knew the answer.

"A land grab," he said matter-of-factly. "That'd be my guess, anyway. They're clearly trying to race the clock on something."

I set my jaw, looking at the unfinished mill in the distance. "Thanks for sharing your insight," I said quietly.

Finnegan put his hands up. "Like I said, I don't know for sure. But... yes, I'd worry. The whole thing is odd."

I puffed out a breath into the cold air. "I wish your visit here were under better circumstances. My father could probably glean a lot from an Otherwolf as clever as you are."

He laughed, which I hadn't heard in days. I liked the sound of it. "Trust me, I'm hardly all that clever," he insisted. "Just well-traveled. And I know my people a bit better than you do, for obvious reasons."

We began walking, following in Odina and Sawyer's wake. At length, he asked, "So otters, huh? Picturing you growing up amongst a whole family of otters is...I'm not gonna lie...really cute."

I blanched, then nodded. "There was a fox that stayed with us for a time, a few seasons back. And a weasel a few years before that. Both tribal refugees."

He made a face. "I suppose that must be happening more and more."

"More and more tribes dissolve every year," I nodded. "Odina had a tribe once, too. I remember they moved through these parts, following the herds, when I was a child. They've always traded with us—everyone trades with us, but each year there's been less and less of them. We thought they were all gone and moved on until Odina started coming each season to trade, starting a few years ago. I guess...probably around the time she must have had her daughter."

"Some kind of awful story there too, I'd wager," Finn said grimly.

"She doesn't seem the sort to share stories, as we do," I said. "But yes. I doubt she'd be raising her children alone now if she had any choice."

He walked beside me in silence for another few beats, before speaking again. "Are you all right?"

I hung my head, "You shouldn't be worrying about me right now."

"Why not?" he asked simply. "You should be over the moon to be home, right? Is it just the mill that's got you suddenly upset?"

"No, I—" I opened and closed my jaw a few times. "I...it just occurred to me that since Broen, I've been walking you towards what we were previously running away from. I feel like I'm..."

"Escorting me to the gallows?"

I whipped my head around to stare at him, shocked. He just gave an easy smile and a shrug. "What choice did you have?" he said. "I don't blame you, Tulimak. I know you think your father's going to help."

"But you don't believe he will," I said, unquestioningly. "You haven't, this whole time."

His only response was telling silence.

"You haven't run away," I said, my hands beginning to shake. "Why? Why come along without protest, all this way, if you thought I was just... just..."

He glanced aside, at nothing in particular. Just away from me.

"Finn, what?"

"I'm afraid if I answer you," he sighed, "you won't believe me. You don't...trust me anymore."

"You said you wouldn't hide things from me anymore," I reminded him. "If you want me to trust you—"

"I wanted to make sure you got home," he said, cutting me off. He finally looked back into my eyes. "All right? What...whatever happens from this point forward, at least I can say I didn't ruin *your* life. If I feel like things are going to go south here, I'm not going to lie to you, I probably *will* run. Again."

"Will you fight Odina?" I asked softly, knowing the mountain lions far ahead of us had keen hearing.

"Not if I can avoid it," he muttered.

"...I have your weapon," I reminded him after a long pause.

"I know, Tulimak," he sighed, "I gave it to you. I said 'run.' I set out to do this thing to save lives. Or make myself feel better about my own wasted life, I hardly know any more. In any case, I'm done taking. If I can make it to Arbordale on wit and tenacity alone, I will."

"Even *I* think that isn't realistic," I said soberly.

"Maybe not," he agreed. "But I've had nothing but my sins to think on over the last few days, and it's been harder to push them off my conscience than usual. At what point does any of this stop being worth it?" he wondered aloud.

"I...don't know," I admitted. "Your sire is selling people like livestock. I don't know how to measure an...evil...like that. Let alone how many lives would be worth stopping it."

"Me either," he shook his head. "And I'm tired of torturing myself over it. It's simpler this way." He gave me a tired smile. "I'm just glad nothing else went wrong before we got you home. I look forward to meeting your otter family."

My hands were still shaking. This happened to me sometimes, had been happening several times a day over the last week, and I didn't know how or why. My body would shake, my chest tightening until it felt like I couldn't breathe. Sometimes I'd take greedy gulps of air and wait for the feelings to pass, sometimes it would get worse before it got better. I could blame it on the injuries I'd sustained, the exhaustion, the tonic I was drinking...but the fact was, this had been happening to some extent since I was a young cub. It's just that nothing had tested me as much as the last few weeks had and because of that, it was getting worse.

When it happened everything just piled up in my mind and I felt like my world was crumbling. Everything felt hopeless and desperate, like only the worst things I could imagine were going to happen.

I'd just been so happy, not moments ago, to make it home. Why was this happening now?

I tried to keep my mind focused on the thought of seeing my family. Soon. So soon. My otterfa would know what to do.

My family would resolve this. I could leave the decision-making to someone else.

"Panuk told me you had returned, but I hardly believed it!"

I was engulfed by my family almost the moment I arrived on the shore adjoining our village. My father was the first to greet me, dressed down in his evening parka and long breech cloth. Most of my siblings were similar attired, suggesting they'd been at dinner.

My father allowed my brothers and sisters to crowd around me and embrace me one by one before he did the same, doing so with an earnest smile. That smile faded however, after he came in close and drew a breath through his nose.

"Son," he reached up for my shoulder, resting a paw just below the edge of my cloak, *"you're injured."*

"It isn't bad," I placed my other paw over his. *"It's healing well."*

"It is no small wound," he said, slowly lifting my cloak back, gingerly revealing the healing burn. When he saw it he seemed even more concerned, dropping his voice. *"This has something to do with your guests, I would wager."*

I nodded with a sigh. "I'm sorry for bringing them to the village unannounced—"

He cut me off with a wave of his paw. "Never mind that. I'll judge once I know the full tale whether there's any need to admonish. Right now, simply assure me two things," he looked past me to where my companions were waiting further down the shore, near the long line of covered canoes. He looked back to me. "Odina, I know. She is welcome here. The canine… the Otherwolf…is he dangerous?"

That, of course, was a question I'd been asking myself since a week ago. But I only hesitated a moment, remembering the pistol stowed in my bag. *"He gave up his weapon before we made it here,"* I said. *"His pistol,"* I amended, since that hadn't been specific.

My otterfa's eyes widened. *"He gave you a firearm?"*

"I have a lot to explain to you," I said exhaustedly.

"Chieftain Takoda," Odina called from behind us, slowly setting her basket and bags down. "My family and I only wish to make camp on your land. We'll not intrude on your hospitality. But we need to pitch camp before the sun is entirely set."

My father looked past me to the mountain lioness and nodded. "As ever, you are welcome," he said. "There is an unfinished pit house in the north field, near the ponies. It would do."

"Thank you, chieftain," the woman nodded to her son. The two began to gather their things to leave, but oddly before she did, I saw her clap a hand on Finn's shoulder and say something to him too quietly for me to hear. Then she spoke up again, calling towards us, "We will return to speak after darkness has fallen. Not long after."

The mountain lion family made their way through the reeds out towards the pony field and Finnegan, now alone, hesitantly approached me and my family.

There were six otters in my immediate family and absolutely all of them were staring at him. My brothers Tarkik and Yutu were both grown with families of their own now, although they'd come down to meet me without them, for now. Likely because their pups were so young. They went everywhere together and both looked equally wary and protective of my sisters. But then, that had always been the case.

My sister Alasie was the youngest, younger even than Sawyer, but easily the boldest of my siblings. She was still standing at my side, her immature features set in a serious expression she was still far too adorable to wear well, but the implication was clear. She'd heard about, (or smelled) my injury and she'd always been very protective of me. She'd also always had good intuition and I think she suspected Finnegan of wrongdoing against me, because her brown-eyed gaze was pinned on him accusatorily.

Kirima and Nujua, both a few years younger than me, were at that age where they were preoccupied with men, more than anything else. They were whispering excitedly to one another, standing off to the side. I didn't need to take a guess what it was they were talking about, because they too were staring at Finn.

To be fair…I was no better.

"Father," I cleared my throat, "this is Finnegan Ambrose."

My sisters giggled when I said his name, which to his credit, Finn only smiled at. He was taking being gawked at in stride.

"Finn," I accidentally shortened his name without thinking about it, which again prompted a muffled chuckle from Kirima. Well, they could make of that what they would. I gestured to my father, "This is my otter-fa—my father. Chieftain Takoda, of the Tawnahowac Tribe."

Finnegan folded an arm across his midsection and gave a shallow bow. "Sir. It's a pleasure to finally meet you."

"'Finally,'" my father repeated, looking to me with an arched eyebrow.

"Your son has spoken of you many times since I made his acquaintance," he explained. "Fondly. Very fondly."

"I must apologize if my words are not as comprehensive as yours," my father enunciated the word "comprehensive" with no trace of accent. He'd gotten better, even in the time I'd been away. "Our Amurescan is learned purely through trade."

Finnegan seemed humbled. "I…am in awe of your grasp of our language sir, I must be frank. Your son also speaks it *exceptionally* well."

"My father taught us all," I said.

"A necessity in our mixing cultures," my father nodded. "I would imagine he has learned even more about your language and your *world* since coming to know you, sir." His voice was friendly, but there was an undertone there, almost an accusation.

Finnegan didn't miss it. "Ah…yes."

"Do you wear the thing on your head to make you look taller?" my youngest sister blurted out.

Finn glanced up at his frayed hat, then slowly removed it, looking it over as though even he'd forgotten it was there. "I'm not actually sure why we wear these," he admitted. "But that might be it. I just always thought they looked rather fine."

My father seemed as though he was about to stop her from saying more, but my sister beat him to the punch. "Do you hide things in it?" She asked. "I would hide things in it."

Finn huffed out a laugh and tipped the hat upside down, then showed her the inside. "Afraid not. Although that's a grand idea. I'll consider it in the future."

"All right, all of you, back to the longhouse," my father gestured at the small gathering. "The fish will be done by now. Go help your aunts."

Slowly but surely, my family began to disperse and make their way back towards the village and the communal longhouse. The last to leave was Alasie, who eventually had to be led away by Tarkik. She seemed hesitant to leave my side.

"I'll be there soon," I told her. "I'll see you before you sleep. I promise."

Once my siblings were gone, I leaned down to Finnegan, asking quietly, "What was that Odina said to you before she left?"

"Oh," he snorted softly. "You know. 'Try to sneak off and we'll hunt you down.' Something along those lines. Worded less friendly. Woman's not one for profanity or exaggeration, but she is dreadfully blunt."

My father was staring us down. For some reason, I'd forgotten he was right there and very capable of understanding us. And apparently, so had Finn. It's not as though I would have kept this from him, but it hadn't exactly been the best way to reveal what was going on.

The graying river otter narrowed his eyes at the both of us, then pinned me with a look only a father of six children could perfect to the degree he had.

He said precisely one word. "Explain."

We spoke to my father for nearly an hour. We were eventually joined by Odina, but she had little to add we hadn't already told my father. I felt it best we explain as much as possible, including Finnegan's history, because we knew she'd arrive in time and I didn't want it to seem as though we were hiding anything.

Moreover, I didn't *want* to hide anything from my otterfa. I wanted him to know as much as possible, because *I* was still struggling to know what to do and I wanted him to have all the facts.

Well...most of the facts.

I don't know why I'd been expecting he'd have all the answers. Let alone arrive at them *that* night. But I suppose I'd always looked to my father for absolute guidance and some part of me really had expected he'd immediately have insight that would solve the situation, in a way that wouldn't hurt so very badly.

Instead, he listened silently most of the hour, only speaking to ask questions and when we'd related all we could think to, he sat in contemplative silence for a long time. Eventually, he took out his pipe, packing it with an ample amount of tobacco.

Finn leaned over to me, asking quietly, "Is this some kind of tradition?"

"No, sir," my father answered him flatly, "I just need a smoke, after hearing all of that."

"Ha...fair enough," Finnegan said ears falling flat.

"I'd like to see these ledgers you spoke of," Odina surprised us all by speaking up. So far, she hadn't said a thing since she'd joined us, in time to hear Finnegan's tale of his father's dealings in the south.

Both Finnegan and I looked at her. I was glad to see he was as surprised as I. "Of course," he said, gesturing to his bag. "I have nothing to hide."

The mountain lioness nodded. "I'll read them tomorrow by the light of the sun. My eyes aren't what they used to be."

Finn looked to me uncertainly and I could see the question there. It was confusing me, too. Neither of us had thought the terse woman would take particular interest in his family's dealings.

She wasn't offering us any answers as to why she was curious, though. And a moment later she dispelled any notion that his story may have forced her to reconsider her position. "We'll be taking the Amurescan off your hands in a few days' time, once we've re-supplied. I'd like to move south before the worst of the weather really sets in, or before anyone else in these parts happens to realize the price on his head and we've competition to contend with."

"You speak as though the situation is already decided," my father spoke evenly, tapping his pipe over his knee.

"I trust you will come to the right decision, given a few days to consider," Odina said matter-of-factly.

"You assume then that you are in the right," my otterfa said with an arched, whiskered eyebrow.

"I don't assume," she said, standing stiffly. "I simply know. It is the only right decision for the safety of your family and your tribe. Harboring this Otherwolf will only bring you troubles, Takoda. You know that."

She began to ascend the ladder up to the surface. We were in my father's pit house now, where he mediated matters with the tribe and prayed. It was a small dwelling and not comfortable for those of us who had to stoop under the low clearance of the clay-caked log roof. But we had a larger, deeper-dug pit house for the family, where I would join them later to say goodnight to my sisters.

Silence descended on the house after she left. The smoke from my father's pipe wafted up and collected in curls along the ceiling, or passed through the small smoke hole in the top of the roof. Favors from various other tribes and mediations my father had overseen in the past adorned the walls, the fire in the center of the room crackled with the familiar woodsmoke of the local kindling, and everywhere here smelled of my family, of otters.

I should have felt so at ease. I was home. I was *home*.

But I was coiled like a fiddlehead fern, my heart in my throat, wanting my father to say something…anything…to alleviate the disquiet in my heart. It felt like he'd been silent so long now, but I knew in actuality it had probably been very little time.

"Otterfa—" I began.

"I'll need time to think on this, Tulimak," he said with a long exhale, blowing out a trail of smoke. "There is much to consider."

"For what it's worth," Finn spoke up, his paws on his knees, muzzle down. "I agree with her. My presence here is a danger to you and your family."

I looked at him, baffled and dismayed. "What are you suggesting?" I said, the words tumbling out of me. "If you were just going to give up, this whole time…"

"I am not," he sighed, "*giving up*, Tulimak. But there's no use denying the truth."

"Why would anyone look for you here?" I asked, spreading a paw in the air.

"Bounty hunters, people like Odina," he said, "this is their *trade*. They're good at it. I don't know how, but they've found me several times already."

"What was this all for, then?!"

"Tuli, calm down," he coaxed, glancing at my father.

"Yes, please calm yourself, son," my father said in a stern, loud enough tone that it reminded me of being a cub and shut me up immediately. I closed my muzzle reflexively, digging my claws into the bundled cloak in my lap.

My father looked to Finn and continued speaking, "I respect your honesty and concern for my family," he said. "But please extend that concern in this moment to my son, as well. He is clearly emotional."

I felt his eyes on me and couldn't bring myself to look up. "Tulimak," the older otter said, leaning forward and tipping my chin up, forcing me to look at him. "You are in pain, and this trip, I fear, has been too much for you. I think before we speak any further on this..." he looked to Finn, "... very precarious situation you have found yourself in, thanks to this new friend of yours..."

"I'm hardly going to deny that," Finn said, unflinching.

"I think it would be best for us to approach this mediation with cooler, more rested heads," my otterfa reasoned. "It is late, you have both been traveling, and if I might say so, the smell of the road is fairly...strong...on both of you."

"Oh Lord," Finnegan wrinkled his nose, "I am so sorry. You get inured to your own scent over time."

My father stood and gestured to the ladder out. "Tulimak," he approached me and put a comforting paw on my arm, "why don't you show your friend to the springs, for now? You can come see your sisters afterwards. I'm certain they'll be too excited to sleep for some time. You can spend a bit with the family before you turn in for the night." He smiled. "We've reinforced your roof for the winter in your absence. I'll send someone over to get a fire started."

He leaned in and embraced me, the warm, familiar feeling of his arms around me sinking into my bones and making the reality of being home all the more visceral. I hugged him back, wishing I hadn't grown so much larger than him. I missed the days when he could envelop me in his arms and make me feel safe.

But perhaps it was time I let go of that yearning.

"I'm so glad you made it back to us safely," he said quietly, before slowly slipping away from me and looking to Finnegan. "And you have my gratitude sir, for the part you played in that."

Finnegan scratched the back of one of his ears, holding his hat in his other hand. "I'm the reason your son was endangered at all."

"I very much doubt you could have forced Tulimak to accompany you," the older otter ascertained. "He may *seem* soft and docile, but my bearchild has a stubborn streak."

"Yes, I've...had occasion to witness it," Finn said, glancing at me with a quiet smile.

"It is a quality I prefer all my children have, if possible," my father said. "The world my generation is passing on to them will bow and break you if you do not have that strength of will necessary to stand your ground and know your own mind."

We made our way back up to ground level, on the clay bank. Our village was built into an area of particularly hard-packed clay soil, a short distance from the river where it never flooded. The earth here was perfect for pit homes to be dug and maintain their shape for some time, but still close enough to the shore that going for water was a short trip.

I walked Finnegan through the home I'd grown up in for all of my life that I could remember. It was a bit surreal. Since I'd met him, it felt in a way as though my story had been separated into two parts: my life before Finnegan, and after. I think some part of my mind had assumed that the two would never meet.

We walked through the field of pit homes and into the village center, where most of my tribe was still gathered in the communal longhouses for their evening meal. This time of year, the longhouses were insulated with caribou furs over the doors, but I still saw many of my tribe peering out to catch sight of the newcomer.

"So, I noticed that your father said 'spring,'" Finnegan said, "not 'bath.'"

"The spring is where we bathe when necessary," I explained. "The water there is not good to drink, but it is medicinal for the outside of the body. The fur, the skin, the claws—"

"All right, magical healing waters—why not?" He shrugged. "I'll buy that. I've heard this land has all sorts of exotic treatments for what ails you. But I'm more concerned that most springs I've ever visited have been... freezing..."

"Our spring is special," I said with a slight smile. "It's why our ancestors built the village here. The fishing is good too, but the spring was why we settled here. There is a tale, if you'd care to hear it."

"It better be *real* special," Finnegan grumbled. "Or this is turning into a military bath. I have been freezing and wet enough lately."

"You'll see."

"Ohhhh myyyy gooooooodddddd..." the wolfdog moaned, sinking down into the waters of the Ghost Fish Spring. It was named thusly for the spirit said to inhabit it, which churned the waters and created bubbles, when nothing had ever been seen living in its waters.

The spring was actually several pits in the earth, ringed with strange, almost otherworldly colors that adorned the rocks and crept out along the edges where the water lapped. The waters themselves smelled strangely and occasionally churned, and were never safe to drink. Sometimes they weren't even safe to bathe in, growing far too hot. But that was thankfully rare and usually easy to discern before you got in.

The most important part was: the water in these springs was warm. Very warm. Some in my tribe found them too hot for their liking even when they were tolerable, but I found if you eased down into it, it lessened the discomfort.

Finnegan, once he'd realized what this place was, had all but flung his clothing off with a speed I hadn't even known him capable of and submerged himself nearly all at once. And he didn't seem to regret it. I took considerably more time to do so, as usual.

"Uhhhhhhh," the canine groaned once more, leaning back and dipping back his head until all but his muzzle and part of his face were submerged.

I smiled a little. "Good?"

"You *grew up* with this in your back yard?" he asked incredulously. "Bloody hell Tuli, I think you might be right."

"About...?" I asked uncertainly.

"About me staying here," he mumbled, "'harboring' me and all. You're right. Don't let them take me away. Just keep me here. Forever. In fact, I'll just stay right here in this spring. They'll never f-hindh m-he herehhhhh—" He sunk further into the water on the last words, bubbles rising from his nose.

I snorted through my own nose. "You probably shouldn't swallow that," I cautioned through a smile.

"Blimey, where've I heard that before?" he muttered, now floating in the water, only his paws and face above the surface.

"Huh?"

"You really are the dearest, most innocent lad," he chuckled.

I had no idea what was amusing him so much, but it felt good to laugh again, to see him put on antics again, so I joined him in chuckling. The two of us laughed back and forth, really just tired, delirious laughter for a bit, for no real reason.

It felt so good. There was a release in it, in being able to be lighthearted with him again, even if it was only because I was briefly forgetting the situation we were in. The truth was, I'd wanted so hard since everything had gone sour between us to forgive him. And he'd done everything right, apologized and been contrite, even going farther than I'd wanted and confessing to my family not only of his past, but that he'd put me in danger. Risking *their* disapproval…the people who were ultimately going to determine his fate.

Even I wouldn't have asked him to do that. But he had. And he had nothing to gain from it, no matter how I thought about it. It had to be that he was just earnestly remorseful.

It was hard to square all of that, to really make sense of the man I'd come to know, with the past he'd admitted to. But it had also been hard to imagine the person hunting us, who'd shot me and haunted us all those nights we'd spent running from her, was a mother of two just trying to feed her children the only way she knew how.

The world was complicated and people even more so. All of this had been hard, but it felt overdue. I wasn't a child any more.

Maybe I wasn't supposed to make sense of it all at once. There was a sort of release in thinking that way. It made me feel less like I was failing at understanding something. Setting that confusion aside for now, it was actually easier to know my own mind, to see what my true feelings were.

I knew a few things very clearly. I loved my family. I was glad to have returned to them, but I also felt as though I'd changed too much in the last month for us to ever go back to how things had been before. That thought didn't frighten me as much as I thought it would.

It was also very clear to me now that going out into the world, not just meeting Finnegan, is what had ultimately brought those changes forth. And I didn't regret that. Life here in our village was safe, familiar, protected...and unchanging.

I wasn't sure that was all I wanted any more.

And I couldn't deny, no matter how conflicted I was over him, that Finnegan made me happy. I enjoyed his company, I enjoyed talking to him, I felt things for him I'd never felt before, and I wanted very badly to protect him.

That was where reality came crashing back down on me. Even here in the warm spring waters, floating beside him staring up at the stars, the inevitability of his situation was poised over us like an archer with an arrow nocked. My father would try, of that I was certain, but what possible outcome could there be for him? I couldn't ask my family to endanger themselves for one foreign man. I couldn't even justify it to myself.

Even if I could forgive Finnegan, even if I could wrap my mind around how a person could be so many things at once to me...what would it matter if he were soon gone?

I spent an hour with my family that night, talking to my sisters and eventually convincing the youngest that it was time to sleep. She insisted I wrap her up in her furs, which of course I did.

My father made us peppermint tea afterwards and I sat with him for a short time, talking. He deliberately avoided the most important issue at hand, because he knew when I went to sleep troubled, I would hardly sleep at all.

Finnegan had nowhere else to go, so he'd come along with me and sat on the lower rungs of the ladder into my family's pit house, watching us in quiet calm. He couldn't understand a word we were saying, seeing as we spoke our own language in our home, but he seemed content just to be warm. The ladder's lowest rungs were close to the fire, in the center of the dwelling.

"He'll need to stay with you," my father said after sipping his tea, shaking his whiskers a bit. "I won't ask any of the other men to put him up with their families and your dwelling is the deepest. He's not quite so large as you, but still a mite taller than all of us."

I nodded. "We've shared closer quarters throughout this trip," I assured him. "I'm not worried about having him in my home."

"Mmmhh, he seems amiable and polite enough," he agreed. "As Otherwolves go, you could have befriended worse. And I say that knowing he's a murderer."

"*Otterfa*," I said, somewhat aghast.

"Tulimak, you're a man now," he shook his head at me. "I can be honest with you about the world."

"Fine, then," I said, calling his bluff. "I know you don't want to talk about anything else dismal tonight, but I want one answer before I sleep. The Mill."

He looked down into his tea, as if he'd seen this coming.

"And the forest they've cleared," I continued. "Finnegan thinks it might be their way of claiming our land."

"That is precisely what they are doing," he confirmed stoically.

"How could you let that happen?" I asked, keeping my voice down so as not to wake my sisters. "I thought you knew some of the Otherwolves in town. We've traded with them...learned their language...I thought we had some measure of their respect. Wasn't that the point?"

"Tulimak, I..." He stopped for a few moments, gripping his tea cup with both hands. "We have made some mistakes in our dealings with them, over the years. Mistakes you and your brothers and sisters will inherit, I fear."

"What does that mean?" I asked.

He let out a breath, slowly. "Long before my time, the Otherwolves fought a war against their mother nation. They wished to govern themselves. When that happened, the Tribal Alliance was founded. Many tribes joined in the Otherwolves' war effort to liberate themselves from Amuresca. Many chose not to. Those that did...when they ultimately won...became a part of their Nation." He looked up at me. "The Tawnahowac Tribe did not join the war effort. It was believed then, and I cannot disagree, that the

Otherwolves' problems were their own and it was best not to get involved. We are not part of the 'Tribal Alliance' founded all those years ago."

"We're on good terms with every tribe I know," I reasoned. "No one has warred with us in generations, we trade with tribal folk and Otherwolves alike—"

"All of that may be true," he said, "but it does not change how the Carvecians—the Otherwolves that broke free of their mother country and founded the new government here—feel about us. We are, in essence, non-persons in our own land."

"*That doesn't…what?*" I asked, uncertain I'd heard him right.

"We are not citizens, Tulimak," he said quietly. "Not of their nation. We have no say in their government."

"Their government is…new," I reasoned, still not understanding. "We've been here for many, many generations longer. We have our own alliances, our own gathers."

"They are claiming this land is theirs now," he stated. "All of it falls under their laws."

"*Our land too?*" I asked, eyes widening.

"**All** of it, Tulimak. All of it."

"So what exactly does that mean?" Finnegan asked as we descended the reinforced log ladder down into my dwelling. I hadn't been inside in nearly a month now, but it was clear my family had maintained it for me. The roof looked newly-thatched and packed with fresh clay, there was a fire crackling in the central pit and someone had hung drying herbs and left pots likely full of dried berries and grains on the shelves I'd dug for myself the year before. Additionally, a covered basket sat alongside the left wall, where the racks I would hang my parka, my cloaks and other clothing were waiting for me. I couldn't wait to put on something other than my travel clothes. But of immediate interest was the basket, which I dug into after getting a whiff of the fresh flat bread inside. I was not disappointed.

"The way he explained it," I said around a mouthful of bread, unwilling to be embarrassed about my manners when I was as ravenous as I'd suddenly realized, "we can't say we own the land, because we aren't meant to be here to begin with. They're asserting that after the war, all the land...from coast to coast...became theirs. So unless we're citizens of their country, we can't own anything here."

It was a great relief to me that he looked as confused as I felt. "Well that's horse shit," he pronounced at length.

"Thank you!" I exclaimed, swallowing a satisfyingly too-large chunk of bread. I had a moment of self-awareness and glanced down at the basket. "Oh, uh. Do you want some?"

"It's food that isn't fish, so yes," he said, crossing the distance between us and digging a hand down into the basket, pulling out one of the pieces of flatbread. He examined it a moment, then licked his fingers. "What's this on top?"

"Honey and ground chestnuts," I said, while starting on my third.

We sat down by the fire, going through probably half the basket between the two of us. Really, mostly me.

"So how do you become citizens?" he asked, brushing some crumbs off his vest after he'd finished his first piece.

I shook my head. "Apparently that's what my father has been trying to work on with one of the Otherwolves in town for the last few years. We'd either have to join the Tribal Alliance now, which is possible, but requires our tribe appeal to some sort of...I don't know...a group of important men—"

"Likely a Court of some kind," he interjected, grabbing another piece of bread.

"Right. I think that's the word he used," I nodded. "But they're very far from here. *Very* far. In the South, where the big Otherwolf city is."

"Arbordale?" he asked, ears perking.

"I think so," I sighed. "He's been trying to put together the means and the knowledge on how to do this thing we have to do, to be recognized, for a while now. But there's another problem. Even if we're able to join this Alliance now, our land won't be...ours. We would have to pay the Otherwolf nation for it. Or clear it and use it the way they are, to prove we're making 'efficient' use of it to qualify for some kind of 'Act' they passed recently."

"That is *also* horse shit," he snorted. "There has to be some sort of way around that. Some sort of homesteading loophole you could exploit."

"None of it will matter in a few months' time," I curled my fists in my lap. "The man my father thought he could trust—the one in the settlement nearby—he apparently talked to some of his fellows about what my father was planning to do. And now they're pushing outwards, as quickly as they can. They know he can't travel during the winter. They're using that 'Act', some kind of law in place where if they clear-cut the land to use it for their crops, or raising their beasts, they can claim it as their own without having to purchase it. All they have to do is be using it for one of these purposes, and it's theirs."

I stared into the fire. Finnegan apparently had nothing to say, but he did reach over and gingerly put a hand on my knee. The warmth of his palm seeped into my fur, reminding me of how much we used to touch.

I wanted that again. So badly.

"Father's contacts in the Otherwolf town have assured him they will not lay claim to the land our village is on," I said softly. "For however long that promise is good. But it won't matter. The forest is where we hunt, where we get all of our food that isn't fish. And even fishing will become impossible soon. Not just because of the Mill, but they intend to clear much more land than they already have, which will mean log runs down the river almost *constantly*. The ones that come through here already cause *so* much damage. A flood might destroy a house and that is a hardship we can endure, but we can't rebuild a river."

"So you'd need a *lot* of land," Finnegan said in consideration.

"Much fewer people used to live in the North Country," I sighed. "This didn't used to be a concern. When we began welcoming Otherwolf travelers wanting to homestead, we didn't know this would happen..."

"Some of your people clearly suspected," he murmured. "And tried to put a stop to it."

"Odina's people," I said quietly, glancing down at my bear paws, so unlike my family's. "And mine, most likely."

"Damn, Tulimak," he made a frustrated noise. "I'm so sorry."

"I want to help my father," I said, my fists still curled, a tremor making its way from my core down to my arms and growing. "But even if I could take this trip for him, even if we could best these men trying to claim our land out from underneath us, I'm...a fisherman. I couldn't earn enough in a lifetime of fishing salmon runs to save the lands my people rely on. It wouldn't matter how hard I worked."

"It isn't about effort," he said, knitting his hands over a knee. "That's what they'll tell you, but it's a lie to make the underclass blame themselves. It's about the rung you start off on when you're born, the chances you're afforded, and the power those above you have to ensure you can't take what they have. And it all reinforces itself. It's insidious." He looked to me after a moment, clarifying. "Evil."

"Is it completely hopeless?" I asked softly. "How do we prosper when they make all the rules, and they make them so they work best for themselves?"

"And they have the guns to back them up," he added. "I don't know, Tulimak. And I'm not going to say I understand completely how you feel, but I do know that frustration." He glanced sidelong at me, his green eyes slim, eyelids dropped low, "You *know* how I tried to climb my way up out of that pit."

I was silent, my vision slowly shrinking around me, the low, dim firelight creating an orb around Finnegan and I. The rest of the world seemed to recede into blackness, like it was all some distant place. I was there alone save for Finn and my thoughts. His words sunk into me slowly, and rather than frightening me or intimidating me as they rightfully should have, they ignited something inside me. My chest was burning up into my throat. I felt like I wanted to yell, to shake this all off of me like ice on my fur.

I felt helpless. I realized then, with startling clarity, that was what I'd been feeling all this time about the situation with Finnegan, as well. There were many things I felt...but more than anything I was paralyzed by the fear that there was *nothing* I could do. Not about what had been done, what was still to come...nothing.

And now, I'd come home to this. Another problem beyond my control, completely beyond my abilities to affect change.

I just wanted to be able to protect, to shield the people I loved. I'd always thought all that would take was courage. But it was so much more complicated than that.

Finnegan was speaking again, but all I could hear was the pounding of blood in my ears. My entire body had begun to shake. This again. I hated how it could come upon me so quickly, when I thought I was doing fine.

But I wasn't doing "fine." All I'd been doing was pushing it down. Ignoring it. And it kept growing inside me, festering like the sickness I'd had in my wound. I had to burn it out, somehow. I had to do something, *anything*, to stop from feeling this way. I couldn't *bear* it...

I just couldn't bear it any more.

"Tulimak? Tulimak?" I heard Finnegan's insistent voice as though it were through water. I looked up slowly, finding he'd moved up beside me, standing and looking down at me where I sat, concern etched in his every feature.

I opened my mouth to assure him I was all right, but the reality that I *was not* came crashing down on me so hard right then, I couldn't find the energy to say a thing, let alone lie. I just stared up at him, jaw trembling, hands limp in my lap. I was so overwhelmed, so tired, all at once. I felt like movement of any kind would make me crumble.

I felt my eyes stinging, knew what was coming. But as humiliating as the realization was, I knew there was nothing I could do to stop it.

I tried to say something again. All that came out was a wordless, shuddering wheeze. And that must have been when he saw my eyes watering, because Finnegan's ears dropped and he slowly crouched down beside me, extending a hand slowly to my shoulder.

"Tuli..." he trailed off. "Tulimak, I'm so sorry..."

"No more apologies," I finally managed to utter, my voice half-choked. "Nothing...none of it...is making this any better!"

He leaned back on his haunches, looking away for a few moments, clearly uncertain what to say. "What can I do?" he asked at length, softly.

"Nothing!" I cried out, frustrated. "Th-that's just the thing. There isn't a thing...either of us...can *do*. About any of it! But I can't...just...accept it, either. What am I supposed to do?!"

"I-I don't know—"

"I am so tired," I huffed out, between increasingly frantic breaths, "of feeling this way. Not just now. My *whole* life. I know there's nothing we can do right now—"

"Not tonight, no," he eased, putting his hands out. "But by tomorrow we'll be more well-rested, we're going to talk with Odina and your father—"

"You are *so* calm!" I belted out, shocking myself at how loud I'd become. Finnegan, to his credit, barely flinched. "I don't understand how you're so…*calm*…all the time. *You're* the one they're going to drag off. You know better than I do what's waiting for you. And still…" I shook my head frantically. "I can't…I just can't…"

I'd squeezed my eyes shut by then, but I felt his paws settling on my shoulders, his fingers sinking into my fur. I could smell he'd drawn closer, feel the heat off his breath. "All right," he said quietly. "All right. You just need to calm down, that's all. Today's been bad. Today's been really bad."

I sat there and shook, and tried to catch my breath. It felt like there was a crushing weight on my chest, stifling my ability to get enough air. Whenever I tried, I'd cough or gasp.

"I can't…protect…you," I gasped out, "I can't…help…my family… Can't…even endure hardship…without this…happening…" I bowed my head, closing my eyes tightly again. "What is…wrong…with me?"

His arms slid around my shoulders and he slowly leaned into me. I almost didn't realize I was being embraced until I felt his muzzle press into the ruff of fur along my neck. I hardly knew how to react, but it did stop the hyperventilating, because I stopped breathing entirely for a few moments.

"Do you know," he said, his muzzle inches from my ear, "how many times I broke down, caring for my mother?"

I didn't have an answer for him, but then he'd known that.

"So many nights," he murmured, "she'd be out of her mind, and I couldn't calm her down, no matter what I did. I'd have to clean the raw patches on her body, and she wouldn't *let* me. I would just…go outside… to the little back patch near the well, sit with my back against the stone… and curse and scream."

I finally dragged a ragged breath through my muzzle, filling my lungs. I could feel his paw against the nape of my neck, stroking through the thick fur.

"I got angry," he continued quietly. "That's what I did. It's what I…do… to this day. I'm probably always going to, to some extent. But you get…better…you learn how to get past it, with time. You start getting over it faster. You think more clearly, when you feel it coming over you. I know that's not the best answer, because it's not a help right now, but I want you to know it won't always be like this."

He let out a long breath against my shoulder, taking a few moments to compose himself before continuing. "Considering what's happened to you the last few weeks, I think you're within your rights to be overwhelmed. I don't think there's anything wrong with you. We handle troubles differently, is all."

"I feel like a child," I managed to say, my voice coming out sounding every bit as small as I felt. "I'm a man. I should be able to..."

He pulled back to look me in the eyes, while stroking his palm up over my cheek. "Men still feel overwhelmed sometimes, Tulimak. Men still have their limits." He leaned forward until our noses were almost touching. "It has been a *hard* few days. I understand why you're frayed and I don't think less of you for it. I may not seem it, but," he exhaled, "I am, too. And I'm not...calm...either. I'm just very good at pretending to be."

"Finn," I uttered, my normally deep voice frail, "I am not letting them take you."

"We'll figure something out," he said, soothingly. "Tomorrow. We'll talk about it tomorrow."

"I really care about you," I said, reaching a hand up to wrap around one of his.

He smiled. "I know."

I huffed softly, wiping my arm across my eyes. "I think," I sniffed, "you're supposed to say something...similar...there."

"I probably owe you that," he agreed, ears twitching, the slight smile still in place. "But it's harder for me. I really envy that you seem to be able to say everything on your mind."

"No, I don't," I muttered, miserably. "Most of the time I can't find any of the right words. All that spills out of me is nonsense."

"That's better than half-truths," he sighed. "All I seem capable of doing is obfuscating, until I'm caught and cornered and staring down reality, and by then it's too late for me to do the right thing. All I've got left then is contrition."

I sniffed again, noisily, "Finn," I groaned, "you *need* to start using smaller words."

I heard rather than saw him give a light laugh and then I felt him lean his forehead against my own. Even after we'd bathed in the spring, his scent was filling my nose, pulling back memories of nights spent pressed against one another in the lean-to. Woodsmoke, leather, that musk that was unmistakably *him*. I could feel the heat of his body even through the sleeves of his jacket and the shirt beneath it, where his arms rested over my shoulders. His breath was on my cheek, his whiskers brushing against my own. I could feel every slight twitch of his muzzle.

One of my paws reached for the edge of his coat and dug in, balling in the travel-roughened leather and tugging it towards me. He inhaled sharply, but didn't resist. Only pulled back his muzzle an inch from mine, lifting both palms to cup either side of my face.

"Tulimak," he breathed, "can I—"

"Yes," I said immediately.

Our muzzles met, with no further hesitation. The first time we'd kissed, even having no experience, I'd somehow fumbled my way through figuring it out. It had been exhilarating, physically thrilling and I hadn't worried over whether I was doing it right or not, because I'd been so absorbed in the fact that it was happening *at all*.

This time, my mind went similarly, *blissfully* blank. With the storm that had been raging inside my thoughts all day, the silence was such a release. I may have fumbled finding the right angle for a while, but if I had I didn't *care*, because exploring Finnegan's pliant, soft mouth underneath my own *was* the whole point. And no part of it felt like I could get it wrong. Even when I felt his tongue against my teeth. I opened my muzzle to his and our teeth briefly clacked together, but that only served to remind me how eager we both were. Knowing it was mutual meant everything.

At some point after I'd first felt his tongue on mine and realized that, too was something I wanted to feel more of, he'd clambered closer to me. Which by necessity meant he'd gone from kneeling before me to straddling one of my thighs. I wrapped an arm around his midsection once he had a good seat there and dragged him up against my torso, and then it really clicked. He didn't need to crouch or kneel over me, I could hold him easily in one arm. He leaned in against me fully and deepened the kiss, his tongue sliding over mine inside my muzzle.

I panted, not fighting the intrusion, but briefly overwhelmed by the sensation. I had *never* known kissing could be like this. I'd never even known it could last this long. How long had we been at it now?

Once or twice he pulled back, blinking hazily at me and looking as though he were going to ask me if I wanted to stop. Each time, I'd chase him and nip at his muzzle if he still seemed uncertain. That prompted a few surprised noises and breathless chuckles from him I immediately decided I liked.

How long were you supposed to do this for? Could we just do it all night?

His coat was bunching around his waist and just generally getting in the way. I wasn't about to remove it, but it seemed obvious and natural to release my hold on it and instead slip my paw up beneath it to touch and hold him under the garment. My hand settled where it had been holding him before, only now all that I felt were his trousers and the soft base of his tail. Without thinking much about it, I wrapped my hand around it and stroked it once down to his white tail-tip. I'd never touched his tail before and I'd long wanted to.

"Nnnhh," he groaned against my mouth, pulling away from my muzzle with a wet lick of his own mouth. He blinked dark green eyes down at me, irises blown wide in the dimly-lit room. "All right," he said in a husky tone, slowly lifting himself out of my lap. "Give me a moment."

I leaned back on my palms, worry creeping in as I watched him stiffly stand and walk over towards the rack where my clothing was hanging. What had I done wrong? I shouldn't have touched his tail.

He shed his coat and laid it out over my parka, then turned to regard me, undoing the cuffs of his sleeves. The look he leveled at me across the room was smoldering.

"I know you've only the one garment," he said, his lean figure all the more striking in the well-tailored vest he wore beneath his jacket. "But you should probably lose it."

I glanced down at my breech cloth, then back up at him. He was unbuttoning his vest.

"O-oh," I said, awkwardly. I became painfully self-aware of my body's condition in that moment. "I…maybe I shouldn't," I mumbled, "I'm…"

"Tulimak, I was in your lap," he reasoned. "I know."

I knew my ears were flushing, but it was less embarrassing this time, for some reason. I looked up at him shyly. He paused before shrugging out of his vest. "We don't have to do anything but kiss tonight," he said quietly, "if that's what you want."

It didn't take me long to decide.

"I want to know what else there is," I said after a few moments. "And I want to figure it out...with you. But," I stammered, "are you really..."

He looked at me expectantly, slowly smiling. "Attracted to you?" he supplied.

"We're just," I sighed, "so different. I never thought someone like you would like...looking...at someone like me."

"Tuli, are you attracted to *me?*" he asked, although we both knew the answer was obvious.

"Yes," I said in a gruffer voice than I'd meant to.

"But I'm quite different than you," he said pointedly, shrugging out of his vest. "People like different things. Often things...and people...very different from themselves."

"That...makes sense," I agreed.

He'd already gotten off his spats, holster, and was undoing his trousers as he approached me. They had been one of the few pairs of clean clothing he had left, if what I'd seen in his pack was any indication. I realized as he approached me that the scent on him had changed and a slightly darker spot had appeared on the front flap of his dark tan trousers. When he finally shoved them down, it was clear where it had come from. A far softer shade of pink than my own, his length was half out of its sheath, the tip slick where it had been pressing against the fabric.

He seemed relieved to be free of the garment and kicked it aside without further ado. "Best I got out of those sooner than later," he muttered, then glanced back at me.

I was staring. I know I was staring, but I couldn't stop. He smirked slightly, approaching me fully nude now, his black fur catching the orange and red hues of the flickering fire. I'd never *really* gotten a good look at him, laid out before me as he was now. And I'd certainly never seen all of his body.

Some part of my mind, I think, had wondered how far these desires of mine went. It was one thing to kiss another man, even to be touched by him. And there was no doubt I was attracted to his figure. But this...I'd thought on it more than was probably healthy since that first night and wondered many times if I could possibly want another man in this way. It was so opposite to what I was supposed to want.

But now, I knew. I very much did.

"Do you want to touch me?" he asked in that same, unusually deep voice that had first surprised me. It seemed even lower now.

I nodded dumbly. He gestured at me, "Then disrobe," he said again. "Or you'll ruin your clothing."

His implication hit me hard, sending the blood right down to the spot in question, with its unspoken promise. I swallowed and got to my knees, untying my breechcloth and removing it with unsteady hands. I was acutely aware of his gaze on me, the whole time. But despite feeling awkward, I didn't want him to look away. I watched him watch me, his expression validating the part of me that needed it. Seeing him hanging out his sheath didn't hurt, either.

I was embarrassingly hard. The breechcloth had honestly been doing little to contain what was obvious, but it was good to have it off all the same. I leaned back on my palms, still looking up at him, bashfully. His gaze was traveling over my figure, those green eyes I'd so often found entrancing drinking me in silently. I wanted to know what was on his mind.

"You're marvelous, Tulimak," he rumbled, slowly stepping up towards me until he was nearly standing over me. He was so close. I wanted to...I hardly know. I just wanted to nuzzle into his fur, press my nose between his legs...

I groaned lowly at the sheer thought of that, my cock twitching.

He chuckled, stroking a palm over the top of my head, rubbing one of my ears. "I keep forgetting how young you are. Bit eager, are we? That's all right," he settled both of his paws on my shoulders, smiling down at me. "If I'm being completely honest, I've wanted to mount you since the first time I realized you fancied me."

"'Mount me'?" I echoed, my mouth gone dry suddenly. "Like a...horse?"

He laughed through his teeth, "Not exactly! Probably doesn't mean what you think it means. Or maybe it does? Heh," he slowly kneeled over me and lowered himself back into my lap, fully straddling me this time. "Here, I'll show you."

He leaned forward and kissed me again, pressing our bodies together, fur against fur, finally. I was going to wind my arms around him again, when he gave me a light shove on my uninjured shoulder. "Can you lie down on your back now?" he asked, tail flicking back and forth over my legs.

I nodded. "My furs here are better, too," I said, glancing behind me at the mountain of soft sheep fur laid out over the woven straw mattress my sisters had so lovingly spent *far* too much time on for me. My den, specifically my bed, was one of the things I'd most missed from home.

He gave me another playful nudge, this time with just one finger. He smirked at me as I dutifully fell back into my furs and lay down beneath him. Afterwards, he remained straddling my waist, placing his paws on my belly and slowly stroking them up through my thick fur, leaning forward now that he could and grinding his hips down into mine with a low hum.

The sensation of his sheath, his cock, deliberately rubbing against mine was...if my mind had been blank before, now it was a *void*. All I cared about in the world was that he keep doing *that*, keep moving, keep making those noises...

"Put those big paws on me," he slurred out, reaching for them and dragging them to his hips, where I eagerly dug my claws into his fur. He steadied himself with his hands on my chest and slowly moved his body against mine. I felt his muscles flexing through my paw pads, the rise of his hipbone under my thumb, where I dug in and rubbed the spot I knew him to be sore.

He hissed low, tail brushing against my inner thigh. "Goddamn," he groaned, "you're like a mountain. My knees can barely touch the bed."

"I'm s—"

"Don't you dare fucking apologize," he admonished, before leaning in and kissing me once again, nipping at my muzzle, "I like the challenge. Mmmhhh..."

He'd wound his arms up around my neck again, flattening his chest to my own while still continuing to rub his cock into my fur, more against my stomach, now. My own was between the heat of his thighs, enjoying the occasional tease from his tail. My paws continued to rove his body, finding him softer than I'd imagined. I'd always thought he'd be all hard planes and unyielding, since he was so thin. But his figure was still soft in places and quite enjoyable to squeeze, and since he'd told me to touch him and all…

He gasped out into my muzzle when I first cupped and squeezed his rear, then broke from the kiss to give a breathless chuckle. "You don't need much instruction, huh?"

"No, I do," I managed to say somehow, even though my head was swimming and my body was on fire. "I have *no* idea what I'm doing."

He smiled and rubbed his muzzle up beneath my neck, biting at my scruff there. The building anticipation made each successive nip feel better than the last. I let my head fall back, exposing my throat to him. He teased me there for quite a while, all the while grinding himself into my thick fur.

When he at last lifted himself back up to straddle me again, he was fully out of his sheath. Finn was half my size, but then he was in all other respects, too, so it suited him. His light pink cock contrasted beautifully against his black fur, beckoning me to wrap a paw around it.

Before I had a chance though, he'd slid further down my body, straddling one of my thighs instead. One of his paws moved along my other inner thigh to tip it aside, which I complied with, easing up onto my elbows to watch him in curiosity. He slowly slid his free hand up to cup my sac. I instinctively twitched back for a moment, but he leveled a cool gaze at me from between my legs and even more gently stroked me there, making it clear he'd be ginger. When I allowed myself to relax, I enjoyed it. And he squeezed softly once he'd gotten me comfortable, which pulled a groan out of me.

He gave a self-satisfied, "Hmm," and moved his other palm up, wrapping it loosely around my length and stroking once from base to tip, feeling the whole of me out. He let out a long breath as he did so. "Damn," he said.

I couldn't reach much of him, as far down as he was now, so I settled for playing with one of his ears. The reprieve wasn't bad, I was appreciating the moment to calm down, but what exactly was he doing? I couldn't even kiss him from here.

The answer came soon, when he nosed his way up my inner thigh. For a moment I thought he was just indulging in what I admittedly had considered earlier, just nuzzling me there. But then he lathed his tongue up the underside of my manhood, and whatever chance I'd had at calming down, it was gone.

"Unnhhh..." I felt some of my bear voice slip out on the groan, my head falling back into the sheepskins. One lick was soon joined by another and before long he was holding me by the base and just putting me *in* his muzzle. Really, given how our kissing had progressed earlier, I probably should have seen it coming. But I was wholly unprepared for how it would *feel*.

My paw was still wrapped around one of his ears, partially holding his head in my palm, and I tried my hardest not to grip him or pull him into me, but I wanted to more than words could describe. I was still propped up on an elbow, watching him slack-jawed, breath huffing out heavily as the top half of my cock disappeared into his slender muzzle, again and again. His tongue was caressing the underside, cheeks sucking at me, the hand that had been gripping me stroking what he couldn't swallow with the aid of his pooling saliva.

I couldn't take it for long. I felt the bliss overtaking me, the mounting pressure building, coiling in my stomach. When his other hand again massaged my sac, that was it, that was all I could bear.

I couldn't get anything out other than growling groans by then, but I frantically shook his shoulder and he released me from his muzzle with a last, long drag of his tongue up and over the tip. I only barely made it, spilling long ropes of seed over my stomach and part of his muzzle as he narrowly avoided most of it. He only chuckled again and continued to lick the underside of my cock while I spilled and twitched.

I was boneless and barely coherent in the wake of it, but I heard him cursing lowly...not angrily...more in sultry admiration. When I managed to look up, he'd moved back up to straddle my waist and was looking down on me, stroking himself slowly.

"Give me one of your paws," he all but commanded. Weakly at first, I complied, reaching over to him. But when he grabbed my hand and placed it on his cock, I got some of my strength back.

"Won't take much," he promised breathlessly as I closed my palm around him and began to stroke. Like this, it was easy. It was only slightly different than touching myself. He leaned up on his knees and let his eyes drift half-closed, still watching me. As I stroked him, he curled his tongue up over the edge of his muzzle to lick at where I'd left my mark on him, and I swear to you, the sight nearly got me hard all over again.

I briefly slid my palm over my own spent length, slicking it before returning to his. He groaned out his approval immediately, bucking his hips into my palm. "Tuli-*fuck*!" He began pumping into my grip. "Just like that…"

He'd been right. It wasn't much longer before I felt a bulge grow beneath my palm, and his knot—something I'd heard canines had, but never before seen, let alone felt—popped free of his sheath. I made sure to curl my palm around it as well as I stroked him, my gaze flicking between his needful thrusts into my hand and the soft, unguarded expression he was making in those few precious seconds. And then his moans reached a crescendo and he shuddered, spraying my stomach and even part of my chest with his seed, joining my own. I felt it, warm against my fur, surely leaving his scent on me. We'd clean up as well as we could soon enough, but I hazily thought it might not be so bad if enough lingered for me to remember all of this by.

In the aftermath, we mostly lay against one another, kissing. Finnegan didn't even seem to care that doing so was getting us *both* dirty. On the contrary, he was apparently relishing in it, chuckling lewdly when I tried to wipe his cheek with my thumb, where he still wore the evidence of our act.

"Nnnhh," he waved a hand, smirking. "You're just rubbing it into the fur. At least lick it off."

I don't think he'd expected me to comply, but when I did, leaning forward to lathe my big, dark tongue over his cheek, he gave a surprised, "Oh-hooo! Someone's got a few gutter inclinations himself there…not so innocent as y'appear." He chortled contently, then leaned forward to kiss me again. It quickly deepened, his content hum growing to a groan as our tongues curled and our bodies pressed together once more.

I rolled him onto his back in the furs this time and he let me, allowing himself to be caged in my arms. We kissed, groaned, laughed at ourselves and generally rolled around together for a while, until I was hard again and he was halfway there. And then we did it all again…in a slightly different order.

Eventually, exhaustion got the better of us and we somehow managed to get to the wash basin and clean up…somewhat…before collapsing in bed together.

I should have worried more. About what tomorrow would bring, about what tonight meant, about how careless we'd been. But I'd never slept with such a clear head. And worrying wouldn't have changed anything.

Chapter 12

Sanctuary

My dreams were quiet and peaceful, but my waking mind remembered my fears very well. The few times I roused throughout the night, it was only for a moment before I confirmed the warmth of the figure in my arms, my unconscious self afraid he'd be gone, I suppose.

Even when the first rays to peek through the caribou furs covering the entrance to my pit home tickled my eyelids, hazily blinking against the unwanted light, I had that brief jump in my chest. I tilted my muzzle down an inch at most and immediately encountered resistance, his head tucked beneath my chin. I let out a long breath, dropping my cheek back down against the mattress. Why was it I kept thinking he'd be gone?

Right. Because today we were going to discuss just that.

Stop focusing on things that hadn't even yet come to pass, I told myself. Right now, everything was warm and perfect, I was home in my own bed, with a man I'd come to admire and…care for…very deeply…safely held against my chest. Nothing could harm us, no one could ruin this moment, it was mine to remember forever. I might as well enjoy it.

Finnegan's breathing was slow and steady, his chest rising and falling where my arm was loosely draped over his ribs. It felt so right to have him here, for some reason. As woefully out-of-place as he was in my tribal home, as strange as it was to see his foreign clothing draped over mine where it hung on my parka rack, it felt like the culmination of something

I'd fought for. Getting him all this way, surviving despite being hunted, despite the elements and illness, I couldn't help but feel that we'd earned this. All those cold nights we'd spent together in the lean-to, I had been subconsciously yearning for this. The comforts of home, accompanied by the newness of this man in my life.

This *must* have been how people felt when they desired to marry someone, I couldn't help but think. That was most certainly an irrational thought given who we were, how long we'd known one another, and the obvious impossibility of a future together. The thing is, if Finn had been a woman, no one would fault me for thinking that way in the slightest. The desire to share your home with someone, to feel safe with someone, to just *be with* someone, were all things men were supposed to feel. I was just feeling them for the wrong person, and that made this all terribly confusing because I was *so certain*.

These *had* to be those feelings I'd been promised I'd feel with a wife, or someone I'd want to make my wife. They had to be. What else could they be? Every married couple I knew that was happy had told me it wasn't something one could describe, this feeling. Just that I'd *know*.

I felt like...I knew.

So what, then, did I do with this? I was supposed to come to feel this way for a tribal woman, or at least a *woman in general*. From there, I could have consulted my family on courtship, or something like it. The steps forward down that road were known. But this? I hardly knew where to begin. Either my feelings for Finn were terribly misplaced and there was something wrong with me...or they were right, and there was something wrong with the world.

"Are you going to leave home with the fancy wolf man, Tulimak?" A young voice cut through my meditative silence. I very nearly bolted upright before remembering there was someone in my arms.

I recognized my youngest sister's voice, of course. I just hadn't known she was *in my home*.

I turned my head slowly, careful to jostle Finnegan as little as possible. Miraculously, he didn't stir. How was it he could sleep so deeply now, but always seemed to wake up at the slightest noise when I didn't want him to?

My sister Alasie was sitting on the sturdy ladder leading up to the surface. The flap of caribou fur covering the opening was pulled back slightly, explaining why the light had woken me. I couldn't be sure how long she'd been down here, but she didn't look to have moved off the ladder, sitting a few rungs up, her legs dangling.

Strangely, she looked sad.

I lifted myself up on one elbow, readjusting the blanket covering Finnegan and I. Could she tell we were both nude beneath it? Would she even know what that implied?

"Alasie," I said, my voice coming out in a rough scrape. "What's wrong? Why are you here?"

"It's after breakfast already," she murmured, finally looking up at me. "You never came to eat. Dad said to leave you to sleep, but the sun's high, already. And you've been gone so long. I wanted to go dig thistle root with you. You can dig so much deeper than I can."

I released a breath I hadn't realized I was holding. "Alasie, I'll come join you soon," I promised her in a whisper. "I was very tired. Dad's right, I needed to sleep late today."

Her eyes moved pointedly to the man curled against me beneath the blankets. She looked accusatory, but she dropped her voice to a whisper, "His fault," she muttered petulantly.

"What?" I asked, uncertainly.

"It's his fault you got hurt and came home so tired," she clarified.

I blinked. "Did otterfa…?"

"I don't need dad to tell me that," she sniffed. "I'm not a pup any more. He's gotten you in a lot of trouble, hasn't he?"

I looked away from my own little sister, embarrassingly finding it hard to keep eye contact with her. The little otter had a way of staring me down that I'd yet to best. Especially when she was upset.

"And now you're going to leave the tribe," she said in a mournful, sulking tone.

"What? No," I stammered. "Wait, did otterfa—"

"I already told you, *no*," she said vehemently. "I just know. Whenever any of the girls meet an Otherwolf man they want to be with, they leave and they don't come back. And then we only see them at gathers."

"It's not," I let out a breath, "like that, for me and Finnegan—"

"Why, because you're a boy?" she asked, scrunching up her nose. "What does that matter? You're doing the same thing. You're going to leave us just like them, and live with the Otherwolves. Just like them."

I glanced down at Finnegan, then back at her, baffled. She was upset, sure, but not over what I expected. I hardly knew how to make sense of it. But I suppose by her immature logic, her reasoning made complete sense. We had in fact "lost" two women in recent memory to marriages with outsiders. Trade had opened our people to meeting many strangers, all of which in the frontier logging towns were necessarily male. The nearby Otherwolf settlement had no women in it as of yet, at least not of their ilk. Two of them had taken wives from our tribe, women who had willingly given up their lives and traditions with us to embrace the new way of life the Otherwolves offered.

My otterfa had since restricted travel amongst our women into the Otherwolf town. I'd not thought much about it at the time, but now in retrospect, it did seem...severe. Both women who'd married outside our tribe had done so willingly, as far as I knew, and in return had nearly lost all contact with their families in our village. Not because of the Otherwolves, but because of *our* traditions. It's possible the Otherwolves had similarly limiting traditions about marriage as well, I couldn't say. But the trouble I knew of had come from within our own tribe. Even now, they were only permitted to return during gatherings.

One of them was even married to another otter. A different kind from a foreign land. But still, an otter.

My sister had every reason to see Finnegan and I together and assume what was most likely, based on her experience. And she hadn't even processed the main issue, yet. All that mattered to her was that a foreigner had come along, grown close to me, and she was afraid she'd lose her brother the same way the other families in our tribe had lost their sisters and daughters.

"Alasie, I'm not leaving the tribe," I promised.

"Dad will make you," she insisted.

That statement, made in such a subdued tone by a child of all people, punched me in the gut so hard it robbed me of my next breath. I couldn't tell her she was wrong. Even though I had no plans to marry Finnegan, would never, *could* never do so...she might still be right.

The fact was, whether or not she realized it, Alasie had ensured that now no matter what happened between Finnegan and I after today, I would *have* to tell my father what had transpired between us. Because she would most certainly tell him, eventually. And I wanted him to hear it from me.

I hadn't planned on keeping this a secret from my family. But now, I truly had no choice.

I hardly knew what to do with myself after Alasie left, so I kissed Finnegan awake. At the very least, it briefly made me feel better.

He came to groggily and as if answering my silent plea, curled an arm around my shoulder and pulled our bodies closer together. Even half asleep, or perhaps especially so, his muzzle melted effortlessly against mine. His jaw was lax and lazy as he tilted it into mine, back arching just so as I slid a paw beneath his body, fingertips feeling the bumps in his spine. We continued on like that for a while, time slipping away.

He at last pulled back, dragging a long breath and half a yawn through his nose, his agate eyes half-lidded. His dark fur was leafy and soft, the spring waters having worked their magic on our bodies the night before. He looked calm and serene, devoid of that aching tiredness he'd worn like a second skin since we'd met. It was…fulfilling…to know I'd been instrumental in that. I wanted to see him this happy, this peaceful, more often.

I cupped fully half of his skull in my palm, stroking my claws through his cheek ruff. He leaned into the touch and closed his eyes. I couldn't help the words that bubbled up out of my muzzle.

"You're beautiful," I murmured.

He opened his eyes, then huffed out a chuckle, his voice still thick with sleep when he spoke. "You're sweet, but 'handsome' might be the word you're looking for."

I glanced aside shyly. "That, too. But I like that word and I think it suits you. Your eyes remind me of pine boughs. I love to watch them shift and sway when storms move in. Beautiful." I breathed. "When you look at me, that's what I feel."

He blinked slowly at me, "What you 'feel'?"

"Like a storm is coming," I said softly.

"And that's a compliment?" he asked uncertainly, clearly amused.

"Storms bring change," I ran my thumb up over the edge of his ear, gently. "My life was pleasant, but repetitive, before you."

His paw moved up over my own, fingers threading through mine. He pressed his muzzle to my palm once more, then slowly slid our entwined hands away. His expression got distant and he went utterly quiet for a time, staring up at the roof of my home. Once again, I wished I knew what he was thinking.

"My youngest sister saw us," I said, because he needed to know, before we went out into the village.

His eyes snapped to mine and focused down to pinprick pupils very quickly. "Are we in danger?" he asked immediately.

"You still are," I reminded him. "But if you mean—"

"She's young," he reasoned, his tone suddenly nervous. "She might not have understood what she saw."

"She asked if we were going to marry," I sighed.

Despite his obvious discomfort, that got a bitter laugh out of him. He sat up slowly, leaning to his side to stretch out his hip. "Oh, to be as innocent as a child again."

"It *would* be nice," I agreed, rolling to my back.

It took me a moment to realize Finnegan was staring down at me, since I'd rolled over and was no longer facing him. I glanced his way, trying to make sense of the dubious, uncertain look he was wearing.

"Innocence?" he asked after a few moments. "Or...marriage?"

He was giving me an odd look, almost worried, so I decided very quickly to go for the more benign option. "The first," I replied.

But Finn was canny. "Look, Tuli," he said quietly, shifting up and loping a leg over my waist, straddling atop me again, although far more casually than last night. I found my hands going to his hips, stroking down his thighs, all the same. "I'm very fond of you—"

"Only my sisters call me that," I interrupted him, which was rare for me. But I'd meant to say something about it yesterday and I'd forgotten.

"Hm?" he asked through a low hum, as I once again rubbed my thumbs over his hip bones in slow circles. I liked watching the expressions he'd make when I massaged him there.

"'Tuli,'" I replied. "My sisters call me that sometimes. You've taken to shortening my name now, too."

"I'm sorry," he said, tipping his ears back, "is it offending you? I didn't mean to."

I shook my head. "Not at all," I assured him with a smile. "I've been doing it to you, too. But we both did it in front of my father yesterday. And even if we scrub up at the wash basin, I think he might smell you on me. So…"

"I have very strong soap," he assured me, tapping his nose. "Only way I survived on that passenger ship. It's one of the few things I brought from Amuresca that I refused to pawn."

I hadn't known that the night before, but it was reassuring. "That's good," I shrugged, "but regardless, I would have told him eventually. He knows everything that happens in this tribe. He'll figure it out eventually, regardless."

"First off, I'm not sure what there even is to tell him," Finn insisted, splaying his palms on my stomach. "This isn't his business. It's *no one's* business but ours. It's a page in our lives, nothing more. Even if I end up staying here a short while, it isn't like your father has to know everything about your personal life, Tulimak. We can talk to your sister—"

"I'm not hiding something this important from my family," I said, voice steady.

He ran his paws up over his muzzle, then smoothed back his ears, blowing out a breath. "What's *important* here," he insisted, "is *discretion*. We talked about this. I thought we were clear on how we'd handle this."

I covered up the hurt in my voice as well as I could. "You're acting ashamed, Finn. I thought…last night…"

"All right, to be clear," he said, adopting a very straightforward, fierce tone. "I am not *ashamed* of who I choose to bed. You included. I grew up in a community of people who made their living on their knees and they were some of the most honorable, decent people I've ever known. To hell with anyone—the Church included—who says different. If God exists and he's watching and judging who and how we bunk up, he's a bloody degenerate and he can fuck *right* off. But Tuli, it isn't about what *I* think. Or what *you* think."

He leaned down over my torso, resting his weight on his palms, which he slid up my chest fur. He moved in close until our muzzles were nearly touching. "Remember when I told you this was dangerous?" he asked, his tone nearly a whisper. When I nodded, he continued. "Back in the Risers, they'd have these gangs of armed men come in sometimes, working for the Bailiff. 'Raids,' they'd call them. They'd rout us all out of our homes, toss the place upside down and try to herd up any Mollies they could find. We had a cellar—" he paused. "Mollies…sorry. Men…well, like us. 'Heretics.' Male Courtesans. It's all the same to them. It didn't even matter if you were in the trade, all that mattered was that you looked like what they were there to find."

He looked down. "My Uncle Mikhail dodged them so many times before he quit the trade. He was lucky. A lot of the other men weren't. They don't just throw you in a work camp with a 'buggery' charge if you've made a trade of it. They hang you. Or worse."

"But that's your country," I insisted. "This is my tribe. My family. They might not like it, but—"

"Tulimak, have you ever known tribesmen like us?" he asked flatly.

I, of course, hadn't.

"Your family seems wonderful," he said earnestly. "And I don't know your customs, to be fair. But people are people and when they're used to having something one way, they don't tend to take well to those that buck it."

"But," I stammered, "I want my father to know who I am. And this is part of who I am, now."

His expression softened to one of sympathy and he leaned in to kiss me. I let him, but the way he'd been looking at me made me uncomfortable. I didn't want him feeling bad for me, for whatever reason he was.

"I loved being with you last night," he admitted in a quiet, husky voice once he'd pulled back from the kiss. His hand stroked over my ears, gently. "I love being with you…in general," he admitted after a further few moments, hesitantly. "But I know I definitely don't deserve anyone as sweet and unselfish as you. And that isn't even the point, really. But I feel I should say it."

"Finn—"

"I've been twenty and passionate," he continued. "I get it. But you're going to meet a lot of people. Better people, with less troubles. Women, even. And you'll feel this way again."

"Even if that's true," I said, "it isn't happening now. Right now I'm with you."

"Tulimak," he sighed, "you would be better off with any woman, literally *any* woman, than you would be with me."

"You keep saying that," I said, frustration working its way into my tone. "What if I don't like women, Finn?"

That seemed to give him pause. "Who doesn't like women?" he said in a forcibly dismissive tone.

"I mean—like this," I said pointedly, looking down at where our bodies were pressed together. "What then?"

He didn't seem to have a ready answer for that. It was disturbing to see him caught off-guard, as thus far he'd been so much more knowledgeable about all of this than I had. Was that really a possibility he'd never considered?

To be fair, I was only beginning to consider it now myself. And it *was* frightening.

He let out a long breath, hanging his head. "Let's not entertain that right now. You've hardly been out in the world a month. You have a lot more to see, a lot more to experience. But one thing I know for certain: You and I, and this thing we have going, it is not the future you want."

"How can you say that right after kissing me?" I croaked out, disbelievingly. "I thought you felt—"

"This," he gestured between the two of us, "is a death sentence. You have to enjoy it for what it is while you have it and leave it at that. It can't ever be more than that."

"I-I'm so confused," I confessed. He was still atop me, his body soft and warm against my own. One of his paws was stroking my chest. "Are we," I found the words catch in my throat, antithetical to everything lain before me, "is this…over?"

And if it was, why was he here with me like this? How could he be asking to end things while still in my arms?

"It…doesn't have to be," he said carefully, lifting his eyes slowly to mine. "We can just enjoy it while it lasts. Like we are now."

I couldn't come up with a response for an uncomfortably long time. I know he felt it, too. When he slowly began to rise up off of me, I found the nerve to act. And finally, to say something.

I reached up and gripped his arm, slowly tugging him back down to me. He looked uneasy, knowing, I suppose, that he'd upset me. I'm certain I was wearing it on my face, plain as day.

"I don't know," I said with a slight tremble in my voice, "how long I can do that. But…I'm also not ready to end this. Not if you still want it." I swallowed past the painful lump in my throat. "I don't like what you're describing," I needed to declare that, right off. I lifted my eyes to his, because I felt I should for what I was about to say. "I think it's unfair. What you're asking of me."

For once, he broke eye contact first. It was hard to see it as a victory.

"But I understand," I said after another awkwardly long silence had passed. "You—neither of us—know what's ahead. Everything's hinging on that anyway, so…for now…I'm willing to wait it out. And see."

"Tuli," he began, then corrected himself, "Tulimak."

"I don't mind that," I reminded him.

"I'm not family," he said uncomfortably. "That feels…I don't know. Sacred? Very important to you, clearly. I didn't realize. I probably haven't earned the right to be so informal with you."

"I'm giving you permission," I said, stroking his chin with the back of my fingers.

He released a slight breath at that, a soft noise that reminded me of some he'd made last night. It was a relief to see my words could evoke such an unintentional, visceral reaction from him. He didn't lose his composure often, and I so often did. It made me feel we were going a little more even with one another.

Whatever he was going to say, it died on his tongue. Instead, he leaned down and kissed me again. I wound my arms around his lean figure and pulled him tight against me, the heat from beneath his fur bleeding into mine. He gave that soft sound again, breathless, not quite a whine, but just as vulnerable.

It probably wasn't wise for us to renew our affections from last night in the middle of the day, with my family just feet above us. But where Finnegan was concerned, caution had not been my guiding principle.

I sat with my father for much of the afternoon, while the women prepared the midday meal. For a while we simply talked about the tribe, of family matters, catching me up on what I'd missed in the month I'd been away from home. It was all familiar trials and tribulations and a bit of expected gossip, comfortingly domestic and mild. Other than, of course, the incursion of the Otherwolf settlers, which hung over our tribe like a dark cloud.

Everyone knew of it. It was impossible not to, with how quickly they were seizing land and clearing-cutting the forests. But my father hadn't told them all the details, just yet. How much more they planned to take and what it would mean for our future here. Or our lack of one.

I understood not wanting to incite a panic when he'd been chasing a solution. But even he admitted to me that at this point, it was a losing race. The outcome was inevitable.

"*You need to tell them all,*" I said, keeping my voice low. My sisters were sitting nearby weaving and Alasie was playing with Odina's little girl and, of all people, Finn. Children found it so easy to forgive, and even as surly at him as she had been earlier, she was still curious about the strange wolf in our home.

Sawyer was nearby too, chatting with some of our hunters while keeping an occasional eye on his sister. He was playing coolly disinterested, but he was clearly far more intrigued by what Finnegan was doing than whatever conversation he was having with the two hunters from my village. It seemed to involve Finn's hat, two upturned bowls and a colorful rock he'd hidden at some point beneath one of them. The trick, however he was accomplishing it, was enthralling the girls. Even my older sisters were looking on, chiming in on which object the rock must have been under.

I was apparently distracted by the strangely charming scene too, because my father had responded to me and I'd missed it.

"—can't uproot everything we have here while the river's frozen anyway, let alone on such short notice. I've put out word to some of the nearest tribes that might have us, but…Tulimak." He tapped my shoulder with his palm, looking up at me critically. "I am not going to speak to you on tribal matters I haven't even shared with the other elders if you're not going to listen."

"I'm sorry," I said quickly, looking back down at him. "But it's not as though I pulled this from you, otterfa. I discovered much of it myself."

"Yes, you've become very worldly," he admitted, begrudgingly. Then, with an arched eyebrow, "More so than I think is wise. Especially in so short a time. I had no inkling when I sent you east that you'd become so embroiled in the matters of Otherwolves. Let alone return with one."

"It hadn't been my plan either," I confessed. I chanced a glance back over at Alasie, knitting my fingers together worriedly. She must not have had time to tell him, yet. *"But,"* I hesitantly spoke again before my father could, *"it hasn't been all bad. I feel as though my eyes have been opened. To a great many things."*

"I'm certain they have," he said. "But you're young yet, son. This is all too fast, I feel—"

"I'm a man now, otterfa," I tried to sound assuring as I said it, but it probably came off sounding a bit petulant. He didn't look pleased that I'd cut him off, either.

"A man allows his elders to finish their statement," he said pointedly. When I went silent following that, he nodded. Then scrunched up his nose, shaking out his whiskers. *"Mmhh. You even smell like a foreigner, now. What is that?"*

I bristled. He couldn't...we had been *so* thorough washing up this morning.

"Smells like one of their colognes," he used the Otherwolf word for it, since the closest thing we really had as an equivalent would have been fur oil, or incense.

"Oh," I said, realization dawning. *"Finnegan's soap. It's got a strong scent to it. I-I like it."* That bit was a half-truth, of course. I actually did like whatever scent it was, but it was because I associated it with Finn now, subconsciously. *"You said yourself,"* I forced a huff of a laugh, cringing at how terrible I was at bluffing, *"how awful we smelled yesterday. I thought I'd try it."*

He gave me a long look. I knew he saw through me, but he also didn't seem to register anything beyond the fact that I was acting strange.

A peel of laughter from one of my older sisters interrupted the moment. Both my father and I looked over in time to find that one of them had apparently guessed correctly, this time around. Finnegan revealed the rock beneath one of the bowls and scooped it up, bowing and offering it to her with a flourish. They both laughed and Alasie stood and pulled at his ragged coat, imploring him to do it again.

"I'll get it this time," she said determinedly, balancing Odina's little girl on her hip. The little mountain lioness, I couldn't help but notice, was wearing a bow made of green ribbon today. She also reached for Finnegan, but for his tail. Which to his credit, he allowed.

"*Quite the charmer*," my father said wryly.

I cleared my throat. "*He certainly is.*"

"That game he's playing with the girls is one of their grifts," he informed me, tone cynical. "The wolf's a Confidence Man, Tulimak. I warned you about them."

"You saw his papers," I said pointedly. "Finnegan wasn't entirely on the level with me when we first met. I told you that. But the papers—he has so many of them, dad. They look official. Even Odina thought so. They have to be real."

He gave a long sigh. "I'm sorry, Tulimak. Truly. I am trying to give your new friend the benefit of the doubt. You know, I've always said we need to try to foster relationships with the settlers. I still believe that whole-heartedly, even given what's happened recently. They are just men and women, like us. But there are so many of them. We have to find a way to co-exist, or they will swallow us whole. But that doesn't mean I trust them. And I fear I've opened the doors to their world and thrust you into it before teaching you enough about trust to truly prepare you."

"Their world is invading ours whether we're ready for it or not, otterfa," I said quietly. "Better to have allies that will help us understand it."

"Also something I taught you," he agreed, smiling ruefully. "Spirits, what have I done?"

"*It's been difficult*," I said, looking out towards where Finnegan was entertaining my family, and Odina's. "*Very difficult. But I've learned…a lot. And I wouldn't take it back.*"

"It's natural for a father to worry, when his child's been hurt," he reminded me with a palm softly resting over my healing wound. "I know you must find my attitude a bit severe, but you'll understand some day when you have children of your own you want to protect."

"Does that mean you're sending him away with Odina?" I asked, making direct eye contact with him.

"You look at me now when we speak," he noted quietly. "You certainly **are** growing into a man, Tulimak."

"You didn't answer—"

"I'm still uncertain," he sighed. "I agreed to speak with Odina at length about it today, but she has yet to return from the Otherwolf town."

"Is that why her children are here and she isn't?" I asked. I'd noted it earlier, but I'd assumed she was off somewhere in town, or back at their camp.

He nodded. "She's been gone since dawn, apparently. She opted to leave her children here, which I cannot blame her for, given how corrupting that place can be. And potentially dangerous, especially for her young one."

"Did she say why she was leaving?"

"Gunpowder, other supplies, I'd wager," he shrugged. "To be honest, that woman has always been a mystery, even to me. Some of those who have suffered great loss construct an inner sanctum around their thoughts and true character. I've known her for nearly your entire life and I can't say I know her well. Even before her tribe fell apart."

"I know even less about her," I said. "Save that she hunted us for nearly a week and shot me." I wanted to remind him that it had been her, not Finn, who'd done that.

"Her tribe were hunters, you know that much," he waved a hand, dismissively. "Back before the Otherwolves came up here hunting for beaver and shot most of the caribou, drove the herds further up north. She was a tribal woman like any other once, married to a hunter. I remember trading with him. Their tribe disappeared for a few years when there were a lot of skirmishes happening between those of us that were more…aggressive about defending our lands, and the Otherwolves. Her tribe chose war, not co-existence." He looked to me. "The next time I saw her, only the women and children came to trade with us. She was pregnant at the time, I assume with Sawyer. Her husband had died by then…" He looked off towards my sisters. "I don't know when she re-married, or even if she did, but she took up with a lone lion, a trapper, a few years back. I don't know what happened to him, but he must have been Nuka's father."

Two mates, gone? I'd had sympathy over the years for people who'd lost wives and husbands, of course. But it wasn't until now that I'd known how it felt to have someone even remotely like that in your life. To think of having that, losing it, then rediscovering it, only to lose it again?

"When she started coming to trade with us again a few years ago," he continued, "she was alone save for her children. And that's when she began hunting men. The coin must be better than any living she could eke out off of the few beaver left in this area, or I doubt she'd risk it."

"Especially with two children," I agreed. "And Sawyer's young, younger than he looks, even. I wonder how long he's been helping her on her bounty hunts."

"Dangerous," my father said softly. "I wouldn't want that life for my children. But I don't judge, and you shouldn't either. Many of the tribes we once knew are in desperate straits these days, scattered or gone completely. She is trying to feed her children."

"You'd be much less forgiving if you'd lost me," I said.

He gave an affirmative hum. "*But that didn't happen.*"

"*Finnegan kept me moving,*" I said, the wolfdog's eyes catching mine for a moment from across the camp. He winked at me, smiling. "*He encouraged me to eat,*" I stared back down into my lap, "*did most of the rowing, insisted we go into town even though it was more dangerous for him personally, so I could get my wound treated...*"

"You are **really** trying to sell me on this Otherwolf," my father remarked. "I never expected my shyest child to bond so quickly with a foreigner. Although I suppose you've been traveling together for quite some time, now. It's remarkable to see the change in you, Tulimak." He reached over gingerly touched my injured shoulder. "And you've earned guardian markings. We'll need to send word to the wolverine tribe in the mountains, I don't know the traditions for warrior scarring well."

I smiled. "I thought maybe, but I wasn't sure. You really think I've earned that?"

"You protected kin," he nodded sagely. "Even if he is a foreigner...he is clearly kin to you, now. You shed blood for him."

"Could," I paused, "could he be kin to the tribe?"

He looked less certain at that. "I would want to know him far better," he said. "And obviously we'll need to get these matters of his with the law settled. Oh no—" he paused mid-sentence, staring past me.

I looked past him to where my two older sisters had effectively cornered Finn. He was standing near one of the communal longhouses, back to the outside wall, and my sisters were boxing him in. I couldn't imagine what it was they were asking him, but they were both talking at him incessantly. He didn't seem uncomfortable exactly, but he was glancing my way occasionally, wordlessly looking for a way out.

I stood and made my way over, clearing my throat as I approached. Kirima glanced back at me, then raised her voice, "Good, brother Tulimak must agree with me! Tulimak, is it not strange for a man of thirty years to remain unmarried?"

"How…?" I gave an exasperated noise. "Why are you bothering our guest about this?"

"Otherwolf mates," she explained, her accent a little thicker than mine, "wear a band around their finger, when they are married! It is true—"

"It is," Nujua nodded emphatically, chiming in.

"Made of gold," Kirima continued, "that is why they want all the gold, you see! They all need it, by tradition, to marry."

"It isn't *always* gold," Finnegan reasoned.

"No, no!" she insisted, talking with her hands. "It is always gold! I have been told this."

"Kirima," I sighed, "the man probably knows his own culture better than you do."

"But, no ring!" she gestured at him. "You see? No ring. So, I asked."

"He has *never* married!" Nujua pronounced, amused. "No pups, either."

"No children!" Kirima laughed. "What a carefree life this man has!"

I stared over their heads at Finnegan while the two of them prattled on. He gave me a hapless look that begged for help and honestly, for a moment I considered just leaving my sisters to it. Fitting revenge for his misdeeds.

But I wasn't that cruel.

"He's a soldier, of a sort," I explained to them. "A warrior, amongst his people. He doesn't want to leave a widow."

That seemed to surprise and intrigue the two of them. They both stopped speaking for a few moments, taking stock of him. After a brief silence spent carefully scrutinizing him, Nujua said, "He is *small* for a wolf warrior."

"How many wolf warriors have you met?" Kirima teased, laughing.

"He would be bigger if he took a wife!" Nujua cackled, her Amurescan falling into disarray, and soon the two of them had switched entirely back to our language between laughter. "*I would feed my wolf husband, I would feed him so well!*"

"A well-fattened wolf husband! Just as you've always dreamed, Nujua."

Finnegan ducked away from my two sisters just in the nick of time, as they launched into another tear about how he would look with a "big, proper otter belly," or some such nonsense. Honestly, I was grinning ear to ear as we left, leaning down to murmur, "I think they like you."

"Oh no, you think?" he snarked. "Thought I'd never escape. I finally see where you get it from. Absolutely no one in your family is *subtle*, Tulimak."

"Your fault for charming them with your 'magic,'" I smirked.

"The cup and ball game?" He snorted. "Lord, that's just a parlor tri—"

We both saw her at the same time. Odina was standing at the edge of the village circle, my father quickly crossing the clearing towards her. It was enough that she was back, but that wasn't all. At a glance, it was immediately apparent that something was very wrong.

The lioness, who despite her age looked to be of a strong build, was clearly winded and dirty. She was covered in mud up to her knees, suggesting she'd traveled through the marshes, not along the roads, for whatever reason. And she was leaning slightly against one of our fish racks, speaking quietly to my father when he arrived, between labored breaths.

"Something's happened," Finn said darkly.

We all gathered in the pit home where my father held meetings, once more. Sawyer and Nuka waited outside, but I'd seen Odina speak lowly to him for a moment before she climbed down the ladder, and he looked worried. Which worried me.

I was the last to start my descent down the ladder when my father called out to me, "Tulimak, perhaps you should wait outside—"

"With the children?" I finished for him, taking the last two steps. Everyone turned to look up at me, my father doing so sternly. "With all due respect, otterfa," I said, "I've been part of this all this time, I'm an adult, and Finnegan is my friend. I want to know what's going on."

There was a long, awkward pause during which everyone waited on my father's word. At length though, it was Odina who spoke. "Your bearchild is right, Takoda. Let him listen."

Before my father could interject, she continued, "The Jackwalds are here for Ambrose. In town. There are nearly a dozen of them, an entire posse. Word is it's the same group that settled the Miners Union dispute in East Wythe."

I looked around the room and found a look of confusion similar to my own from Finnegan, but my father…he seemed to recognize what Odina was speaking of and had slowly hung his head, the dim lighting in the room resting in the pits of his eye sockets, making him look ten years older.

"Otterfa?" I asked quietly.

"Are you sure?" he asked Odina.

She nodded. "It was hard to miss them. I think it's likely they actually beat us here. They all have good trail horses, and a guide besides. A coyote tribesman. Another hunter, no doubt, who knows the area better. Although if they're the ones from East Wythe…"

"They're already well-acquainted with this region," my father said grimly.

"The foxes," I said suddenly, all eyes turning to me. I looked down at Finnegan, "When I first met you, those two foxes mentioned 'The Jackwalds.' They thought I was one of them. It feels like a lifetime ago, I'd nearly forgotten.'

"The Jackwald Detective Agency," Odina said, bile in her voice. It was odd to hear her get emotional about anything, but the disdain was evident even in her normally placid tone. "They're a militia. Privately-owned, privately-funded. They have nothing to do with the actual Otherwolf law in these parts, or anywhere. But there are rumors they actually outnumber the Army." She slid her gaze over to Finnegan. "Your bounty's reeled in some dangerous folk, Ambrose."

"How did they find him?" I asked the obvious question. "How did they know to come *here?*"

"If I hadn't caught up to you in Broen, this is exactly where I would have come," Odina said flatly. "There aren't any other settlements for miles and this isn't the kind of country an Amurescan just *roughs* it in. They likely don't know you're here, in this village, yet. But once they've scoured the town, this is the next place they'll check. There's already talk you were traveling with a tribal 'guide,' Ambrose. You're noticeable, bearchild. And known. There aren't many bears in this region at all any more, let alone white-furred bears."

I grit my teeth. I know she hadn't meant to, but it was hard to interpret her statement as anything but "this is your fault." Simply for existing, for being different, I had once again inconvenienced the people I cared about.

"You know, we might have made it here without attracting so much attention if not for *you*!" Finnegan finally spoke up, real anger in his tone.

"And none of these people would have been put in danger at all if you weren't a murderer," she replied, matter-of-factly.

"No, you know what—" he growled, but I put a hand on his shoulder, trying to calm him down. "No—stop, Tulimak—she doesn't get to blame *you* for any of this," he snarled, stabbing a finger in her direction. "We weren't even going to stop in Broen, except that you shot at us! And you're the one who fired on us in the street! You think that might have attracted some fucking attention?!"

"Enough!" My father put his hands out, stepping between the two of them. Despite the calm stance he was trying to take, I knew him better than anyone else here. He looked rattled. Scared, even.

"I'm sorry, but there won't be time to discuss this at length, Takoda," Odina said. "Not as you had planned. You must make your decision swiftly. Now. It was hard enough for me to confirm the Jackwalds' numbers at the tavern they were occupying without being noticed, and I cut across the flood plains to get here as swiftly as possible. Even now, my son is packing up our camp. This man," she turned her gaze back to Finnegan, who was staring daggers through her, "cannot be here amongst your people when they come here looking for him. Earnestly, the sooner we leave, the better for your tribe. I can cover our tracks between here and my camp, so it does not seem that you were harboring him. You know how these men are..."

"I don't," I spoke up.

My father looked to me, then dropped his head again. That was a very, very bad sign. My father was not the sort to bow his head unless speaking of those who had passed. "There was a mining town," he said, "southeast from here, called 'East Wythe.' It was an Otherwolf community, but I knew some tribal refugees who had taken jobs there. The man who ran the place, their 'chief,' although they have a different name for it...he was a gold miner who came here and made a fortune some years ago. He bought up most of the mines in the area and paid his workers very little. Since they could go nowhere else to ply their trade..."

"Why doesn't it surprise me that that's happening here too, now?" Finnegan said bitterly. "God, wealth is like a disease. It eats people up from the inside out, and the only thing that cures it is *death*."

My father sighed. "Some of the mining communities banded together to form a tribe, of a sort. They called it a 'union.' As many voices, they hoped to improve their lives, to force the man who owned these mines to pay them a wage they could live on more easily. Instead of negotiating with them…this man hired the Jackwalds."

"They came to put a stop to this 'union,'" Odina said. "Through force. I wasn't there, but the way I understand it, these people weren't armed. Just…brave. And stubborn. And they died for it."

"Not just them," my father said softly. "I wasn't there either, but I met a man who was. A tribesman who'd lost his family. The Jackwalds didn't just kill those that resisted. They gunned down everyone in the mining town. Every single soul they could find. The women, the children, the old and infirm. Everyone. Very few escaped."

"Why?" I asked, horrified.

"To set an example to the other mines," Odina said.

"I don't understand how a heavily-armed…army, by the sound of it," Finnegan spoke up, "could exist in a civilized country. How is it your law hasn't put a stop to these people?"

"They work within the bounds of the Otherwolf laws," Odina said. "Legal bounties, protection, private jobs. The people killed in East Wythe were causing civil unrest, and I'm sure they spun a good tale of self-defense to any Marshall unfortunate enough to be this far north. Besides…none of them were citizens. They were all tribespeople and immigrants."

Conversation died at that. My father looked more helpless than I'd ever seen him, and Finn had gone disturbingly silent. I knew that intense set to his jaw, the way his eyes got fixed on a point in space that wasn't there, the stiffness in his shoulders. He was about to do something dangerous.

"My back is against the wall," my father said breathlessly. "I hardly know—"

"Don't torture yourself," Finnegan spoke, lowly. "I'm leaving."

"Finn, no—"

"I've been thinking about all of this a lot since yesterday," he went on. "And honestly? I probably would have, anyway. Odina, this bounty...you said it's a lot more if you bring me all the way south, right?"

She nodded. "I've a feeling I know what you plan to ask. And yes. If it means you'll cooperate, we can see to it your documents make it where they need to in Arbordale. It will simply be a matter of doing so *before* I turn you in."

I opened and closed my mouth, no words coming. It's like I was watching a terrible disaster from a mountain-top, the inevitability of it all right before me, but powerless to stop it.

"Then we have an accord," he said, offering her a hand. "I'll come with you willingly."

Before the two of them could shake, I grabbed his arm. "Like hell!" I bellowed.

"Tulimak!" My father similarly raised his voice, but in a much more restrained way. Although no less effective. He stepped in closer and bodily put space between Finnegan and I, lowering his voice once he was in close. "This is out of our hands, now."

"Gather your things," Odina said to Finn as she began to climb the ladder out. "We're leaving as soon as possible. They have horses, we need to put as much distance between us now, while we can."

"I'll send you with ponies," my father offered.

She shook her head before ascending the two final rungs. "Faster if we take some of the trails I know. Ponies will only hold us back."

"As you wish," my father said.

"Is anyone going to listen to me?!" I demanded, looking between my father and Finnegan. "Dad, there *has* to be another way! Even if they outrun these men somehow, she is walking him to his *death*!"

"Your friend has made a choice, and we must honor him for it," my father said, speaking fiercely but quickly. "Would you bring down these men's wrath on your family, Tulimak?"

"No, obviously," I strained for anything, any other alternative I could come up with. "But we could—there must be something else..."

I looked to Finnegan. He only dropped his muzzle, wilting under my gaze.

I felt like my world was falling apart. Just minutes ago, we'd been sitting with my family, laughing. Just this morning, I'd been with him, worried about what the future would bring, but trying to focus on enjoying the present. And now, all of a sudden, the worst was here. Now.

The paths before me shrunk, trails I'd thought I might take washing away. Everything narrowed down to this moment, where my options had all at once come down to two branches. Only two possibilities.

At every other point in my life when I had been faced with even a minorly difficult decision, I would have sat in agony, indecisive. But this time? I made up my mind all at once, faster than I ever had before.

"I will make sure you're well-provisioned—" my father was saying.

"I'm going with him," I said, prompting both of them to turn my way.

My father all but immediately rejected my decision. "Absolutely not," he growled out.

I set my jaw. "I'm not your bearchild any more, otterfa. I'm a man, I can make my own decisions, and *I am going*."

Past him, I thought I saw Finnegan looking at me with a slight hint of hope in his eyes. But my father was past frustrated now, he was angry. He took up most of my field of vision despite his slighter stature. "You will *always* be my child!" He was actually raising his voice now, a true rarity. "And I am not just your father, I am your *Chieftain*. I am telling you, if you embroil yourself further in these foreign troubles, you are going against your tribe! Against your *family*! Stop being selfish and think of what this will do to me, to your sisters, to your brothers. Imagine how much we will suffer if we lose you! Imagine how hurt and lost we will forever feel, if you do not return to us, and we've no body to give back to the river."

It wasn't that his words didn't affect me. I felt them in my chest, tightening like claws around my heart. I knew very well how it felt to lose a family member you could not bury at the water's edge. And he knew that. It was written all over his features, the pain still evident in the graying fur and the glossiness in his dark brown eyes. I'd watched him grieve for my mother. And now I was asking him to give up a son, over something I still hadn't even had the courage to explain to him.

"I'm sorry, otterfa," I said softly. "I…have to do this."

His tone fell to one more pleading. "*What has this man promised you?*" *he* demanded, looking accusingly at Finn. We'd bled into using our own language midway through our argument, so he looked lost, but very worried. *"Is it something about the land?"* My father pressed. *"Has he said he's going to do something for you in this southern city, to help our tribe? Son, he can't do that. He's a criminal. Just because he's one of them—"*

"He hasn't made me any promises," I said honestly. "But yes, that's one of the reasons I want to go. This city, Arbordale, is the only place I might be able to fight for our tribe. And I want to fight for Finn's cause, too."

"You aren't a warrior!" my father insisted. "You're a fisherman, Tulimak. You don't need to go to war for your tribe, we will find another way! We **always** find another way! This instinct in you, this urge to fight, it is what destroyed your tribe. I thought, I had hoped, you were different. You've always been so gentle..."

He reached for me, but I took a step back, pushing his hand aside. I stared into his eyes, unable to speak for a time. When I did, my voice came out breathless.

"You found me in the river," I said.

He went still.

"You found me in the **river**," I said again. "How do you know what befell my tribe?"

Chapter 13

New Moon Basin

I jumped down into my pit home, foregoing the ladder. It was a deep drop, just about my height, but I was angry and I wanted to feel the impact of my paws on the packed earth. The walls shuddered and some of the dirt from the roof shook loose, the remaining embers in my fire snuffing out from the sudden displacement of air. I felt rather than saw Finnegan wince, above me.

It wasn't enough. Nothing would be enough, right now.

"Tulimak," he called down, concerned.

"Is your bag packed?" I asked, my voice a growl that barely exited my muzzle.

"It's not as if I own much," he sighed, taking the steps down the ladder and dropping down beside me. "Let me just fold the clothes your sisters washed for me."

I began moving about my small home, grabbing up my clothing, belongings and food haphazardly. I hardly cared how I packed them, I just began stuffing it all into my travel bag. I could worry about unpacking and sorting later.

"Whoa, calm down there," I felt Finnegan's hand settle over my arm, fingertips gingerly wrapping around my bicep. Unthinkingly, I shoved his arm away. I immediately regretted the careless gesture, especially when the unintentional force of it knocked him off-balance and he stumbled back, nearly into the ladder.

I gasped, immediately turning around, my muzzle in my paw. "I-I'm so s—"

Finnegan recovered after only a brief waver on his feet, shaking his head. "Forget it. I'm fine."

"I didn't mean..." I squeezed my eyes shut, gritting my teeth. "I'm so sorry. I-I'm just..."

"Angry," the wolfdog replied. I still had my eyes closed, but I felt him crossing the space between us again. This time when he reached out for me, he closed his hands around my wrists slowly and hesitantly, dragging my paws away from my face so that he could look at me. "I know," he said. "I understand anger. Trust me."

"Someone like me can't," I swallowed, "*get* angry."

"It's not your fault you're big, Tuli," he said softly. "I said I'm fine, didn't I? Hey. Hey? Look at me."

I blinked my eyes open, looking down into his. "He's been," I snuffed, "lying to me. My *whole life*."

He sighed out through his nose. "He must have a reason..."

"How can I judge that for myself," I demanded, "when he won't *tell* me?!"

"I can't give you those answers," he said. "But I'm here for you. All right? Whatever this is, we'll figure it out. Right now, you need to try to calm down. We don't have long, and trust me, you don't want to leave here angry at your family, or say something careless you can't take back."

I was shaking. "I don't know *what* to say to that man right now," I grated out. "And I *am* angry. I don't know how to not...*be angry*. Why does it matter what I say to him now? He won't talk to *me* about what's most important."

"Tuli, I don't need to explain the danger we're in here," he said quietly. "You knew that when you decided to come with us. You've been shot once already. You *know* what could happen to us out there. I know you understand the importance of leaving here with a clean conscience and the right kinds of memories with your family."

That got me to look down at him again. His eyes had never left my face the whole time he'd been talking to me. I lifted one of my damnably big paws up to his cheek. "You're not fighting me on coming with you," I said.

He shook his head, giving a slim, rueful smile. "I guess I'm selfish like that. I know I couldn't stop you if it's what you really wanted, and anyway...I want you with me." He paused. "But I hope I'm not the only reason you're coming."

"You're always so smooth," I said between sniffs, my nose embarrassingly wet.

He chuckled. "Well...yeah..."

"No, I really do want to look into how we can avoid this land grab," I insisted. "Father's clearly already given up. Just rolling with the waves, like he always does. I'm sure he can find...somewhere...for us to settle. But that's giving up our ancestral lands to these men who've taken advantage of him. Taken advantage of *us*."

"Yeah, fuck that," he agreed. "Cockers," he gave a bitter "tch" through his teeth. "I promise I'll try to help you figure out the legal bits. As well as I can, anyway. I'm hardly a legal *scholar*, mind you, especially in this country. But I'm a canine and that might be all it'll take to open a few doors. We'll do all of that first. All right?"

"I don't want to talk about turning you over," I muttered. "Spirits. How can so many terrible things happen all at once?"

"That's usually how it is," he said. "Tough times bring more and more hardship, just by their very nature. Shite like this causes you to rush, to get desperate, to make mistakes, forces truths out of people."

"Or not," I said bitterly.

"Give him until you're at the town edge," he reasoned. "Trust me, all right? Just seem like the reasonable one and give him nothing but silence, force it out of him. People, when they're tense, when they're feeling scrutinized, tend to want to fill silence. Then they talk too much. Usually give you just about everything you wanted. Sometimes more."

"Your insight is scary sometimes," I said, my voice still rough.

He chuckled. "You love it."

"I *am* scared," I admitted for the first time in the flurry of the last hour, "about leaving home. I mean, really leaving home. This isn't just down-river. Even my father has never been to Arbordale. It's going to be overwhelming, traveling so far from everything and everyone I know."

"Not to mention all the gunmen on our tail," Finnegan reminded me.

"None of them have anything on you," I said, brushing the edge of his ear with the back of my claws.

"I like your confidence in my abilities," he said. "And that we've gotten to the point where you can see the utility in it. But there are a *lot* of them, Tulimak. And I highly doubt they'll be civil enough to duel me one at a time."

"We have Odina, and each other," I leaned down and rested my far larger forehead against the top of his. "I trust your confidence more than my own. You aren't telling me to stay. That means we must have a chance."

"I hope so," he said quietly.

I tried to stoop lower to kiss him, but from this angle I wasn't entirely sure how to. Every time we'd kissed in the past, we'd been sitting. This was a first. I craned my neck down, trying to tilt my head the right way. He smirked against my cheek and wrapped his arms up around my shoulders. Then all at once, coming so naturally that I hardly questioned it, he leaped up and I grabbed him around the waist and beneath the knees, dragging him up against me so we were eye level with one another. He got that overly-pleased-with-himself smile and I kissed it off of him, his body warm in my arms.

When he lazily pulled back, he took a brief glance downwards at the ground below him, his tail swishing about over my forearm. "Is this even hard for you?" he asked, amused.

"Not really," I admitted, shyly.

"Speaking of 'utility,'" he grinned, "I can think of quite a few things we could employ your ridiculous arm strength for."

"Are you ever serious?" I asked, dryly. "Now's really not the time for levity."

"I am being seri—oh my *God*," he gaped over my shoulder. "Put me down, put me down."

I dropped him to his feet, my heart jumping in my chest. Had one of my family come down the ladder? But when I turned, he was just heading over to one of my dug-in shelves, where some of my older possessions were stored.

"I didn't notice this last night," he said in wonderment, gingerly reaching into the nook and pulling something out to inspect it. When I saw what he held, I was hit with a wave of memories so suddenly it nearly knocked me off my feet.

Finnegan cradled the little woolen toy in his palms, turning it over once to inspect the bead eyes and the sewn in nose and mouth. A delighted noise bubbled up out of his throat. "Oh my God, it's a bear. Isn't it? It's a little bear!"

"That's…my little brother," I said quietly, knitting my hands in front of me.

He turned to look at me like I was a yawning newborn cub.

"I mean, not actually," I said awkwardly. "Obviously. But, when I was little, all of the other children in town had siblings or relatives that looked like them. I…obviously…didn't. So my parents gave me that, so I'd feel less alone." I walked over to him, laying a hand, (now larger than the toy itself) on its worn, but still soft head. "My mother made it for me."

Finnegan's expression sobered at that. After a further moment, he went to place it back on the shelf, carefully.

"She knew," I said after a solemn space had passed between us. "Dad knew. She must have known, too. They didn't keep secrets from one another. They both must have known about my real tribe, whoever they were, from the beginning. They were both lying to me about how I came into their lives." I hung my head. "But then, I thought dad didn't keep secrets from me, either. So maybe she was just as in the dark as I was."

I felt Finnegan slide his hand into mine. "Tuli?" he said. "I've only known your father a day, but—and I'm going out on a limb here, I'll admit—I really think he wants what's best for you. He seems to truly love you. I mean, that's just a surface read, but," he shrugged slowly.

"I know he does," I admitted quietly. "I don't doubt that."

"That being said," he sighed. "Love can manifest in a lot of different ways. Not all of them good. Just because you love someone doesn't mean you won't make mistakes in the way you treat them. Your father's fallible. The way you talked about him before all of this, I think you might have idolized him a bit. Part of hitting adulthood is seeing the shine come off the people you look up to. Hit me a little bit earlier, but I went through something similar with my mother."

I ground my teeth together inside my muzzle, then slowly let out a long breath. "Well he has less than an hour to make it right," I said. "Then we leave. Let's get finished packing."

As we stepped out of my pit home and covered the flap back over with its caribou hide, I produced something I'd been holding beneath my cloak, offering it to Finnegan. I'd dug it out of my previous travel bag, which I'd swapped this time for a larger one.

He looked over the pistol for only a moment before taking it and pushing his jacket aside, re-holstering it.

"You kept wearing your hip holster," I noted.

"I had a feeling you'd return it to me," he admitted. "This thing takes a few minutes to strap on. Sometimes you don't have the time. Better to be ready. Thank you for trusting me enough to return it to me in your village, though."

"It makes a statement," I rumbled.

"To your father?" he guessed, uncertainly.

"To Odina," I corrected him. "She's still planning on turning you in, Finn."

"That's the agreement," he nodded. When I began to open my mouth again, he held up his hands. "Look, it's a long way off and we have other problems right now. We can hash that out another time, all right?"

I looked past him, taking stock of the tribespeople I could see dotting the village, peering out of the communal longhouses or poking their heads up out of other pit homes. We seemed to be the center of attention, unsurprisingly. By now, news of what was happening had likely spread all around our little community. I'm sure very few yet understood the implications of the situation. My family, perhaps. Most of them simply watched us as we walked towards the main gathering area, where a distant crowd of figures waited. I could hear arguing, but not make out voices yet.

One of my uncles, leaning against a longhouse with a pipe in his mouth, called out to me in Nontawlik, our language, *"Tulimak! Good luck to you on your travels. We're sorry to see you leave again so soon."*

I managed a smile in his direction. *"Thank you,"* I said earnestly.

"Whatever these matters of yours in the Otherwolf world," he inclined his head towards Finn, "settle them and return as swiftly as you can. For your father's sake. And for the tribe. You will be missed here." He gave me a whiskery smile, and mine grew.

"Thank you, uncle," I said, my throat hoarse. As we walked the remaining distance into the center of town, it really began to set in. These people, this place that had taken me in and treated me as one of their own...I might never see any of them again. And that wouldn't be hardest on *me*. When someone died, the suffering they left behind fell on the shoulders of those that loved them, that relied on them, still in the living world. I knew that first-hand.

It's not as though life for me in this tribe had ever been perfect. I'd felt lonely, cumbersome and out-of-place my whole life, and some of the otters here hadn't been as kind about my presence as my close family had been. But we'd adapted and grown, together. I'd carved out a niche here, found a place within these people so different from me. And over time, I'd become valued. Not just in spite of, but sometimes *because* of our differences.

A too-small pile of split logs attested to that. I saw it out of the corner of my eye as we entered the main circle. Everyone in the tribe took on what we called "village work," like maintaining homes and fish racks, or getting water. My task, since I'd grown taller and stronger than any of the otters in the tribe, had always been to cut wood for the communal fires. In my absence, the pile had dwindled significantly.

Considering something for a moment, I leaned down near the wood stack and wrapped my hand around one of the axe handles, tugging it up out of the stump it had been resting in. Someone must have been cutting wood earlier this morning.

I lifted the tool, so familiar in my palm. Never before in my life would I have balked at holding an axe, never would I have felt any sense of trepidation. But as I slowly pushed the handle down into my belt, stowing it, a pall of uncertainty fell over my heart.

This axe was no longer a tool. As of this moment, it had become a weapon.

I was still processing that when my father's voice cut through the cooling afternoon air, my chest tightening at the sound. He was behind us, I knew the rhythm of his footsteps, and he wasn't alone.

"*Tulimak,*" he called out, a twinge of desperation in his tone. I stopped in my tracks and hung my head.

Finnegan leaned his muzzle up, speaking lowly. "Remember what I said, all right? Don't turn this into an argument. Just talk matter-of-factly. And say goodbye, no matter what."

I turned slowly, taking in the sight of…my entire family, as it happened. My father, my brothers, my sisters, even Alasie. He'd brought all of them and they were each carrying bundles in their arms.

"This isn't," he said in a staggered breath, "some last ploy to stop you. You've made your intentions very clear, and I-I…"

His words died at that and he looked to me imploringly, perhaps hoping I'd break and change my mind. Or just say something to assure him. I had to force myself to keep my muzzle shut, my guts twisted into knots. There was a pain in my stomach that I knew I'd be feeling for days.

"*We gathered some essentials for you,*" he said at length. He and my brothers and sisters all set down a bundle. They looked like foodstuffs, medicine, furs…even my littlest sister had wrapped up what seemed to be a very large, frozen fish for us. I couldn't help but smile at her.

She was the first to break away from my family and run up to me. I kneeled and brought her into my arms, hugging her tight to my chest. "*Stupid bear,*" she hiccupped against me. "*You shouldn't travel in winter. Mom always said. You're going to lose toes.*"

The rest of my family soon joined her, gathering around me. Only my father hung back, while I hugged each and every one of my siblings. My brothers wished me good fortune and that the spirits be at my back, my sisters told me to keep my wits about me.

My father eventually stepped closer. I looked up at him since I was still kneeling, biting my tongue inside my muzzle. He was usually such a collected man, but right now, his expression was all pain and fear. It reminded me of how he'd looked while mom was sick.

I had to say something, anything, to assure him.

"I'll return, otterfa," I promised.

"You cannot know that," he said. "You cannot. Tulimak, your place is here. It has always been here."

"That's why I have to protect it," I said, heeding Finnegan's words and stating my position as simply as possible. "I can do something for our tribe that will really matter, otterfa. I have to try."

"You don't know that there is anything you can do!" He raised his voice. "You have no reason to believe that, Tulimak. No experience that says this is a task you are suited for! You're abandoning your tribe on a whim—"

I stood, slowly. "*Goodbye, dad.*"

"No. Please. I promise, I am not going to force you to stay," he insisted. "You're a man and you can travel the world as you please, but Tulimak, I want you to feel the weight of this choice—"

"*I do,*" I said, looking down at my siblings and stroking Alasie's head once more before parting from them. "*I'm sorry, dad. I have to do this. Please respect my choice, regardless how it turns out.*"

He took a step back, staggering like the wind had been punched out of him.

I looked over the parcels my family had offered, sighing. "I don't have any more room in my bag," I said. "I don't know if I can bring much of this."

I turned to look towards where at the other gathering, a second drama was playing out. Odina was in a pitched argument with Sawyer. Truth be told, Sawyer was the only one making a scene. Odina was speaking to him calm and low-voiced, as ever. I could take a guess at what they were discussing.

My intention was to head over their way when their argument finished and ask if she could help us carry supplies, but my father must have taken it as my parting from him, completely. Because the moment I turned around, he cried out, "*Tulimak, please! Not like this.*"

I craned my neck back around to look at him, brow lifting.

"Not like this," he repeated, softer. "Your mother and I never…there was so much I wanted to say to her…"

I turned to face him completely, remaining silent, but looking towards him openly.

He slowly released a held breath. "*Please do not leave here angry with your family,*" he pleaded.

I swallowed, shaking my head slowly. "I love you, dad," I said. "The fact that I'm upset with you right now doesn't change that."

"I took an oath," he said, voice wavering. "I swore to them, it was the only way they would entrust you to me. They would have killed you otherwise, son."

"*What?*" I breathed.

His gaze fell. He looked so much older in that moment, the shadows settling into the lines on his face, the waning sun catching all the grey in his muzzle. "*There is a place,*" he said at length, "*far to the south of here. A basin in the earth, created long ago when the sky rained stone.*" He looked up to me. "*It is where you are from. Where your tribes…both of them…once dwelled.*"

"I've heard the stories," I said. "The trappers don't go there."

He nodded. "Those lands are not safe for anyone, Tribesman or Otherwolf. The spirits there are restless, angry, from all the blood spilled on their soil. The feral beasts have overtaken the forests. As, perhaps, they rightly should. In the struggle to retain our place there, the tribes lost everything. The Otherwolves lost everything. All that remains of their settlements are graves." He took a moment. "What few survived…your tribe is there, hidden in the New Moon Basin, where they are safe from further recriminations. They made many enemies amongst the Otherwolves when we were still warring, Tulimak. It was the only place they had to retreat to."

"*How do you know all of this?*" I asked. I heard Odina and Sawyer approaching us, not trying to hide their footsteps. Sawyer followed his mother, looking angrier than I'd ever seen him. Nuka trailed behind him, holding his hand.

My father looked to Odina, but then sighed and continued. "We were all part of one great alliance, back then. But, when certain tribes began massing for war against the settlers…"

"*Tribes like the Tawnahowac abandoned us,*" Odina spoke. Her voice wasn't decrying in tone, just matter-of-fact, but it was hard not to see her words as the condemnation they surely were.

"I had only just become Chieftain," my father said defensively. "Our people have never been warriors, Odina. I did not see your path as a way forward. Not for us."

"It wasn't," she said, surprising us all. She looked around, then shook her head. "I am not going to argue against the facts. Our efforts to ward off the incursion of the Otherwolves were in vain. You all know what became of my tribe." She looked to me. "And his, I suppose. Although I'll admit, the bear tribes preferred an isolated existence, I didn't know them well. I only heard tales of their ruin."

"They were proud," my father said. "So...proud. Fierce. Determined to remain unyielding. So determined, in fact, that they united two tribes as one, by way of marriage. And before that, they'd fought for generations. So it was quite the concession. The chieftain's daughter from the Great Northern Bears and one of their largest and most renowned warriors of the Ice Bear tribe. I only met him once." He tensed his jaw for a moment, lifting his eyes to mine. "You look just like him."

"You said they're still there," I pressed.

"What remains of them," he said sadly. "I have not had word from them in some time. Your father was gravely injured when they sheltered here, Tulimak. And he was the last of the men. They have been an Uklashan since his death, which came soon after you were left with us. I don't know how many remain in the basin. But not many."

"*Then,*" I stammered, "*why didn't they* want *me? If they were so few in number?*" I hadn't meant for my words to come out so strangled, but my voice was escaping me.

My father gave a frustrated wheeze, gripping his chest, "This was why I didn't feel you needed to know this, Tulimak! Your life here, was it not good, before all of this?"

"*Of course,*" I insisted, "*but—*"

"Did I not treat you as one of my own?!"

"*Yes!*" I said.

"When your tribe came to us for sanctuary," he shook his head slowly, "your father was at death's door, your mother had a terrible wound, your tribe was barely six strong. They had fled their last three encampments—they weren't even taking the fight to the Otherwolves then, they were just trying to survive. But the Carvecian militias had taken their previous attacks on their settlements very seriously, they were hunting them."

"*Your parents,*" he let out a breath, "*confessed to me that they were considering smothering you. As a mercy.*" As he said the last part, he reached out to grip my hand. Which I very much needed at that point. "*You were so small, you were sickly, underfed...if they'd kept on the run with you, you would have died a far crueler, wasting death. A-and I knew...we could not help them, but we could help you. Hide you away, raise you amongst us while the Otherwolves forgot their anger towards the bear tribes."*

He gripped my hand in both of his, squeezing tightly. "Your mother made me swear to her that you would never know them. She was ashamed, Tulimak. They could not care for you. And more than that...they were ashamed by their failure to defend their land."

"They were more ashamed they lost their land than losing their son?" I demanded, sharply.

"They were fighting for a homeland they could raise their families in, Tulimak. Yourself included. When they lost that, your mother made an incredibly hard decision I pray you never have to make," the older otter emphasized. "Giving up someone you love, letting them slip from your life, because you know you cannot give them what they need to thrive, any longer."

The double-meaning in his words was not lost on me. I leaned down slowly, taking a knee once more. My father's eyes widened and without any hesitation, he moved forward into my arms, wrapping me tightly in his hold. For a moment, I felt like a cub again. I wanted to disappear into his fur, to be enveloped by him, to feel safe again.

I *was* that cub again, tired and torn up by brambles, clutching to his chest after pulling myself up the hill I'd fallen down. I'd had to make the climb myself, but then he'd been there, holding me. Promising me he'd never let me fall again.

When he pulled away, he had tears in his dark brown, oval eyes. It didn't matter that they were so different from my own. Those were my father's eyes.

"There was nothing lacking in the life you gave me," I said to him, through staggered breaths. "Nothing. You, and mom, and the whole tribe, were all I ever wanted or needed."

"That isn't true," he said with a pained smile, looking past me to where Finn, Odina and Sawyer stood. *"But I'm glad we were able to help get you this far, at least."*

"Thank you for telling me all of this," I said, slowly slipping from his hold.

"I haven't told you just to clear my conscience," he said, leaning down to pick up one of the bundles my family had left for me. As he spoke, he

began gathering up the others as well. "*I've told you because…I think it is time you go to them.*"

"*What?*" I wasn't certain I understood what he meant.

"*The basin,*" Odina said in a flash of realization. "*I should have thought of that.*"

My father nodded. "It may be a good route to take to escape your pursuers. It's a few days south from here, in the direction you're headed. And the Otherwolves fear it."

"Perhaps not these men," Odina said. "But it's worth a try. At the very least, the mountains would be a good place to make a stand."

"You said it was dangerous, though," I said.

"In the winter, most of the feral hunters will be hunkering down," Odina said. "But if the bear tribes do indeed remain there, they will not take kindly to our presence. They were individualistic, even before they were scattered and broken."

"*Which is why I must accompany you,*" my father said, shocking the both of us. Even Finnegan seemed to pick up on the sudden change in the timbre of the conversation, although we'd been speaking in our tongue most of the time, so I'd have a lot to explain to him later.

"*They owe me a great debt,*" he continued, gathering the bundles into one and un-shouldering a bag from over his back. Had he been planning this the whole time? "*Or at least, that is the way they choose to see it. I can't imagine being given a greater gift than what they entrusted to me. But nonetheless, if I cannot talk you out of this, Tulimak,*" he said as he began to pack, "*then I will take you at least that far. Even Odina does not know the land in those parts as I do. And I am a Chieftain. If anyone is to negotiate with your tribe on our tribe's behalf,*" he nodded, "*it will be me.*"

"I had hoped to leave my children in your village's care," Odina said, switching to Amurescan likely for her son's sake. He seemed more comfortable speaking it. "For the duration of this trip, Takoda. I would of course not expect to do so freely—"

My father waved a paw. "Done. You'll be protecting my son, after all. They are welcome here."

"I'm part of this hunt, mom," Sawyer growled out. "You could use another gun—"

"Enough," Odina snapped, a true rarity for her. It shut her son down and fast. "You have a responsibility to your sister. Consider all we've been through to get to this point. Do you want that to be for nothing? You will stay here, you will look after her, and you will live the life we fought so hard for. Whether or not I return."

The two of them began to talk again, in hushed tones. It didn't seem like my business, so I turned my ears away.

Finnegan, who must have been terribly confused having only understood the end of the conversation, had at least gleaned enough to know that both of our families were feuding over the current situation. And he seemed very ashamed over the fact, if his body language was any indication.

"I am so sorry," he said to my father, "for all of this."

"You weren't the one who wanted to come here, I was," I reminded him.

"Yes, let my son take the credit for his foolhardiness," my father said, his voice back to being stern. "This *was* careless, son. Bringing him here. We will have to leave deliberate evidence to draw them away from the tribe, you know. Which will cost us precious time. And there is still a chance in the future this may come back somehow to harm your family. I was quite serious before when I said I wanted you to understand the weight of your decisions. Every choice you make has a consequence."

"I know," I said, slumping. "I-I knew at the time, too. I'm not going to say I didn't. I just thought—I didn't realize it could get so—"

My father put a hand up. "You act on your gut," he said, patting his belly. "Very otter of you, honestly. And we aren't always given good options in life. This situation may never have had a good outcome, no matter what you'd done differently. I know that frustration all too well."

"Are you certain you should come?" I asked, looking to his satchel. "The tribe needs you."

"I can only see you as far as the Basin," he said. "I will not endure the entire trip, I fear. Not in the winter months. And I don't want to slow you down. Tulimak," he looked up at me intently, "if there is *any* chance of solving this issue with the land, it is my duty to aid you. I made mistakes in my dealings with the settlers. I can't be so proud now as to deny someone else the chance to try, where I failed."

He glanced sidelong to Finnegan. "Him, I am still uncertain of," he said, switching back to our language. "I can't say I buy his story. But you believe in him and as a father, I want to respect your beliefs."

He shouldered his bag, walking past us towards the rest of the family. "Now tell him to stop slumping like a beaten pup. He's supposed to be a 'warrior,' isn't he? We might need him to kill people."

Finnegan couldn't understand us, but he at least seemed to pick up on when someone was talking about him. "Huh?" He blinked at my father.

The otter glared at him for a moment, before pronouncing an Otherwolf phrase I'm sure he'd heard somewhere, "Buck up!" he said. "You have a small coalition of people here putting their necks on the line for you and my son is *very* devoted to you, for some reason. He is a kind, giving young man who is risking his life for you, and you *do not* deserve him." He brushed past Finn at that, grumbling, "I don't care *how* charming you think you are."

Finnegan watched him go in dumb shock, before turning back to me. "Honestly," he muttered, "I'm starting to like your father."

Snow fell that afternoon and into the evening, which made leaving behind evidence of our flight that the Jackwalds might find easier than expected. My brothers and sisters carefully covered our presence in town by brushing away our footprints and burning large bundles of sage to cover our retreat. We scattered the remains of Odina's camp out on the clay flats so that it looked like we'd left in a hurry, and left deliberate footprints from there to the river, as well as doing nothing to mask our scent.

Odina had told us one of the men amongst the Jackwalds was something called a "bloodhound," which seemed to worry both her *and* Finnegan. I didn't have to guess very hard at what sort of specialist that might be. Although apparently in Amuresca, it was more than a profession—there were entire family bloodlines of them. If I hadn't been so distracted with everything else that had happened today, I'd probably have asked Finnegan to explain the idea of canine bloodlines to me more in-depth, because it sounded fascinating.

We were all worried for the Tawnahowac village and the family we were leaving behind. But even my father seemed to think it likely that these hunters would not spare the time, even out of spite, to harm them when they were on a hunt.

It was hard to know when they'd pick up our trail. For all we knew, they might have opted to stay in town another night. They had horses, reliable trackers and good information. It was impossible to know how confident they'd feel.

Once we'd crossed the river, we were careful to cover our trail up the banks into the woods. We did our best past there as well for at least a mile, sticking to areas of pine undergrowth, where the ground was flat and needle-covered. It might have seemed counter-productive since it meant we were leaving very clear tracks, but with the fresh snow, that wouldn't be the case for long. Broken underbrush would be a lot more noticeable, which there wasn't much of under the large pines.

For all of Odina's expertise and my father's added wisdom though, both seemed fairly certain we'd still be tracked and followed. The question would be whether or not they'd follow us as far as the New Moon Basin.

We weren't able to make more than ten miles' headway the first day before we had to encamp. We were heading into the mountains, so some of the terrain was steep and difficult, we never ever foraged this far. And we'd gotten a late start as it was. We tried to press on through the darkness, but after the first time someone fell down a sheer hill of loose snow and pine needles, we'd given up that idea.

Me, by the way. I'm the one that fell. Because of course it was me.

Camping was…interesting. Initially I'll admit, as selfish as it may have sounded, I'd been very relieved that my father was coming along. The moralistic part of me knew I shouldn't feel that way, but I couldn't very well deny it to myself. Ever since I'd embarked on this terrifying and often painful adventure, I'd wanted my only remaining parent by my side. For absurdly childish reasons. Comfort, primarily. But also guidance.

Now, I had him. And I'd realized somewhat lamentably, far after the point that I probably should have, that having my father traveling in close quarters with me alongside my new, secret romantic partner was… complicated.

I'd yet to talk to him about Finnegan and I. He hadn't brought it up, so I could only surmise my sister had not yet explained what she'd seen to him and honestly, even if I could manage the courage, what was I supposed to say?

Hey, dad. This foreigner who brought down near calamity on our village and whom you now know to be a wanted murderer is someone I'm interested in courting, like one might a wife? Oh, but don't worry, he's made no promises of fidelity to me and neatly dodged any idea of a future with me because he seems to think our being together is a death sentence. So, it's not as if I'm *really* going to court him. We're just sharing a bed until he either flees for his life or we turn him in to the law, who will likely hang him. By the way, he wanted to hide *all* of this from you and I've sort of been going along with that because I have trouble saying no to him.

Yeah. That's about how that would go.

So that night Finnegan and I slept in separate bedrolls. We had no lean-to for this trip, but we'd found a good area of thick spruce and an overhanging rock-face that sheltered us well enough. The snow was still falling when my eyes got heavy, but it was gentle, big flakes falling soundlessly and calm, the sort of snow me and my siblings would have relished playing in during our more innocent years.

At the very least, we had the best bedrolls my tribe could put together for us, not the worn sheepskin I'd brought along on the raft because I was afraid anything better might get wet. And I was emotionally exhausted and for once, well-fed, with my father sleeping right beside me. I had no trouble drifting off.

Something roused me, some far-off noise in the forest, rustling at my consciousness. I lifted my head slowly, peering through the dim twilight, searching the swaying, powdered boughs for any sight of the hulking shadow. I knew it was there—could feel it—but it eluded my vision. Everything was indistinct, the world a shifting collage of pine and snow, purple and blue hues.

I found my feet underneath me easily enough, moving inexorably towards what I somehow instinctively knew was *there*, beyond the tree-line. I could feel it pulling at me, predatory, overwhelming and terrifying, but I felt compelled to answer its call all the same.

The climb up the rock face was hard, my every movement exhausting me more than it should have. My legs burned, my arms ached, I felt my footing give way more than once. But when I arrived, claws digging at frozen rock, paw-pads raw, at the slate summit…I found myself face to face with the creature itself. And it was far more than some spectral shadow.

The Ursark were storied predators, feral ancestors to all bearkind. I had seen a few of the smaller, more stooped, black-furred feral animals throughout my life, sharing our land. They were just similar enough to evoke curiosity, but subtly different in form and vacant in expression in that way feral animals were. It was the sort of encounter that left a palpable air of uncanny discomfort inside you, especially when like me, you'd known few other actual bears in your life.

This creature, though…it was no stooped, small predator of rabbits or minor threat to fish lines. The Ursark that stood before me was a beast unlike any I'd ever imagined, let alone seen. Its body seemed to tower into the heavens themselves, fifteen heads tall at the shoulder at least. Its muzzle was shorter than my own, eyes wide-set and black as the night, with starlight dancing through them just the same. Upon its titanic shoulders was a mantle, a mane of thick fur, long enough in places that it collected snowflakes. But what truly stood out was its pelt, impossibly dense fur split like a shadow had fallen over its body, following its spine and cutting its muzzle in half: One side rich mahogany brown, the other cream white.

It was standing atop the thick, ancient stones pushed up to form the rise, its massive shoulders hunched. Its head hung below them, empty eyes boring through me without any indication of what motives might lie behind them.

It took me a moment of still, shocked reflection to realize it was bleeding along the seam of fur down its body, almost as though the two halves had been cut in twain and only pushed back together. Crimson oozed out from where it seemed fused together and pooled beneath it in the earth, collecting where the great stones jutted forth from the ground.

As I watched, frozen in place, it slowly lowered its broad muzzle to the caking blood in the dirt and began to nose at it. Terrifyingly, after enough nudging, the blood-soaked earth began to *move*.

At first it simply roiled, like boiling water. Then it formed what clearly resembled a small muzzle, opening its maw and crying out in the night air. Transfixed, I watched it roll itself into more of a body, mewling and clawing towards the enormous creature whose blood had birthed it. The little cub grew with each passing second, the stars in the sky beginning to move past us in a blur.

Once it had freed itself from its earthen womb, it began to gather up paw-fuls of the bloody earth around it, its own efforts aiding its growth. Bit by bit, its body began to resemble something closer to my own. For a time, the enormous Ursark helped it, seeping more of its blood into the soil and using its far larger paws to gather earth.

There was no doubt now. The thing being made, and now creating itself of earth and blood, was a man. It soon built itself a form nearly as large as my own, unstable and marbled with cracks, pieces falling off almost as fast as it could replace them. When it finally turned to look at me, its muzzle was all at once hard to perceive and terrifyingly familiar. And its chest had a hole where its heart beat, exposed to the world, blood leaking out in rivulets.

It reached for me.

I took a step back.

A voice shattered through it all, piercing and solid in an indistinct collage, pulling me back with a crash of sensations into the waking world. All at once, the vision shrunk before me, the stars slowing their spin across the sky and all the world re-coalescing into hard lines and shapes. The air was cold, the earth beneath my feet felt real and solid, my breath puffed out in front of me, lungs rasping.

"Tulimak!" The sharp whisper and a hand tightening around my wrist were the final viscerally *real* things that pulled me into consciousness. I blinked slowly, still processing what was happening—where I was. I was... that's right. I was traveling. With my family. With Finnegan! Right...we were on the run. Again. I was...where was camp? Where was everyone?

I looked around, noticing with a start first off that I was feet away from a rocky ledge and a long plummet. It looked, upon retrospect, like the one that was sheltering our camp. We had no fire, but I could smell the distinct scent of my father's fur. Our camp was nearby.

It was still dark. Had I been dreaming? I'd been dreaming. I'd walked, climbed, all the way up here? Asleep?

So who was—?

The face staring up at me in the dark was not the one I expected. Not Finnegan. Not even my father. It was a young, gangly mountain lion.

"Sawyer?!" I exclaimed.

"Tch-shhhhh!" he hissed, glancing back down the rise. "Don't wake the others!"

"Oh," I mumbled sleepily, "I'm sure Odina's already awake. I don't know why she let me leave…she must've assumed I had to relieve myself."

"Les' keep it tha' way—what're you even doin' up here?!" he demanded in another sharp whisper. "You were about t'stumble down the damn cliff over there."

"Dreaming," I slurred, still coming to my senses. "Or maybe…I don't know. It felt like more than a dream. What are *you* doing here? I mean I'm…supposed to be here, I'm pretty sure. You're supposed to be back at the village."

"I'm tailin' you, obviously," he growled out. "Like hell I'm lettin' my mother do this alone. Doin' a pretty good job at stayin' down-wind and unnoticed, too. Or at least I *was*, until I saw you about t'walk off a damned cliff."

"Oh, Sawyer," I looked at him sympathetically. "She is going to be *so* angry."

"By the time she finds out it'll be too late."

"Kid," I sighed. "You know I have to tell her, right?"

"Ah just saved your life!" he said, scandalized. "You wouldn't!"

I did. I was appreciative that the young mountain lion had blown his cover in order to help me avoid what would surely have been a much worse fall than the one I'd had earlier in the day, but he was fourteen and I wasn't very well going to hide his presence from his mother. Especially given the situation.

Odina left camp as we were all rousing in the early morning twilight, returning a short time later with a sulking, angry Sawyer in tow. They were arguing again. And once again, I tried to distract myself from the family drama that wasn't my business.

My father glanced past me for a moment as the bickering mother and son moved past, then looked to me. "A vision?" he repeated. "You're certain?"

"I…no," I admitted. "Not certain. It could have just been a dream. But it was so *vibrant*, otterfa. *So* real. It reminded me of two years ago, when I received my markings. But clearer. Like it should have been."

"You'd been fasting for days, then," he said pointedly, "and smoking. But…the spirits can make themselves known to us in many states. In times of sickness and great strife. Perhaps your ordeals of late summoned forth a spirit of *your* people," he put a paw over my heart. "Perhaps it is watching over you because you are returning to your homeland." He sighed. "I am not a shaman, son. It is hard to say."

"Or you're having stress dreams," Finnegan muttered from where he was reclining nearby. He hadn't bothered getting out from under his bedroll yet, preferring its cocoon to the frigid cold of the morning air. "Now I can't stop imagining what you're like smoking hashish, Tuli. Must've been a *riot*."

I looked his way. We'd been speaking in Amurescan out of habit, because I preferred not to hide things from him or essentially talk behind his back while in his presence, as my father seemed to have no trouble doing.

I felt my father's paw on my chest press into my fur, bringing my attention back to him. I couldn't help but remember the "man" I'd seen the Ursark birth, its chest open, blood pumping from its heart, spilling out like a waterfall. My father's paw over my own heart was comforting.

"You can tell me everything while we travel today," he assured me. "We will try to understand this together. River spirits I understand well enough, but this…this is new. I can only promise I will do my best."

I smiled a little. "Thanks, dad."

Finnegan gave a long yawn that ended in a slight whine, which he self-consciously covered his muzzle after. "Oof…sorry," he cleared his throat. "I didn't know you sleep-walked, Tulimak."

I began to speak, but my father cut me off. "Oh, you wouldn't believe the places we've found him," he waved a paw. "This isn't even the worst.

The river, once. And you have to be so careful waking him up, you know. Especially if he's in some precarious position."

Finnegan seemed vastly amused by the concept, but I wasn't. "It doesn't happen often," I insisted.

"It isn't even always just walking," my father continued, further embarrassing me as thoroughly as possible. "Once, as a child, he raided the fish racks—"

"Dad!" I covered my muzzle with my paws.

"'Sleep-eating,'" he chuckled. "How do you discipline that? This one gets up to the most trouble while he's in bed, I swear."

Finnegan physically ducked his head under his blanket to laugh. I, meanwhile, wanted to die.

Odina became my savior when she rejoined us not long after, already hiking her bags up over her shoulders. "We need to move out," she announced.

I looked past her at Sawyer. My father was the first to ask, though. "So, the boy's coming along, then?"

"No choice," she said in a curt, clipped tone. It was the closest I'd ever heard Odina to furious. "Care to tell them what you've told me?" she inquired of her son.

He spoke up hesitantly, "Ah saw them horsemen comin' at us from town," he said. "Ah stayed behind'n hour or so, so's my ma wouldn't find me out too soon. Might've stayed longer too, 'cept I saw them. Couldn't've been no one else."

"So, unless my son is lying-" Odina said with a glare his way.

"I wouldn'lie 'bout somethin' like that!" he insisted.

"- then they aren't far behind us," she continued. "Now they might have needed to slow down to catch our trail, but I can't risk sending him back with so little space between us and them out there."

"And you need me," he insisted impertinently.

"Your *sister* needs you!" she snapped back, showing her fangs. "What is all of this even for, if you get yourself killed, boy? The coin's a temporary fix without land. You had one responsibility—"

"Mom," he interjected, his voice coming out shaky, but earnest, "I was *scared* fer you. These boys, they ain't foolin'. This's a real posse, mom. I wanted to *be* with you fer this. I didn'wanna wait around like I used to, thinkin' you'd never come back. I *couldn't*. Not again. Not anymore." He swallowed, readjusting his rifle sling over his shoulder. "Ah'm a man, now. But I still...need you."

Odina, and indeed the entire camp, had gone mute in the wake of his words. My father was still a hairsbreadth away from me and I suddenly wanted to reach out for him, to embrace him. I *felt* the young lion's fear so palpably. I'd been trying not to become involved in Odina's family's trials, since our paths crossed. In a very real way, she was the enemy. She wanted to take Finnegan away from me. Send him to his probable death.

But as immature and boorish as Sawyer was, his love for his mother, and indeed the entire family's bonds, were undeniable. I couldn't push back my compassion for them, regardless how much I disagreed with their way of life and the circumstances that had brought us together.

I wished in that moment that I didn't know all of this. That I hadn't seen it. Every new thing I learned about them made condemning them harder. And I needed to condemn them, in the same way that I needed to be able to justify fighting these men coming after us. Because otherwise, how could I defend myself and Finnegan?

But not knowing wouldn't have changed the situation. This was where we were. This was the truth of it. And there was probably so much more I still didn't know that would make it all even harder, even more complicated.

Was it possible for two people on opposite sides of a conflict to be in the right? I'd always thought of wars, or even smaller-scale things like what was happening here, to be between a bully and a victim. A well-armed private militia killing unarmed miners. An overwhelming power like the Carvecian military, against a few small tribal nations trying to defend their homeland. Surely, that was as clear-cut as it came. It was unthinkable to imagine that I'd ever sympathize with the predators, there.

But Odina had been a faceless predator to us, once. And now, I was watching her son pour his heart out to his mother about his fears of losing her. I might disagree with how she made a living, but that didn't mean I wanted to take this woman away from her children.

It was so...so confusing.

The voyage into the mountains took us another four days, which we spent primarily in wary, hyper-vigilant silence. We kept a watch at night, we talked very little during the day so as to keep our senses tuned to the land around us, and we never lit a fire.

My body was aching and cold, taut as a bowstring, by the time the basin came in sight. It's not that the trip itself had been any more strenuous than it should have been. The cold nights were hard, certainly, but the weather had cleared considerably since the first day, consisting of bright, sunny days and blue skies, star-speckled horizons at night and a nearly full moon. Winter aside, it was good weather for traveling.

But the fear...the paranoia...it gets to you. Being on the edge of a blade for so long wears down your reserves, saps your energy and makes you jump at every shadow. We were all feeling it as we entered the valley.

The basins were, even from a distance, some of the most beautiful and striking land I'd ever seen. It was testament to the stunning view that we stopped for nearly an hour to eat and look down across the valley when we reached the first vantage point in the mountains. The land seemed to go on forever here, evergreen forests overlapping and fading into blue waves of sweeping mountainsides off in the distance. The basins themselves were like great depressions in the earth, the forests growing down around the edges but slowly fading off to browner, sparser earth the further you got towards the center of each. Two had lakes in the center, the same cerulean as the sky.

The largest of the craters was the one my father denoted as our destination. The New Moon Basin was aptly named, as a full half of the rim of it seemed pushed up out of the earth, gray even in the distance, denoting a ridge of rock blasted out in a semicircle. The other half was covered in forests which stretched down to a small lake. I imagined I could see smoke trails, proof of my long-lost relatives still living there, but the valley was rife with drifting, low-hanging clouds, so if I'd seen anything it was probably that.

"The last I had heard from them," my father breathed out, "the tribe still took up residence here."

"It's defensible terrain, regardless whether its occupied by his blood anymore," Odina said, pointing down towards the basin. "That rock ridge there? Assures only one way in or out of the basin. Good place to get trapped, but if your goal's to hold a place, I can see why they'd choose here." She was checking her rifle, cleaning a piece of it. "If the Jackwalds are willing to follow us this far, they'll catch us once we leave the mountains and get to even terrain. Best we make a point here, and dissuade them."

I kept my gaze on the valley, trying to find some meaning in each sense. The smell of this place, the sight of it, the sounds of the forest...this was where I'd come from. My birthplace. I'd thought it would "call" to me somehow. That after all this time, coming here might make me feel whole, connected to something I'd lost.

What I felt, overwhelmingly...was fear.

Chapter 14

Part Of Me

We found the first jaw trap early the next afternoon. Thankfully Odina caught it before any of us triggered it, which was especially good since this one seemed either made for very large game…or people. It would have badly maimed whoever had stepped in it.

The lioness sat hunkered next to it, carefully selecting a long, heavy stick and positioning it just so, before thrusting it down into the pile of frozen leaves and detritus concealing it. When it snapped, it cracked the stick in two with a shockingly loud noise that echoed through the trees.

"Well," Finnegan murmured uneasily, his hand on his pistol, "if they didn't know we were here before, they certainly do now."

"I had to trigger it," she sighed, "in case we circle back around this way. Any sort of marker we leave could get covered by snow." She crouched down again, looking at it more closely now that it was spent. "It's rusted," she declared, "but not horribly so. I think it's just in disrepair, I don't actually think it's been here long."

"If'n they've got one, they've got more," Sawyer said, worriedly. "You wanna press on, Ma?"

Odina scrunched up her muzzle for a moment before standing and shaking her head. "No. Not worth the risk. This one was sheltered from most of the snow, but a lot of the others won't be."

"So what can we do?" I asked. "We're close to the Basin. A few miles, at most."

Odina shook out her duster and looked out past us, towards the distant mountains. "We made good time," she said. "If they chose to follow us this far, if they kept their horses, they'll be days behind. They can't know the trails as well as Takoda and those animals won't handle the mountains well."

"That's quite a few 'ifs,'" my father noted. "What's your plan?"

"We start a fire," she said matter-of-factly. "And wait for the bear tribe to find us."

"Is that wise?" Finnegan asked. "They might shoot first, ask questions later. Or not at all."

"They won't shoot Tulimak," my father said, reaching over to put a hand on my arm. "I am certain of that. We will just have to make very sure it is clear that we are all here with him. Everyone stays together."

I glanced around, noting all eyes were on me, now. It made me incredibly uncomfortable. "What?" I said, my voice wavering.

"You may need to accept being the center of attention for a little while," my father said with a lopsided smile.

Building a fire was welcome, at least. We hadn't had one for days and in addition to chasing the cold away, I was very much looking forward to some warm food, too. My father brewed tea and Finnegan offered to make us all a simple stew with some of the provisions my family had packed up for us. It was just jerked meat, root vegetables and a little salt, but he seemed to have a fair idea how to portion things out and cut the ingredients, which impressed me.

"When I make stew," I said, my muzzle resting in one paw, "I just sort of boil water with things in it. You keep taste-testing and adding...things..."

"I'm trying to get the salt right," he said, taking another slow sip from the ladle. "It's rarer than gold in some places, we're lucky to have it. Don't want to overdo it. It was a real treat in the Risers," he reminisced. "We'd get some occasionally from my mother or my uncle's clients. We always tried to make it last."

"I didn't know you could cook," I said.

"I didn't know you *couldn't,*" he countered, smirking at me. "You talk about food a lot and you...clearly seem to enjoy eating—" He paused at that, as if worried he'd offended me.

I stared back at him. "Uh-huh," I said.

He smiled fondly, like I'd done something cute. I didn't understand him sometimes. "So, I don't know. I guess I sort of figured you'd have a bent for cooking."

"I can grill fish," I shrugged, "but cooking is women's work most of the time. Some of the men in our village have specialties they prefer to prepare, and everyone salts, smokes and grills fish, but I never learned much other than the basics to keep me fed when I was traveling." I smirked a little and nudged him in the shoulder with a fist, "That's why I need to get married, eventually. My wife can do all of those things, while I fish and sell at market. She can forage, garden and grind maize, make bread and keep our home warm and tidy, raise the cubs..."

"Sounds nice," he said, his voice hard to read.

"I'm sorry," I said at length, not certain if I'd said something wrong. He was always the one who talked about how I should marry someday, how what we had was temporary. Was he upset I'd started saying it?

It's not as though it was actually something I wanted. The wife part, anyway. The rest...yes, I suppose. At the very least, it made me sad to think I was going to miss out on all of it.

He shook his head, focusing on the stew. "Don't be sorry," he shrugged. "It really does sound nice."

"I know it's probably a very mundane life for a world traveler like you," I said.

He laughed, leaning back and looking up at me. "Tuli, I didn't come all this way looking for adventure or out of some wanderlust," he huffed. "And I'm earnestly not disparaging your 'mundane life.' I think it sounds...amazing, honestly." He reached down and tugged up the edges of his worn collar around his neck, puffing out a breath into the cold. "Peaceful," he said after a further few moments, his tone soft. "If someone's content being a homemaker, spending all their time and energy on the little'uns, keeping house, whatnot...they'd be lucky to have you. Where I come from, everyone has to work outside the home. Doesn't matter who you are, or how many kids you've got. You don't have the option of staying home."

He tapped the spoon on the edge of the pot. "That's why I know how to cook. My mother wasn't the only one who was out on the job all the time. There were a lot of other kids in the Risers. I made us a little extra coin, watching over some of them. From the time I was barely older than most of them." He chuckled. "Don't get your hopes up, though. I'm hardly *good* at it. Just passing."

"I'll bet you could get good at it," I said.

He glanced at me out of the corner of one green eye. "What's that supposed to mean?"

I shrugged, averting my gaze. "Just that you're a very focused person. You could probably get good at just about anything if you wanted to badly enough."

"You could learn to cook, Tuli," he reasoned. "It's not that hard."

"I don't really want to, though," I admitted.

"Lazy bear prefers to be doted on," he teased.

"Hey, poke fun all you will," I snorted. "I'm unusual enough as it is. So what if I'm a little more traditional about family roles? I'm allowed to be a little boring in my interests, right? I've just always preferred male pursuits."

I gave him a good few seconds. He only grinned at me.

"What?" I asked as if I didn't know.

"Not. Saying. A thing," he sing-songed, continuing to stir the stew.

"You two are snickering like Tulimak's eldest sisters," my father muttered as he moved in closer to the fire and sat down beside us. "Care to let me in on whatever is so amusing about our current circumstances?" He sniffed, leaning over the pot. "That smells good. Seems you're good for something, after all."

"Otterfa," I said, exasperated.

"Oh, he takes it all in good stride," the older otter said.

"Honestly, given our situation," Finn cleared his throat, "you're being very kind. And anyway Tulimak, you forget that I spoke to your sisters, at length. This just seems to be the way your family communicates with one another."

"We've always been kinder to him," my father said, speaking to Finn around a hand, like it was a great secret. He didn't bother whispering. "He's a very sensitive boy. We only give as much as we can take in our family."

"I've got quite the negative balance, I'm afraid," Finnegan said regretfully. "So I won't participate. But it sounds brilliant. Any other time, I'd be all about it."

My father gave a slight smile. "I am beginning to understand what it is my son sees in you. You've quite the clever tongue. You'd make a good storyteller."

"I've been telling stories my whole life," Finnegan said dryly.

"I'll just bet you have," my otterfa sniped back.

I watched them speak, realizing with a sudden jolt of clarity that now…might be the moment. It wasn't ideal, of course. We weren't alone, we couldn't go *off* somewhere alone. But maybe that was good? Maybe he would be less angry, because he wouldn't want to make a scene in front of Odina's family?

Maybe I was dead wrong. I could be a bad judge of these things sometimes.

But it really felt right. At the very least, if I didn't tell him now, in this moment, I would have to admit that I was consciously hiding it from him. Now *was* the time to say something.

Or at least, it would have been, if Sawyer hadn't whistled sharply from a nearby tree.

Finnegan immediately got to his feet, dropping the spoon in the snow. His hand was beneath his jacket, but he was wise enough not to draw right off. Not that it would matter. I'd seen how fast he was at it in the past.

It took me considerably longer to get to my feet. By the time I'd stood to my full height, one of them had stepped past the wood line. If it hadn't been for Sawyer in his roost, we wouldn't have seen them until they were right up on us. And that was impressive, given their size.

The one that revealed herself first was towering, nearly as tall at the shoulder as me. With the fresh coat of snow over every surface, it was hard to even make her out except where her form broke through the dark undercarriages of pine boughs. Her fur was entirely white, unlike mine. Cream-colored in places, especially around her muzzle. She also wore white tanned hides, although like me, she didn't cover herself much. She didn't need to. Her hide was dense and powdered with snow, carved with elegant patterns that nearly disappeared beneath her thicker winter fur.

But what I could see were distinctively jagged, unlike the swirling patterns of my otter tribe.

She was marked as a warrior. And not only by her tribal markings, but more importantly, by her far less aesthetic war scars. There was no denying how she'd obtained the disfiguring marks across her face, the divots in her legs and arms, a torn ear and one clearly blind eye.

She was unnaturally lean for a bear, and not just because she was an ice bear. They already had more sloping, slender muzzles, longer arms and legs and a taller torso. But she was either underfed, aging, or both.

The other, golden brown-furred and stockier, was not long following behind her. She was also large, but not nearly as tall. Her posture was more stooped and she had a thicker brow, grey peppering around her muzzle and eyes. They both wore the same camouflage, bleached-out hide parkas and a decent dusting of snow. They'd probably shaken out a few branches over themselves. And they'd moved through sun-crusted snow without any of us hearing them until Sawyer had noticed them. True hunters.

They each had rifles, as well as bows, slung over their shoulders. One for game, one for killing people, most likely. Arrows did less damage to meat.

They didn't have their weapons out, though. And their expressions, once I could make them out, surprised me. They were wide-eyed, both of them, like they were scared or shaken. Staring at me.

"Ujarak?" the ice bear called out in a wavering tone.

"No," the other said, pulling back the hood of her parka and taking a few steps forward. "That is...that is little Tulimak. Aren't you?"

My throat went dry. My body froze. I didn't know what to say to these women. What could I *possibly* say to them? This wasn't the culmination of some dream, for me. Until a few days ago, I'd never even known they existed. They were strangers to me. I felt no familial tie to them, even now, when they were standing before me.

They looked like me. But...that was it. I felt no spark of recognition, like I'd hoped. No flash of memory of them. Everything before my otter family was blank. I was too young.

"You can approach," Odina called out to them in our tongue, resting her rifle down and making it clear she had no intention to use it. She waved

a hand back at the rest of us, and Finnegan similarly relaxed. "*We are here to talk.*"

"*Uki?*" My father stepped up to stand beside Odina. "*That...was your name, yes? Uki?*"

The ice bear began crossing the clearing towards us. Her friend followed her a bit more warily. "*Takoda!*" she said at length, as she came nearer. "*Yes, of course. Of course it is you.*"

She surprised us all when she came right up to him and dropped down to a knee, scooping my father up in one arm like he was nothing. I saw both Finn and Odina jump a bit, like they were ready for something...but it was just an exuberant embrace.

A bear hug, if you will.

The way she'd kneeled first and drawn him against her reminded me of how I had to hug my family. I felt the first bit of warmth bloom in my chest. The first inkling of solidarity with this woman. She had looked so intimidating upon first blush, but she was unrestrained in her affections, or her smile, which she wore very well.

"Ahhh," my father chuckled, patting her back. "It is good to see you again, too. I remember, when your tribe left ours, you were the one—"

"*Crying,*" she said, pulling back just slightly and looking up at me, her eyes wet even now. "*Like a babe. I was the one who carried him everywhere, for my brother and sister. Especially after they were both hurt.*" She dragged a breath through her nose. "*Look at you. You've grown up so beautiful.*"

I still could not find words. I was admonishing myself mentally, knowing she must have thought me some simple idiot, but I just...couldn't...

She looked at me imploringly, but her broad smile didn't waver a bit. Like she knew.

"Just the two of you here, then?" my father asked from beside Uki. "Hunting party? Where are the others?"

Uki hung her head for a moment. "*Oh...*"

"Chieftain Takoda," the other woman, the honey-brown furred one, spoke. "There are no others. We are all that remains."

Uki's smile returned, weakly. She looked to me, specifically. "*Welcome home, Tulimak.*"

The bear tribe Uklashan was precisely where my otterfa had said it was, in the New Moon Basin. They'd never left. Their "village" was nestled beneath the rocky ridge of the basin, where apparently over the years, they'd dug many cave homes into the existing natural caves that had always been there. There was a quaint, honestly beautiful gathering area at the base of the cliff face, near the small lake the runoff waters that came down along many slow-drizzling wet rock faces and waterfalls drained into.

The lake was as bright and blue as the sky, clear, cold waters biting at my toes as we walked along its shore towards their home. The Uklashan, or rather, the two women that remained of it, had walked us past what they assured us were many more traps and through weaving, secretive trails they marked with scents that would stand out particularly to bear noses. "In case any survivors ever found their way home," they'd told me.

I suppose...I had.

Uki, the ice bear, and as we'd later find out, Kissima, the great northern bear, led us around the rim of the lake, which hugged the edge of the tree line. There was a well-worn path, but I occasionally stepped into the lake regardless, wanting to feel water between my toes again. It was cold, but it felt right. I wasn't used to being away from our river.

"*Haha, he is just like Ujarak,*" Uki had not stopped smiling at me. Her paw drifted to my shoulder, not for the first time. So familiar, despite being strangers until just half an hour ago. But then I noticed she and Kissima touched a lot, as well. It seemed to be normal for them. "*So drawn to the water. My brother could not see a puddle without putting his feet in it!*"

"*Ujarak,*" I spoke the name for the first time. "*Was he...?*"

She nodded. "Your father. Yes. My baby brother. I held him in my arms, as a cub. But he grew into a mighty, mountainous man!" she said with a chuckle, spreading her arms as if to indicate his...shoulders, I suppose?

"Was he bigger than me?" I asked, curiously.

Uki gave me a long look, scrunching up her muzzle. "I think you are bigger, actually. Taller, certainly. Ah, think, Kissima," she elbowed her sister-in-law, "if he only knew. My father. He was worried, when Ujarak married a smaller woman. Worried his children would be weak!" She chortled. "And look at you now!"

"*We shall have to brew tea and speak to him, when the stars come out,*" Kissima said, her tone more subdued. She'd been more subdued in general. Not unfriendly exactly, but harder to read. Uki was infectiously cheerful and spoke her mind freely, she'd been the one who'd done most of the talking so far, while we'd walked the few miles to the basin.

"Our ancestors will be in the western skies, tonight," Uki explained before I could ask. "We will show you."

Their small camp, which until now we'd only seen at a distance across the lake, finally came into view. Two massive, carved poles stood guard over the entrance, intricately-crafted but clearly aging depictions of many spirits adorning them. Bears supported the base, followed by wolves and mountain lions, likely depicting past tribal relations and allies. The paint was weathered and chipping away, leaving mostly wood grain behind, but they were still a sight to behold, speaking of a once-prospering tribe.

The grounds beyond were a husk of what they once were. Snow-covered and stripped-down, mostly dismantled longhouses stood empty and open to the elements on the edges of what had once clearly been a large settlement. Everywhere were remnants of another time: Piles of broken and powdered pottery collecting on the shoreline, covered in brown algae and slowly being reclaimed by the water; a grown-over archery field with little evidence of its long-ago use, save a few scarred, marked trees. But most notable were the graves. We passed rows of them, denoted only by small stone carvings poking up out of the snow. A dozen in particular had been cleared, (recently given all the snow we'd gotten) and burned, ashen bundles of sage sat at the base of four.

In the center of camp were uplifting signs of life. A chicken waddled past, crooning at Uki as it did, until she reached into her pouch and tossed a few berries at it. More came darting our way from various other places in the settlement, drawn by the lure of food. They seemed to have a dozen or so of the birds.

There were fish racks, a few campfires, cooking pots and a stone smoker, and a bucket left over the fire with what looked to be reeds soaking in it. A half-finished basket sat beside a stump with a sheepskin thrown over it, and beside another was a stack of fish spears, finished and unfinished.

This felt more like the home I knew.

My eyes traveled up the bluff that overlooked the town, and the many caves dotting it. From a distance they'd simply looked like black depressions in the rock, but up close I could see the carefully-carved pathways that climbed the cliffs connecting them. It was hard to say which ones

Uki and Kissima lived in, but the reality was, most of them were probably empty and bare now.

At least we'd all have somewhere to stay while we were here.

"*Well?*" I heard a voice and it took me a moment to recognize it had been Kissima. I turned to her. "*How does it feel, returning here?*" she asked.

I had to think about that, not wanting to give her a careless answer. "*It's hard to know how I feel,*" I finally said with a sigh, defeated once more by my own uncertainty. "*I was so young, I…I wish I had memories of this place. But I don't. I don't even remember my parents, and I feel…*" I had to search myself for a few moments. "*I feel guilty for that, for some reason. Because they must have meant a lot to you two, and I want them to mean a lot to me. I want this place to mean a lot to me.*"

"You were a cub," Kissima said softly. "Don't punish yourself."

"*It's not just that,*" I said. We'd had to briefly explain to them why we were here, but we hadn't had time to elaborate on it yet. I looked back at my party, grinding my teeth briefly, before averting my gaze to the ground. "*I feel bad that I've only come to you now. In a time of need. I should have done this a long time ago. Now it feels like I'm infringing on your solitude, because I'm in trouble.*"

"Tulimak, that isn't your f—" my father began.

Kissima cut him off with an outstretched palm and looked up at me intensely. "Your father and your mother made certain demands of Chieftain Takoda, before they would release you to him. We honestly did not think we would ever see you again. So this is a gift."

"*And we always expected if one of us ever returned here,*" Uki spoke up, "*they would bring trouble.*" She said it with an odd grin which…generally I liked her smiles. This one was unsettling.

"You weren't the only tribe member that we lost during the hard times," Kissima nodded. "Many of us were scattered to the wind."

"Did any of the others ever return?" I asked.

She shook her head. "In the end, most were hunted down, I think. Or went so far from these lands that they will likely never return."

"And now they are hunting our little Tulimak," Uki said, flashing her long fangs. So like mine. "My brother was right. It will never end." She put her big paws on both of my shoulders. "We will kill them together, these men who hunt you. It will be an honor to fight beside you, to go to war with my blood kin at my back, once again."

I let out a long breath. "It's…it's not me…they're after. Not exactly."

Kissima narrowed her eyes. Uki only looked confused. "*Explain,*" Kissima said.

About an hour later, the sun beginning to dip in the sky, we got a verdict. And not the one I'd expected.

"*I don't care,*" Uki announced, midway through my father's explanation about who the Jackwalds were. Her statement stopped him dead. He glanced between the two bear women, uncertainly, before Uki spoke again. "*It doesn't matter to us who they are,*" she crossed her long arms over her chest. "*They are Otherwolves, intruding on our land. Any of their kin that come here die. That is the oath we took, when Ujarak died.*"

"*I am glad to know they fight amongst themselves, these days,*" Kissima said, her voice a quiet growl. "*But Uki is right…what do we care* ***why***?" She glanced briefly at Finn, then spoke directly at him. Although not in a language he'd understand. "*They are a scourge. A blight. I hope they grind themselves to dust.*"

"*You know,*" I said uneasily, "*he's—*"

"I had thought he was a wolf," Kissima said, arching an eyebrow as she assessed him. "Many wolves have taken to wearing the Otherwolf clothes, of late. He doesn't look like a dog. Are you certain?"

"*He's…half,*" I explained. "*Like me.*"

"*Hmm,*" Kissima seemed to consider that.

"His wolf half must be the stronger blood," Uki said, in a tone of "that decides that." "Yes. He looks more like a wolf, and he kills them, you said. They hate him…they are hunting him. He's a wolf."

I barely knew how to begin addressing that, or how it made me feel. How it would have made Finn feel, if he could understand them. It was so simple a classification for them, clearly. But it seemed to be how they were processing all of this, and if it meant they'd accept Finn, did I really want to argue the point?

I decided to stay silent on the matter for now. We were in a precarious enough position, and I didn't want trouble between Finn and my long-lost relatives.

"We aren't certain they'll even come into the valley," my father said. "But if they do, we want you to understand the danger we might be putting you in, coming here. I did not bring Tulimak here lightly. We just weren't certain where else we could go that might be safe."

"It is fate," Uki said. "We came to you in **our** time of need. The spirits led you here, back to us. Of course we will fight beside you."

"I hope it doesn't come to that," I said, hanging my head. To think I could be responsible for even *more* of my tribe dying…

"You said it's less than a dozen men," Kissima said.

"A dozen very well-armed and experienced men," Odina spoke up. "They hunt men for a living, they know the land—"

"Not this land," Uki said, narrowing her eyes. *"Not our Basin."*

"We have fortified ourselves here over the last twenty years," Kissima nodded. "You were fortunate you made it as far as you did before encountering one of our traps. There are many. And Uki and I could move some, so that they are more centrally located, surrounding the basin. There is only one half we need reinforce; there is no easy path down the cliffs. Anyone coming from that direction would have to climb very slowly if they could make the climb at all, and they'd be exposed the whole while. And the lake never freezes fully this early in the winter. They will have to move around it, through areas we know like the back of our paw."

"I noticed it wasn't frozen," my father said, curiously. "Why is that?"

"It is very deep," she said. "Much deeper than it appears. We are able to ice fish in it throughout the whole winter."

"You do have a very defensible position here," Odina agreed. "And if you're fine with letting us set up camp here, I'm not going to fight you any further on it." She hefted her pack up over her shoulder. "We've been moving like hell for days. Do you mind if we find some place to start settling in?"

Uki stood. "I will show you all to the caves. We can speak more over dinner, and even more tomorrow after you've all rested."

"I'd definitely like to talk about your routes of entry and how you might place your traps," I heard Odina say towards Kissima, but at that moment, Uki filled my field of vision.

"*Tulimak,*" she took my hand in hers. "*Come.*"

She began tugging me towards the caves, walking at a stride I was capable of, but hardly ever used because I'd been so accustomed to living around smaller people my whole life. In a way, it was liberating, but I knew we were leaving my friends and father somewhat behind.

"*Was Takoda good to you?*" she asked when we'd put some distance between us and the others, walking down a winding path through the trees that led towards the bluff.

It became clear to me in that moment that her pace was intentional. I slowed, until my arm tugged at hers. When she turned to face me, I spoke intently. "*He was an incredibly loving, dutiful father,*" I assured her. "*The best I ever could have hoped for.*"

She looked a little sad at that for a moment, but forced a smile. "I'm glad you were well cared for. And I'm so sorry we couldn't keep you. I tried to convince my brother. I never wanted to give you up, Tulimak. He didn't, either."

"I know what their circumstances were," I said.

"I cannot say it was the right thing," she said hesitantly. "In the end, we made it back to the Basin and managed to hold this place, mostly because the fighting had taken so much from both sides that we were simply unable to continue it. There were hard times even following that. Ujarak's death... your mother's not long after..." Her muzzle twitched, with the memories. "Many lean years. Bad times to be raising young. Once things had gotten better, we thought...we considered going back for you. But you'd grown older by then. We sent messages, we spoke with some members of your tribe and heard how well you were doing, with the Tawnahowac. We weren't certain we could give you a better life. This land is beautiful, but it gives up very little without a fight." She frowned. "Kissima convinced me you should not have to become a warrior, like your father. Like us. She was happy when Takoda told us, some years ago, that you were a fisherman."

She glanced briefly past me, as the others' approached. "But I suppose," she smiled again at me, "*the spirits had other plans for you. And now, you will walk your father's path regardless.*"

I didn't say it aloud, but it bothered me somewhat how happy she seemed at the thought. Certainly, Uki held her brother's memory in high esteem. And part of that was clearly tied to his role as a fabled warrior.

She'd be very disappointed if she knew how little I took after him, in anything but appearance.

Finn moved up beside me as I was lost in thought. "So," he said, his voice wavering, "going...all right? Seems like?"

"Oh," I blanched. "I am *so* sorry. You can't understand a word we've been saying."

"Your father filled me in a little," he assured me. "But uh, while we're on the subject. I was thinking maybe...you know, since it seems like we might be holed up here a little while, and then if all goes well, traveling together for a time...I was hoping perhaps you might teach me a little about your language."

"Really?" My ears came up. "You want to learn how to speak Nontawlik?"

"I'm not sure how much progress I'll make," he shrugged weakly. "But... yes. If you're comfortable teaching it to me. Seems it could be useful."

I felt a smile tugging at my muzzle. He scoffed at me. "Come on," he rolled his eyes. "Don't look at me like that."

"It's just not the sort of thing I expected," I said. "What with all your fatalistic talk."

"I can pick up a few useful things fast enough to matter," he reasoned. "And I'd wager next to no one in the colonized cities here can speak a northern dialect like yours. Could be useful to have a secret language, you know? Never know what the future will bring."

"Says the man planning to turn himself in," I hummed.

"My plans are always evolving," he said with a sniff.

"That's the sort of thing my father would say 'I'll bet' to," I muttered. "You really do bring it on yourself."

"Natural born scoundrel, what can I say—oh. Wow." He stopped in his tracks.

I turned to look where he was, my breath catching in my throat. Ahead of us stretched the opening of the first cave mouth, and it was clearly the main one, judging by its size. Two of the carved poles we'd seen outside the village rested on either side of the hewn entranceway, which looked to be a natural opening in the rocks, but the tribe had clearly carved into it further over the years. A soft, warm light emanated from somewhere deep inside, illuminating the entranceway in the waning light.

Uki stood before it with a proud smile on her muzzle. And it was deserved. All along the curve of the entranceway, and by the look of it deep inside, the walls of the cave were painted in swirling patterns and illustrations, in red and white clay. The markings resembled those on Uki's hide, tribal markings evolving over many generations, along with illustrations of more things than I could properly take in at a glance.

We all slowly stepped inside, the scenes surrounding us. Depicted centrally in most images were white bears, engaged in hunts with enormous herds of caribou, making their way through forests of jagged trees and over mountain peaks, dancing in large gatherings under prominently-displayed, careful renditions of star formations. The moon in all of its phases moved in a circle over the ceiling of the main area, where a smoldering, low fire burned in a dug-in pit. That first large room seemed to be where Kissima and Uki lived, judging by the shelves of possessions and the two piles of furs and blankets on opposite sides of the fire. It was a comfortable home that in many ways reminded me of the pit homes my otter family lived in, but far larger.

Uki untied a large fur, which probably belonged to a feral bear, looking it over. She let it fall over the entranceway, shutting us in for the most part. She gestured up to the ceiling, "There are cracks we left in the caves, for air and for smoke to escape. It might not get as warm in this chamber as some of you would like," she said most pointedly to the mountain lions. "But the caves deeper down are always far warmer, especially if you have a small fire. All have fire pits, but we haven't enough furs and blankets. I hope you've brought your own." She gestured to several tunnels out of the main room, presumably different branches of the cave system. "We keep our seeds and root vegetables in the higher caves, where they stay cool. All of the rooms here, in the Chieftain's caves, are yours to use."

"You and Kissima will serve as our guardians, then," Odina noted. "The only way in or out is through your sleeping area. You don't want us out there with access to the camp."

Uki chuckled, although there wasn't much mirth there. "We trust Chieftain Takoda, and of course Tulimak, but many of you, we do not know. I'd say we're extending you a lot of trust. You must allow us some measure of concern. We haven't survived this long by taking chances."

"Fair enough," Odina nodded.

"And in any case, the caves down here *are* warmer," she assured us. "Go find yourself a place and settle in. We won't be turning in until after dinner, which you're welcome to join us for." She looked to me. "I'd especially like you to join us and tell us more about…everything. I want to know you, Tulimak."

"I'll do my best," I promised her.

I began to head for one of the larger-looking cave paths, when my father tugged on my wrist. "After dinner, let me check that wound of yours," he offered. "I have some salve in one of my bags. And I brought one of your mother's blankets to share. The large one. We really need to have better blankets made for you. I know the ones in your pit home are wearing thin—"

"Actually, otterfa," I cleared my throat, nervously. "I-I was hoping I could have my own space. Um. My own…cave. If that's all right. There seem to be a lot of them. And I'm grown now."

He blinked up at me. "It isn't like at home, though," he insisted. "These caves are large."

"I know," I persisted. "But I'm an adult, now. I've had my own pit home for a while. I know that's mostly because it was hard to dig one big enough for me to live with all of you, but…but I've gotten used to it."

"All right," he said uncertainly, in a subdued tone.

"I'll still sit with you around the fire until it's time to turn in," I insisted.

"Of course," he nodded, moving on ahead of me.

Just like that, the conversation was over. But I sensed his coldness in the stiff way his shoulders were set as he left, and I suddenly felt bad for asking for privacy. Not just because of *why* I wanted it, but because I understood why my father might have wanted us to be together in this strange, potentially dangerous place. And, although he hadn't done anything to make me feel guilty about asking, I still felt like I was abandoning him.

But I wasn't about to change my mind. Something in me had shifted over the last month and I didn't want to keep relying on the comforts of my youth. My father was stuck in our old roles too, and since our arguments back at home, it had begun to feel less nostalgic and more controlling. If I wanted him to begin to let go, I had to do the same.

"What was that about?" Finnegan asked, sidling up beside me.

I sighed. "I told him I wanted my own space to sleep in."

"Oh." He paused. "So...I'm going to go...make a show of doing that, myself."

"Yeah," I said.

"Yeah," he said.

A beat of silence passed between us.

"See you later tonight?" he ventured, quietly.

"Yeah."

We didn't talk much over dinner, except to go over a few important points. And that was mostly Odina, Kissima and my father. Kissima seemed to be taking Odina's information very seriously, nodding along as the lioness laid out everything she knew about the Jackwalds and what they were likely to bring to bear. The two of them were still talking as Uki and I walked off from camp later that night, when she'd insisted I come with her to see something.

She'd talked to me in between bites of dinner about my life with the Tawnahowac. I'd tried to tell her what I could, but it's harder to summarize your entire life than you might think.

"It sounds idyllic," she said. "I'm happy for you, Tulimak."

"*It's had its difficulties,*" I admitted. "*I've always felt very, very different. From everyone, not just my tribe.*" That feeling had resurged in a big way lately, although I couldn't explain to her why.

"I cannot say it would have been better with us," she sighed. "Even if the tribe hadn't any troubles with the Otherwolves, you...did not have the easiest start in life."

"What do you mean?" I asked.

"Takoda would not have known this, so I doubt he told you," she said, "but you were not the result of a tribal alliance. You were the reason for it."

I stopped, realizing where it was we were headed. The field of stone markers stretched before us, including the four more carefully-maintained graves. The carved stones that rested atop them were actually much less intricate than many of the others, likely because neither Kissima nor Uki were artisans. And there hadn't been anyone else left to do it.

At some point, one of them had returned here while we'd been settling in and lit two more bundles of sage, which were sticking up out of the earth, smoldering and smoking, the curls wafting up into the clear, starry sky.

"Your father, Ujurak," she gestured to one of the graves. "And your mother, Amka. Kissima's sister. Our tribes were...not at war, but...for a time, our territories overlapped and there were misunderstandings, skirmishes between hunters, many negotiations that went nowhere..." She shook her head. "Foolish. If we'd known what was to come. We were so much stronger together. If we'd had more time to reinforce one another, to build our alliance, we might have stood stronger against the invaders."

"So how did..." I trailed off.

"Your father met your mother while he was hunting in the mountains and she was searching for a special kind of root," she explained. "Both had gone too far from their territory in their pursuits. It was a chance meeting." She laughed a little. "I don't know exactly what transpired, but soon he began going on 'long hunts' often. To see her. And so it might have remained, but when the Otherwolves came, with their mines and their logging..." she curled a lip. "We entered negotiations again. And Ujurak, frustrated with the stubbornness our father was displaying, announced his intentions to marry Amka. Father did not take to the idea well at first, but Amka was with child already by then, so."

She looked to the graves, then to the sky. "The spirits led them to one another. And they blessed Amka's womb. With you. So that we might find one another, as people, and unite against a common foe."

I looked out across the field of graves. *"But..."*

Uki took my paw in hers. "I know what you must be feeling. But Tulimak, we had no choice. It was only a question of how bad it was going to be. They push," her paw tightened around mine, "and push. And push. They take, then they take more. They make promises, they rescind those promises, they forget. And eventually, they just bring out the rifles. We'd seen it happen so many times before. We were not going to be pushed aside. Not from the land where our ancestors reside. Not from this place."

She looked up to the sky, pointing up with her free paw. "*Do you see?*" She gestured, tracing a path between the many points of light. "*The charging Ursark? Our greatest protector.*"

I recognized the formation above us as one I'd seen in the cave, traced there into the shape of a large, feral Ursark. Flashes of the dream I'd had played through my mind. "*I do,*" I breathed out.

"From this place, it is always in the sky," she said, her dark eyes sparkling with reflected starlight. "The further south we move, the less it will watch over us. The further north we move, the leaner the land. **This** is our home. We were here before them, and we will be here after them. Even if all we leave behind are our bodies."

She looked to me, unshed tears in her eyes. It was twice now, in the few hours since I'd met her, that she had cried. I felt a kinship with that. I could see myself in some part of her, other than her physical form. It was good to finally feel that way about something here. "*We are part of this place,*" she said. "*They will **never** be part of it. They do not respect it as we do. They do not understand it as we do. My brother—your father—tried to negotiate with the Otherwolves, when they first arrived. But he became convinced very quickly that they would not protect this place as we do. It isn't the spirits' role alone to protect us. We must protect **them**.*"

We didn't speak for long after that. I had little to say to Uki's blind conviction. Especially since, although she certainly came off as unyielding and polarized, I couldn't tell her she was wrong about any of it. I hadn't been more than a cub when this land war had begun and it was in fact very likely that my tribe had been taken advantage of and pushed around by some very aggressive Otherwolf homesteaders, the same way my current tribe was. The main difference was, of course, how each tribe had chosen to react to it.

It would have been easy to make a blanket statement that my father was making the right choice. So far, his entire tribe was alive. Kissima and Uki may have retained their land in the end, but their tribe would die with them, unless more of my people eventually returned here. Or I had cubs. But even then, one family would not save an entire tribe.

Uki wanted to watch the stars, but I was tired and had a lot on my mind I wanted to think over somewhere warmer and less depressing. As I began my walk back, a voice softly emerged from the trees.

"Tuli..."

"Finn?" I whispered back, my eyes adjusting. Eventually I was able to make him out, leaning against one of the few oak trees nearby. His slim figured was easily hidden by the thick trunk, even with his coat on. "How long have you been there?" I asked him.

"Relax, I wasn't eavesdropping," he assured me. "Can't understand a word, remember? I was just worried, you know, with you going off alone with her. We still don't know them well."

I sighed. "They don't really trust all of you, either."

"That's a healthy way to be for now," he said, pushing off the tree and heading towards me. He slipped his hand through mine, squeezing. "Just wanted to make sure you were all right."

"Did my father send you to check on me?" I asked.

"Actually no," he said. "He's gone in for the night. But I...do think he knew where I was headed and was all right with it. He's starting to trust me. At least, as a useful murderer."

"Ugh," I growled.

He just smiled. "Hey, I've learned to take whatever credit I'm given."

We headed back towards the cave, separating our hands once we left the trees. He chatted with me lowly as we walked, I think mostly because he missed talking. It had been nearly a full day where he was left out of almost every conversation. That had to wear on you.

He was bearing it with good spirits, though. And considering it was his life on the line, he'd been patient in asking us for updates. He deserved a lot of credit for that.

So when we got back into the cave, I led him towards where I'd settled my own things. I'd chosen one of the larger caves, probably one that had belonged to an entire small family at some point. I'd gotten a fire started there earlier, just coals from the main pit and a little bit of kindling, and it had since crackled down to little more than embers, but it was enough for the two of us to see by.

We talked casually until we were deep inside the recessed chamber, and then I reached down and firmly took him by the lapels of his jacket, tugging him into a long, deep kiss. After days without him, having to keep myself from so much as touching his cheek or brushing his paw, the sensation of his mouth on mine made stars explode behind my eyes. I breathed him in, felt him whine into the kiss, the sound eliciting a slight leap of my heart. I wrapped an arm around him, crushing his smaller body to mine.

We parted only to suck in air, before kissing again in short, needful bursts. He began to shrug out of his jacket, huffing out lowly, "Sound carries in here, so…mmhh…we'd better…"

I was in the midst of kissing him again, when shockingly, he suddenly shoved away from me. The force of it startled me, not because Finnegan was especially strong, but because of how emphatic it had been. He even smacked at my shoulder a few times to get me to pull away. Which I did, staring down at him, confused.

He was looking past me, ears flat, mouth open.

"Shit," he said breathlessly. "*Shit*. Tulimak, you need to—" he shoved at my chest. "You need to…go. You need to…leave…go. *Now*."

"This is," I glanced around, "my room."

"Your father," he physically pushed me to turn around. "Down there. Now."

My heart froze.

"Tuli, he *saw* us," he stammered. "I'm sorry. Go. Just go. Talk to him."

I didn't need to be told again. I left Finnegan standing there in my room, jacket discarded on the floor, his form illuminated by the dim firelight. It didn't take me long to make it out into the main area, but no one was there. Odina and Sawyer must have still been down at the lake, talking to Kissima. Uki was still in the graveyard. I looked down several of the other cave branches, finding where the mountain lions were staying, and then the room where my father had left his possessions. But he wasn't there. I could smell that he'd been here recently, but he must have come looking for me…and then stormed outside? Maybe just to get air…

By the time I made it back into the main area, something occurred to me. The fur covering the entrance had been pulled back when I'd first come out here. Now it was down.

Distant voices told me all I needed to know to put two and two together. He'd come back while I was searching. It was the worst possible scenario I could imagine. I raced back down the tunnel leading to my cave, the voices growing clearer as I got closer, my heart hammering in my chest.

"…he went out looking for you—" Strangely pained, wheezing.

"It doesn't matter," an echoing growl, barely recognizable as my father's voice. "You are leaving here. *Tonight.*"

"I...can't..."

"I have been tolerant of the *hell* you've brought into my son's life! Into all of our lives. Because I thought you were a *friend* to him. I *knew* you were taking advantage of him, you *all* take advantage of us, but spirits help me you *despicable cur...*"

It was at that point that I made it into the room and found them. To my horror, my father had Finnegan shoved against one of the uneven surfaces of the cave wall, his back and hips jammed up against a sharp protrusion of harder rock than the rest. I knew very well how that must have been excruciating for him, given his old hip injury. My father was both slightly smaller and far older than Finn, and the wolfdog was still armed. He was allowing this to happen, but he looked more helpless than I'd ever seen him.

"Tuli..." he implored, his hands out, palms up.

"Don't *call* him that," my father snarled out, shoving him once more and leaving him there, turning towards me. His eyes were afire. As he approached me, he pointed back in Finn's direction, where the man was bracing against the wall, arm wrapped around his midsection. It's possible he'd been hit, too, although it was hard to tell.

"That," my father spit out, "*that* is why you endangered yourself? Endangered your *family*?! Your TRIBE?!"

I didn't know how to reply to the man I loved so much, faced with his sheer, heart-wrenching anger. But I knew that I needed to. So, I decided all I could do was be honest. "Yes," I said simply.

His eyes widened, and he trembled. "Your sister," he breathed out, "told me...before I left. But I thought she had misunderstood what she was seeing."

It felt like my world was unraveling, piece by piece, coming apart at the seams. "No, otterfa," I said quietly. "She didn't misunderstand."

My father seethed silently for a time, running a paw over first his eyes, then his whiskers. As he did so, I looked past him, towards Finnegan. The wolfdog was nearly doubled over, every part of his body curled in on itself, ears and muzzle downcast. He was still gripping his ribs. He'd definitely been hit.

"You always told me," I was somehow speaking again, my tongue dry, every word a struggle. But I was doing it. I had to. Looking at my father, trying so hard to get him to meet my eyes, too. "You always told me…I would find someone, out in the world, that I would care for. Someone I would want to provide for, to protect—"

"We will find you a shaman," my father said, voice gravelly and worn. "We will purge you of this…curse…this spell he has you under…"

"These feelings are my *own*, otterfa," I said, insistently. "They are a *part* of me—"

"They are *not real*, Tulimak!" He raised his voice, the shout bouncing off the walls of the cave, carrying distantly down the corridor. "For *so* many reasons! He isn't a tribesman. He isn't your kind, he isn't even a *woman*. You cannot have a life worth living with him. He is using you—preying on your loneliness!" He tossed an arm in Finn's direction again. "What do you think he can offer you, other than suffering?! That is *all* he has brought with him into our lives!"

"That isn't true," I said softly.

"Do you know what happens to men…like this? In *their* world?" He growled, claws extended as he drew a line between the two of us.

"Finn's…told me—"

"I don't care what he's told you!" he spat out between grit teeth. "You already *know* he's a liar! *Think,* Tulimak. Have you ever even heard of a tribesman living this way?"

I shook my head. "No," I admitted.

"Why do you think that is?!" he demanded.

His meaning was clear. In a very different way, he was telling me exactly the same thing Finnegan had. Many times. I felt like my body was turning inside out. I wanted nothing more than to curl in on myself, as much as Finn was.

I heard before I saw Finnegan slump down against the wall. Without a second thought, I pushed past my father and headed for him. I knelt down beside him, putting a hand to his shoulder. His muzzle was contorted in pain, but he only shook his head at me as I approached. "Don't—I'm fine," he insisted through gritted teeth.

"No one has to know about this," I heard my father's voice from behind us, dropped somewhat in intensity, now. "Alasie will not tell anyone else, if I explain the consequences it could have on you. We can go home."

"You hurt him," I said, hoarsely.

"We can…leave this man…with Odina and Sawyer," he said, in his "mediator" voice. "They can take it from here. You can even come back here to the Basin later next year, after all of this is behind us. He's a criminal, Tulimak. You would have been separated in Arbordale, anyway—"

"Get out," I growled gutturally.

"…Tulimak…"

"Get. Out." I turned, staring him down.

He looked between the two of us, uncertainly. "I am not…leaving you with him…"

"Leave us ALONE!" I boomed, using every bit of power my voice could command.

My father was stunned silent. Slowly, he began to step back into the threshold of the tunnel. "I…" he slid his palm slowly along the wall. "I'm not leaving you, son. I can't."

"Then leave us alone, for now," I said, turning my attention back to Finn. "I can't talk to you right now."

"…tomorrow…then…" his voice receded into the tunnel. The sadness in it was palpable.

But right now, I was much more worried about Finn. I reached down, gathering him up in my arms. "I'm so sorry," I sniffed. "I'm so, so sorry.'

"You're hurting worse than I am, I'd wager," he said against my fur. But he wrapped his arms up around my shoulders and held on tight, all the same.

Chapter 15

Tension

"You know, I really hate being right all the time," Finnegan grunted as I helped him down into bed. I'd gone to get some of his belongings, but there had been no question between us after what had happened with my father that he was staying with me tonight. I didn't care how it looked.

I pressed my paw pads gently against his ribs, feeling along his bare chest beneath where we'd hiked his shirt up. So far, I hadn't found anything that felt especially bad. "I think it's just badly bruised," I said after a little while, looking back up to his face. He was doing an admirable job of covering his discomfort, but I knew by now, if not based on the injuries he'd sustained while with me then by the myriad of scars I'd found over his body, that this slight man had a far higher tolerance for pain than was probably healthy.

"Your father has a hell of a right hook," he muttered. "Quick, too. Caught me by surprise. I was never really one for fisticuffs, though."

"He might be getting on in years, but he's still a fisherman," I said ruefully. "It's all in the arms."

"Nnhh," he shook his head, smiling through the pain. "One of my favorite things about you, turned against me. Oh, the irony."

"You don't need to be so flippant," I said gently, reaching down to cup his cheek scruff in my palm, a passing gesture between us that was swiftly becoming as necessary for my continued survival as air and food. "You shouldn't have to make light of this. Be angry, if you need to be. My father had no right."

"Humor's how I handle things I…can't handle," he said hesitantly after a few moments. He closed his eyes. "Honestly Tuli, this isn't outside of what I expected. Less talk about God and sin, and…I guess some of the things he flung my way were…deserved, but—"

"No," I growled out. "I don't care that he's my father, Finn. He doesn't get to do this to you, just because he *thinks* he's protecting me from something."

"Tuli, I'm a piece of shite," he muttered, his eyes still closed. He looked so tired. "Maybe it shouldn't matter that we're both men, I don't fucking know. I'm not a priest, I don't know the will of God or…nature…or spirits, or whatever arranged the laws we're all supposed to follow to lead good and virtuous lives. But your father's right about a lot of the other things he said. I'm a murderer, I'm a charlatan, I *did* use you in some ways and I'm continuing to endanger you and your family—now your actual blood family, too—"

"Finnegan, I could have left you in Broen," I stated fiercely. His eyes opened slowly, looking up at mine. I leaned down over him, our noses nearly touching, dropping my voice. "I thought about it. After I found out about the bounty on you. When Sawyer told me you were a killer. I considered leaving you there, taking the raft and going home. Everything… *everything* since that point…has been *my* decision."

He blinked slowly. "That…isn't…that can't be true."

"Think about it," I emphasized. "At what point since then have you made any decisions for the two of us?"

"I decided to leave your village," he said, after thinking about it for a bit. "That's why you left home, ultimately. You and your father fought over it. God, I felt terrible watching that. All of that was because of me."

"Stop being so self-important," I said with a forced smile, stroking a scar on his cheek with my claw. "My father and I fought because he refuses to stop seeing me as a child. And I didn't just come all of this way for you."

"I don't know how much luck we're going to have with this mission for your tribal lands," he murmured.

"Finn, do you honestly think of this relationship between us as being entirely for your benefit?" I asked. The question might have seemed unfair on the surface, but I knew I could bring him around if he stopped thinking of everything within the confines of self-blame. I knew that cycle all too well.

"No," he muttered.

"Then stop acting as if everything we've done has been for your sake. *I need you,*" I said, my voice thin and drawn on the last word. "For as long as I can have you. I've been making decisions that keep you in my life, because I *want* you in my life. I want to be a part of your story. I want you to be a part of mine. All you're able to see is the damage you think you've done. But you've helped me *so* much. Look at where we are." I gestured with my free hand.

"Your father might have told you some day," he said quietly, but his resistance was fading. I could see the warmth in his eyes, each of my words soothing away that cold, cloying guilt he wore like a second skin.

"Not if I'd never had the courage to confront him about it," I said with certainty. "My father does not like to take risks. That's how he keeps our people safe, how he keeps his family safe, but it means everything we experience first has to pass his scrutiny, and we don't get to decide for ourselves if something is worth the difficulty we'll have to endure for it."

"You mean me?" he guessed.

I smiled fondly. "I mean you. Getting to know you made me...brave. Definitely more decisive. It hasn't just been about discovering..." I looked for the right words. "Figuring out...who I wanted to be with. I'm discovering who *I* am. Finally." I dropped my gaze from his. "And the fact is, if you were a woman, I think he'd be proud of how you've helped me mature, and far more accepting of you and I being together."

Finnegan was silent for a time. Eventually, he said, "I'm actually not so certain of that."

I scrunched my brow, making it clear I wanted him to elaborate.

"I mean," he sighed, "I don't think he would have punched me, if I were a female canine. But Tuli, I think he's wanted to hit me since you first came home injured. Your father has a few really valid grievances against me."

"I've already said—" I growled out.

"I understand," he insisted. "And I'm not saying he wasn't out of line tonight. But he was also really fucking shocked, I'd wager. Betrayed, even. And again, that's on me. You wanted to tell him earlier. This wasn't the way he should have found out," he sighed. "You need to give him time to settle down and think. You both need to. You don't want to do or say anything you'll regret right now."

"You mean like he did?" I snapped.

"Let him be the one in the wrong," he said, rubbing a paw over his ribs. "Let him think about it all damn night. About whether or not he wants to lose his son over this. I listened to him, Tuli. Couldn't do much else, doubled-over like that. He sounded...mostly...scared. About your future with someone like me, about what could happen to you if people—*other* people—found out. I didn't hear a whole lot of the sort of self-righteous rhetoric I'd hear back home."

"Like what?" I asked, laying my palm over his where it rested on his chest.

"...shame," he said after a long pause. "It's all about shame, back in Amuresca. About making you feel like less. Your father's certainly not fond of *me*, but when it came to you, he mostly seemed afraid *for* you."

"He tried to make me feel bad for endangering the tribe," I pointed out.

"Yes," his ears tipped back, "but again, I think that was directed at... me. He thinks I've taken advantage of you, lured you in, cast a spell on his innocent son."

"I'm not—"

"Trust me, I know you're not innocent," he said with a wry look. "I've a feeling we've hardly plumbed the depths of *that* well, yet."

I let out a long snuff. "It's true," I admitted, embarrassed. "You've no idea the things I dream of doing with you."

"Do tell," he chuckled, then winced, cutting off his laughter. "Ughhh... although for some reason I've a feeling it's less dirty than I'm imagining and more...like...gardening or something else profoundly wholesome."

"It is not gardening," I assured him.

"You're caught somewhere between adorable and randy, and I hardly know what to call that," he said with a fond smile.

"Twenty?" I ventured simply, with a shrug. "I was nineteen just a few months ago, best we can figure, and my father's told me this sort of thing is normal for young men."

"Fuck, that's right," he snorted. "I keep forgetting. See? No Amurescan father would tell their son it's all right to wank off." He made a gesture at that to explain the, I'm assuming, cultural saying he'd just used. It was instructional. "I mean my uncle Mikhail, maybe…but he was a whore. Sorry, 'courtesan.' Hardly the usual role-model we Amurescan boys get. It's all shame, fear and repression across the pond. Your father's damn open-minded in comparison."

"Finn, he punched you in the ribs," I put a hand to my brow, massaging my temple.

"The man *did* fuck up royal tonight," he agreed, grimacing. "But it's worth talking to him about this a second time, once you've both calmed down."

"Why do you care?" I asked quietly.

"Because I care about *you,* obviously," he rolled his eyes.

"No, but I mean," I sighed, "you keep telling me I'm going to marry, some day. Find a woman. Live a normal life."

"Sure," he said. "You just might."

"Then why do I need to try to convince my father that this," I pointed between the two of us, "is all right?"

"…because you also might not," he said after a long pause.

"Finn," I pleaded quietly. "Please. You know a lot more about this, about the world in general, than I do." I took a deep breath, steeling myself. We'd tip-toed around this many times, but I had the nerve to ask flat-out, finally. And I wanted an answer. "Are there men…" I asked hesitantly, "…who…*can't*…feel this way about a woman?"

His silence spoke volumes.

"What if that path is closed to me?" I whispered.

"Have you ever thought about a woman in that way?" he asked me, softly. "The way you think about me?"

I didn't need to think on it long. I'd been thinking on it for over a month now.

"No," I said, resolutely. "But…" and here I paused, "…but I've felt this way…for other men, I think. Recently. In Broen."

That seemed to surprise even him.

"Nothing important," I said, hanging my head. "I only looked, is all. Just…since I met you…it's like a lot of things made sense. Things I felt before, but didn't understand. Some of the men…at the river, in Broen…

the ones loading the barge. I guess I started to notice their bodies a-a little more. We were fighting at the time and I—"

"Tulimak, you don't need to apologize for that," he said with a forlorn look, slowly pushing himself back up to a sitting position.

"I…I-I think I've liked men a long time…" I admitted, my voice getting very small. I felt tears stinging at my eyes, but I wasn't sure why. Maybe everything that had happened with my father was finally catching up with me. "I just didn't understand," I was repeating myself. "I didn't understand until I met *you*."

He wrapped his arms up around me, pulling me back down into bed with him. I lay against his shoulder until I fell asleep.

"No. Sloppy," Finn's voice bounced across the clearing from where he was sitting with Sawyer. I turned to watch them for a little while. They'd been working on Sawyer's rifle. "You're wasting powder," the wolfdog said, crouching down beside where Sawyer was sitting, reaching over him to guide his hands. They were a decent distance away, so their voices were muffled from here, but I could make out the gist of most of it.

Sawyer seemed frustrated. "Isn't the whole damn point fer me to get my re-load time down, here?"

"Yes, but efficiently," Finn instructed, his voice firm but not unkind. "A shot does you no good if it's packed wrong. All it's going to take is one mis-fire at the exact wrong time for you to learn that lesson the hard way."

"Fine, aright," the mountain lion muttered.

The young man tinkered in silence a little longer, Finn standing over him, watching his work. I smiled fondly, observing them from across the clearing. I was sitting with Uki and Kissima out on what had once been the archery field. The two of them were working on fixing a jaw trap that had fallen into disrepair and I was readying us all some fish I'd caught from the lake for lunch. The water had finally begun to freeze today, but I'd still been able to spear a few in the more sunlit spots.

"I'll tell you what," Finn said with a sigh, once more hunkering down beside Sawyer. "If you can get your load time under forty-five seconds today, I'll show you how to quick-draw tomorrow."

"Really?" Sawyer's head shot up.

"Do you even have a pistol?" Finn asked, looking him over.

"Naw, but I will. Some day."

The wolfdog gave an exasperated sigh. "You can use mine to practice. All right?"

"Hell yeah."

"When's the last time you cleaned your firearm?"

"Uhhhh..."

"That's about what I expected. I'll get my kit."

"If you would like, Tulimak," Uki said from beside me, her voice breaking me out of my reverie watching the two across the clearing, "I could teach you a few things today as well. Takoda has told me you were never formally trained as a warrior."

"I'm...not," I said, bashfully. "A warrior, I mean. At all."

"Nonsense," she shook her head. "You're a predator. You have hunted, yes?"

"*Yes,*" I shrugged.

"And fished, obviously."

"Obviously." I agreed. "But that's not the same thing as war."

"That is true," she nodded. "Would you like to learn how to make war, Tulimak?"

The question was so straightforward, so simple. But it still took me aback. At any other point in my life, the answer would have been obvious. But now...

"I don't...want to," I admitted. "But I've learned the hard way over the last month that what I want matters less than what needs to be done."

"War is like that," she nodded sagely. "After our meal, then."

I swallowed. "All right. Thank you, Uki."

My father didn't show for the midday meal. He hadn't come to breakfast, either. I'd seen him once or twice briefly, near the caves. Smoking, walking the trails along the upper part of the bluff. I know he'd seen me too, but he was sending a clear signal that he wasn't ready to talk, yet. So I'd let him be.

Odina and Sawyer had been our constant companions throughout the day, though. Odina in particular seemed to be getting on very well with Kissima, which made sense. Their personalities appeared very similar to me. Serious-minded, reserved. They only spoke to one another when strictly necessary and when they did, it was over their plans to reinforce the Basin's safety. I think if we weren't all in danger they would have made good companions too, though. It was honestly nice to see the gruff lioness warm to someone. It made her seem slightly less frightening.

Slightly.

Finnegan was still instructing Sawyer on how to clean his rifle through the midday meal. I knew next to nothing about firearms so most of it was lost on me, but apparently the young lion hadn't been terribly diligent on the upkeep of his weapon.

"It's as much the tool of your trade as a smith's hammer and forge," Finn explained, between bites of grilled fish. "Or a fisherman's nets," he gestured to me. "Don't you want to be serious about your trade?"

Sawyer seemed subdued by that question and a moment later, we found out why.

"Sawyer is not going to be a bounty hunter for much longer," Odina explained. "We're getting out of the trade. It was never meant to be permanent."

All of us looked up at that.

"He is going to open a tannery," she continued. "Before I was married, I tanned hides. We are going to make a family business of it, when all of this is said and done and we have the coin to purchase a building in Broen."

"Oh," I said, realization dawning. "That's...that's what you're planning to use..." I looked to Finnegan, "...his...bounty for?"

"We have some coin saved from over the years," she nodded, "but yes. This will be the last job we'll ever need to take. Once we've put the coin into it, my son will have a safe, legal business."

"That's the plan," Sawyer said in a dull tone, his chin resting in his palm.

"But," I said, "you're tribespeople. I thought...my father said we couldn't own land, if we didn't fight in their war."

"Sawyer has citizenship," she said, matter-of-factly.

"We paid off this piece o' shit mayor in Auldrick," Sawyer chuckled, "to draw up the papers. Years'n years ago."

"It cost us everything we had at the time," Odina admitted, putting a hand on her son's shoulder. "But it will be worth it. For his and Nuka's future."

"Clever," Finnegan said, tossing his fish spine in the fire. "You're sure the papers are legitimate? Or decent enough forgeries to pass the muster?"

She narrowed her eyes at him. "I'm no fool. The papers are legitimate. It was the man himself who was corrupt. Filthy…contemptible…" she got a distant look at that, which bothered me for some reason. "But he is behind us. Ahead is brighter."

"Well, hell," Finn sighed, wiping his paws on his already destroyed coat. "I'm glad I'll be helping your little girl out, then. Nice to know I'll be doing some good with all of this. Make sure you count every damn crown. It's the most value I've ever had in my life, I'd at least like to know I fetched the best possible price."

"I won't be swindled, don't you worry," she promised.

The whole exchange, while friendly, sat heavy in my stomach. This situation was unreal. I liked everyone here, even Odina, when I thought hard enough about it. I wanted them all to live happy lives. I wanted Sawyer and Nuka to have a future. Just not at the cost of Finnegan's.

I hated this. I just…hated it.

"*Tulimak, come,*" Uki put a paw on my shoulder, shaking it. She was smiling down brightly at me. "*And bring your axe. The one you chipped ice with earlier today.*"

Since the lake had begun to freeze over near the edges, we had access to ice, which had ended up being useful for Finn's sake. He'd woken with a bad bruise, which we'd iced for a short while this morning. He wasn't gripping his stomach nearly as much anymore, so it must have had an effect.

"Are you sure you want me to bring this one?" I asked, removing the weapon from my belt. "It's really just a woodcutter's axe I brought from home. I saw you had racks of stone hand axes inside the main cave."

"Yours is metal," she said, "and you're accustomed to using it, I assume. Durability and familiarity can be more important than size. That weapon may be meant for otters, but you are used to tools meant for otters. You might find the axes inside unwieldy."

For the first time, I noticed she had something in the crook of her arm on the left side of her body. She must have brought it from the camp site, but I hadn't gotten a good look at it yet. When we reached the center of the field, she turned towards me and revealed what she was holding.

"*Is that—*" I began.

"*Oh, this,*" she held up the grey and brown bird. It had dull, greenish legs and a small red comb. I didn't know much about chickens, but it seemed... normal to me, otherwise. "*This is Blueberry,*" she said, stroking its back. She wasn't holding it terribly tightly, so it must have tolerated being pet better than most chickens I'd ever known. "*We call her that because they are her favorite food. She's very good at finding them in the woods,*" she explained.

She set the bird down. It stood in place for a few moments, then began to peck at the ground looking for insects, milling about aimlessly, but not going far.

"She does not know it yet, but she is dinner," she said, watching the small animal move about. "Catch and slaughter her for us, Tulimak."

"*What?!*" I blurted out.

"Surely you've slaughtered animals before," she asked me patiently.

"Well, yes," I said, exasperated. "But you gave her a name. You told me a story about her. Why did you do all of that? I don't want to kill Blueberry."

I was earnestly upset, and she was beginning to chuckle. It made me feel somewhat humiliated. I'd slaughtered and butchered animals before, of course. I wasn't put off by that and I didn't particularly like being mocked because I didn't want to kill something that was closer to a...pet. Why had she insisted on making this harder?

I went to grab for the bird and she put her paw on my arm, stopping me. "Tulimak, it is all right," she insisted, giving a toothy grin. "I was just trying to illustrate a point. It is harder to kill something...even an animal...when you know it has a name and a story."

"*Oh,*" I said, blanching. "*I...I see.*"

"This is the true difficulty of war," she explained. "It is not just a matter of strength, tenacity or wits. You have those in abundance, I'm certain. You are Ujarak's son." She pointed to the axe on my belt. "And you already know how to use that tool. Your father told me you can split most any log in one swing."

"Well, otter-sized logs anyway," I muttered.

"If you can split a log, you can cleave flesh," she said. "It is not a question of physical ability. It is whether or not you hesitate, whether you can bring that weapon down on a living being—a person. Someone with a name, a family, a story. Even those who wish you harm. Trust me." She looked me in the eyes. "Even if they have taken something from you. Killing requires either fury, or cold indifference. We are all capable of it, but it can be hard."

I couldn't help but think of Finnegan and his eight murders. Eight lives. Eight different stories, ended. I had never taken a life, not even accidentally, not even someone who'd threatened mine. Many of the people he'd killed, Finnegan hadn't even known. He'd killed them for money, for sport, for petty grudges and entertainment for the men with power in his land. But he'd been the instrument, ultimately. I saw how it weighed on him. How he'd get quiet sometimes or laugh at his own misfortune. Did he hate himself for what he'd done?

I'd hesitated to kill a chicken, because I found out she had a name and liked to eat blueberries.

"I don't think I can do this," I said, my shoulders falling. "Uki, I…I don't think I have it in me."

"Everyone can kill," she said softly, her paw moving down to grip my hand. "It is only a matter of which darker impulses you give in to. If you are the sort of person who will kill out of anger, you must be pushed to that point. If you will kill out of desperation, the same. For some, it is easier than others. Hate. Hate is easy. But I do not think you are hateful, Tulimak."

"Finnegan's certainly killed out of desperation," I said quietly. "It's hard for me to understand, even now. Even though I…care about him, even though I've gotten to know him so well and I want to understand."

She nodded. "It is also easier to kill with a firearm, Tulimak. That is worth understanding. Killing from a distance feels very different, in the moment. Afterwards, though…" she clucked her tongue, "…much the same. But it can be easier to pull a trigger than cleave a man's skull."

"'*Can be*'?" I queried.

She held up a paw, showing how it wavered just slightly. "*Nerves*."

"He doesn't seem to have a problem with that," I said darkly.

"Conviction," she hummed. "Whatever it is that steadies his hand, he believes in it."

"I think it's just…survival," I said. "He grew up in a very difficult place, from all he's told me. He's endured a lot of hardship."

"He will likely always exceed you as a warrior, then," she said. "But there's no shame in that, Tulimak. There is no shame in having lived a good life with loving family." She smiled. "It's all we ever wanted for you. I hope you go on, after all of this, to raise another loving family. And that your children never know hardship, either."

I bit the inside of my mouth, guiltily. "*I…I don't know if I'm ever going to find a wife, Uki,*" I admitted.

She gave me a long look, her big brown eyes appraising me. Then she took both of my paws in hers and turned me to face her. "*Then raise a family with your wolf, Tulimak.*"

"*I-I…*" my heart stopped. "*What?*"

She tilted her head. "It is…Finn. Finneg? I am sorry, their names are strange."

"*Finnegan,*" I said, searching for words for a moment. "*How…?*"

She blinked up at me. "I see. This must be what you and your otterfa were feuding over, last night. And still this morning, it seems. I noticed you keep your distance from the wolf when you are around him, despite your obvious bond. You were not being honest with him."

"*Look what happened when I was,*" I gestured at the caves, where he was likely still stalking about, smoking like a chimney. "*Why doesn't it bother you like it bothers him? And how did you know?*"

"You smell of each other's clothes," she explained. "Like mates. Kissima and I both noted it. We bears have a better nose than otters. Also, he stayed in your cave last night. We weren't entirely certain until then," the corners of her muzzle crinkled in a smile. "But there are plenty of caves. There could be only one reason."

"*Fair,*" I murmured. We'd known that was a risk.

"My grandfather," she continued, "had two mates. A wife, and a twin-tailed lover from a neighboring wolf tribe."

"'Twin-tailed'?" I repeated.

"Not literally," she laughed. "It is what we called those whose spirits were not what they first appeared. This wolf had been born a man, but was raised amongst the women once it became clear it was where she belonged."

"I…" I tried to digest that. "I don't think I'm 'twin-tailed.' Or that Finnegan is, either."

"Our spirits know the kinship that is right for them," she said. "It is not for the tribe to decide who must love whom. A shaman whose eyes are truly open would tell you this. When two spirits are drawn together, the body is irrelevant. Do you love this wolf, Tulimak?"

"I…I don't know," I admitted. "I've never been in love. My otterfa always told me I would know. I feel like I do, but…but there are so many reasons we can't be together. My father disapproves. Clearly. Finnegan's people, by all rights, would disapprove. Vehemently, if what he's told me is true, and I don't doubt it is. And," I looked down at where her hands were still holding mine, "I do want a family, Uki. It's something I've always wanted. I'd need a wife, to have cubs."

"Tulimak, your father, the one who raised you, is an otter," she said, pointedly. "Why would you ever think that you'd need to marry a woman to have a family?" Her smile returned. "You are living proof that is not true."

I rejoined Finnegan and Sawyer down by the lake some time later. Finn had removed his hip holster and lent it to Sawyer for a time, and despite the fact that they were playing with a pistol, there was something profoundly touching about watching him humor the young mountain lion's request.

I couldn't hear them from where I sat down at the edge of the tree line, but I watched for a time as Finn patiently went over the subtle motions and movements he used to quick-draw the weapon. There was more that went into it than I'd assumed.

Eventually, he left the lion to his own devices and called something like "I'll be watching from up here" over to him, before heading over towards me. He sat down beside me on a fallen log, washed up ashore long ago and worn smooth by the water.

The conversation with Uki was fresh in my mind, but I wasn't sure I was ready to talk to him about it yet, given all the very heavy things it had me thinking about. He seemed to know I was troubled though, likely assuming it was still over my father, (which to be fair, was also true).

"You doing all right?" he asked, reaching down to thread his fingers through mine.

"I...mmmhhh..." I hung my head slowly, not sure how to answer him.

He moved a bit closer to me and brought my hand up to his muzzle, kissing my knuckles gently. It was a small, brief gesture, but it made me feel worlds better.

Until I saw my father nearby.

Finn saw him too, his ears immediately tipping back, posture stiffening. The older otter was meandering along the lakeside, coming back towards camp. He must have been out for a walk.

He noticed us too before long and stopped where he was. It looked like he was considering turning around. He couldn't possibly head back towards camp without passing right by us.

Finn growled slightly in the back of his throat. "Is he—he's turning around."

I sighed. "He's been avoiding me all day."

"No, enough of this," the wolfdog grated out, standing.

"Finn—"

"Talk to your son, you fucking coward!" he shouted before I could stop him. My father stopped dead, turning to look back at us.

I couldn't blame Finn for snapping at the man. He wasn't usually one for unnecessary confrontation, in fact he'd had to calm me down many times in the past. But he was right, avoiding this was not doing either of us any good. I didn't want my father and I to be strangers.

I pushed myself up off the log and crossed the distance between us in measured steps. If we were going to fight again, I didn't want to do it within earshot of Sawyer. I heard Finn following behind me and wondered briefly if this was something I ought to do, just my father and I.

But...no. Finn was involved, after all. And moreover, I wanted him with me.

We stopped a few paces apart. My father looked tired, drawn and hunched in on himself. More than anything though, he looked guilty, which was not something I was used to seeing on the man I'd looked up to my entire life. He smelled like smoke, the scent of his pipe clinging to his fur enough that he must have been smoking again recently. My father had smoked as long as I'd known him, but not usually so much in one day. Only during bad times, like when my mother had been sick.

"Just so you know," Finnegan spoke up, "I gave you the first one, but if you try to hit me again, I'll retaliate this time."

"I...am sorry, about that," the otter said, his voice ragged. "I was..." he started to say something, then let it die on his tongue. "It doesn't matter. That was wrong of me."

"I'm sorry I didn't tell you earlier, otterfa," I said, exchanging the apology. "I was afraid."

"Also, I warned him not to," Finnegan spoke up. "Where I come from—"

"I am aware," my father said sharply. "I am more worldly than my son. I have spent the better part of my life trying to find a place for my people within your encroaching society. We haven't a choice, any longer. Your ways are becoming ours by force, you are re-crafting this land in your image."

"I understand that you're worried for me," I began to say.

"Worried?" He actually scoffed at that. "'Worry' is not the term I would use, even in their tongue. 'Terrified' would be more accurate. Disappointed, as well. You may not be an otter, son, but in all other ways you embody the spirit of the Tawnahowac. You could live a proud, decent, happy life. You are giving all of that up." He looked to Finnegan, narrowing his eyes. "For *what?*"

"Why do you assume I'm the end-all, be-all for your son's future?" Finnegan demanded. "Just because we're together right now—"

"Are you *admitting* you're just toying with him, then?" my father challenged, angrily. He stomped a foot forward into the frozen mud, but didn't do anything more than that, for now.

Finn seemed to realize his mistake the moment it left his mouth. "No, I—"

"It wouldn't matter to me if you were a woman if you were still a criminal with a bounty on your head," my father exclaimed. "You are going to break my son's heart, and you *know* it, and yet, you *persist* with this rather than stepping back and doing the right thing and letting him *get on with his life*! How long has it been that you've strung him along like this?!"

"I-I haven't," Finnegan seemed to gather himself. "He wants to be with me."

"He has no experience!" the otter said between grit teeth. "Of *course* he wants to be with you! My son may not be a child anymore, but he has an open, unrestrained heart. You are *letting* him give it to you, knowing what could happen, knowing what *will ultimately happen* when you reach Arbordale. And that's if he doesn't die for you first!"

Finnegan looked to me, as if looking for help. But I couldn't refute all the things my father was saying, because so many of them were worries I had in fact had for some time, now.

There *were* things I wanted to say, though.

"Otterfa," I spoke, finally. "I hear you. I understand your words. But are these really the reasons you don't want us to be together? Because last night, you said many other things that...hurt. They hurt *me*."

The older otter let his hands fall at his side, at that. He looked torn. "I don't...want this for you," he said. "For so many reasons."

"Uki says there are tribal men who've been mates with other men in the past," I said. The statement seemed to surprise Finnegan, and my father. But less so my father.

"That," my father said, putting his hands out, "is an old, dead tradition. And it is not one our tribe has ever practiced in recent memory. I don't personally believe it to be sanctioned by the spirits. It is not good for tribes to encourage marriages that cannot produce children."

"Hold on," Finnegan huffed. "Your people have *married* men together, in the past?"

"Not our tribe," my father insisted, stubbornly.

"But others," I pressed. "Uki thought nothing of it."

"If you want to look to why that practice was abolished entirely, look no further than *his* people," my father gestured at Finn. "Our traditions are dying at their hands as surely as our people are. Whenever they deem them 'barbaric' or 'sinful' there's a purge."

"A raid," Finnegan said quietly.

"I don't personally think what you're engaging in is right, or natural," my father said, his uneasiness clear in his body language. "But it is not me you need worry over. And that's what terrifies me. I can protect my children from most of the world's dangers, Tulimak, but this..." He shook his head, pleading. "I thought you wanted a family. I had such high hopes for you."

"There is no reason I can't still have a family, otterfa," I said, crossing the space between us, finally. I reached down to take his hand in mine. "Look at us."

The old otter stared up at me, his expression softening marginally. Then he looked back down at our hands…his fingers webbed and brown, half the size of mine.

Finnegan moved up beside us. Before I could look to him, he spoke, his voice low and deadly serious. "Takoda, you were followed. No—don't look up, Tuli. Don't. Neither of you."

The fur down my spine stood on end and I chanced a briefly glimpse over my father's shoulder towards the woods, but saw nothing. My father similarly fought the urge to stare behind us, but his sudden concern was evident in his features.

"Spruce tree, about fifty yards back along the bank," Finn continued, softly. "He's up high. Probably trying to get the lay of the land."

"What should we do?" my father asked.

"Walk with me," Finn murmured. "I don't have my weapon on me and it'd be a hell of a shot from here either way, but Sawyer has a rifle."

We all turned and made our way down the bank towards where the mountain lion was practicing.

"'Ey all," he said chipperly, spinning the pistol in a needlessly showy fashion before depositing it cleanly back in his hip holster. He was actually getting pretty good at that. "Family troubles? Got those. My Ma's been—"

"Sawyer, I need your rifle." Finn said calmly.

"S'right up there near mah bag," he pointed, Finn immediately grabbing his hand and eased it down. "What?"

"Scout," Finn explained briefly. "Don't turn," he said before Sawyer could. "And stay here with Takoda, like you're talking. I don't want him to think we're heading back into the caves, I want him right where he is. Tuli, come with me. It'll look suspicious if I go off alone and I need a blind, anyway."

We did as he said. My father stayed behind with Sawyer on the bank, the two of them trying to appear as though they were talking casually. I was a bit nervous leaving my father and the young lion so exposed, but I had to assume Finn knew what he was doing.

"They're out in the open," I said to him as we casually walked towards Sawyer's things.

"One scout isn't here to start a fight," Finn said. "He's here to see how many of us there are and what the layout is. Sit on that stump."

I did as instructed, slowly settling down on the large, hewn stump he'd indicated. The area here was overgrown with some kind of evergreen, sharp-leafed shrub which kept the snow from collecting too much on the ground, likely why Sawyer had set his rifle and powder down here. Finn moved behind me and the scraggly shrubs, dropping to his knees and checking the weapon over for a few moments.

"Can you fire that as well as you can a pistol?" I asked without turning around.

"Rifles are far more accurate," he said as he slowly brought the weapon up between the branches of the foliage. "He's looking here, I think. He knows something's going on. Go on…that's it…lean forward…"

"I can barely see him," I admitted, although now I definitely could see *someone*. They were very well-camouflaged, midway up the tree in question, but they must have moved to get a better vantage point, because they were more obvious now than they had been before.

"Tulimak, cover your ears when I say," Finnegan whispered.

"Please don't miss," I begged, worried for my father.

I heard something click, followed by his voice. "I don't miss. Now cover your ears."

I did so. A second later, the shot rang out from less than a foot away from me, like thunder when a storm was right overhead. I grit my teeth and smelled powder, the smoke billowing up around us.

Something fell out of the tree.

Sawyer and my father had both gone for cover, but Finnegan was getting up, grabbing at my arm to do so as well. "Come on," he grated out. "You've got your axe, right?"

I nodded and we bolted back down towards the shoreline, feet pounding into snow-slickened earth. Finnegan stopped briefly by Sawyer, barking at him, "Pistol, now!"

Sawyer pulled it free, struggling with it in a moment of panic before he got it into Finn's outstretched hand. And then we were running again, *towards* the tree. *Towards* the enemy.

This was mad.

We made it there in time to see a man, lean and smaller than Finnegan, some kind of canine with white and brown fur and flopped over-ears. He was wearing leathers, but had a forest-green cloak that by now was tangled and pillowed around him where he was splayed. He'd clearly fallen, then drug himself down the shore across the icy snow towards the lake, a blotchy trail of crimson in his wake. The blood seemed to be coming from his thigh, where he had a hand clamped over a bad-looking wound.

"Stop moving," Finn warned, holding his pistol out as he approached. I followed up behind him, my axe held in a now sweating palm.

In response, the man backpedaled further, going for a weapon on his own belt.

"I said *stop,*" Finnegan growled out. "If not for my sake then for your own. You can survive that wound, if you staunch the flow of blood. Moving's making it worse."

"If y'know what's good for you Ambrose, you'll walk outta this savage camp with me'n turn yourself in," the Otherwolf snarled out, pulling his pistol finally. Unlike Finnegan though, his hand was shaking wildly.

"All right, first off," Finnegan said defiantly, "you're not 'walking' anywhere with that. Secondly, you can fuck *right* off. I'm not going anywhere with you."

"This doesn't have to happen," I spoke up. "You and your men don't need to bring him in. He's already in our custody. We're bringing him to Arbordale."

The canine was still backpedaling, half-crawling at this point. "We ain't leavin' until he's under arrest. That's the job," he said, narrowing his eyes. "*Proper* arrest. Not'n the hands o'some savages."

I heard more footsteps crashing through the woods, coming our way. Likely the women. "You're outnumbered," I pointed out. "Wounded—"

"I seen how many you got in camp," he replied. "And we talked to folks at the nearest trade post. Said all that e'er comes outta here are two women. You ain't got shit."

"You're on the ice!" I tried to warn him. He'd been walking, or rather crawling out onto it this whole time, trying to get as far from us as possible. It was working, because I sure as hell wasn't following him and Finn seemed to know not to, either.

"This doesn't have to go down this way," Finn said, not dropping his gun arm.

"Ohhh, bit late fer that," the man said around a wince. "Boss got caught up in one o'them traps, got it *out* for you now, boy. You're lucky you're worth more alive."

"Come back to shore," I pleaded. "The lake gets deep very f—"

He made the mistake at that point of trying to push himself to a standing position. With a popping, otherworldly noise that anyone raised in these parts knew to fear, the thin sheen beneath him gave way and the man disappeared in a few seconds flat, with little more than one last, cut-off cry and a mad scramble at the jagged edge of a large sheet that flipped over top of him as he went down.

Finnegan and I both ran to the edge of the icy bank, staring out at the cracked, black-blue hole he'd left behind and the trail of blood leading to it. We waited.

And waited.

In time, our companions arrived. No one said a word. It was not hard to deduce what had happened.

Finnegan released a long, frustrated breath, letting his gun arm fall. "Well that's nine," he muttered.

Chapter 16

Blood Moon

The cave was a flurry of activity that night. Mostly, a lot of talking. Kissima, Uki and Odina were sharing their knowledge and going back and forth on plans for the coming day. Finnegan would add a kernel of opinion here or there about what these mens' capabilities were likely to be and what to expect in firepower. Odina served as a translator for most of the conversation. My blood relatives spoke some Amurescan, but their understanding was spotty. Kissima was better at it than Uki.

My father and I were, for the most part, severely out of our element. Even Sawyer had more to add than we did. The young man had been doing sweeps up and down the edge of the basin each morning, looking for vantage points and gaps in the trees we might be able to exploit from above. I wouldn't have even considered something like that.

We ate, talked and prepared, the latter role primarily being taken up by Finnegan, who was checking over, taking apart and carefully cleaning our firearms. He'd mentioned wanting to modify them somehow, but apparently there wasn't time or the right supplies for that.

"This weather is miserable for flintlocks," he said distractedly as he looked over Odina's rifle. "And your powder could be better, Kissima. I don't know where you're buying your supply, but they might be substituting something. Or they're not storing it properly."

"We've had problem in the past with rifles not igniting," Kissima said, nodding. "I had wondered."

"Percussion caps load faster, ignite hotter and they're better in weather like this," Finnegan said with a sigh. "It's a simple enough modification, but I can't do it here. I'd need to change the cock out for a hammer, and I don't have the tools, regardless. But you should consider it in the future."

"I had my own modified some years ago," Odina said, looking to Sawyer. "But it was expensive. We never modified his. I did not see the point, since he loads so slowly anyway."

Sawyer began to object, before Finn laid a hand on his shoulder. "No worries there. Sawyer's going to stick with me and load for me, army-style. His idea."

Odina's brows lifted at her son, suitably impressed. "Yeah, Ma," the young mountain lion smiled. "I ain't gonna be all self-important when stakes're this high. Ambrose's got the eagle eyes and all, I want to be as much use as I can. Make every shot count, right? I know you're gonna be perched somewhere on yer own, so..."

"I'm still deciding between a few places," she nodded.

"Uki and I moved some of the traps," Kissima said, "but not much time. That scout got past ones we set, so we should not think we can rely."

"He followed me," my father said a bit guiltily, "along the paths I knew were safe. I'm sorry, I should have been more observant."

"He's dead, in any case," Finnegan cut in, voice curt. "So he can't report back on the route he found. And he mentioned that one of their men, he indicated a leader of some sort in fact, fell afoul of one of your traps in the wood."

"What about me?" I finally spoke up, looking to Uki and Kissima. "I mean...I essentially know how to fire a rifle, but we only have four and like Sawyer said, we should let those of us," I looked to Finnegan and Odina at that, "who can make their shots count have those. As it is, it's a dozen men with guns versus only four of our people who are any good at a range."

"They cannot simply fire on us from the cover of the trees," Uki said. "We could remain in the caves and wait them out as long as we need to; we've far more supplies than a few men on horseback are likely to. They will have to take the village. They may have us outmanned and outgunned, but this village was established here **because** it is so defensible."

"We're going to do our best to keep them from reaching the caves and our gunmen first and foremost," Kissima said. "Even the shores of the village, if we can help it. We have the advantage of knowing which direction they'll come from, but it's a large area. We can perch high in the caves and have a vantage point overlooking the forest and the lake, but the trees will provide them with ample cover. We'll only be able to take shots when they reveal themselves, which won't be often. But that means they'll need to move slowly down there, rushing between cover. And if they want to have any chance at reaching us unseen, they'll not be able to move in large groups, either. That is where Uki, Tulimak and I will have our chance."

"You're not going to be in the caves?" I asked, uncertainly.

"Those who stay in the caves will have no path to the forest without exposing themselves to gunfire," Kissima explained. "And as I said, it is key that we prevent them from reaching the caves. Some of them will surely slip past our gunners, there are too many. As they draw close, someone must meet them in the woods. Fire on them, ambush them, or force them into the open so that our gunmen can pick them off."

Odina translated all of that in broad strokes for Finnegan, who nodded. "You two are seasoned hunters," he said, eyes narrowing, "but I don't know how I feel about Tulimak being in the kill zone. Especially without a rifle."

"Tomorrow, I will instruct Tulimak on axe throwing," Uki piped up. "I had hoped we'd have more time, but things being as they are..."

"Hopefully we won't be under attack by then," my father murmured.

"I doubt they will come in the morning," Kissima reasoned. "The sun rises over the bluffs. It would blind their approach. They will come closer to evening."

"One of your caves up top is full of fishing spears," my father said. "Do you mind? I'm a miserable shot with a bow, but..."

"Take as many as you wish," Kissima said, nodding. "We carved an abundance last year during the winter, when the snow kept us sealed in for a time. We've hardly gone through half of them so far this year."

"Otterfa, you're going to fight?" I asked, surprised.

He looked to me, his grey-peppered brow lowering. "*You thought I wouldn't?*"

"All of us will fight," Uki said with a toothy, intimidating smile. "I do not care what these men want with your wolf, Tulimak. Their kind will take nothing more from this tribe. Ever again."

"There's a part of me that really feels I should just turn myself in," Finn said quietly as we walked back to our cave. "I don't want to watch any of these people die for me. Not even your father."

"Odina is fighting for a future for her children," I reminded him, "and this is a task she *chose*. For better or for worse. You might be able to help my tribe's future as well, Finn. Besides," I ground my teeth, uncomfortably, "even as 'unworldly' as I am, and I have to tell you I'm getting very tired of being reminded of that—"

"Sorry," he said.

"My father was the one to say it this time, not you," I sighed. "Anyway, my point is, if even *I* realize these men are not likely to just take you and go, the reality of that must be setting in for you by now."

"It's probably worse than you realize," Finnegan admitted, sadly. "Outfits like this? They're part of a larger group of thugs, so it's never just the men you're dealing with that you have to worry about. In Amuresca they're called 'gangs,' 'mobs,' or 'syndicates'. They don't forget and they don't forgive. If any of these men make it back to their organization and they think for a moment that Uki and Kissima were harboring me, protecting me...Hell, they could come after your otter tribe, too. For the same reason. Even if they win here and capture me. Just getting the coin is not going to be enough."

I looked to him, worried. "You think they'd go after my otter tribe after this, even if they got what they wanted?"

"I can't say for sure, obviously," he reasoned, "but I lived in the Risers long enough to know how armed gangs work. It's about sending a message. I'm sure that story about what they did to the miners was spread around by their own group, as well as any survivors they let escape. Even if what they did there technically broke the law, an organization like that wants to be feared more than they want a clean reputation. They don't want anyone harboring future marks they're set on hunting down. So they'll do things to put the fear of God into people, make it clear what happens when you work against their interests."

"All it took was the mention of the Jackwalds to frighten both Odina and my father," I agreed.

We both stopped in front of the opening to our cave, staring at something that hadn't been there before. Someone had hung a caribou fur over the entranceway. There'd been these little divots dug into the rock along the edges of the "doorway" that I'd noted were on most of the others around the caves as well. I hadn't realized until now what they were intended for. The caribou fur had holes cut into it that were spaced the right distance apart to be hung on them. The other doors had probably all had them a long time ago as well, back when the caves were more occupied.

"Uki's work, no doubt," I said as I slowly pushed aside the flap, stepping inside. The tunnel here gave us some privacy, being that it bent more than once, but this was certainly better.

"Where was this the other night?" Finn asked aloud, grumbling.

"I think this was likely an improvement made in response to that," I said pointedly. "But I'm not arguing."

"Mnnh." Finn seemed less pleased than I was.

I shed my cloak once we were inside and kneeled beside the dim coals in our firepit, gathering kindling from the small bundle nearby and slowly coaxing it back to life. "What's with the grumbling?" I asked him. I didn't turn, but I heard him unbuttoning his coat and going about the process of removing his leather spats, gun belt and holster.

"It's nothing," he assured me. "Just interesting that they weren't so insistent on anyone else having a cover for their doorway."

"Uki was very accepting when I spoke to her about…us," I said, blowing gently on the ashes to re-kindle the fire. "I'm absolutely certain it's meant as a kindness, and nothing else. I mean, it's a practical consideration. We *are* the only mated pair here."

"'Mated Pair,'" Finnegan whistled, chuckling from behind me.

"I don't know what else to call us," I admitted, finally turning to regard him. He'd stripped down to his undershirt and britches and was shrugging out of his vest by the time I looked over. My body tensed in a few places, just at the sight of him undressing. It was frankly humiliating how easily he could affect me without even being aware of it.

"I like it," the wolfdog smirked, tail flicking about. "Certainly a kinder expression than those we have in Amuresca for two men bunking up."

I stood slowly and crossed the space between us. He was still fussing with his vest, so by the time I reached him, he seemed surprised I was so close.

"Tuli—" he began questioningly, but by then I'd wrapped an arm around his middle and another behind his knees, scooping him up. He gave a whuff of surprise and looked briefly alarmed, until I'd crossed the two strides necessary to deposit him in the combined mound of furs that had made up our sleeping space last night.

The surprise on his features hadn't entirely gone, but he began to chuckle as I climbed over him. "Well, good evening to you too, sir," he snickered, glancing down between us. Specifically where I was tenting my breech cloth. "How may I be of service?"

"You're so strange sometimes," I muttered, nosing at where his shirt gaped.

"Says the bear who has bodily lifted me like a fainting damsel on more than one occasion now," he pointed out, stroking a palm up and over my shoulder, his claws tracing the line of one of my marks. "You could just ask me to get into bed, you know."

"You seem to like it when I pick you up."

"I do like it," he admitted, still smirking.

"You joked last time we were alone together about using my arm strength for..." I paused at that. "Actually I'm not certain," I said, resting my jaw as lightly as I could on his chest. "You want me to hold you up and...I...guess rub against one another? That sounds more like how I scratch myself on trees..."

"Oh, you sweet darling," he said between snorting laughter. "You really have no idea, do you?"

"Hey," I blew out a breath across his fur. "I'm getting better at figuring out what I want."

"What do you want, Tuli?" he asked in a far-too-sultry tone.

"I want..." I trailed off, then rubbed the side of my cheek against his chest, huffing lowly. "I don't know, Finn. I want *you*," I said, frustrated. "I've really liked what we've already done with one another. Is there more?"

He smiled slowly, nodding.

"There's one thing I've wanted to do since Tawnahowac," I growled softly, nuzzling at his belly. I wanted my nose in his fur, so I got up on my elbows and balled my fingers in the cotton of his undershirt, tugging it up from where it was tucked into his britches. He saw what I wanted and easily assisted me, pulling the loose shirt up over his head and discarding it. While he did so, I got back to my knees and undid my breech cloth, freeing myself of its restraint.

"Fuck," Finn let out in an utterance, his paw wandering down his body to grip himself between his legs, despite the fact that he was still clothed there.

"You like that word," I said, moving back over him. "Especially when we're, well..."

"When I fancy my pants off," he said, fussing with the tie on his britches, "the chap from the Risers comes out in me, so you'll have to endure the gutter talk, I'm afraid."

"I don't care what you say, I just like hearing you," I admitted. "I've always liked your voice."

"Well one hide isn't going to prevent sound from carrying down here," he said, glancing at the caribou fur just barely covering our doorway. "So, unless you want tomorrow to be *real* awkward in addition to real dangerous, we ought to try and keep it down—damn. Tuli, that is still goddamn intimidating," he said, changing gears rather abruptly mid-thought, his gaze still pinned between our bodies.

I followed his eyes, realizing eventually that he was indicating where I hung stiffly between my legs. "Oh," I said, blanching. "I-I'm sorry. I'm big... everywhere..."

"Let it never be said Finnegan Ambrose was one to back down from a challenge," he said with a grin that revealed his canines. He peeled himself out of his britches, kicking them aside. His own cock, a lighter shade of pink than mine and half the size, was also fully out of its sheath by now, rising up from the dusting of white fur between his legs. I'd never wanted anything so badly.

The urge to push my oversized muzzle down between his legs came on even stronger than it had last time. I decided this time that there was no use in fighting it. I dropped my nose back down into his fur and snuffled my way down his belly, dragging his scent through my nostrils. He smelled more like himself, the scent I knew to be his, than he had the last time we'd been together like this, right after we'd bathed. In a way I preferred it. It brought back a lot of memories of time we'd spent together on our journey thus far, a general feeling of "us," of this strange, life-changing connection we'd built.

I wanted him so desperately. I wanted to wake up to his scent, every morning.

"Ah-Tuli...ahh..." his palms moved around my head to stroke at my ears, fingers moving through the thick rolls of fur around my neck. I could feel his cock beneath my clavicle, knew the moment he realized what I intended for him by the way he splayed his legs for me. "Are you sure?" I heard him ask in a husky, low voice when my muzzle made it to the scruff of fur above his sheath.

"Mmmhh-hmmhh," I nodded, letting out a warm breath on his cock. His entire body *shook*.

I swiped my tongue out first, tasting him. My tongue was easily able to cup half of him, lathing it root to tip. He tasted like he smelled, mild and musky and utterly unlike myself. I curled my tongue along his tip as I finished one long, first swipe, then went in for another.

Finn's hips stuttered, lifting off the furs as he bit down on a whine, then released a long, shuddering breath. I loved watching his reaction, so I lifted my gaze to him as I took another slow lick of his manhood.

"God...mffhhh...is your tongue blue?" he asked around a puff of breath.

I couldn't help but smile slightly at the odd question. I suppose before now, he'd never really had a reason to examine it closely. "It's spotted," I said, amused. I cupped it around his cock again, closing my eyes for a moment as I focused on the feel of him, encased in my tongue.

One of his paws was still cupping my cheek and toying at one of my ears. "Fuck, you're so damned cute—ah...ahhh..." He lifted his hips into my ministrations, squeezing his eyes shut. "I'm gonna cum way too soon, watching you..."

I was growing more and more needful myself, seeing how strong a reaction I could pull out of him with something so simple. It was surprising and empowering, like I'd stumbled upon a great secret to cracking the wolfdog's often cool demeanor. So far, each time we'd spent a night together like this, I'd felt relatively at his mercy. His experience and knowledge exceeded mine and he was far more confident besides.

But for the first time, the tables had turned and I found there was a part of me that reveled in it. I'd enjoyed following his lead in the past as well; it had been a real relief to have someone who knew the way when I was in uncharted waters. But this...this was good, too.

I thought back on what he'd done that night in my pit home. It seemed, honestly, somewhat dangerous? I had very large fangs. But all I had to do was be careful. He'd been careful and it had been fine.

It was worth the risk sheerly for the groan that emanated from deep in his chest when, at last, I closed my muzzle around him. I tested it slowly, but soon found it was no challenge whatsoever to take the whole of him in my mouth. He'd only been able to take half of me, and I realized of course that I had an unfair advantage, but still. It was satisfying.

"Fucking *suck me,*" he growled gutturally, loping one of his legs lazily up over my shoulder, his paw curling around one of my ears, like he wanted to hold me there.

I'm honestly glad he said that aloud, because for a moment, even though I'd taken him into my mouth, I wasn't sure what to do with him. But then I remembered how he'd done it and began to try, myself. I could still employ my tongue, thankfully, although not as dexterously. Even though I'm certain I was bad at figuring the process out and taking far too much time doing so, he seemed to be enjoying it. Perhaps so long as I was gentle, there wasn't really a way to get this wrong.

He leaked down my tongue, salty and warm. I hollowed my cheeks as well as I could, glad for once for my oversized muzzle. My own cock throbbed between my legs, something about this…the noises of the act itself, the noises it was pulling from *him*…just…driving my want even further. I hadn't expected that doing this for him would have such an effect on *me*.

My gaze moved up along his body as I bobbed my muzzle between his legs. He'd thrown an arm over his face at some point, muffling his moans into it. His chest rose and fell in panting breaths and his tail was swiping about erratically beneath him in the furs.

I felt a deep, rumbling growl build in my throat, which I hadn't intended. I worried for a moment that it might frighten him, but instead I felt his hips stiffen, his body going taut. He tried to push at my skull, to warn me, I suppose.

I'd decided when I'd begun this that I didn't want to make a mess of our bed. Maybe that was just an excuse, I don't know. But either way, I only took him deeper, wanting all of him, his knot included. It was just more of *him*, after all.

He buckled against me, paw gripping the back of my head, hips locking me in tight, with the one leg he'd thrown up over my shoulder clamping around me. If he was at all concerned at that point for my comfort, instinct had won out.

With my muzzle pressed to the base of his knot, he did actually come rather close to gagging me, and I had to struggle to swallow him all, but at least I didn't taste most of it. I let him slip from my mouth finally, after sucking at his knot gently through the last of it.

To say the wolfdog looked flustered would be an understatement. He was devastated, absolutely in shambles. Honestly, I felt rather proud of myself.

"I *can't* be all that good at that," I teased him, licking my muzzle as I looked down on him.

"I haven't had my cock sucked in over a year and it's just about my favorite fuckin' thing in the world," Finn uttered between heavy pants. "Don't get a big head." He paused. "R'actually. Your head can stay exactly the size it is now, it's perfect for my purposes."

I snorted. "Yes, I think this is a bit easier for me than it is you."

"Natural advantage," he agreed, nodding blissfully. "But life's about overcoming adversity, and I'm a scholar in that." He slowly and dizzily got to his knees, gesturing at me. "C'mon and stand, for me. Let me show you how it's really done."

"Stand?" I repeated, uncertainly doing as I was told. Although I had to admit, the view from above him was spectacular. He looked blissful and flustered, fur all askew, his knot still out and cock still hanging between his legs, resting against our blankets. His tail was sliding back and forth behind him and one of his ears had just entirely given up, crooked to the side. To see the normally fastidious man lose all composure, just for me, was utterly satisfying.

"It's how I prefer it," he smirked, palms spread flat over my thighs, nose trailing down the scruff on my belly. "Everything's right there, laid before me." His green eyes lifted up to mine, pinning me there on the spot. There were a lot of things about tonight I'd remember for quite some time, I was certain. I hoped to make many more memories like this with Finnegan.

Unless tomorrow was the last day I'd ever have with him.

I woke to my name being called, repeatedly. By a voice more familiar to me than any other.

I blinked slowly, the ground reasserting itself beneath my feet, reality spinning back into focus in a dizzying barrage. The sensation of hands on my biceps, steadying me.

"Tulimak, are you with me?" My father's voice. His eyes, looking up at mine. His figure, encased by early twilight. I was outside. We were outside.

"I'm…awake," I said slowly, growing more certain of that by the moment. When I had these dreams, it could be so hard to tell. I looked over his shoulder, out towards the forest and the lake beyond. The scenery looked much the same as it had through the haze of my waking dream, but everything was more substantial now.

The same waking dream. It had happened again. I was glad at least at this point that I'd learned to put my breech cloth on before turning in, or I'd be sleep-walking everywhere nude.

"I saw it again, otterfa," I said quietly.

"The vision?" he asked knowingly.

I nodded, hazily. "The Ursark, with a seam of light and dark down the middle. The young bear it made from blood…"

"You're all right," my father assured me, patting my arms and releasing them. "Just a dream. You're having them because you're troubled. Just like when you were young. They'll pass."

He scrunched up his nose for a moment, then began to walk away from me. I didn't miss the passing look of discomfort, but more importantly—

"Otterfa, please," I said, reaching out for him without grabbing at him. I didn't like grabbing at people unless it was necessary. "These dreams, or… visions," I continued, "they're haunting me. It feels like it *must* mean something. You said we'd talk about it."

He turned to regard me, his expression hard to read.

"Please," I pressed. "I need your help. Your wisdom."

"Tulimak," he said with some difficulty, "I don't understand you anymore. Let alone your dreams. I don't know…I don't know *how* to help you. I wish I did. But I don't know what to say to you." He let his arms drop, head hanging. "You don't want my advice, right now. It is clearly of no value to you."

I was too stunned to respond to him. It was as blatant a dismissal as ever I'd heard. It wasn't said cruelly or even in an unkind way. It was worse.

It felt like my father was giving up on me.

"I *do* want your advice," I insisted.

"Stop worrying about a dream," he said, voice impassive. "Worry about the situation we are in and reflect on why we are in it. You are troubled because you're in danger, and because you've endangered your entire family, over a person who is not worth any of it. A man who will see you ruined. You smell of him, by the way. I didn't think it appropriate to say anything, but better to tell you than not in case you want to avoid embarrassment later."

Ice grew in my chest, like spires threatening to burst out through my ribs. "I..." I drew in a quick breath. "I wanted to help someone, otterfa. Someone in danger. I believed him, I-I still do, and I thought helping him was the *right thing* to do. I'm not saying I haven't made mistakes..."

"I believe your heart was in the right place," my father said quietly. "I'm not saying you're a bad person, Tulimak. But at this point you've seen the consequences of aiding this man, and still," he gestured around him, "we are here. We could return home."

"And leave Kissima and Uki?" I pointed out.

That gave him pause. "Well..." he murmured.

"You could leave," I said, even though my heart fought every word. "You could go home, otterfa."

He lowered his brow. "I can disagree with your choices and still love you, Tulimak. I won't abandon you."

"I love you too, otterfa," I said softly. I felt tears threatening. I wasn't even sure if they were happy or sad at this point.

He walked past me, heading back towards the cave. As he passed me, he briefly put a hand on my arm, comfortingly. "Tell your...partner...that when you rise in the middle of the night, he should check to ensure you're actually awake. I think most assume you're simply getting up to relieve yourself, and I know from raising you how dangerous it can be to let you wander when you're in these dazes. He should know that, too."

"...sure," I said, watching him go.

"Take a moment to look at your target. Now, put one foot—your dominant foot—forward. Swing your arm down and to the side."

I tried to do precisely as Uki told me, arranging my big, cumbersome body as she showed. She straightened my foot for me with her own, then continued, "*When the axe head goes past your leg, bring it back up quickly—yes. Good. Now when it's over your head,*" she steadied my arm where it was, showing me the proper apex, I'd imagine. "*Yes. Here is good. When you've gotten it this high, move your arm as though you are throwing a ball. You've played with leather balls before?*"

I nodded. "Not as much as my brothers, but sometimes."

"Just like that," she said, guiding my arm down in a slowed-down version of the swing, then stopped it halfway. "Now when it's here, parallel to the ground, that is when you release. And remember, hand grips the axe handle straight up and down. Not tilted to either side. You want the axe to fly straight." She pointed ahead of us to the tree I was aiming for. "A tree is a good way to see if you're holding the axe straight."

I nodded again, but in truth, this seemed like a lot to remember.

"Just practice going through the motion many times," she eased. "It will be like second nature eventually. You just have to get your body into the rhythm." She patted my shoulder. "You are Ujarak's son. His blood runs through you."

"*What?*" Those words broke my concentration, for some reason. The image they conjured in my mind's eye…

"Ujarak was a great warrior," Uki began to explain, "I only meant—"

"No, I understand," I shook my head. "But Uki, can I ask you something?"

She smiled back at me, waiting. I'd honestly never seen such open, warm, inviting features on such a scarred face.

"Do you think," I began, then halted for a moment, uncertain of my words. "That is to say—are we the people we're going to be, before we're even born?"

She actually laughed. "I take it back," she chuckled, "Ujarak was never quite such a deep thinker as you."

"I mean," I sighed, "you're not the only person who's told me I'm going to be something, because of my blood. Or that I'm supposed to be something, because of my blood." My mind went back to the two-toned Ursark bear, forming the young bearchild from its own blood and earth. "I'm not a warrior. I don't think I'll ever be much of one, even if I try, but even you seem to think so. Just because I'm a bear?"

"I am not a deep thinker either," Uki confesed, humming softly, "but I think…yes? In ways. I think it is half of who we are, at least."

"Half?" I parroted back, now utterly confused.

"Well, you may not have been trained as a warrior," she explained, "and you may not like it, but that doesn't mean you aren't very large, and very strong. That came from your mother and father's blood. No matter how well Takoda raised you, if he'd wanted to raise you to be twelve heads tall, he could not have. Your blood gave you that."

"All right," I said, following along uncertainly for now.

"But Takoda raised you to be loving and kind," she said. *"And to embrace new things,"* she glanced past me, towards where I knew Finnegan was helping build a tree stand with Odina, *"and people,"* she finished with a smirk. *"Our tribe, perhaps, would not have raised you quite so trusting of the outside world. You would have become a different person. I happen to still think you would have been a very good person. But different."*

My father was nearby, sharpening spears. I knew he'd heard the entirety of the conversation I'd just had with Uki, and some petty part of me hoped he was reflecting on how much more she'd helped me break down the visions I'd been having lately, without even knowing she was doing so.

"So, maybe it's a bit like pottery?" I offered, while she steadied and corrected my arm for another practice swing.

"Ha!" She showed off a broken fang with her laugh. *"Tulimak, you are a funny man."*

"I just mean," I blanched a bit, *"if people were made out of clay,"* I was offering the metaphor seemingly lightly, but in fact it was directly taken from my dreams. *"If you made a child out of, say, blood and earth, the ingredients would matter—"*

"I do not think blood would do well to make clay," she made a face.

"—but the hands that craft and shape the clay would also matter," I continued, exasperated. "That's what you mean by 'half'?"

"Maybe?" She was chuckling again. "I do not know, Tulimak. I most confess, you have lost me. But I think we may be saying the same thing. Yes. The blood matters, but how you are raised matters, too. I do not think anyone would question that. It seems rather obvious to me. But what do I know?"

Great. Even Uki thought my visions were just common-sense observations. What was the Ursark spirit trying to tell me? Or was it really just a simple-minded spirit, showing me complex visions to teach simple lessons?

Whatever the case, I really wished I could get more of my father's usual wisdom on the matter. But he'd all but shut down recently, since he'd found out about Finnegan and I. I felt like the two of us were on drifting canoes, taking different forks down a river.

"Your mate is proof enough that the bodies we are given at birth do not necessarily determine whether we'll be adept warriors or not," Uki said pointedly.

I felt my fur fluff up a bit, a warmth spreading through my chest. *"I like...hearing you say that,"* I confessed.

"What?" She paused. "Oh. That he is your mate?"

I smiled. "You said it again."

"If it truly makes you so happy to hear it," she said, *"then I cannot see how you could be in any doubt of your feelings for him."* She put a hand over mine where I was holding the axe handle and leaned in almost conspiratorially, her voice dropping. *"I know the rituals. If you like, Takoda's blessing or no, I will marry you."*

I coughed, *"Uhhh,"* I glanced out of the corner of my eye towards where Finn was straddling a tall branch, legs dangling on either side, lifting a few planks Odina was handing up towards him. *"I think probably...a little premature there, Uki."*

She scoffed. "You are lucky you are a man. If you were a woman saying that, I would remind you with some consternation that you're already sharing a bed. But I suppose when there is no risk of cubs coming along..."

I sighed. *"I'm not even really certain how he feels about me."* I admitted. It was strange that the words came so freely with Uki, I never would have said anything like it to my father. To him, I was always on guard of Finnegan, defending my right to be with him. If I'd shown any of my uncertainty over my relationship, I knew full well it would just add fuel to the fire. But with Uki, I felt a lot safer in admitting my fears.

"I can find out, if you wish," the female bear offered.

I turned my head towards her quickly, putting my free paw up. "*No, please,*" I insisted. "*Don't beat it out of him or anything—*"

"What?" she asked around a laugh. "I would never hurt your mate. That would be disrespectful as well as cruel. You think that is what I meant?"

"*I...*" I decided in that instant not to tell her about what had happened between my father and Finn. Everyone was on edge already, and I didn't want to sow trouble between my blood family and adopted family. Maybe someday I'd talk to her about everything. But not now. "*I don't know. I guess it's natural to be protective of your family, but...*"

"I meant ask him," she clarified. "Speak to him, only if it is difficult for you to do so yourself."

"I've tried," I let out a long breath. "But to be honest, I don't think even he knows how he feels. It's all muddled by the fact that we don't have very much time together. That's **always** been the problem, since the day I met him," I groused. "Everything with him has always felt temporary. First it was until we got to Broen, and then the Tawnahowac land, and now it's Arbordale," I knitted my brow. "It's so hard to know your feelings for someone when you can't plan for anything lasting."

"*But you do,*" she pointed out with a slight quirk of her muzzle upwards. "*Know your feelings, I mean.*"

I gripped the axe handle tighter, dropping my nose. "*I do,*" I confirmed.

"And you feel what? Foolish?"

"Maybe?" I snuffed. "My father certainly thinks I am. I think even Finnegan believes that. He keeps saying things I know are meant to push me away. But then he says other things..." I swallowed heavily. "He pulls me back and forth between despair and hope—"

"You should tell stories," she said. "You have the tongue. So poetic."

"*It's* bullshit," I snapped, using an Amurescan word instead of a curse from our language, because honestly, it felt right in the moment. "*He knows what he's doing. My father's right about that. If he wanted to push me away, he could have by now. Which means he* **does** *want to be with me, he just doesn't care that it's temporary. It's not fair. Maybe he* **is** *using me...*"

"Or he is in love with you, but has no control over his future," she offered, quietly.

I turned to regard her. She gave a very gentle shrug, squeezing my arm before letting it go. "I do not know, Tulimak. But the position you are both in I think is so hard, you are both bound to make mistakes."

"I certainly have," I admitted softly. "I endangered my family, I endangered you and Kissima."

"Kissima and I have the chance to defend one of the only remaining living members of our tribe," she said. "And kill these bastard Otherwolves in the process. Do not worry for us. I am gladder than I can say that you came to us in your time of need."

"Still," I muttered. "A lot of people are getting hurt because of this. I don't even know if these men coming for Finn are bad people. We shot down that scout without really knowing who it was. He could have been a trapper or something. We assumed."

"It was very unlikely anyone here, at this exact time, in an abandoned corner of the world would be anyone other than the men feverishly hunting you," she reasoned.

"My point is more," I said, "before we got to know her, we could have also killed Odina. And since we've been traveling with her I've realized she's a person whose motives I...can understand, you know? She isn't just some nameless threat anymore. The men coming after us? Some of them might have good reasons to be in their trade, too."

"*Tulimak, every person here has made choices that led them to this point,*" she said, her one brown eye, one glazed-over eye locking on mine. The scar there had obviously been what caused the loss of vision. The original wound must have been horrific.

"All you can do, at this point, is survive."

One of the only things I'd insisted upon that I helped place out in the woods to defend the Basin was a collection of small signs. Emblazoned on them in red paint we'd made from some of the local holly berries and clay were warnings in our tongue, as well as Amurescan. Finnegan helped us write the latter, so we'd be certain it was legible. We hung them high and visible in the largest clearings, to be certain they'd be seen.

Turn back. Trespassers will be fired upon.

I wanted to say we had done all we could. And as the second day of waiting turned to a third and the shadows grew long, it seemed like the Jackwalds might have left.

And then, as we'd all sat down to eat dinner on the third night, a shot pierced the still calm of the frigid air.

Everyone, even Finnegan, went stiff for a full few seconds after it had happened. And then all at once, people were getting to their feet, grabbing for weapons and falling into the well-practiced routine we'd worked out in a state of fumbling shock.

I knew, somehow. This was it.

"That was close, had to be Kissima," Odina said as she grabbed up her rucksack of ammo and her rifle, pushing Sawyer towards Finnegan. "Stay with him. You stay *right* at his side, do you hear me? No heroics."

"I know, ma," he promised, grabbing up a bag himself, as Finnegan quickly re-checked his pistol and stowed it in his hip holster, gesturing at the young mountain lion to get the rifle, too.

"You two take your position in the caves," Odina said as she began heading towards one of her tree stands. "Takoda—"

"I'm the last line, I know. My spears are waiting for me near the cave entrance," the older otter said gruffly. He quickly scraped a paw through the ashes of our cooking fire, I knew not why.

I felt Uki at my shoulder, slinging something over my back. It felt heavy. She straightened it at the collar for me, her eyes alight as she looked me over. "*Ujarak's heavy parka,*" she explained. "*The hide is from a great ocean beast. It will not stop a bullet, but it may ensure you do not die. Push it back over your shoulder when you mean to throw your axe.*" She demonstrated for me what she meant with her own parka.

Another shot, this one from the same distance, confirming it was most likely Kissima firing into the woods below.

"She would not be wasting so much powder unless she saw them," Uki said with a snarl. "We must go. This is real."

We'd had a few false starts over the last few days where whomever we had on watch had caught sight of an animal and mistaken it for one of the Jackwalds. But Kissima was especially careful. If she'd fired twice...

"Ma!" I heard Sawyer call out. He sprinted down towards her before she could make her way into the woods and slung an arm briefly around her shoulder, kissing her on the brow. She embraced him back. Then the two of them parted ways again.

I looked to Finn. He looked back at me, uncertainly. Sawyer was jogging back towards us and now was hardly the time to be shy, but in the end, I didn't go to him, either.

"Take care out there," he said to me instead.

"You too," I returned.

"We have the most defensible position," he said. "I'm not worried."

"Son," my father's voice interrupted us. I looked down and found he was holding up a paw smeared in ash. "Uncover your shoulder a moment," he directed.

I did as I was told, unconsciously uncovering my shoulder with the burn scar on it, out of habit. I'd gotten so used to pulling back my cloak to treat it for weeks now. It was fairly well healed now and didn't bother me at all any more.

My otterfa reached up and drew a spiral with a jagged wedge shape around the injury, tracing the lines of my shoulder-blade. The pattern was not particularly intricate and only took a few moments, and the ash wouldn't remain on my fur for long, but I knew what his intention was.

"Your warrior marking," he said, finishing the mark off by hooking it around the scar itself. "You earned it. You saved the life of someone important to you," he looked briefly to Finnegan, his face a complex confluence of emotions. "Warrior markings call upon the spirits of war to protect those of us that *must* fight. I will pray that they see you this day. But I think they have already found you."

"Otterfa..." I breathed out, my throat closing up.

"Come back to me, son," he pleaded. And before I could say any more, he turned and took off for the caves, following in Finnegan and Sawyer's wake.

Another gunshot echoed across the basin, this time from a more nearby location—Odina's tree-stand, I realized. Uki grabbed at my arm. "*You stay closer to the rim of the Basin, where the trees are thicker. I will keep closer to the lake. You will have more cover. Use it.*"

I nodded dizzily, throwing the parka back over my shoulder and taking off towards where we'd practiced. The trees thinned out the closer you got to the lake, so there wouldn't be as many places to hide and take cover there. Uki was a far more experienced hunter and ambusher, so she was taking that ground.

We had two choices, north or south. But the north was covered by a rocky ridge of the basin wall that was hard to trespass, and Odina had a good eye-line in that direction besides. The trees there were also thinner overall, so it seemed like a bad place for the Jackwalds to advance on our camp. Uki and I would stick mostly to the south.

Kissima was posted facing the south and she'd fired first, so it seemed likely that's where they were advancing from. Both women could fire towards the north or south whenever anyone broke cover, but there was no guarantee any of the shots I was hearing had hit anyone. Especially if the men were still far off.

There was also the possibility, as Finn had pointed out, that the hunters would separate into two groups and cover both sides. It depended on what their plan was, and we couldn't know that.

Finnegan was posted higher still, with Sawyer helping him re-load and rotating firearms between the pistol and rifle. But he was the farthest, so to say the shots would be difficult was an understatement. It might've seemed counter-productive putting our best shot the farthest away, but we didn't have a choice. Finnegan was their goal. If he was isolated in a tree stand and they got to him, this whole thing was over. They'd take him and retreat, and we'd never see him again. But the skirmish was bound to move in closer soon enough, and if anyone could make long-distance shots until then...

A crackle broke me out of my reverie and I dashed behind a tree just as Uki had made me practice again and again over the last few days. But the shot that punctuated the next few seconds hadn't come from the man I'd heard far too late, but from behind me, from my own people. A pained shout later, the white dog tumbled over into the snow, pistol falling from his hand and burying in the fresh powder.

I sucked in a cold gasp of air, realizing how close I'd come. I'd been thinking of my friends and right off, I'd lost focus and not paid attention to my surroundings. The man now lying in a puddle of his own blood and a crumpled leather duster had had that pistol pointed right at me until he'd been shot down by one of my companions. By the sound of the shot and where it had likely come from, it had been Odina.

They were this close already? I'd barely reached the thickest part of the forest.

I hunkered low, grabbing at a pine bough and shaking the snow over my shoulders. My parka was already a light tan, but I remembered how Uki and Kissima had been when they'd first come upon us, nearly invisible against the snow. It certainly couldn't hurt.

I stalked slowly through the forest, eyes scanning the darkening boughs and trunks. There was a sort of pattern to it I instinctively knew to look for, and I was trying to pick out breaks in it. The tree trunks moved in my field of vision, lines of darkness blotting out the glimpses of light between them. It was there, in those checkered gaps, that I was looking for movement.

Another shot. Followed all too soon by another, this time from the wood-line. They'd begun firing back at our people. They all had blinds, I reminded myself. We had much better cover than our enemies. That shot had been near enough to me that I thought I might be able to find the man who'd fired. This was why Uki and I were here.

Clutching one of my axes (the one from my otter tribe) vice tight in my palm, I paced as quietly as I could manage through the snow. The soft coat we'd just gotten the night before eased my footsteps, and I found I fell into an uneasy but steady rhythm as I approached where I'd heard the gunshot emanate from.

Heartbeat, slide a foot forward, *heartbeat,* press that foot down through the snow, *heartbeat,* lift the foot behind, *heartbeat,* slide that foot forward…

My perspective shifted and with it the black lines of tree trunks and boughs and the thin strips of light between, and then all of a sudden, there it was. Movement. A figure, leaning slowly out from behind a trunk. Peering past.

He hadn't seen me.

He had his back turned to me.

From behind, all I could make out was that he was canine. Slim. Pointed ears, a wolf-like tail. He might have even been a wolf, or a coyote. It was hard to say.

He was wearing similar clothing to Finnegan, if more rugged, more meant for the outdoors. Leather breeches and vest, long jacket. Holster on his hip. The pistol was clearly held in his hand, at the ready. He'd had time by now to re-load it.

He hadn't seen me.

This man had a story. He had a reason for being here, whether I agreed with it or not. Someone somewhere in the world knew him and might even care about him.

The snow crunched beneath one of my feet, the man twitched and spun on me, and my thoughts just…stopped. Everything narrowed to one point in front of me. His hand, the pistol in it. He'd begun to raise it, I'm not even certain how fast. Certainly not as fast as Finnegan. But too fast.

I heard my father's voice in my mind, begging me to return to him. Fear surged through me like a howling gale, and I erupted through snow-laden pine saplings and charged the man.

The sound that left me in those frenzied moments, I cannot begin to describe. It was somewhere between a fearful bay and a bellowing roar. It almost drowned out the frantic gunshot the man fired off slipshod into the snow, erupting feet in front of him between the two of us.

I threw my axe before I made it to him, almost forgetting to do so until it was too late. The blade flew from my hand with all of my strength behind it, but I'd overshot. It hit the tree behind him and stuck in at an angle, and by then I was on him.

I bore him down into the snow, jaw agape, snarling. I could feel the saliva connecting my teeth, the howling roar puffing out between us into the cold air. I was afraid of myself. But not nearly as much as I was afraid of him.

I knew he couldn't possibly get another shot off at me, but the first thing I did was pin his gun-arm down into the snow, putting all my weight into it. He cried out, clawed feet kicking at my chest, his other arm escaping my grasp, hand fumbling down at his waist.

For some reason, I'd thought if I got the gun away from him, I'd be safe. But a flash of steel confirmed he had a hunting knife too. I gritted my teeth, knowing there were only inches between us and that blade would be coming up into my gut in a few seconds unless I could do something.

I twisted my bulk away from him all that I could and tried to grab again for his struggling arm, succeeding only in tearing at his sleeve. It was enough to push aside his first swipe, but his second arced upwards in a quick stab for my arm itself, the blade catching me with a sharp sting across the bicep. It would have gone deeper too, if not for the parka, which it had caught and tangled in for a brief second in time.

Both of my hands were on him, one holding his main hand down, the other just barely keeping his knife from my chest. I had very few options left.

I'd thought it would be harder. But in the grip of mortal terror, I hesitated less than I'd ever imagined.

My jaws closed around his wrist, biting down until I heard a crack, and felt the squelch of blood between my teeth. I'd closed my eyes, but nothing could block the smell, the taste, the sound of his screams. I'd hear them for the rest of my life, however long that ended up being. I gagged against the coppery flood, but kept my jaw locked, until I heard the knife drop from his hand.

When I opened my eyes again, the man had gone strangely still. His head had fallen back into the snow, body limp and contorted. He wasn't dead, of that much I was certain, but he'd passed out, from pain or shock or both, I couldn't say. I slowly unclenched my jaw, his buckled wrist falling from it, blood frothing between my teeth.

Somehow, I dragged myself to my feet shakily and tugged my axe out of the nearby tree. I don't know how much time passed. Not long. Another gunshot in the distance, a shout in the woods. Someone—one of my comrades most likely—had felled one of the invaders. I think. No one but the Jackwalds, Uki and I were down here in the woods. I hoped it wasn't Uki. It had sounded male.

More movement, but this time too far off for me to make it there in a sprint. Even if I *could* move my legs. Spirits, how many of them were there? I wasn't even far from camp, I'd barely made it into the woods. They'd gotten so close to us before we'd been able to mount our defense. They'd reach the caves soon if we couldn't stop them.

I chanced a brief glimpse down at the man I'd bitten before I left him. Uki had said to kill them. Make sure they were dead. But this man wasn't a threat anymore.

I managed to convince my legs to move and began sprinting towards where I'd last seen movement. I was certain it had been two. One larger than the other, but moving at the same time, darting between the trees.

One of them turned a lean muzzle towards me, hearing my approach. He had a rifle, which slowed his spin in my direction just enough that I was able to dive behind a fallen clump of trees and snowdrifts before he got off a round. Snow billowed up from the shot, a shower of bark flakes and pine needles accompanying it. I instinctively clutched my paws over my head, before shakily pushing myself back up onto all fours. Other than the gash in my arm, I wasn't hurt. I'd gotten down in time.

There was shouting, half-muffled by snow and the ringing in my ears, but I made out a few words in Amurescan. One of the two men was saying, "...god-damned tree stand! To the north, big maple."

I lifted my head in time to see the larger of the two men, a barrel-chested canine with a rifle slung over his back *and* a pistol in his hand, attempting to lean out from behind the clutch of trees they were using as cover to take a shot. The second he did, another gunshot rang out, pitting the large, wide-brimmed hat he wore on his head and forcing him behind cover again. I thought it had missed him entirely, until I saw the dark, spattered stain across his wrinkled muzzle. One of his ears was chipped near in half and hanging a stringy bit of flesh from the end.

The other man with him, a thin deerhound of some sort, was furiously re-loading his rifle. I considered coming out from behind cover, but the big canine with the wrinkled face still had two loaded weapons as far as I knew and the space between us was too big. I remembered all the times Finn had counted between shots, had kept track of whether someone had fired or not. If I wanted to go after these two, which was risky in and of itself, I had to at least wait until they'd exhausted their rounds.

I tried to get my bearings. I was very close to the main campsite; after the white dog who'd been shot and the other man I'd bitten, I'd circled back towards where I'd heard these two men. Uki was nowhere to be seen, which means she'd probably followed the lake and ended up farther from camp. These two men had made it fairly close, had slipped past both of us and the snipers, and if they got much closer my father was the last line of defense for Finnegan and Sawyer.

"Where's the big'un?" I heard the larger man ask through a pained hiss, clamping a hand over his bleeding ear.

"Think he's down, behind there," I heard the other reply. I could barely see them through the clutch of holly bushes, but I could feel his eyes on me. He either thought I was dead or hiding, but he knew exactly where I was.

"The one up high tha'clipped me's gotta be Ambrose," the bigger man growled out. "Tree-stand missed."

"I can see 'er through the branches," the thin canine said, ducking his head around for just a moment as he finished packing his rifle. "Malcolm's gotta have a shot soon. We take her out it's a clear path up to th'bluff."

They were wrong. They didn't realize we had another gunner in a tree stand, Kissima. And she was actually closer. Probably packing another shot right now. But that wasn't what mattered.

What mattered was that apparently, there was another man somewhere gunning for Odina. And I was pinned down.

Now that I'd gotten my bearings, I had a vague idea where everyone was. I couldn't see her, but I knew the direction of Odina's tree. And if the last shot had been Finnegan, that meant she was probably finishing packing another shot just about now. Which meant she'd fire again soon…

Steeling myself, I sucked air into my lungs and shouted as loud as I could, "*ODINA! STAY BEHIND COVER!*"

The smaller man cursed and raised his rifle. The loose bank of bushes and debris I was hiding behind would hardly stop a rifle shot now that he knew *exactly* where I was, so all I could do was run. They had three chances to shoot me, so I ran for the nearest, most durable cover I could see, a hill, rather than risk charging them. Two gunshots nipped at my heels, but neither man was apparently the kind of shot Finn was, because both of them missed. I tumbled down the embankment towards the lake, my knee knocking hard into a boulder on my way down, white-hot pain shooting through me and making me nauseous.

I wrenched myself up, struggling to my feet just in time to see the smaller of the two Otherwolves bounding down the rise towards me. He had his rifle slung over his back, and had a very large knife in one hand, presumably intending to gut me with it. Until he saw me.

I stood to my full height, for once in my life glad for my monstrous size. I must have looked quite a sight too, with blood staining my muzzle and throat. I began to move towards him and he seemed to think the better of it, retreating back up the hill towards his companion, who presumably still had a loaded shot in the rifle he hadn't used yet.

I hadn't quite made it up the hill when another gunshot, followed by a feminine cry of pain, made me stop in my tracks. The crumpling of branches followed, a noise I feared was likely something falling from the treetops. I re-doubled my efforts to make it up the steep incline, the threat of the armed men up there aside, and found they were no longer there waiting for me. I caught sight of them distantly sprinting for another grove. The larger man had yet to pull his rifle, so there must really have been a third gunman out there who'd been able to take a shot.

I didn't have to take much of a guess to know who'd fallen out of a tree, and where the two men were headed. I had no choice.

They were fleeter of foot than me, so even at an out-and-out run, knowing the lay of the land, I couldn't catch up to them easily. Even less so when I had to slow to spare a glance towards Odina's tree.

She wasn't in it.

I wasn't going to catch them in time. Finnegan still hadn't fired, which meant no one was loading for him. I couldn't imagine what Sawyer must be thinking right now. But Kissima was still out there, and she hadn't—

Just as I thought it, the smaller of the two canines took one right in the shoulder, the blow spinning him around. The larger canine had to stop briefly and double back to grab him by the vest, dragging him behind one of the large, carved spirit poles at the entrance to the main campsite.

I could smell the fear on them. Could see it in the way the big canine turned his wrinkled face from side to side, assessing his situation. Looking for his men. They'd had some kind of a plan when they came into this, I'm sure of it. But so had we.

The thinner man was moaning in pain, clutching at his shoulder. "Caaaap'n—" he groaned out.

"Sonofabitch, how many of them are there?!" the big canine snarled out, dropping his comrade and finally pulling his rifle. He'd barely gotten both hands on it when I got in range.

This time, I made sure to adjust my grip on the axe before I threw it, lining the throw up with the arrow-straight, carved pole they were hiding behind. The hollow wooden eyes of the Ursark at the base locked with mine and the spirits practically sang to me as the weapon released from my paw.

The axe flew true, burying nearly to the hilt between the man's densely-muscled shoulder-blades. With a gurgling cry, he reached backwards for the weapon with one hand, as though he'd be able to pull it out, and stumbled around to face me, managing to raise the rifle one-handed.

He'd hardly need to be a good shot at this range, but I was already mid-charge. At the last minute I ducked low, hoping to avoid the worst of it. The rifle fired and he lost control of the weapon all but immediately, unable to handle the recoil one-handed. The shot went wide, and I tackled him at the knees.

I reared back my fists and brought them down into his face, again and again. I felt his teeth tear at one of my knuckles, but I didn't care. I punched him repeatedly, until my lungs were ragged, my fists were bloody and he'd stopped moving.

Somewhere in the haze of it all, I'd heard familiar voices. Sawyer, crying out frantically. Finnegan, sharply shouting at the young man.

I looked up from the badly battered, massive Otherwolf, just in time to see what was undoubtably the most terrifying thing I'd seen all day. Sawyer, rifle in hand, running across the long stretch of open land between the caves and the tree-line. He was screaming for his mother, whom I still hadn't caught sight of, but I suspected was somewhere on the ground beneath her tree-stand. Possibly still alive, possibly not. But that wasn't what made my heart seize up.

There was another Jackwald out there who hadn't fired for quite some time now. And he'd been a good enough shot to hit Odina while she had cover.

There was nothing, absolutely nothing, I could do. I felt my body move as quickly as it could, too slowly...far too slowly. He was too far away.

It was like he hit a wall, mid-stride. The shot punched the young mountain lion back, erupting out the back of his head. I hardly even heard it, and he'd crumpled.

Finnegan screaming Sawyer's name was much more clear. He'd broken cover too, I briefly caught sight of him moving between trees along the edge of camp, making his way towards the now two fallen mountain lions. But I was closer.

I didn't know how many more men had made it this far, or how many had shots, but the one I knew of had just fired and Kissima had to be done re-loading by now. Maybe she could cover me? I *should* have been determined not to make the same mistake Sawyer had just made. I *should* have reflected on the fact that we were all gathering towards one spot with next to no cover, which could be disastrous. But all I could think about was that two of us had been shot, and if I somehow got to them, maybe there was something I could do.

I dashed out into the clearing, my throat and lungs screaming in protest, chest heaving. I'd been running and fighting now for far too long, I wasn't built for this. Still, I pushed myself to make the sprint as fast as I could, skidding in slushy snow and frozen, crisp leaves down the small embankment towards Sawyer. When I got to him, my one given physical asset did finally pay off. I hefted him over my shoulder fairly easily and broke for the area I thought Odina must have fallen.

No one shot at me. The man was either still re-loading, or didn't consider me a priority. But I heard another shot from our side, which also could have meant Kissima was covering my run.

I nearly ran headlong into my father, raising my axe before I realized who he was. He didn't flinch away from me, but grabbed me by the wrist, shouting my name. Everything sounded like it was through water.

Why was he...? Of course. He'd been down here, guarding the caves. He must have gone to Odina when she first fell.

For the first time since I'd known her, I heard the mountain lioness crying. It was honestly more of a wail, a guttural scream of her son's name. She was propped against the tree, hand clamped tightly over her hip, blood soaking through her clothing. But she wasn't crying for herself.

"Give him to me..." she choked out, reaching out for me with her one free hand, her words unraveling into sobs near the end.

I lowered the young man's body down gingerly, my father helping me set him down beside his mother. I had hope until his head lolled back against his mother's shoulder and I saw the wound. I'd thought...maybe it had been a graze...

She clung to him, pressing her muzzle into his fur. It was the worst image I had ever seen in my life.

My father's hand on my arm, yanking me closer to the tree, pulled me somewhat back into the moment. "There's still someone perched out there—" he began, but all at once he froze up, staring past me.

I began to turn, but my father was faster. Without a trace of hesitation and in a bodily motion born of a lifetime of practice, he wheeled back with the spear in his hand and sent it gliding through the air. It was like a lightning strike, connecting with the bloody-faced, large canine who'd stalked up behind us, pegging him center-mass.

I turned to see the enormous canine finally fall once and for all. I'd gotten him between the shoulders, I'd turned his face into meat, but it was my father's spear that killed him.

Because he'd been *trying* to kill him.

The ground erupted in front of us, far too close for comfort. Apparently, the sniper, wherever he was, had been holding his shot. But killing one of their men was enough to get his attention. I dove for my father, dragging the two of us back against the far too-small tree we were all forced to hunker down beside.

Odina was still there, gone silent, her son slumped against her side. But she was shakily removing his rifle from where it was slung over his shoulder.

"Your wolfdog's in trouble," my father wheezed, as he pulled another spear from the bundle on his back. He pointed out towards a clutch of pine.

I could barely see, but there was definitely an outline there, hunkered down in the branches. He wasn't far, but we still didn't know if there was more than one man out there capable of taking shots. Had Uki and Kissima gotten the rest of them, or driven them off? I knew he had to be out there, thinking the same thing I was. The clearing where we'd eaten most of our meals and talked late into the night was a killing zone, now. There was absolutely no cover between us.

"He should have stayed in the caves," my father grated out.

"He went after Sawyer," I shook my head, wracking my mind trying to figure out what I could do. "I don't even know if he has a shot left," I said aloud.

For just a moment, I vaguely saw the outline of Finn's ears. He was trying to see us, as well. But then another shot, somehow impossibly soon after the last one, blew off a branch near him and he ducked back again.

"Was that another gunman?!" my father asked, frantically.

"I don't know," I moaned. It was so hard to gauge time between shots with so much going on. I didn't know how Finn did it.

"Tulimak," a ragged voice broke through our conversation. I looked to my side to see Odina pushing her son's rifle towards me with her foot. "Can't…focus. Sight's blurry. Get this. To him."

I took the rifle, taking one last look at the bloody mountain lioness clutching her dead son, then looked out across the field. I began to stand, but my father grabbed at my leg. "No, there could be two of them," he reminded me fiercely.

"He hasn't taken a shot since he got stuck there," I insisted. "He has no ammunition. They have to know that by now, too. What are we going to do, stay pinned down here until they pick us off? I'm a faster runner than you."

It was true, if barely. I had longer legs than my father and was significantly younger, otherwise he'd probably have me beat.

My father opened his mouth to object again, but a shot followed by a distressingly familiar yelp of pain interrupted us. I turned towards the thin clutch of trees Finnegan was trapped behind, the splintering of branches confirming my worst fear. He'd been shot through his cover. Considering I could see his outline through the branches, it was hardly surprising. They'd either given up on not trying to kill him, or they didn't know who he was. Or care, at this point.

Maybe it was one man who was just an incredibly fast re-loader. Regardless, I wasn't going to wait any longer. He'd just fired…now was my chance.

I held the rifle to my chest and made my second run across the clearing. This time, I was all but certain I was going to be shot at, if there was in fact a second man. They were taking shots at all of us now.

But I made it, with only the sound of my thudding footsteps, my heavy puffs of breath, and the trill of evening birds. The odd calm between punctuated tragedies was more eerie than anything else about tonight.

When I found Finnegan, he was hunkered over, teeth grit, his whole body buckled in against itself. He had a hand clamped over the side of his chest along his ribs. It was impossible to tell how bad the wound was, but I knew his pain tolerance, so I could take a guess.

"Finn!" I skidded to my knees beside him, reaching for his shoulder and closing my palm around it, *needing* to feel his physical presence to confirm for myself that he was real, that he was alive and in front of me.

"Sawyer," he croaked out, looking up at me through pain-saturated eyes. "Is he…?"

I choked out a non-word, averting my gaze from his. Finn's eyes squeezed shut for a moment, his muzzle peeled back, and a ferociously angry noise tore forth from him.

A shot broke through the branches above us, this one doing little more than scaring the shit out of me and raining debris down on us. But it brought us both back to the present.

"How is he—" I began, shocked. I hadn't been counting, but I *knew* these shots were coming too close together to be one man.

"It's two men, rotating guns," Finn growled out, getting stiffly to his feet, using me for leverage. "Like Sawyer and I. And one of them's a marksman for sure. They've got us pinned down here with a hell of a fucking vantage point, they're up on the rise. I caught sight of one of them. They can just pick us off at their fucking leisure from there. And I can't get a good shot at them from here, even if I had a round—"

It was at that point he seemed to notice what I was carrying.

"Is that loaded?" he barked out.

I nodded, unshouldering the weapon and handing it to him. He checked it over once and wrenched himself fully to his feet, removing a bloody palm from where he had it clamped over his side. His left side was stained all the way down, the tang of copper so thick in the air it was stifling. But unlike with the canines I'd fought, this was his blood, it smelled of *him*, and that made my whole body react in ways I can hardly describe.

He walked stiffly out towards the clearing and I followed without even asking. Everything, every worry for my life or rational fear had been cast aside. He needed a clear shot and that was all that mattered.

"*Kill him*," I begged him between clenched teeth, walking beside and partially in front of him, providing as much of a blind as I could.

"Keep your arms up, protect your head," he said shakily as he braced his hip on his bad side against me, raising the rifle. I could see his arms quivering from exertion, from the wound he'd sustained. He blew out a long breath, steadying himself as much as possible.

The Jackwalds' bullet struck me a moment after I heard Finnegan growl a low, "There you are…" and the rifle he held erupted in a shot.

I didn't even feel the pain, just the numb shock of my body as it succumbed to darkness.

Chapter 17

Parting Ways

It wasn't long before I came back to my senses, but my perception of the chaos that surrounded me was vague and drifting. I couldn't tell you much about the next day. I'd been taken to the cave at some point; I remember seeing the paintings on the ceilings. Someone had told me to open my mouth and I'd been given something for the pain I was in, but while it helped, it turned every waking moment I had from that point forward into a blurry, confusing dream.

Finn was near me. I could smell him, could even feel him when I reached to my right. He was close, very close. I saw his familiar features, muzzle tipped to the side, lying prostrate beside me. I could smell his blood. My blood. Vaguely make out the features of people I knew, people I cared for.

The figures on the ceiling danced and fought wars. I watched their stories unfold in between unconsciousness.

The first real moment of clarity I remember was during one of those times, when I'd been looking at one of the paintings, a shaman performing rites for a group of young ones. The figures were all sketched in painted clay, but I could tell they were bears. Some of them white, some of them brown. Things were starting to make sense again. They weren't moving any more. The rock walls had definition again.

Someone was holding my hand, squeezing it.

I turned my head and found evergreen eyes staring back at me. The wolfdog looked haggard, his features drawn and exhausted, fur clumped and rough. Despite that, he still managed the slightest of smiles when I turned towards him. When he spoke, his voice was rough as gravel.

"G'morning sweetheart," he said, his fingers weakly tightening around mine again. "You really with me this time?"

"…I…" my tongue felt like dried-out leather, "…Finn…"

"Yeah, it's me," he forced another slight smile.

"I…was shot," I mumbled, nearly incoherently.

"We both were," he said, blinking slowly. "Odina, too. Really just a graze, in her case, but she hurt her leg pretty bad in the fall. No one else was injured. Kissima, Uki, your father, they're all okay." He slowly slipped his fingers out of mine and leaned towards me, wincing with the slight movement. He brought his palm up to my face and cupped my cheek. "They caught you in the forearm. That cloak…parka…you were wearing spread a lot of the shot out, or it might've gone through and hit you in the chest. But they had to dig what was left of the bullet out. You don't want lead in you," he grimaced, "trust me."

It was then that I realized my other hand, the one he hadn't been holding, was bandaged all the way up my forearm. When I tried to move it, an ache washed over me, the pain making itself known through the muddiness in my head.

"M'I going to lose it?" I asked. I'd known and heard stories of people losing limbs to rifle wounds. Sometimes they'd take off a limb even if they weren't sure, because it wasn't worth risking the infection.

"Kissima thinks the hides you were wearing probably saved you that," he said. "But for what it's worth, even if you do, you'll still be handsome to me."

I gave him what I'm certain was a sleepy but incredulous look, and he gave me a fond one in return.

"What about you?" I asked, flexing my palm a little to see if I could still feel my fingers. They all seemed to respond, it just hurt to do it, so I stopped.

"Went clean through me," he said tiredly. He reached down and slowly, gingerly pulled up his shirt, which looked to be one I didn't recognize but was clean. He showed me where he was patched, along the side of his ribs. He was clearly still bleeding through the bandages.

"That looks bad," I murmured.

"Nnnhh, I got lucky honestly," he said. "No surgeon can dig a shot out of the torso. I've never caught one in the chest before, but I'm once again glad I'm slender. Barely clipped my side."

"That looks like more than a graze," I said worriedly.

"The important thing is it came out th'other side," he said, his voice clearly denoting he was under the influence of something, too. "But you've been out more than I have, Tuli. How're you feeling?"

"Like I had a lot of that 'tonic' from Broen," I replied.

"Yeah, they mixed the last of that with something Kissima and Uki made," he said. "Don't know what it is, but it's bear strength, that's for damn sure. You really don't do well on drugs'r spirits, do you?"

"You should see me when I smoke," I said.

"I'd like to someday," he said sedately. "I'd like to do a lot of interesting things with you, Tuli. See you all kinds of ways I never have."

"I'd like that too," I said.

We both stared up at the ceiling for a while. It had taken me until now to realize we were in the common area; there were no paintings on the ceiling in the cave I shared with Finnegan. There was no one else near us right now, but there were mugs and bowls near the fire and a few scattered possessions, suggesting we'd not been left alone much.

If I turned my head all the way to the left, I could see the blanket-covered form of Odina, her back to us, presumably asleep in her own improvised sickbed.

The reality of that night came roaring back to me, all at once. I nearly choked on it, the memories causing a physical reaction that left my muzzle in a gasping gag.

"Tuli?" Finn went to grip my hand again. "What's—"

"Sawyer..." I hoarsely whispered. Somehow, even though he'd named everyone but the young man when he'd assured me of who was alive, it had taken until now for that realization—that one of us had not made it—to catch up with me.

I hoped, somehow, that I'd remembered it wrong. That he was somewhere else, also sleeping off a wound. But the way Finnegan's features immediately darkened and fell confirmed my worst fears.

"It should have been me," Finnegan breathed, barely audibly.

"No," I said, still coming to terms with the fact that it was real. With the memories…

Odina, cradling her son against her. Her fourteen-year-old son, with a hole the size of an apple in the back of his skull.

"I was lining up a shot when he broke cover," Finn continued, lowly. "I couldn't grab for him in time, he got past me, h-he…he just ran…"

"He wanted to get to his mother," I said quietly.

"He was a *fucking child*," he growled out. His eyes looked glassy. I had never seen Finnegan cry before. "He was my responsibility, and I-I…I fucked up."

"He was in the safest place he could be." I shook my head slowly. "He broke cover."

"He shouldn't have *been* here," he snarled out.

I watched his expression carefully, trying so hard, as I had many times in the past, to understand what was roiling beneath the surface. For someone so seemingly expressive, Finnegan could be incredibly hard to understand, sometimes. I could see anger, regret, deep and intense sadness. But it was hard to know where it all turned. The regret was obvious. But the anger…

I had anger, too. But it was complicated, messy. Like…grieving mother or no, wasn't he at all angry at Odina for bringing her children on her hunts? Or the Jackwalds themselves, for obvious reasons. Both would have been reasonable. But I suspected he really *was* entirely blaming himself, as nonsensical as that sounded to me.

Maybe it was the drug cocktail, maybe it was coming so close to death, but this time I decided just to follow my impulses and outright ask.

"Aren't you at all angry with the men who did this?" I asked plainly. "Or Odina—Finn, it's all right—"

He looked to me, still with unshed tears. "I'm only angry at *myself*, Tuli," he said, as though it were the most obvious thing in the world. "None of you. *None* of you would be in this position if not for me. Odina would still have her whole family. You would be safe back with yours. None of this…*carnage* would have come into your lives. At *all*. I feel like I'm an…an unwanted…stain…that trod mud into everyone's lives, making everything worse everywhere I go. Everyone I've ever known, literally everyone, would have been better off if I'd never existed. I ruined my mother's life," he gritted his teeth for a moment, "I ruined the lives of so many strangers I never bothered to know. I've been an instrument of death for exactly the kinds of men who exploit people like me, like you. Poor people with no recourse. I became a part of it. And even when I gave that all up and tried, *tried* to fight back against just one of these men, the only way I knew how, look what happened."

He stared past me, to where Odina's form lay.

"Sawyer didn't die because of you," I insisted softly.

"No, he died because he's *poor*," he snapped. "And just like me, he had to do something dangerous to make coin. The only real differences between he and I are that he's still young and had a chance at something better, and someone alive that still loved him. But for some reason he's gone, and I'm. Still. Here." He annunciated each word with a pound of his fist on the furs between us. "And I don't...know...why. It doesn't make any fucking sense, Tuli. It doesn't..."

His voice got very small on the last few words and he turned his muzzle into the furs of our bedspread, squeezing his eyes shut tightly. Every fiber of his body curled in on itself, his tail and ears, his whole thin frame, pulled wire taut inwards, like he wanted to will himself somehow to disappear. He clutched at the blankets and began to shake, his breaths hissing past his teeth. I wasn't sure if he was crying or trying not to, but it made my chest burn to watch him.

I'd gotten my answer. For once, the thoughts that were playing out past those green eyes I was so entranced by, he'd spilled out in a torrent for me. I'd suspected for a long time now that Finnegan might have a lot of self-loathing. He took great care to put up a polished façade, so it was easy to miss. But this went beyond that. It went beyond even my own worst thoughts about myself. In all my years of feeling cumbersome, of feeling in the way or different, I'd doubted nearly everything about myself. My body, my intelligence, my wisdom, my feelings for other people.

But I'd never doubted I was loved, or wanted. I couldn't imagine a world where that was the case. Even through the recent arguments I'd been having with my father, he'd been certain to tell me he loved me. And I truly felt he meant that. If a canyon were to rise up and separate the two of us, we'd always have that thread. And if I lost him, which I would someday, I'd still have my brothers and sisters. And now Uki and Kissima.

Finnegan had no one.

Of course he thought everything terrible that happened around him was his doing. If I had no one to shore me up when I was low, I would unravel. Finn was forged in a hotter kiln than I had been, he'd been denied many of the things I'd taken for granted my whole life. He was probably a lot more resilient than I was in a lot of ways. But everyone had their limit.

Losing his mother must have been a tipping point. When I'd lost mine, I'd still had a family to fall back on. More than I knew, apparently.

He really thought there was no one left in the world who wanted him here.

"Finn..." I reached for him, being careful of his wound as I gathered him against me. I used my good hand and the upper portion of my injured arm, tugging him to my chest. He was still shaking and he wouldn't look at me.

I lowered my muzzle to his, brushing our whiskers together. "Do you really think no one loves you?" I asked in a low whisper.

"Don't you dare," he breathed out fiercely.

I'd expected he'd rebuff me. It's why I'd said nothing for so long now, even far past the point where I was fairly certain of my own feelings. Steeling myself, I pressed on.

"I love you, Finn," I said, the words leaving me like a sigh I'd wanted to release for far too long now. I leaned over him, stroking his back with my good hand, while his body shook and he continued to hide his face from me. I could tell he was sobbing, now. "I think you love me, too..." I said a little more uncertainly, "...but it's hard to know what to do, or how to feel, when everything keeps falling down around us the way it has. I know you blame yourself for a lot of it."

I paused. "And I know how that feels. I feel...incompetent, clumsy, stupid...all the time. Even just saying *this*, I know my father, even you think I'm foolish for the way I feel—"

"Your feelings for me," he dragged a breath through his nose, "aren't getting people killed."

"You keep saying they could," I pointed out. "That two men can't, *shouldn't*, be together. But I can't stop feeling this way, no matter how many times I'm reminded how dangerous, how pointless it is." My gaze softened as I looked down on him. "I can't stop loving you, Finn. Nothing that's happened has made the feeling fade."

"I knew," he said, his nose dug in against his sleeve. I saw a sliver of green past his lashes. "I knew and I did nothing to dissuade you."

"It's okay," I assured him, stroking one of his ears. "I'm not a cub. Considering what's happened over the last few months, I'm more afraid of losing the people I love and the place we rely on for survival than having my heart broken."

He finally looked up towards me at that. I continued, finding the will to push the words out coming far more easily than I'd thought it would, "You were right a while back when you told me I'd be able to move on. I don't want to, but...I will. If that's what I have to do. Whatever happens from this point, I'll survive it. I've made choices that led us here, too. I've made mistakes. We've both made mistakes. I just wanted you to know how I feel while we're still together, because...because it sounded like you really didn't realize it."

I leaned down, touching our foreheads together. "You aren't alone, Finn. Not anymore. Not so long as I can possibly stay at your side. And... even if...even past that, if it comes to that. Always. There will always be someone out there who wants you in the world. Even if you can't be with me anymore."

"...why?" he croaked out, at length.

I sighed softly. "Do you really want me to say it again?"

He was silent, swaying slightly on the one elbow he'd propped himself up on. After a very long time, long enough that I wondered if he was going to answer me at all, he did, in one word.

"Yes."

I sat up a little bit more, so that I could embrace him fully. "I love you," I said again, in Amurescan. And then, a few moments later, in Nontawlik, "Inkonuvit ek nua."

His palm gripped my good arm, fingers wrapping around my bicep. "Teach me how to say that," he murmured. He tilted his head up slowly. The ardor in his gaze was always enough to emotionally floor me, but right now it looked razor thin. Like anything I said or did wrong now could crumble him.

I'd just given someone at rock bottom a thread to hang from, and I realized with terrifying clarity that he'd need me, now. In a way no one had ever needed me before. I hoped to all the spirits who were listening it hadn't been a mistake.

I kissed him, because I was afraid to say any more. He folded against me and let me, and we lay back down together to rest our wounds.

He fell asleep again before I did, but as I lay there, holding him, one thought rose above all others in my mind.

Spirits, please let this not be another mistake.

When I woke next, everyone was there in the commons area. It was quiet, distressingly so. I felt various eyes on me as I slowly sat up, the blankets collecting around my waist. I could tell by the chill in the air, despite the crackling fire, that it was night outside.

Kissima and Uki were sitting opposite us, the two bear women staring somberly into the fire. Their paws were covered in earth, the clay-laden soil in this area staining Uki's feet a coppery color.

My father was nearer to me, kneeling with his gaze cast down to his lap. His expression was strange. When he briefly looked at me, he seemed almost ashamed. But he forced a slight smile when he saw me sitting up and moved closer to me. He was obviously still uncomfortable, but he seemed to be stifling it, like someone trying forcibly to lower their hackles.

"How are you feeling?" he asked quietly, taking the palm on my injured arm between his hands.

"The pain woke me," I admitted, "but my head is clearer. I prefer it like this."

He nodded at me, his brown eyes sympathetic. "You've never liked the effects of medicine," he said with a half-hearted huff.

I stared past him, towards the person whose gaze was burning through me. Odina was awake, sitting on her bed, her leg stretched out and splinted. Her eyes alone were predatory and intense, but that wasn't what worried me. She had her rifle slung over her lap.

Finnegan was already sitting up beside me and had likely been awake far longer than I had. I couldn't be sure if there'd been discussion while I was asleep, but I'd been sleeping fitfully so it seemed unlikely.

He looked only slightly better than he had when I'd last seen him. He was still submissive in posture, back bowed, ears back, tail tucked. His arm was wrapped around his middle and he'd begun to bleed through the thin, oversized shirt he'd been dressed in. It was an Otherwolf shirt, so it had probably belonged to one of the Jackwalds.

He was staring at Odina, and she back at him. The two of them were practical mirror images of one another: The obvious exhaustion, the unbrushed fur and the pain plain to see in their entire countenance. But where he wore guilt, she radiated a ferocious anger that made my chest tense just to look on it. My instincts screamed at me to run from her. But I could not abandon Finn to her wrath, regardless how justified it was. Right now, I feared he'd simply let her avenge herself on him.

"Say what you mean to say," Finnegan said, his voice ragged.

"My son is dead," she spoke the words, strangely, with the same calm she'd always embodied. But no one could miss the deep and profound grief beneath them.

"I'm sorry," Finn all but whispered.

"Your guilt will not return him to me," she said.

"No, but it's all I have to offer," he murmured. "You trusted me with watching over your child and I failed to protect him. I am more sorry than I can ever say."

"I entrusted you...*to* him," she corrected him, her tone harsh. "You were the commodity, Ambrose. You were the job. A job which has now cost me more dearly than the price on your head can ever repay."

Finnegan closed his eyes, his knuckles clenching over his knees. "Do you mean to kill me, then?"

"No—"I began to say, but my father shook his head at me, squeezing my hand. He gave me an affirming look, and I went silent.

"I am not saying you bear no guilt for this," she continued with a low snarl. "You can decide how much you wish to carry that with you. It will have no effect on my grief, either way. But Ohitekah was my child. I brought him into this world and ultimately I failed to protect him from it."

"Ohitekah?" my father said.

"His birth name," she said quietly. "Named after his father. We chose an Otherwolf name for him when we got him citizenship. He picked it himself. It made him fit in more in their communities. But he will always be Ohitekah to me."

For some reason, I saw Uki smile. "*Well-named,*" she said.

"What?" Finnegan looked to me.

My muzzle fell slowly. "It means 'brave,'" I explained gently.

Finnegan looked like the air had been punched out of him. He slumped further, even though I know it must have been agony for him to bow with his injury. "I'm so...so sorry," he breathed out.

"Enough," Odina growled out. "I am in no mood to hear this all again. I believe your grief is genuine, Ambrose. But it does nothing for me, or my son. The only thing that will ease my pain now is action."

"Hear it again?" I repeated back. "What's wrong with letting him apologize?"

"I heard his confessions of self-hatred already," she said. "The last time you woke."

My fur prickled. "You were awake for that?"

"In...the interest of being open," my father said from beside me, surprising me. "I also overheard most of your conversation. I was in my own sleeping area, but it's a shallow cave, and the sound here...carries."

"*Kissima and I did not, we were burying the dead,*" Uki said to me, as if assuring me that only half of the people here had overheard my *extremely* private conversation with my lover was of any comfort.

I looked to my father, his odd state making a lot more sense to me now. "You heard?" I asked, the unspoken part hanging in the air.

"Yes," he said staidly. "All of it."

"If you wish to pour your heart out to your mate in privacy, you could have chosen a better place and time for it," Odina said, her tone annoyed, but little more than that. "But I am glad for your lack of discretion, because now I feel I understand the both of you better."

I tensed, awaiting her verdict.

"My husbands..." Her words fell off for a moment, then returned with renewed strength. "Both of them...died for nothing. In the end, their sacrifices did not save our family. My first mate died with my tribe, trying to re-take our lands. My second was shot by ranchers, in a property dispute.

We lost the land, anyway. I was left alone with my two children and no way to feed them. I starved for years so that they could eat. I told myself they would never live as I had to. That I would do absolutely anything to provide some kind of decent life for them. With Ohitekah—with Sawyer dead, that hope has died, too."

She looked down for a moment. "My daughter will know the same struggles I have. Unless she binds herself to a man of means, and even that will be no guarantee. Marriage did not save me, either time I attempted it."

"You'll always have a place with the Tawnahowac," my father offered.

"No offense meant to you or your traditions, Takoda," Odina said, turning her sharp gaze on him, "but you've shunned your own people for marrying outside the otter tribes. You've been distancing yourself from your own son since, I'm assuming, you learned of what I just overheard last night."

It was my father's turn to look ashamed. "I..." he glanced briefly towards Finn and I, "...I may be re-thinking our traditions in the future."

"My daughter and I cannot spend our remaining years sheltering in one of your spare pit homes, as outcasts," she said, her tone becoming a bit more civil. "I want more for her than that. And in any case, I didn't miss the Otherwolves' talk in town about annexing your land. You will have your own troubles come the thaw. We would be an additional burden on you."

"You can still turn me in," Finnegan said, steeling his voice. "What was all this for, if not that? It's literally all I can offer. It's something."

"The coin will mean little if we cannot purchase land and build some sort of future for ourselves," she replied coolly. "It is more likely to be a danger to us in fact, if anyone knows we have it."

"Then we'll get you citizenship somehow," Finn pressed, his tone growing desperate. "Fuck, we'll find a way, all right? Tuli's people, too. I'm slick, I know my way around cities and my own people. Let me do this for you."

"That is not enough," she said.

"What will be enough?!" he demanded. He didn't sound angry, just determined. "Tell me what I can do."

"We have a common enemy now, Ambrose," she said, a rumbling growl beneath every word. "The man who did this...to all of us. The man who hired the Jackwalds."

"My sire is in Amuresca," he blew out a breath, tail thrashing behind him. "He's untouchable. Believe me, I've tried."

She gave him a long, quiet look. At length, she reached down and pulled her satchel to her, undoing the ties that bound it. "Your story," she said evenly. "Is it true? All of it. Everything you've told us. If you're lying about anything—"

"I am not. Lying," he said, his posture gone rigid, the fur along the back of his neck rising. "I'm not always the most trustworthy man, I *know* that. But I swear to God, to you all, to whatever spirits you pray to, let them strike me down here where I sit, *everything* I have told you about my fath—about my sire...is true. Everything about why I'm here, about his company is *in those documents*. You've seen them!"

"I have," she agreed, pulling a folded, crumpled piece of parchment out from her bag. "So you're saying if we were to look into it all, everything you've claimed would be proven out?"

Finnegan gave a long sigh, lifting a hand to his brow. "I don't know—I guess, sure...maybe I've misinterpreted a thing or two along the way? I can't say for certain that I really understand his operation. But you've seen the manifests, damnit. What do *you* think is going on?!"

"I think you truly hate your father," she said matter-of-factly. "And you were looking for something you could use to destroy him, legally and otherwise. And you think you've found it. You've pursued it to the ends of the earth. I believe that you believe in this mission of yours." She narrowed her eyes. "But I also don't think you did all this for noble reasons. Be honest with me. Are you trying to unearth all of this to help these people your father's company is exploiting? Or is it just to avenge your mother?"

"You said we had a common enemy!" he growled out. "You want revenge, too. What does it matter?"

"The point I am getting at is," she said, leaning in, "would you care nearly so much if the man responsible for all of this suffering was *not* your father?"

Finnegan's face went blank at that, like he couldn't make sense of her words.

I could.

"You know something," I stated.

"I have one piece of information you didn't, Ambrose," the mountain lioness said, unfolding the paper carefully. It looked fragile on the edges and folded sections, like it could fall apart. "Your bounty papers."

"Let me see," Finn demanded.

Odina offered them to him, freely. He reached for the three folded documents and took them carefully, slowly opening them up. She continued speaking.

"There was a name that kept coming up when you were explaining the issue with the manifests to us," she continued, "I recognized it. It's the man who actually took the bounty out on you. Your father's name is nowhere in those records."

"He could be using a middle-man," Finnegan insisted, reading quickly.

"He could," she shrugged, "but then it seems odd that he'd use his Fleetmaster for that, doesn't it?"

Finnegan's shoulders fell, his eyes stopping at one point on the first paper.

"The man named 'Gezan,'" she said, "seems to be the one who signed off on the manifests, again and again. There are letters between him and your father, in which your father asks, repeatedly, about discrepancies in the manifests. That name also appears on your bounty, as both the commissioning and receiving agent for your return. First in Treneval, in Amuresca. And now—"

"Arbordale," he finished, his voice gone distant. Then he clenched his teeth. "He had this bounty out on me in Amuresca?"

"Look at the history," she gestured. "How long have you been looking into this fleet?"

"Years," he rumbled.

"And you've only been here what? Half a year now? How do you think the bounty made it here so fast and got picked up by a company like the Jackwalds?"

"He was already here," he said, realization dawning.

"This 'Gezan' has been trying to bring you in for quite some time," she said knowingly. "Although he's getting desperate. They added the 'dead' part to the 'dead or alive' only recently. Probably when they found out you were booking passage here. This information you have, they don't want it found out by the authorities here. Which leads me to believe you're right about your assertions."

Finnegan stared down at the papers in his hands. I chanced a glimpse at them. It would take me ages to translate the Amurescan, but there was a very striking illustration of him ink-block printed on the first page. It was uncanny.

"So I'm right," Finn said, letting the papers fall to his lap. "What makes you think my father isn't involved? It's his fleet. This Fleetmaster Gezan just runs it for him. Just because he took out the bounty—"

"Those letters between the two of them were in your possession, I'm certain you've read them," she said pointedly. "Did you never wonder why your father seemed so confused about the manifests? I'm hardly a scholar, but that stood out to me right away."

"I assumed he was using code," Finnegan explained, as if it were obvious. "Trying to...to point out the discrepancies between the two manifests, to scold Gezan for being too obvious about it."

"In private letters?" She lifted an eyebrow. "How did you even get those?"

Finn paused for a moment before admitting, "I blackmailed someone in his manor. A housekeeper with a weakness for younger men. My sire's fastidious, he pens everything several times until he has a final draft with no errors. She stole some of the original letters he'd received and some of his rough drafts from the rubbish bin and gave them to me."

"What reason would he have to use code with someone in on this whole scheme?" She shook her head. "You're a clever man, but you've let your passions rule you in this. I think you were looking for something to use against this man and willfully blind to all else."

Finnegan was silent for a long time following that. I could see him coming to grips with everything she'd said in real-time, and I felt for him. But what she was saying...sounded right. I didn't understand the situation as well as either of them, but I'd seen firsthand how much animosity Finn held for his father. It was an obsession for him, a compulsion to punish this distant figure who'd spurned he and his mother from on high and failed to fulfill any sort of parental role, up to and including alleviating their suffering when it would have been little inconvenience for him to do so.

I would likely never meet, let alone come to know, Finnegan's father. He was in essence a non-person, no more tangible in our lives than a traumatic memory. But you only had to know Finnegan to see the damage he'd done.

"You don't know any of this for certain," Finn ground out, looking back to Odina. "Not for sure. It's *his* company. His fleet. All of this is ultimately his responsibility."

"You're not wrong," she agreed. "And unearthing these illegal acts will still damage the man, whether he was involved or not. But I want it made clear, I do not care what happens to this foreign man across the world. If that's what you ultimately want out of all this, you may not get what you're after. Is it still important to you, this quest of yours, knowing that?"

Finn swallowed, looking back down at the papers. His hands had begun to shake.

I reached for him, setting a paw on his shoulder. "This is a lot at once, Odina," I said quietly. "What's your point?"

"Sawyer died for this job," she said, lifting her chin. "That cannot be for nothing. So I am going to finish it. I am going to Arbordale, and I am not leaving until I have taken three things. Citizenship, coin...and this Gezan's head."

Both of us lifted our muzzles at that, looking at her.

"I do not care, at this point, how I get them," she said, between fangs. "My family is *owed* them. Are you with me, Ambrose? If what we find is not what you were looking for...will you still help me?"

I felt his shoulder lean against mine, his smaller frame resting against my body for support. He was still shaken by the information she'd laid out for him—a bit late, by my estimation. She'd clearly known all of this since we'd talked in Tawnahowac. Had the woman not *just* lost a child, I would be pointing out how hypocritical it was that she acted so untrustworthy of Finn when she'd been keeping secrets from us. And planning, up until this point, to turn him in to the very man she seemed certain was a slaver. The man she was now condemning for hiring *other* mercenaries to do exactly what she was doing.

But then, Odina had never claimed to have the moral high ground. Not once in the time we'd known her had she acted righteous, or explained away her self-serving motivations. This woman lived for her family and had little sympathy for others. She clearly respected my father and even seemed to respect me, sometimes. But I didn't think for a moment she'd put either of us over the interests of her or her children.

And now one of them was dead, and the situation had changed for her. That was all there was to it.

This was who she was, and she made no qualms about it.

I didn't hate her. I couldn't. But I knew very acutely that I never wanted to be her. I couldn't even blame her—she was a survivor. She had prioritized the few people left alive in her life that mattered to her and at some point she'd written off the rest of the world. I hoped I'd never know the kind of loss that brought about such self-imposed isolation.

I looked down towards Finn. In a moment of utter relief, I realized that for once, everyone around us was in on our secret. I didn't have to hide it anymore. The release of tension in my chest at that realization was so profound...it's hard to explain.

I nuzzled my nose down into the fur between his ears. "Finn," I murmured. "What are you thinking?"

He tipped his head back for a moment, closing his eyes.

"Yeah," he said, at long last. "We're going to Arbordale. We've got work to do."

About the Author

Rukis lives on a farm, where she spends most of her time working on art, caring for her animals, and hanging out doing tabletop gaming with her friends. She is a huge fan of old school D&D, White Wolf, and Warhammer, as well as studying and collecting exotic fish (Cichlids, mostly) and drinking a lot of Dr. Pepper. Her menagerie includes a rabbit, some fish, two wonderful dogs, and a whole mess of chickens.

She is the author of *Heretic* and the *Off the Beaten Path* trilogy, which also take place in the world of *Red Lantern*.

About the Publisher

We are a small press publisher serving the niche market that is furry fiction. We sell furry-themed books and comics published by us and most major publishers in the community. If you can't get to a furry convention where we are selling in the dealers room, visit our online stores: FurPlanet.com for print books and BadDogBooks.com for eBooks.

www.ingramcontent.com/pod-product-compliance
Lightning Source LLC
Chambersburg PA
CBHW060554310726
48982CB00008B/1118/J
* 9 7 8 1 6 1 4 5 0 5 5 0 1 *